Warriors of Westopolis

The Wrangler

Drew Bale

This book is dedicated to all those who helped me along the way. In particular, Nick, Tom and Ben. The time that you have given to me and the messages you have shared will never be forgotten.
I still cherish the hip flask.

The following acknowledgement pays respect to the traditional custodians and ancestors of this country, and the continuation of their cultural, spiritual and religious practices. I wish to involve awareness and recognition of Australia's Indigenous people and their cultures. People, language, culture and events have been researched in preparation for this book from multiple sources. To the best of my knowledge they have been used correctly, and at all times in a manner with a purpose of being respectful, to assist in the telling of this story.

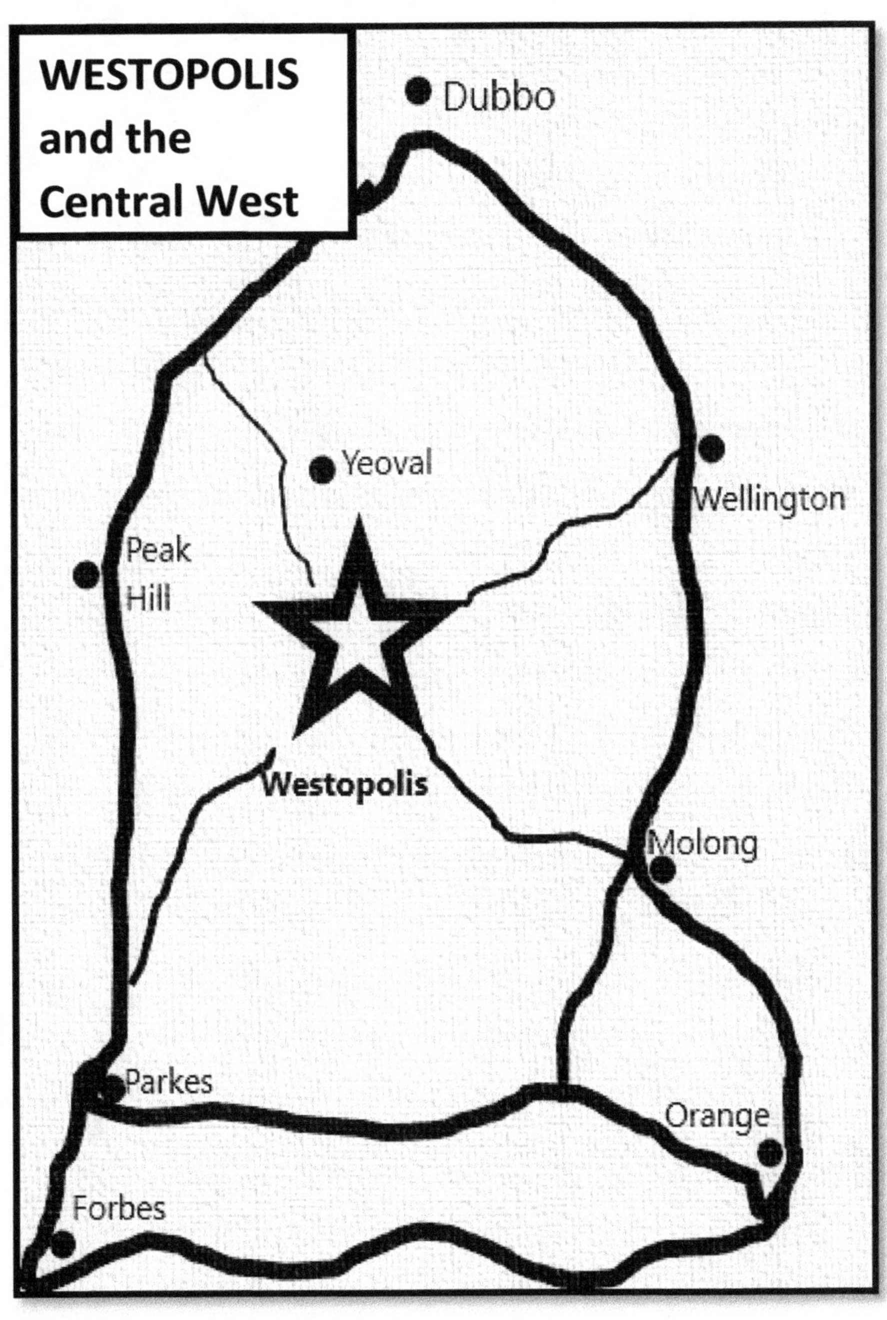

WESTOPOLIS
and the
Central West
Dubbo
Yeoval
Wellington
Peak
Hill
Westopolis
Molong
Parkes
Orange
Forbes

PROLOGUE – A BLAST IN THE STARS

Now

The teacher was about to intentionally injure a student. That student had a desire to do the same. Dennis, the teacher, knew it wasn't the right thing to do. But he was left with very little choice. Jet, the student, didn't care one bit about what was happening.

Dennis couldn't do it.

He shouldn't do it.

It would be frowned upon, he knew. However, he could see almost no other options under the circumstances.

He closed his eyes briefly, quickly, lest he lose his focus. He let out a breath that escaped his mouth as a large puff of steam, under the influence of the increasingly cold night and illuminated by the moon.

He might have to. He shook his head at the thought, and sighed.

Dennis might have to strike some one. Not just any someone; but a student, a junior player, someone he mentored. He may even have to do it more than once.

He would try not to.

Across from him was a much younger man; only just a man, all of eighteen years old and not much more. Within that youth there glowered a barely restrained fury that craved and desired to be unleashed towards Dennis. Dennis could see it in how the younger man stood; in how he clenched his fingers into fists of pure malice waiting to pound them into the teacher, in an attempt to release the rage they contained. Dennis could see the anger in his heavier breathing, the flexing of juvenile muscles contained within the strong young man's shoulders, arms, and neck. It was like he was preparing to spew forth fire, the cold steam which surrounded him adding to that illusion. The youth was bare chested, well-built with his abdominal muscles heaving under some unseen pressure. It would come to a head soon. It had to.

Both of them stood waist deep in the icy cold waters of Lake Burrendong. It had all escalated so quickly, but everyone knew it had been bubbling just below the surface for a while. In fact it had been coming to a boiling point with increasing stress ever since Dennis had met the youth only a few months before. That entire time had been memorable for all the wrong reasons, but despite the chill that surrounded them neither man shivered. Sweat dripped down to mingle with water droplets that had been thrown up in their initial scuffle.

The current situation had been almost entirely of the younger boys doing. Dennis knew it, most of the onlookers knew it too. But that didn't mean that there wasn't some sort of resolution here. Dennis didn't want to fight. Those bystanders at the water's edge, surprisingly, weren't encouraging it either. Many of them, most of them, had already left. Only a few remained.

There had to be another way out of this, Dennis thought to himself. Something that he could say to turn it all around.

Something flickered out of the corner of his eye. It was night time, and apart from a medium sized campfire, that had been left to die nearby, the only light he could see were the stars that penetrated through the dark blanket of the sky above him. The Milky Way appeared to glow brighter out here so far from the closest city. Dennis tried to keep his face pointed towards his opponent as he watched the sky. He found the object that had flashed and caught his attention initially. A shooting star travelled slowly up there, travelling slower than others he had seen. It was also much larger than the other stars that shone beside it, and none of those exuded a vibrant violet luminosity which stretched into the tail behind it, as this one did.

"Pause a minute mate," Dennis said in a soft commanding tone. "Check out that up there." He hoped that the sight would distract, or possibly even interest, his would be opponent. He knew he was hoping for far too much.

"I'm not falling for that garbage," the youth snapped back. "You think I'm an idiot but I am the only smart one out here."

"Not after what you said," Dennis replied. His arms and hands were outstretched showing that he wanted to negotiate, to talk, not to fight. "We can fix this if you apologise, then we -"

"I am not apologising," the young man spat. "What I said was true. If you can't see it then there is more wrong with you than anybody else here. You aren't a teacher, you are a liar and a thief." Dennis had some idea about what the young man was talking about but he knew that it was just an immature point of view. He watched for a moment as a single vein pulsed on the young man's forehead, which was slightly more feral than the sight of his flaring nostrils. Then, slowly, with feet sinking into the sludge like mud which sat at the Lake's bottom, and water mollifying any swift movement as it resisted, the teenager surged towards Dennis.

Dennis turned his feet so they sunk deeper into the muck and allowed his exposed toes to try and grab a hold of anything that was there. He didn't rush forward. Dennis preferred to wait; to be seen to defend against rather than attack the student who came at him. Dennis saw the dying firelight transform the young man's features into something more terrifying and aggressive as it flickered across his face, assisted by the fractured reflection from the dark water. Still Dennis watched, sweat and water dripping from his thick moustache. He was focused.

He was focused, until he wasn't.

The shooting star that he had already located had continued travelling slowly above them. Dennis had been ignoring it despite knowing it was there, after all it was only marginally larger than other shapes that sparkled in the sky. He could ignore it no longer. The light which had been small suddenly erupted like the exploding cap and overflow from a volcano. It burst into a spectrum of lively colours at the same time, brightness and brilliance overwhelming his senses. Dennis couldn't see and tried to hide his face; how could such a display arise from so small a thing? He could no longer visualise the young angry man that was coming towards him as he was temporarily blinded. Dennis staggered around, stunned, as he tried to avoid something that he knew was coming but he couldn't see.

Then it hit him. The fist struck him in the face; only glancing off his cheek bone as he had been a moving target. That didn't mean that it hurt any less. Dennis stayed on his feet. The light blurred in front of him and he found he could see a mirage of outlines that resembled the figure of a person. He groped his way towards them in defence, but they seemed to pulse in around him and away before he had any success.

An explosion tore through the air. A sonic-boom greater than any thunderclap; as if two jumbo-jets, or even something much larger, had collided into each other only metres above their heads. It couldn't have been from the starlight as that was too far away. Dennis brought his hands to his ears. His eardrums had exploded in a cacophony which felt like it was tearing his head apart. The vibration could be felt in his teeth and the sensation was painful, his nerves screaming as they tried their hardest to subdue the overwhelming sensation. Then he was struck again. The blow had been a wide hook intended on striking Dennis in between his jaw and ear. Pain exploded through the back of his hand, Dennis realising that the action to shield his hearing had stopped him from obtaining a broken jaw or worse. It didn't stop him from losing balance though. Dennis toppled awkwardly and splashed deep into the water.

Even below the water his ears were ringing. His eyes were open and water invaded his eyelids. He had no idea if his eyesight was returning as his eyes were just as obstructed and blurred below the water as they were above it. That didn't mean he couldn't see though. Despite the dirty water he could still see a myriad of colours lighting up the night sky. Explosions as if there were fireworks being ignited and bursting could be seen everywhere. Apart from the pain and the overpowering of his senses all Dennis could feel was confusion.

Something darker came forth hiding the light show. Hands plunged beneath the surface reaching down to grab him. They came easily as Dennis still fought to regain control of his body. Instead of the hands pulling him out they instead tried to hold him down and pin him to the bottom.

Dennis had not wanted to hit the youth. He had wished to lay no harm against the teenager that was also one of his students.

So far he had stayed his hands.

He was now left with no choice.

CHAPTER 1 - A BEGINNING

Then

Dennis had driven around the block at least half a dozen times. On each occasion he hung awkwardly out of his window as he searched for the right spot to park. He wanted his car to be safe, not blocking anybody else's driveway, not in a restricted spot where he was either going to be fined or have his car towed, and, because he was brand new to the job, he didn't want to park in anybody else's spot and gain some undesired grudge if he could help it. He knew, in theory, that these were trivial issues but in reality any of them in isolation could be career killers and sometimes people had died for less. He was confident no one had died for such an action, but still, there was always a first time.

He decided upon a nice spot half a block away in the shade of a humongous old oak tree. Dennis reversed his mustard coloured 1982 Corolla until he was sure he was only centimetres away from hitting his bumper against the bluestone rock curb; not that it would have hurt the car as it was built stronger than most present day army tanks.

Dennis awkwardly got out from beneath his steering wheel, despite the fact that his seat was pushed back as far as it could go he was still cramped with his knees ending up almost covering the air conditioning vents just below the top of the dash. It meant that he got cold legs on occasion but they also worked as a buffer of a kind. He didn't actually have air conditioning despite the name, just holes that opened up to the outside which meant he got dirt, dust, rain, and even insects sometimes joining him on his travels. His left knee, apart from covering the vent, also blocked and muffled the sound from his old radio; too old for cassettes and CDs, it only got the AM wavelength rather than the FM. It only managed to get the easy listening music radio stations wherever he went, but Dennis saw that as a luxury as it pleased his taste in music greatly.

His long arm reached into the backseat area, which could only be used for storage due to his chair being pressed firmly up against it, and grabbed his leather over the shoulder bag which contained a laptop, a lunchbox and an assortment of stationery which he may have needed.

As he walked he found all the sensations which accompanied him on his first day very appealing. It was an Australian Summer day and the sun was already trying to make its mark. Despite Dennis walking in the shade he could feel the prickle of heat surrounding him, sifting through the trees to reflect back up from the ground. He could smell the dusty spores as the light struck and sometimes penetrated the leaves of the oak trees that towered above him. The slightest breeze teased through his slim fitting shirt which revealed the early indicators of sweat as there was a cool feeling from beneath his arms and down the centre of his back.

Dennis waited for the traffic lights to let him cross the busy intersection. On the corner where he stood there was a petrol station which was a hive of activity. On the other side of the road, off to the right, there was a beautiful golf course which was covered in some of the oldest and tallest trees in the region, as well as being covered in the most vibrant greens he had ever seen. This intrigued Dennis, as the last time he had been here there was a ravenous drought and the only colours that were revealed in the landscape were yellows, browns, reds, or blacks.

As he crossed the road and left the shade he instantly felt the return of the Sun's sting as it brushed at his skin. No doubt a bead of sweat, if not numerous, would spring forth from his pores momentarily as his body tried to compensate and cool his skin down. The result was not appealing to Dennis, as instead of feeling relief he would instead be consumed by a humid sensation, which in turn would make him more uncomfortable and more sweat would emerge. He stepped off the road and onto the curb. Dennis continued walking past the open gate that led to the staff parking area, which he knew he could have ventured into with his car, but didn't want to risk that yet, and then carefully across the u shaped bus bay with a huge fir pine sitting in its centre for buses to drive around.

Eventually he came to the front gates that led up to the front office. Four or five small steps were before him but Dennis just waited. He took it all in. The open gate, the manicured front lawn and garden area off to his left, the sign that stood to his right welcoming all to what was going to be another successful year. He heard a bus pull up on the road behind him, rather than in the bus bay with the others. Students with a variety of uniforms jumped forth; younger students wearing colours of red, blue and yellow as well as the usual grey moved along to routinely jump aboard another bus which would deliver them to their school.

It was his first day as a teacher here and it all seemed so familiar. It wasn't just because he had taught before, he had done so in various locations across the state; he already had a cool hand in the profession of education. It was familiar because he had once been a student at this very school. A successful student, like the sign was suggesting, was very much in question, but he had fond memories all the same. High school students started walking around him, avoiding him as he frustratingly took up a small part of the entrance. Most of them knew with a single look that he was there to teach, and because of that they either ignored him completely or, thinking they were being discreet, cast quick glances to get a better look at the mysterious new arrival as they walked on by. Others were too busy catching up with friends that they hadn't seen all holidays to take any notice at all.

"Hey," a small student called out to Dennis from his side. "You just going to stand there all day? Taking up space so no one else can get past?" The student wore the school uniform that Dennis remembered from his own time there. He towered over the boy, but he did that to most people, adults as well as children. Dennis was a gangly yet solid individual standing at just over six feet five inches, which is taller than two metres and almost everybody else that he had ever met. Dennis rolled his fingers through his thick brown moustache as he pondered the child.

"I hope not," Dennis replied finally, "you see I just have a great fondness of steps and sometimes I just can't bring myself to walk upon them."

"So what, are you just going to stand there and look at them?" the student responded without hesitation. He had seized upon a moment where he could reprimand a teacher and was seemingly trying to push as far as he could. Dennis could feel a sparkle escape his eye as he smiled at the student.

"It seems to me that steps are some of the best things to stare at," he said, the smile becoming broader, emphasising the word stare so the child understood his meaning. He let what he had said sit between them for a moment, very aware that other students were still nearby. The student looked confused and then it hit him.

Dennis laughing casually as he realised the student had finally understood what he had intended. The student, and many others, suddenly looked appalled and could no longer stand being in his presence. Some laughed as they walked by.

"Oh, so you are one of those teachers?" the boy suddenly seemed even more annoyed, and appeared to regret starting the conversation in the first place.

"Dad jokes are the worst," one girl said as she walked past.

"The joke is never about the recipient if it's a dad joke," Dennis called back. He smiled jovially as they all walked away. Then when they were gone he took one last look around and walked up the steps that would lead up to the front office. Once inside he was hit by a refreshing aroma combined with the cool sensation delivered by a silent air conditioner. The room that Dennis had arrived in appeared to have been meticulously cleaned. The front office shutter was closed, it was apparently too early to serve arrivals, but Dennis could see people moving around beyond the barrier through its gaps. He realised they could also see him and it wasn't long until one of the staff within could be seen moving elsewhere. Eventually a well-dressed woman approached the front door.

"Hello," she said, "I am the Principal. Can I help you with something?" Dennis once again was looking down at the person in front of him. He awkwardly offered his hand.

"Hi," he offered not really knowing what else to say, "I'm Dennis Dodger, I am starting work here today."

"Good morning Mr Dodger," the principal took his hand finally with a large smile. "I have been looking forward to meeting you, I have heard great things."

"Oh, thank you," Dennis said, finding he was bouncing slightly. He wasn't sure if it was at his uncertainty to drop his height to meet hers, or if it was out of nerves. Either way he checked himself and stopped immediately.

"Follow me please," the principal beckoned him to follow her through the door, and Dennis eagerly followed. "Welcome to Orange College."

In no time at all Dennis found his groove. Appointed to teach year seven and eight students he spent most of the morning either helping the younger students find their classes or talking about what they would be studying. He was quick to figure out what needed to be taught, the content was usually the same but the order was what generally varied. The year seven students were in a whole new world and everything was foreign to them, they had no idea that Dennis was not something that already existed at the school the previous year. The year eights were more alert to the fact but not really brave enough to test out the new guy who was bigger than all of them and sometimes two of them combined.

Either by plan or accident Dennis found himself on duty during lunch. There were extra teachers than normal, so that connections could be made or re-established where required, as well as to assist new students young or old who needed help finding their feet, and of course to supervise and dissuade any antisocial behaviour.

Dennis understood almost immediately that he was getting attention from almost anyone who saw him. He knew that given a couple of weeks the novelty would wear off and they would ignore him almost completely. Dennis noticed the students who had spoken to him about standing in the way earlier, and then laughed as they rolled their eyes in disgust and fled his proximity. Several younger students came and spoke to him or asked questions about various things. Sport was a frequent topic: did he play, who did he play for, who did he support? Others simply asked something as a dare or because they could, and usually walked away giggling from the response they received, whether they received one or not. Dennis was happy that it was as confusing to others as he found it.

Eventually, despite still being observed secretly by many, the curious students (and even the ones that were less curious but just talked anyway) left him alone and almost immediately and instinctively Dennis started looking around his surroundings. He was familiarising himself once more with the area, it was not too different to when he was there as a teenager but he ignored those memories to focus on groups or individuals. As much as he didn't want to seem negative he was also looking for issues. It was always better, in Dennis' point of view, to stamp down on issues before they could become bigger, and also be seen as the teacher who would gladly stand in if needed. Dennis also knew, from experience and from a long held belief, that there was a very fine line between fear and respect and although they were different it was sometimes handy to have comparatively sizeable amounts of both. Despite the distinction Dennis usually found himself possessing his fair share. It was therefore a smart idea to let the students know that Dennis could wield both, whilst still being fair and approachable.

Despite Dennis not wanting to find problems or seem negative, unfortunately, as usually happened, they revealed themselves to him before too long anyway.

A small group was gathering behind one of the buildings. It wasn't an area that used to be out of bounds as it was a thoroughfare to both the basketball courts and the large grassed oval where a multitude of games could be played. Clearly times had changed, regardless, when a small group comes together, and others come towards it too, it is very rare that anything good ever comes from it. That seemed to be more likely as every step he took towards the group got him noticed more. Those who saw him mostly just dispersed, trying to appear like they had nothing to do with the world and had just somehow appeared nearby. Some just got a better view to see if the teacher was about to add some extra entertainment to whatever was going on. It took no time to get to the front of the crowd and Dennis took even less time to dissolve it.

"Big crowd," he said simply and loudly, "I can't believe that so many people want to get to know me so quickly." Some laughed nervously but the great majority saw it as the prompt it was meant to be and left without a fuss, even if that moving was no more than fifteen metres away. It had seemed like they were all being pulled in on individual ropes, and then, no sooner had the teacher arrived, all the bonds were cut and they fled from whatever force held them.

"So what is all the excitement about?" Dennis continued in a much softer tone with those who remained. He wanted the remnants to know that he was in command but he was also only there to talk, unless something untoward was going on. He could almost tell exactly what was going on by simply taking in the situation. Some students, who he assumed were brand new year seven kids, had stumbled upon a much older group and offended them somehow, whether by accident or desire he couldn't yet tell, though he suspected the former. Most of the younger kids were cowering on a slim brick wall while a small group of much bigger and older students stood over them. No one answered Dennis, so he continued as he sought a response, going towards the most intimidating older student.

"Hey pal, you seem upset, what's going on?" Dennis asked.

"They are in our spot," the boy boomed, his voice cracking slightly in the process, a result of nerves or perhaps even his age.

"So, they took your spot?" Dennis spoke very slowly making sure that he emphasised every word. "And you are how old?"

"Seventeen, almost eighteen," the older boy replied bouncing lightly from foot to foot as if unable to contain himself.

"So a year twelve student? A senior person of this school? Are you getting cranky, maybe a bit sad, because a little year seven kid is sitting in your spot? Is that right?" Dennis correlated, adding a touch of condescension. Some of the students around them smirked and giggled at how silly it sounded. The student stepped back, humiliated and showing anger toward the unwanted presence of the teacher, but still not really wanting to give it away yet. Dennis decided to help him save face a little bit.

"Look, this is a misunderstanding, these guys didn't know it was your spot. They are already eating their lunch so I suggest we let them finish. I am sure that they will not be here tomorrow or even during the second break today, am I right lads?" he directed the question towards the younger students who replied in a vigorous showing of nodding heads and agreement through mouths filled with food.

"Fine," the older boy finally said with reluctance. His friends had all left him alone to deal with the teacher, realising that they weren't winning in a mediocre scenario. "But Jet is not going to like it."

"Oh, that's sad for Jet," Dennis said dismissively, not caring about the unknown individual who, to his knowledge, wasn't in the immediate vicinity. The conversation had gone on too long already. "Off you go mate, take your friends as well." They mumbled under their breath, but they left all the same so Dennis didn't pursue them further. Instead he leaned against a nearby tree and just relaxed. He half dared, half wished, any of them to come back, but that was not the case. He basked slightly in the knowledge that his impact, though small, had been immediate.

"You guys won't be here tomorrow will you?" Dennis mentioned quietly to the younger students, who he noticed had been devouring their meals ravenously, perhaps in preparation for the return of their tormentors. They shook their heads in reply. "Fantastic, I may not be passing by this way to help you out next time." The casual comment made them very aware of the consequences should they miss this lesson that was being reinforced. Every opportunity was an opportunity to learn. Dennis let it sink in a little longer.

The year seven students continued to eat their meals and conversed about what had happened, before changing the topic to talk about something else. Dennis decided that these were in fact good kids, and the whole situation just a misunderstanding. He was sure they understood that as well.

It wasn't long, however, before one lone figure could be seen stomping down the hill towards them.

His shirt was untucked, his long blonde hair bouncing wildly as he stampeded towards them, though he appeared only to walk. He was tall, not as tall as Dennis but he wasn't much shorter either. He didn't even look at Dennis as he made his way towards where the younger kids sat.

"Move or I will move you," he growled. It appeared like he might have been chewing gum but Dennis suspected that he had nothing in his mouth so he was simply making the motion for his own reasons.

"They don't have to move," Dennis called forward as the younger students seemed to once more be ruffled. "They can stay there for this break and they will move away later."

"No, they move now," the boy replied abruptly. He was talking normally but there was an edge to his tone. The year seven kids looked up at the teacher who simply shook his head and held up his hand saying they should stay. He shook his own head again in disbelief at the nerve of the newcomer.

"Look, mate," Dennis said as he approached the youth slowly. He changed his posture to appear taller, giving a slight show of his extra height. This new boy was strong looking but stood hunched, to stand over and intimidate the younger students, appearing shorter than Dennis knew he was. "They can stay. There is nothing you can do about it. It's their first day, let them have it. You can have your precious spot back tomorrow." Again people that surrounded them chuckled at how absurd it sounded, particularly as the teacher reprimanded the youth like a small child when he was all but an adult. A quick glance around from the boy stopped all forms of noise, even more students vanished from the area at this point. They hadn't fled before Dennis but they disappeared in front of presence of this youth.

"Don't you know who I am?" the boy said evenly, he seemed upset but also acted quite calmly. His voice was low so only the teacher and a few others nearby could hear him.

"I don't care who you are buddy," Dennis replied.

"Well you should my friend," the youth replied dropping his voice slightly. "The other teachers all know me, they know how to behave."

"First of all, I am not your friend," Dennis replied, appalled, "If you want to address me it is as sir or by name. Hi, nice to meet you, I'm Mr Dodger."

"Whatever, sir," he replied, trying to land the title with some sting. "But either you move them or I will." Dennis didn't budge and again he motioned to the younger kids to stay where they were. It was also interesting to see that some of the older girls had come over to join the year seven students. It strengthened their cause, but also made the young man angry. He moved to walk through Dennis, and just as he went to throw his shoulder into the teacher Dennis moved causing the blonde haired youth to stumble. He growled when he finished staggering.

"You don't want to be threatening a teacher, or touching them in anyway, it won't work well for you," Dennis said simply. "Secondly if you lay a finger on any of those kids you won't be looking for a new spot you will probably be looking for a new school."

"You can't threaten me," the blonde boy sneered.

"I don't threaten, I promise, and I don't break either of them," Dennis walked closer to him. "I assume your name is Jet, I am also assuming that you come to school in year twelve to learn because you are a smart kid. I am further assuming that you don't want a phone call home saying that you were fighting over a spot that means nothing to no one. That sort of behaviour would probably remove you from any team you were wanting to be a part of," Dennis hesitated. The urge to say something else was gone, but he felt like he had struck a nerve with one of the things that he said. He couldn't do anything else apart from what he had done. He would follow through with the consequences should they happen, but he silently hoped that this young bull would back down and move along. For the first time since he had arrived the boy stood up at his full height and looked straight into the eyes of the teacher in front of him. The boy suddenly smiled handsomely.

"Sorry, sir, Mr Dodger sir," the boy said. "My name is Jet just like you said." Jet extended his hand for Dennis to shake. Dennis did and was surprised when the boy pulled himself so close that he could smell what he had had for lunch. "Jet, and don't you forget it." Jet whispered in Dennis' face before smiling wildly again. He released his hand and started walking away.

"Enjoy your spot kids," Jet said to the year seven kids politely as if nothing had happened. He waved at them, before turning to do the same to the teacher. "Enjoy the rest of your day as well, sir." Jet smiled again, and then sneered, before turning and disappearing back the way he came.

Dennis held a sock up to his nose. He was not overly surprised by the horrible smell, but that didn't stop him from recoiling with disgust. The socks had been pulled straight from his footy bag and he did not remember when the last time he had opened it was. When he thought about it he realised that his last game had probably been over a year before, if not longer. He had other pairs but it was always worth a try to avoid having to wash more clothes.

His first day at Orange College had been hard work but he felt it had gone a long way to helping establish himself early. He had not liked the altercation between himself and the young man, Jet, and had already told himself that the next day he would seek out the youth and try to build some form of relationship where he could be seen as a positive influence, instead of looking like someone keen to raise conflict. First impressions are important, but sometimes they did not actually reflect who a person really was. Sometimes, however, they did.

Dennis was seeking out football socks because no sooner had he walked out the door from work than he had received a phone call. It was one of his mates who he had gone through school and university with, they had also been teammates for a long time. The call basically requested that Dennis came down for some pre-season training so that he could play again. The thought of any sort of training was not really appealing. He could do it easy enough, and it would help with his diminished fitness, but just because he could do it didn't mean he liked it. He jumped back in the car with some small form of enthusiasm, wearing one of his oldest, but most favourite, rugby jerseys and putting on his oddly bright, yellow sunglasses. Dennis turned the dial up on the volume knob, roughly one turn got it to the max (which was still not loud enough for sound to leave the car), and was lucky enough to get Dexy's Midnight Runners pop onto the station. He sung terribly, smiling at his own poor attempt, while tapping the steering wheel lightly to emphasise his satisfaction as he moved appallingly to the beat.

It wasn't long until Dennis was pulling off the road and onto a long driveway which led towards the carpark of his childhood rugby club. He turned the radio back down to look up at the big solid green grandstand which was a beacon to all that this was where the Orange Emus played and trained.

Dennis was late as he hadn't left school until well after the final bell, needing a great deal of time to prepare for the following day, and it had taken a small amount of time to get ready. Plus he had never actually planned to come down in the first place. He had been reluctant at first, happy to give the whole year a miss from sport as he steeled into his new job, only agreeing because how much harm could one training actually do.

Now that he was here he knew it would be hard to convince himself not to play.

He pulled up and as soon as he was out of the car he was he set upon by people who knew him. They were old friends who he had both played and trained with. A few of them were friends from when he went to school in the area or those who he had met at university.

"Hey Hitman," a large bodied Aboriginal man called out as he approached. He was shorter than Dennis, probably even under six foot tall, but his arms were spread up high and wide as he approached slowly preparing to give a huge hug. The Aboriginal man wrapped his arms around Dennis and snuggled in making very affectionate sounds. Dennis allowed it, but had to keep pulling his head away as the long thick black beard threatened to tickle, irritate and suffocate him all at the same time. He finally let Dennis go but continued to smile the most infectious grin as he looked up at him.

"Hey Jiemba," Dennis replied, pretending to box the other man away from him. "I told you not to call me Hitman."

"And I told you not to call me Jiemba, call me Jim instead, or I will call you worse than Hitman," Jiemba smiled and laughed again, apparently there was a joke that was not seen or even heard. He was a couple of years younger than Dennis, but his presence captivated all as if he was in charge of the whole place.

"Anyway, I am so happy you are here," Jiemba continued with a wide smile, starting to lead Dennis away towards the grassed area where others had started an impromptu game of touch football while they waited for the coaching staff to take charge. "I think you know a fair few of the blokes, but there are some new ones too." Many of those that Dennis knew came forward to greet him and he responded warmly to them. Others that he didn't know he simply nodded his head with exaggeration and smiled to them, trying very hard to remember their names. He fell into conversation with some he knew, and others that he knew very well, many of whom were surprised that Dennis still played.

Jiemba left and rounded up the others who were playing touch as he started a meet and greet again, agreeing that the touch game would continue in a moment. As soon as the group came over Dennis stopped nodding and smiling and instead just watched one of the players as they approached. Names were passed around and Dennis would remember none of them as he tracked just one new player. But that new player he knew the name of.

"And this young stud is almost as good as you were Hitman," Jiemba threw in the name as he could see that Dennis was hardly listening. "His name is . . ."

"Jet," Dennis interrupted. "Yeah I know him." Jet smiled back at Dennis and Jiemba.

"Fantastic, you guys will go great," Jiemba continued, "you could show him a thing or two." Dennis held the young man's gaze but did not reply. Jet did though.

"I can't wait, that sounds fantastic," Jet said. "Show me a thing or two please."

"Sir."

Dennis groaned silently.

CHAPTER 2 – WELCOME BACK

The first few weeks settling into a new place is always hectic; that is no different even if you have lived in the area before. Dennis spent great deals of time sorting out his own house and whenever he could he would abandon his chores to reconnect with a friend he used to know, at least better than he currently did, or even places he used to frequent regularly.

His house in all honesty wasn't filled with too many of his possessions. It mostly consisted of essentials: a bed, a desk, a television, clothing and cooking necessities were his main items. He also had a bookshelf which he filled with all sorts of novels and texts. Dennis was a history teacher primarily, while he also dabbled in some younger ability sciences, geography and sport, and his bookshelf reflected this. He had the complete works of Shakespeare, Banjo Paterson, Winston Churchill's World War Two accounts as well as a well-worn book reflecting the rise and fall of the third Reich. He had a working knowledge of Don Bradman's career as well as the campaigns of the Peninsula War and many of the conflicts that Australia had been involved throughout its history, internal and external, good or bad. Dennis also had a handful of biographies of people he thought were interesting and a small collection of his favourite books, including historical fiction, science fiction, and a small amount of comic books showcasing the abilities of explorers and adventurers as well as the super abilities of countless heroes.

Everything else that he owned was elsewhere, stored in a house with his mum, several hours drive west of Orange, or some shed in which he was on the verge of forgetting altogether. While he had lived in the area during his youth, after moving around for a bit with his parents before they settled down for a while, about the same time that Dennis embarked on his university career his Mum moved back to the country.

Dennis remembered the change that had occurred during that time. He got into university and was preparing to move away for a while, leaving his family behind. His mum, dad, and younger sister would remain. But then it continued to change. His dad had been involved with an accident on his motorcycle and he had been tragically killed. As a result his mum and sister had moved back to the country unable to bare the memories that lurked all around them.

But that had been several years ago; although never really dealt with, it was lodged firmly in the back of Dennis' mind and rarely came forward to be seen.

Upon his return to Orange his love of history had caused him to venture around the town in his solitude, discovering new bits of information wherever he could. It was great that signs littered almost every corner with in the CBD, showing some important landmark or event. The local library, which he did venture towards frequently as it was a constant source of knowledge and support, had so much history at your fingertips to peruse that he spent countless hours buried in some sort of ancient tome or a more recently written article. Dennis was a very personable individual though and preferred talking to others to help build his knowledge; despite his awkward style of communication where he liked to try and be positive and polite, building a trusting conversation, he frequently had the opposite effect. He stood out from a crowd with his height and thick moustache, and although initially off-putting or intimidating he was quick to build a rapport with others.

This was the same at work. It took almost no time at all to connect with his colleagues and Dennis made it a goal to learn as many names as he could and at least one small bit of information in which he could build a conversation and therefore a relationship with.

His quirky style was also a hit with the students. It was easy to build a bond with any of the students he actually taught, as his unique teaching style, stories in abundance, almost expert knowledge of what he taught, as well as his fun and fair attitude towards teaching, helped establish respect within the classes. That only went so far, especially with younger students who were happy to latch on to something that made them feel safe, but as he was a newcomer to all the other older students he had to work harder in the non-teaching areas like the playground, ovals and sheltered quadrangles to continue to establish himself firmly within the school.

The altercation that Dennis had been involved in with Jet had gone a long way to cement an opinion of no nonsense in the students' eyes, but he didn't want to just be seen as that guy. He took on more duties, for the short term at least, so that he had more opportunities to interact with as many students as he could manage. He shared stories of all kinds with many who would listen, volunteered opinions of sporting teams and expectations, and offered jokes whether they were requested or not. It was hard work but finally he was in the position he wanted to be in on the first day. Dennis was now liked, feared and respected. It was harder to establish than maintain, but it had still only taken a few weeks.

His work was still not finished though.

Jet had been a constant focus of his attention. Dennis had discovered that, apart from those students who disappeared due to a sad lack of interest in their education, Jet was the greatest obstacle to teachers and students alike. He was the biggest kid at the school and apart from Dennis alone he was taller than every other individual on the premises. Dennis had observed that he did what he wanted, when he wanted; and although he wasn't an active bully in the sense that he went out of his way to harass or abuse people, if you were in his way you were expected to move or else prepare from some harmful outcome. Most of the students knew that and simply avoided him, but it also meant that some of the teachers would also chose to ignore his actions if the worst happened.

Dennis wasn't one of those teachers. That didn't mean that it was easy. Jet's friends all treated him like their leader and would attempt to follow the example that he set, which was not a great one. They would bravely try and undermine students and teachers thinking that they held the same power, but that courage quickly faded in Dennis' presence. They were like speed humps in Dennis' pursuit of the tall youth.

The more that Dennis observed him the more he saw both the good and bad properties of his character. He was big, strong, fit, he easily led others (in fact he did it effortlessly), possessed charisma that others wished they could have and tried to hide a smart intelligence which was mostly disguised as cunning most of the time, or disregarded entirely. He was handsome, spoke well and in a polite manner on most occasions, and if you knew nothing else about him you would probably like him at first sight. But then there were those other traits which brought him down: he was powerful, arrogant, self-entitled, underhanded and spiteful.

Regardless, as it was the goal that he had set himself, Dennis had attempted to establish any form of relationship with the youth. He walked that fine line even more so, and was particular with what he said to the young man and how he acted around him. That was done at both school and at pre-season training, but in both settings Jet would act the same way. He would smile and speak politely to his face, show indifference to his company, and try to undermine him at every opportunity. It had been a real slog.

All of the positive steps that Dennis seemed to make also appeared to make the divide between the pair even greater. The more players or students liked Dennis the more Jet seemed to disregard him. The more effort Dennis put into trying to strengthen that bond the more Jet pulled away, attempting to break it.

It had been more apparent during rugby training than at school, but that sort of environment was more suitable to conflict and passionate rivalries taking place. On the first day when Jiemba had shown him off to the other players as someone of worth to the club, Dennis was already relinking with all those he had played with before. Even the old boys who still played were easily swayed and showed a desire to get to know him better from the get go.

"Hi Dennis," a solid looking ginger haired man came forward eagerly ready to shake hands, accompanying him was another ginger haired fellow who was slightly slimmer. "It's great to have you here. We saw you when you were younger and heard great things. We can't wait to see what you can do for us." The conversation was honest and the feeling of acceptance was warming, but over their shoulders Dennis had already seen Jet trying to influence the younger players as to what he thought the teacher was actually like.

Over the next few weeks at training Dennis had worked hard, almost as hard as anyone else near him. He wasn't quicker than the outside backs who were built for speed but he could keep up with them and was generally in the front of the pack. Dennis was trying to show his worth for sure, but he was more interested in blowing away the cobwebs and regain some level of athletic fitness. Jiemba and his mate JT, who was also an old friend, encouraged Dennis constantly, even if the encouragement was a small step short of insulting.

"Run you baby giraffe," Jiemba would call out from the side of a shuttle running exercise. He laughed at the comical gait of the two metre tall man. He would laugh even harder as he felt his jokes were getting funnier. "Just kidding, you know I love you Hitman," Jiemba continued, laughing until his eyes shut. When he opened them again he would clap eyes on JT who was struggling after an offseason of nothing but trips to the bottle and fast food shops. "C'mon JT man, you are more like a baby hippo," his loud laugh was cut short as the coach chased Jiemba back into the drill as he was supposed to be doing it as well. "Sorry coach, I love you to, don't hurt me." Jiemba would join in with everyone else, his laugh continuing for a short time until he was just as tired as the others. His shirt would come up over his head instantly showing the hypocrisy of calling someone else a hippo. Dennis would laugh at the sight, knowing full well that based on past years of playing with Jiemba that his extra bulk would be dropped, turned into muscle and put to great use; despite his jovial nature he could hit harder than almost anybody else in the region.

Dennis admired Jiemba. He knew that the young Aboriginal man had endured some hardships in his life, but if you hadn't known that fact then you would have had no idea otherwise. His display was always positive and his mirth infectious. Dennis was aware that this cover made it hard to know Jiemba's true feelings, something that concerned him on occasion, but it appeared like his fears at the moment were unnecessary. Jiemba kept smiling as he continued to search for an opening to drop a joke or make someone else laugh.

Dennis, despite watching Jiemba in his merriment, was also very aware that Jet was shadowing his own training the whole time. Jet would place himself either next to Dennis during fitness activities so he could finish ahead of him at the end, or take place on the opposing team in a competitive game, again with

the idea of beating Dennis in front of others. No one else seemed
to care, even when Jet made his success over Dennis known.

There were lots of little battles between them early on, which
were only being fought by Jet, all just more frustrating and
annoying than harmful.

Finally after several weeks of getting settled Dennis felt like
he was good to go. He decided then that it was worth going for a
drive, putting all his recent accomplishments and small issues
behind him, and visit his mum.

A drive consisting of a couple of hours and filled with enjoyment
at listening to rock music and Australian anthems, whilst having
the breeze flow through his hair and teasing at his moustache,
was a luxury in his opinion. Dennis enjoyed taking his time and
being left with his thoughts and the duration of that trip did not
concern him. His car was not designed for speed, which became
even more apparent when he was forced to shift gears countless
times when attempting to climb even the simplest of hills. None
of which would deter him from his enjoyment.

But when left to his own thoughts his mind tended to wander.
Most of that drive consisted of thinking of how to best teach the
students in his care, what else he needed to do on the football
field, and strategies of how to get through to Jet. It wasn't long
though before he was focused on something else. In his youth
Dennis had played his fair share of football, both for his club
and, more reluctantly, at a representative level. During that time
he had travelled all over the Central West, and in that time he
had observed the environment by the road side more times than
he could count in every direction. Usually that meant a person
would be very used to what they saw and not overly interested.
This time was different.

Much like Orange currently, the majority of the scenery was
displaying a vibrancy of colours and life. This would have been
odd at the best of times as it was not uncommon once you drove

over the Blue Mountains to be greeted by a baron and ill looking countryside. Due to the fact the area was still involved in one of the longest droughts in history all the greenery made no sense at all. It was nice to see, but he had never seen the Central West appear like a paradise like this ever. It was not isolated to Orange either. Usually the impact of strong flowing creeks and rivers, delivered by the local range known as Mount Canobolas, was provided in prosperity to the areas which stretched around the region. That was as far as it lasted, usually, with the bright green pastures, radiant paddocks of canola, and overly fluffy cotton gone before long. This time, however, all these wondrous sights stuck alongside Dennis in the nearby paddocks until he reached the town of Forbes. That had never happened before.

Beyond Forbes though it was a different story. Forbes had its own river flowing through the town adding to its appeal, but almost as soon as you crossed the boundary of the shire the colours Dennis had been getting used to disappeared, with the yellows and browns he had expected returning sadly. The landscape became 'normal' and plants that were thriving became the exception to the rule. This lasted all the way, which was not a massive distance, before he reached the outskirts of the small town that his mother had since called home.

It wasn't really a town but rather a few blocks that seemed to be linked together at their centre by one much larger set of buildings. Even the sign welcoming strangers to the area was unusual.

It read: 'Clapptown: How did you find us?' Not 'welcome', not 'home of the best something', just a simple acknowledgement that you must be lost to have ventured to the area at all. Dennis had been told a story once that the sign had been changed and instead of the curious statement that questioned why you were there at all, it used to say 'Clapptown: Go and get nicked.' It was marginally better than it used to be.

Dennis laughed to himself as he found his way through the small place as he followed directions to his mother's residence. He had been there only once before and he knew it was not within the town but just on the outskirts. But then again even if you were in the town you would probably be considered as residing on the outskirts. He couldn't help but slow down his already unhurried pace as he drove through the town centre. There stood a block that would have been impressive in a city let alone in a small village like Clapptown. At the block's middle stood a three storey pub and hotel, and each of the levels were big too. The building created its own shade in the almost desert like community. On one side of it was the general grocery store and post office, and on the other was a service station and mechanic shop which spread around the corner. Directly behind the pub stood accommodation and surrounding that were numerous novelty stores including a sweet and milkshake bar, a clothing store, hardware goods and a few more novelty shops. They were all run by locals and were mostly visited by locals. Together they were like an island of buildings in the middle of nowhere. Dennis also knew that every single one of them was owned by his uncle, who not only lived in town but basically ran it. While he wasn't the mayor he was still very much in charge.

Dennis finally came to his mother's farmstead almost as soon as he drove away from the safety of the tarred road and onto the dirt. There was a short driveway, long by city standards, which travelled past one solitary but large shed before coming to a dwelling. No sooner had he clambered out of his car, and before even the dust he had been thrown up behind him had settled, he was set upon by a pair of dogs. They jumped halfway up his body, which, while still being a mighty accomplishment, meant that their sharp claws dug in just that little bit more as they fell. The pair of them luckily, somehow, remembered Dennis from several years before when he had travelled to the house, when they were no more than pups. A figure appeared at the flyscreen doorway and waved to him.

"Good to see you," his mum said with a large smile filling her face, as she clomped along the timber deck. The smile disappeared in an instant. "There is a bike in the shed, go grab it and then come with me, there is work to do." Dennis slumped slightly. At least he got a 'good to see you', but his mum hadn't wasted anytime in putting him back to work. He was definitely home.

The sun had long since set before Dennis was finally able to return to the house. He immediately had a shower, which was rushed as there was not an abundance of water in the area, but the short time he had almost wasn't enough to remove the film of grime that covered his body as it attached to his sweat from the hard afternoon's work. Dennis actually enjoyed helping out; countless hours on a motorcycle herding sheep back through several paddocks, towards an area providing better feed, was rewarding in its own way. That didn't mean relaxing afterwards was not just as greatly appreciated.

His uncle had joined them towards the end and had used his ute to form another line to move the sheep along. His uncle, Scott, shrugged off the idea of getting washed, but one look of him revealed that he was already either very tanned or the muck was so thick upon his skin that it had actually become a part of him. By the time Dennis had returned refreshed his uncle was at least halfway through his second beer. Dennis had always been close to Scott in his youth, he was only about ten years older than Dennis anyway, but ever since his dad had died he hadn't had much contact with him. Even if they hadn't gotten along Dennis suspected that Scott's strong build, arms covered in tattoos, fierce piercing blue eyes, and handsome charisma would have won him back over anyway. Scott was the brother of Dennis' mum, but the way they all used to hang around with each other you would have sworn that his dad and Scott were actually brothers instead.

Dennis' mum, who looked remarkably like her son but with long black hair and more dominating stance, was busy preparing some sort of meal inside to accompany the meat that Scott was already cooking with the barbecue on the deck outside. Scott smiled as he saw Dennis approach.

"It's good to see you kid," his uncle welcomed him whilst also handing him a beverage. "I haven't seen you in ages, your mum tells me all about what is going on whenever I see her, you know, whenever you let her know what is going on." It was a simple enough statement but there was a silent shot at Dennis hidden within; Dennis knew he didn't call home enough.

"It's good to see you too Uncle Scott," Dennis replied truthfully. Scott had always been a more roguish version of his own dad, and his dad could be a larrikin in his own right, but like his dad he also held instant authority whenever he walked into a room.

"You aren't a kid anymore," Scott said pointing tongs towards Dennis, "I'm proud to be your uncle but you call me Scott now, or sir, or the man, or almost anything else, but not Uncle Scott."

"Sorry, 'the man', I won't do that again," Dennis replied. Both of them fell into small polite chat about non important things, until inevitably there was a long pause. It wasn't awkward, it never was with family, but Dennis still felt like he needed to say something to fill or cover the silence.

"So I noticed that it is a lot drier out here than around Orange and other areas, I know it always used to be but I don't understand the massive difference now," Dennis spoke about what he had seen.

"That's simple, but a little complicated to explain," Scott said taking a huge slurp of his drink. Then he turned the already browned sausages quickly and lowered the heat on the hotplate before turning back to Dennis. "But you are a smart guy you should be able to understand." He walked to the other end of the deck and pointed in the direction that Dennis determined to be North or North-East.

"You ever heard of the Great Artesian Basin?" Scott asked. Dennis semi shrugged, he knew it had something to do with water flow through Australia, but despite teaching small portions of it, geography was not one of his strongest fields. "Well that Basin holds a massive amount of groundwater and goes through a huge area of Queensland, Northern Territory, South Australia and even New South Wales. Years ago, even when you were still in Orange, they found that there was a confined aquifer, heaps of water underground, which was feeding off all the local rivers and mostly coming from the Great Artesian Basin. It extended further than what the boundaries of that basin suggested. So a company started developing that aquifer and farming the water. They built a huge water station out near Yeoval and started working on making it a sustainable source of water for the area. While they were doing that they found a series of underwater tunnels and caves, and ever since then have used them, along with massive pipes, to pump water out to most towns and cities in the Central West. They have re-established huge natural environments in this area, and it hasn't come as a cost to anybody or anything."

"Sounds great, but I've never heard of any of that, which seems surprising based on what you just said. Out near Yeoval did you say?" Dennis queried.

"Yeah, except it isn't just a water station anymore. About five years ago they started building a town over the top of it and around it, connected it into the nearby hills and small mountains. They started building really aggressively too. It is the size of a small city now, they named it Westopolis. In the middle of it there is a huge building owned by GreenCorp, they own and run the water station as well as other things. They seem nice, but that is just on the surface," Scott stopped talking for a moment, apparently deciding whether or not he had said too much on that subject. "Anyway, that building is huge, when you travel out that way you will see it from far away, looks like a big sleek mountain popping up out of nowhere, but that is just the main tower. They have revolutionised water in the west, basically taken drought off the table so to speak. It's like the environmental equivalent of the Midas touch, everything they try works out for them. That can't be said for everywhere though, we still run off stormwater and dwindling dams out here. Who knows, maybe they will come out this way before too long."

"You don't approve, even if it's better?" Dennis asked.

"They say that it's better, studies say it helps, the proof is everywhere when you travel around the Central West now. It sounds a bit weird, granted, but I guess I am still a little sceptical, too much of a good thing and all that," Scott said, he moved back towards the barbecue and set about getting the meat onto a warming tray. The topic didn't seem to be something that would mean a great deal to Scott, but clearly it did. From the information that he had been given Dennis was more surprised that he hadn't heard more about it. He let it slide, for the moment at least.

"You couldn't have at least changed before you started cooking Scott?" his mum chided as she walked towards the outside timber table and chairs. A potato bake and a garden salad were held in each hand. Scott was wearing dirty jeans and a skin tight navy singlet. He dropped the tongs on the tray and flicked his singlet off swiftly.

"There, is that better? No dirty clothes now," he smiled as Dennis' mum growled disgust at him. Dennis wasn't really paying attention as he was looking at Scott's skin. More specifically his tattoos. There was one alone which caught his eye. Amidst the others which had words, sayings, interesting creatures and suggestive images, there was one which jumped out at him. There was nothing particularly special about it, it was simply a motorcycle which was doing a wheelie and covering Scott's flesh from his lower back to above his shoulder blades. Scott, who had been smiling in triumph at the reaction he had stirred from his sister, quickly threw his singlet back on and got back to the task at hand.

"Was that . . . ?" Dennis started.

"Not important," Scott answered. "Dinner's served, let's go champ." Scott moved to the table and sat down, grabbing a plate and some cutlery that were within reach. Dennis stood unmoved for what seemed like an age before joining his Uncle. His mum joined them with an assortment of dressings and the meal started in a hurry.

"So what's up with the moustache?" Scott asked as he tore some meat from his fork with sharpened teeth. "Is that something they allow at school?" Dennis was still thinking about what he had seen; slowly answering the question after a moment.

"It is kept neat, plus it doesn't impact on my ability to teach so why not?" Dennis replied, stroking his facial hair along the bridge of his lip before he grabbed a serving spoon to begin selecting his own dinner.

"Bet that helps with the ladies huh? Tickle the upper lip a little?" Scott laughed. Dennis' mum rolled her eyes at her brother's remarks.

"Leave him alone, Dennis has come out to see his mum and escape from stupid behaviour like that," she growled at Scott while supporting Dennis.

"Stupid, Eve, really? You know that isn't true. You can't rule an empire like Clapptown if you're stupid," Scott scoffed down a sausage noisily. Before his sister could interrupt him and challenge the prestige of his proclamation he turned to Dennis.

"Are you having trouble at work, Dennis? Staff or students?"

"Work is great, the staff are great, the school is great, the students are great," Dennis confirmed.

"But?"

"There is just one kid. He is a bit like the school bully, but he isn't. He has a lot of unrealised potential. But he has a huge chip on his shoulder. If he can get over himself, focus, apply his skills, he could be something great. He is also on my club footy team so I have to be careful how I treat and talk to him," Dennis told them both. He waited for a moment, waiting for some advice or comment. Soon his uncle leaned in closer.

"Dennis. . . I have no idea how you deal with that now. In my day teachers wouldn't spare the rod, but you can't do that anymore so good luck. Or just leave him be, he might come good on his own," Scott suggested before returning to his food.

"Maybe," Dennis half-heartedly agreed. It wasn't uncommon for people to right themselves, he just didn't feel like that would be the case this time. Jet just had too much power over those around him and a big reputation; Dennis didn't think he would just change it all on a whim.

"No maybe about it, that student will come good, or you will find a way to help them. That's what you do, I don't understand how you do it, but you have always had the gift of talking to people and getting through to them. I know you can do it," Scott added. Dennis just nodded allowing a small smirk to spread across his top lip, hidden partially by his facial hair. It was nice that others had faith in him, that didn't mean that the issues would resolve themselves immediately. The thoughts that he would have to make would have to wait though.

"So back to what we were talking about, that moustache and the ladies," Scott continued his pursuit of answers. Dennis' mum rolled her eyes. Dennis just groaned, smashing as much food into his mouth as he could, hoping that somehow he could still enjoy the evening.

CHAPTER 3 – THE CIRCLE

Good intentions rarely work. As much as Dennis accepted the backing from his Uncle Scott, and knew within himself that he was capable of making a difference, whoever was in charge of fate was definitely trying to get him to fail.

Upon returning to school on the Monday Dennis was asked to act as an assistant coach for the school rugby league team. It was a title in name only as the actual coach simply needed someone else to help him justify the choices that he was to make. Dennis had coached loads of times before and had teams become successful under his tutelage, so he applied this to the more than large group. He provided constructive criticism to all eager participants and in more than one occasion improved the player's skills with a few simple modifications to their game.

Dennis deliberately stayed away from Jet throughout the trials. Not because of anything else apart from trying to provide an unbiased opinion. Dennis knew how good Jet was, in fact despite his poor attitude he was one of the first that should have been picked on skill alone. He also knew what they had been working on at training; at no point did Dennis want to give a suggestion that he couldn't give to everyone, and also didn't want to be seen as playing favourites with a player who was on his weekend team.

After hours of rigorous training and several opportunities in possibles and probables heavy contact full games, it was time for selections. The main coach, who Dennis didn't know very well, stood a few steps up a small hill at one end of the field after the trialling had finished. The players, all of which were exhausted, gathered slowly around. A few of them had chosen the wrong sort of training gear as they now sported ripped shirts and stained socks, some of them choosing the wrong sport it seemed as they hadn't even made it through the tests.

It seemed obvious to Dennis' eye who would be going through to be a member of the Orange College league team. Out of the forty plus young men who had taken part Dennis believed he could put a line through at least a third of them. A quarter of all of them would go straight in as they were stronger, faster, more positive, had an x factor, or were a seriously hard worker. There were about five positions or so that were up for grabs. Jet, in Dennis' eyes, was one of those who would go straight in.

"Alright everyone gather around," the league coach called out as the students continued to amble towards him. "I would like to thank all of you for giving up some of your class time, which I know is really concerning you, and some of your after school time to be part of this trial. I would also like to thank Mr Dodger for helping out as well. I know he was able to give many of you pointers on how to improve, and he gave me some invaluable insight as to who I should and should not pick." That comment caused a stir in the group and Dennis felt many of the eyes land firmly on him. The comment was a lie as the coach had never asked for Dennis' opinion despite that being exactly what he was there for. Some of the students looked at him as if somehow that was going to help their chances when the coach already had a team listed out in front of him. Promptly without any more words he started going through the list.

Dennis didn't know many of the student's names from experience. He quickly identified some of them as those he had worked with, individually tweaking or working on simple skills, and some of them he had flat out just asked for their name as he gave them a complement. Dennis watched as one by one the team was read out. Each boy responded to his name by some show of enthusiasm or excitement. Dennis clapped all of them. Regardless of anything it was definitely an achievement to make it into a school team. He nodded towards many of them as he agreed with the decision of selecting them. Others, where he wasn't so sure, he simply smiled and offered his congratulations. It was hard to see so many not get in, and a little harder as many who had no chance still believed they were going to be the next name called when it was never going to be the case. The last name was read out and no sooner was it called then Dennis' face dropped. He walked quickly over to the coach.

"Sir, are you sure you haven't made some sort of mistake?" Dennis asked.

"No," he replied quickly, "I have picked my team and it isn't half bad."

"Surely it could be made better?" Dennis found he was subtly pleading as he motioned towards those who were left.

"No it can't," the coach admonished. "It's my team and he is not in it." The coach turned away and approached those that had been successful; preparing to provide information about their upcoming campaign. Most of the boys that were not successful had left slowly in small groups, or swiftly by themselves to avoid notice or hide their disappointment and embarrassment. There was but one who still remained.

"Couldn't stand to see me succeed, huh sir?" Jet spat.

"That is not it at all," Dennis replied, "you were one of the best out there."

"So it isn't because you are blind, it's because you are biased. Ever since we first met you have been out to get me," Jet sneered at the teacher.

"That isn't true at all," Dennis defended against the accusation, "If I was coach you would have been in my team."

"Well I wouldn't have wanted to be in your team," Jet whispered. He lingered for a moment, Dennis thought he saw water start to dribble beside the quiver and ferocity burning in the boy's eyes, but then Jet turned and left without another sound. Dennis watched him leave. He did not pursue. He was just left to wonder what was yet to come.

From then on it felt like Dennis was trying to catch a knife whenever he was trying to work with or manage Jet. He had dropped it, and whatever damage it did when it landed would be largely his fault. Instinct told him both to catch the knife, though it might hurt him it might also do less damage to the blade and whatever it hit, and also to just let it drop because it would cause Dennis himself less pain.

Jet turned up his behaviour to make it harder. Dennis could tell that the boy was hurt; despite the fact that he had tried to help and the problem had come from someone else's choice Dennis was the target of his backlash. Dennis for some reason felt partly to blame. Where Jet had been a low threat but high impact problem before he now turned the notches up much higher. In the halls, corridors and general walking areas Jet was determined to walk in a straight line and if you were in his way you would then cop a shoulder to move you or a slap which sent all the contents of what you were carrying up into the air. Neither boy or girl, student nor teacher were immune.

Jet also largely turned away from his friends. He finally saw them as a hindrance who were leeching off of him. Though he didn't stop them from acting out in the same manner in which he usually did, he also didn't stand up for them or intimidate others like he used to. Jet had developed tunnel vision and was hell bent on maintaining his rage and stretching the run of his grudge as long as he could. Dennis alone was safe from his aggressive manner, at least physically. Jet would see him and turn and walk away; if they were stuck in the same area Jet would spit at his feet and barge past in a hurry. For the most part Dennis held back from reprimanding the youth but knew on occasion, those where he could not let an action slide, that a confrontation was inevitable. But even then there were few of those.

Dennis continued to get the cold shoulder treatment at training, but again others got hurt instead. The space between them was filled with tension. The rest of the players could feel it and while Dennis continued to get on with all other members of the team it was not the same as it had been. There was a threat which lingered causing everyone to feel like they were walking on eggshells. No manner of comical bravado, tomfoolery or jokes could desaturate the emotion which hung there. Jiemba had been one of those who had tried incessantly to help rebuild the relationship with his positive actions and warm hearted demeanour. Dennis appreciated it but Jet did not. He simply ignored him all together before moving to the small group of younger players. You couldn't hear what he said from outside the huddle but all could see that there was a conversation of mockery that was targeted towards certain individuals. They were easily and greatly influenced by what Jet said and did.

The coaches tolerated most of it as it didn't detract from what they were trying to do. Most of the training consisted of long periods of fitness and a similar duration of time that was set about developing a skill set which would be adopted across the entire club, and thus building depth for the season ahead. In both of these areas it was easy to see who was succeeding and who was not. Dennis, just like when he had helped select a team at school, could slowly but surely start seeing where certain players would fit into the club and based on his opinion which grade they would represent. The other aspects that the coaches were looking for were: a positive and enthusiastic attitude, as well as the ability to build combinations throughout the team and not just between key positions.

On a few occasions the coaches were forced to intervene with the younger players as some were spending more time standing around jeering at others, trying to bring them down rather than training, while others were spending a greater effort talking themselves up then actually putting their words into actions. Most of the other players saw this, and all knew that it was the example of what not to do.

Jet, however, put his own words into actions more ferociously than anyone else. He was still making a point of training next to Dennis and was succeeding in beating him in most objectives. He had changed his approach though of always being in the opposite team, choosing to be on the same one as Dennis so he could starve him of the ball and be seen to be doing more with it, making Dennis irrelevant and his contribution almost non-existent.

Unfortunately, Jet was also making heavy contact with everyone he could during opposed or semi-opposed training. While initially it looked like he was simply passionate about proving his worth, with several players without the same desire being the victims and therefore culled quickly, it swiftly turned into an opportunity to target those who Dennis was close to or who might be competing for the same position.

Jiemba was usually on the same side as Dennis, so managed to avoid Jet's focus, but others weren't so lucky. Horatio Findman was one such player. Horatio was an old friend of Dennis and Jiemba. All three played at university together and had been through years full of ups and downs. Horatio was younger, slightly shorter standing at about six foot, was more heavy set and played a position where his strength and size were beneficial over his lack of speed or evasion. He sported a moustache similar to Dennis which was often joked about in a 'twins' sort of fashion. Horatio was also a local journalist and would take strategic breaks from training to take photos both from an employment standpoint, a club publicity standpoint, but also from a 'I need a breather' standpoint. Perhaps it was one of these reasons that Horatio found himself on the receiving end of one of Jet's strong tackles, or perhaps he was just unlucky. Horatio frequently ran the ball with intent into contact, which he could do well and was well experienced at. On one occasion though Jet had Horatio thoroughly set in his sights. They both came together, like an unstoppable force and an immovable object. Jet won the battle and as a result he started driving Horatio backwards. In the process Jet lifted one of Horatio's legs, toppling them both off balance, and then speared Horatio dangerously into the ground.

The crunch and crack of Horatio's shoulder buckling and then breaking was enough to send chills up the spines of all present. Play stopped immediately. Players flocked to Horatio's side as he lay their stifling an outcry of pain, rolling, groaning, and no longer able to pretend that he wasn't hurt. Jet said nothing to him as he got up and moved away. He walked straight over to Dennis and spoke so only he could hear.

"There is a new Hitman around here," he said intensely, "you didn't pass the torch though, or hand over that title, as you are incapable of giving others what they deserve. I had to take it. I will use that name, and don't think that because of what has happened here or at school I won't get you in exactly the same way." Jet didn't wait for a reply, Dennis would not have given him one anyway. Dennis simply watched Jet as he turned to re-join the huddle that hung at the field's edge where the other youths had gathered to watch. Dennis watched as some of those younger players patted Jet on the back and heckled the still slumped form of Horatio. Jet did not, he simply ignored them and retrieved his water bottle. A moment later he was back on the field preparing for the game to resume.

Dennis could only be amazed at what the young man was truly capable of. But still he was more afraid for the boy as he had yet to put them to use in a positive way.

There had to be a way to get through to him.

Surprisingly in the next training session there was to be no contact or even any practicing of skills. Dennis had been standing and talking to Horatio who carried a heavy sling around one shoulder. Their discussion initially surrounded the injury he had sustained but as that wasn't a fun conversation it had changed frequently. Topics had changed between work, the complexity and uniqueness of Dennis' training gear and attire, and back to rugby. The last thing that Horatio was sharing was that there was due to be a meteor shower in a few weeks' time. He was consumed by the idea that it was either dangerous or there was something suspicious about it, as it had not been publicised in the media anywhere and it usually would have been. This was a concern he shared loudly, as he was part of the media and he had taken great pride in writing a particularly long article about the phenomena, an article which apparently had become lost. He was part way through his thoughts on a conspiracy about the spectacle, which Dennis found that he had been drawn into considerably, when the coaches called everyone in and proclaimed they would be naming a starting squad with more players than would be needed in a team. The reason being so that the first grade team and the reserve grade could train together, with all players knowing what was expected between the two teams and what the other was doing. An actual team was to be named later on.

Dennis was one of the first names called, right behind Jiemba and before JT. Many of the incumbent players from the previous season were also selected. Horatio was not as he would be out of action for a short duration due to his injury, but Jet was selected into that squad. He was in fact the only one out of his huddle of youths who was. Dennis put that down to their general poor attitude to training and playing, but if that was the only reason then Jet himself probably wouldn't have been in that squad.

What followed straight after was a talking session. The squad moved into an old hut like room which sat below an area of the grandstand. Almost all acted as if nothing had changed despite the selection separating the group, while some were busy congratulating players who were in the squad that hadn't been before. Although not in the team yet it was still an accomplishment to be thought of so highly by the coaches due to your ability or effort you have put in.

"Ok everyone," one of the coaches said as they walked in behind the last player, promptly shutting the door behind them. "Let's get down to business." What followed was a conversation involving congratulating everyone for what they had achieved so far, be them old or new players. After this the coaches outlined, in brief, their plans as to what they were looking for, what they were going to be working on, what the ideals and goals of the team and club were, and what they believed would help them achieve those goals. Finally it all dispersed and a different chat emerged, one which most knew would come.

"Men we are going to go around the circle and each of us will introduce ourselves, regardless if we know you or not, tell the squad your name, where you are from, what you do for work and fun, and something interesting," the coach said. The circle that the group sat in was hardly even a formed shape of any description, but they were each able to determine who would follow who and the order they would speak in.

"Hi I am Jiemba," Jiemba stood up and pretended to shake hands and wave at others where he stood, as if the others were captivated by him like some grand stage performer. He laughed at his own antics, it was uncommon for him not to conclude a sentence without a shot of laughter to accompany it. "I would prefer it if you call me Jim, all my friends do, if you are new you are now my friend, you don't get a choice you just are now, deal with it. Plus it is somewhat easier to shout out Jim on the footy field than Jiemba, and if you shout out Jiemba I get real scared that my mum is going to come and get me. It happened once. She is a scary lady, I love her, don't tell mum I said she was scary," he laughed again through his big bushy beard, the rest of the crowd mostly joined in. "I am a tradie, hasn't helped with the ladies yet but, not through lack of trying, but those are different stories," he giggled again, but Dennis noticed that it was more anxious and less fun than the others. Dennis wondered if others had noticed too. After a short pause Jiemba continued. "I love this club, like really love it, and I look forward to a great year with all of you." Applause accompanied as Jiemba bowed sarcastically to all around him before returning to sit.

The rest of the squad followed in kind, some trying to be funny some just saying the bare minimum.

"Hi, they call me the Badge," said one fit looking man. He said nothing else to accompany his introduction, but even that was enough to get the group excited.

"Yeah the Badge," a majority of players called out in reply. JT stood up next and it became less about him and more about how much he hated Jiemba. It was all in jest, which was all for the best because if anyone was to say what he said, to someone who wasn't a good friend or hadn't realised the joke, the atmosphere would have been very different. Jiemba laughed, but again Dennis noticed its tone.

Dennis was next to introduce himself to the group, saying that he was happy to be there and would do what he could to help out. His introduction was once again followed by an awkward bouncing of his body and small flailing of limbs as he waved and sat down. The motion was greeted by a chorus of people either saying his first name, last name, or by the call sign, 'Hitman'.

Last to introduce himself was Jet. He wasn't sitting in the circle like everyone else as he had decided to stand off to one side. No one really knew where he would fit into the introductions, and although persistently asking him to speak next at multiple interludes he had denied every instance; and so the group had instead decided to ignore him until the very end. He waited under the gaze of the others for a few moments, resisting the urge to talk. Dennis had almost settled upon the idea that Jet would refuse to speak to the group at all, before suddenly he started.

"My name is Jet," he began. He remained leaning against the wall with arms crossed tightly in front of his chest. His arm muscles twitched and bulged at the action, which most of the others noticed was deliberate and displayed just for them. Few were impressed. "You can call me 'Hitman' instead, as that is what I am." Glances were shared between most in the room, with some barely muffled laughter creeping around the group. It was a common thing within a group to have a nickname, but you didn't have one that somebody else did, and you never ever made up your own. That was a great way to be called something else, and those names were normally not pleasant. "I am probably the biggest and best player that has ever come to this club. You would be lucky to have me and you need me more than I need you." Everyone was shocked and none said anything for a moment.

The silence was broken by Jiemba, who, although he had tried very hard to contain it, suddenly burst out in laughter. Most of the players accompanied him. It was laughable at best but when Jiemba laughed it became harder to resist. Dennis knew it would have taken something small to set off Jet, but the laughter was so far beyond that; Dennis therefore wasn't surprised when Jet stormed towards the door. The mockery followed him throughout and from the room, and as it was a solid brick structure it echoed and reverberated from the walls. The big steel door was slung back on its hinges and smashed with a clang on a pillar next to it. The light from an outside spotlamp streamed blindingly into the darkened room. In the door there stood Horatio.

"Ready for a photo, friend," he asked Jet innocently as the youth stormed past, otherwise unaware of his fury. The squad exploded in laughter again. Jet barged past him, causing Horatio to juggle his camera in front of him despite the cord that hung around his neck. He winced a few times at the movement, as it clearly caused pain to his injury, then swept a hand across his brow in relief.

"Um, if anyone else is cranky at getting their photo taken can you please not run into me, it hurts a little," Horatio told the rest of the squad. The foray of smirks and giggles continued. The room was exploding with mirth as everyone smiled their faces off.

Everyone except Dennis.

CHAPTER 4 – THE CHARACTER BUILDER

Now

The relationship was becoming more volatile. Dennis had firmly established himself as part of the school with staff, students and the community. He was approachable, well-liked and knowledgeable. He had even been looking into the local history more and more, and adding it into his lessons; conveying what he had learned about GreenCorp and the aquifer and how that helped provide a sustainable environment in regard to the geography of the Central West. The enrichment of his lessons was something he took pride in; his research was therefore meticulous lest he give the wrong information.

Jet, however, had gone the other way. He was competitive in every facet, at school and at training. He was going out of his way to stop by the classes that Dennis taught and straight out question the validity of what he was saying. The students within knew better than to follow Jet's lead, and in every instance Dennis was able to back up what he was saying and then flick the focus onto Jet in regard to his own knowledge. Jet would leave in disgust at the place the teacher had put him in, which in turn made things deteriorate even quicker. Dennis would not be undermined in his own classroom. Despite the desire he had to help Jet, his control was absolute, and was reflected in the confidence his other students had in him.

Jet had also occasionally found Dennis in the street, before or after work hours, and continued his pursuit to intimidate him in public. Urging the teacher to push him away as he irritated him or made false claims. Those claims were never bad enough to get others involved, but each was a shot at his values and character. Dennis wouldn't rise to the bait, nor respond as the boy wanted, but his anger still simmered below the surface. This sort of behaviour Dennis knew was out of character for the youth. Before he had depicted a charade of a tyrant who could bend others to his will, but now he carrying on like an annoying spoilt brat. Those around him would probably be happy if Dennis was to react and knock Jet away, but still Dennis would not.

Instead Dennis made sure that the appropriate people were informed at school if something should arise from the defamation, but despite his best efforts Dennis could not make contact with the boy's parents. Multiple calls, hand-written notes and a one-time visit to the household residence bore no fruit. When asked about the matter and if this had been normal in the past, staff stated that although contact had been made in the past it was fleeting or sometimes dismissed. Dennis found that no contact had been made so far that year.

Dennis was also finding it harder to demonstrate restraint at training. Jet had turned his intensity up even more. He was aware he was fighting for a position in the team, but he acted like he was fighting off everyone else for that position; as if everyone was out to get him. His ferocity increased in contact as did his focus on improving his fitness. His physical growth was impressive, but his teamwork and attitude were deplorable. He took all the opportunities to carry the ball he could, and when he did he was absolutely devastating, but that meant the team and those around him suffered. Jet still chose to stay close to Dennis, and in doing so he set him up to get hit, throwing poor passes in his direction that were either too hard or impossible to catch, or refusing to assist him at all when it was necessary to do so. The intent clearly was to make Dennis look bad as the two were hard to separate on ability alone. Dennis even suspected on raw talent and many other aspects that Jet had the edge on him, but he wasn't doing himself any favours by allowing others to focus on his negative traits.

Their battles weren't just raging physically however, it had also become a mental battle. It showed more on Jet's features than those on Dennis, but the trials of a teacher had taught Dennis to be positive or appear to be positive in almost any situation lest it impact those around him. Others tried to intervene but their actions were limited as they were just as confused at what was happening as Dennis was. It felt like life was really starting to drag and everything else had been lost to focus.

The day finally came when the team was to be decided. The year was moving into late March and the club had trained hard through their pre-season. This would be the final squad training before the Easter break and when they resumed it would be team training only with far reduced numbers, the rest allocated to reserve grade or lower, or even back to colts which was for those players still eligible under the age of twenty.

This training was special though as it wasn't any run of the mill sort of trial. The whole squad was going to a local recreation camp at a place called Lake Burrendong, just outside of Wellington. It was a bit over an hour's drive from Orange and everyone in the team would take a bus out to the camp; spending the night to encourage some bonding within the team. During the day after arrival, and before departure the next day, they would be training heavily to flush out any last minute decisions for who would be successful in obtaining selection to the team. The only people on the bus were those in the squad, the senior coaches of the club, and the club physio to help with strapping and any small injuries. Horatio had managed to sneak in to the tour as well, as the club publicity person and photographer. He promised he would only focus on the positive things and would stay out of the way mostly. When it came to late night bonding he made no promises as to how little or how much he would participate.

The bus trip proved to be a somewhat social affair. There were enough seats for everybody to have their own without having to share. Some, very few, were busy on their phones as they texted others, searched social media or simply used it as an excuse not to talk to others. Jet was one of those as he sat by himself taking up the entire back seat. He leaned against one window and had his legs stretched out across the positions beside him, allowing no admittance; probably in an act to show his dominance, but ultimately created a sense of isolation. The others didn't care, some sitting in silence but most talking to those in the seats in front, behind, or across from them.

Dennis was sitting in the middle and was surrounded by people. There were people sharing seats so they could be closer to the conversation. The topics jumped between many things. Initially it was about how a couple of players were going to fair, away from their partners and girlfriends, as they were considered to be under the thumb or generally in trouble for going away at the best of times. It then changed to how well a couple of players would cope, as they had gone out on the town the night before, in anticipation of a weekend where they wouldn't be able to do so. Those few were not in a great state. The majority were discussing pre-season selections of national sporting teams in rugby union and league, and how those teams were likely to go in their own campaigns. Dennis contributed as much as he wanted but was a much keener listener than participant in the conversation. On occasion he would add something profound, but Dennis was also known to jump in and berate someone for sharing untruths, humiliating them in the process while obtaining laughs and applause, something which he did several times during that trip. The teacher in him was set aside for the moment so he could relax and settle into his old style and more comfortable character.

Jiemba made the volume of the bus louder. He had created a culture of positivity around him either by desire or happy accident; it meant that he was listened to fondly or in anticipation of him dropping a joke or laughing uncontrollably at one. Even the moments where he was silent managed to bring forth a chorus of uncontrollable laughter. There were times when he was dead serious and some of the other players didn't know whether to laugh or not. Jiemba would return the conversation to something more positive again to reclaim the fun and comradery being shown on the bus. He claimed that he had organised a special surprise for all the players later that evening when training had finished. The players talked amongst themselves as to what they thought that might mean. They were both confused and excited, some with more crude ideas than others. Horatio had sat next to Dennis and once the collective discussion had died down nearly half an hour into the trip, no doubt to return sooner rather than later, both of them shared their own conversation.

"This should be good," said Horatio so only Dennis could hear him. "I think the team is more or less already picked, but either way it is still a great way to get in some better training, build up the spirit a bit, and just have some fun together. It adds depth and a better culture to the club."

"Yeah, should be good," Dennis agreed. "Do you know what Jiemba's surprise is?" Horatio nodded knowingly with a slight smirk.

"Sure do, because you guys are all training I have been asked to help out a little bit behind the scenes. JT was going to help as well because he wasn't coming out for the whole time, due to his work at the mines, but they changed his shift and now he isn't coming out at all. I am not going to tell you what it is, but it is really cool. I haven't been involved with something like it before in my time with the club or elsewhere. I think it will definitely add something. It couldn't happen on a more special night," Horatio explained, but, despite Dennis agreeing and maintaining his excitement throughout, Dennis was left confused. Horatio couldn't just be talking about the training camp, because to him that really wasn't all that special.

"What's happening tonight?" he asked finally, giving into his apparent ignorance. The great thing about sitting in different chairs near each other was that facial expressions were usually missed. Dennis had a feeling that he had been told already but he couldn't recall the necessary information from his memory.

"The meteor shower!" Horatio exclaimed, ignoring how Dennis had forgotten. He had called it out a little louder than they had been speaking, drawing the eye and a small chuckle from others on the bus. Dennis remembered almost instantly. It was great how many of the players had their own little hobbies or interests that may have drawn teasing usually, but this group was so supportive of one another they generally just encouraged what made others comfortable. Dennis knew he was about to be reinformed about the meteor shower and made himself more comfortable in his seat. He pressed himself closer to the window for no other reason than to see out of it better. It wasn't actually going to make him that much more comfortable, which was generally impossible on buses due to his long legs and awkward posture. The bus had recently just left the small town of Molong after following the highway through it. Dennis instantly remembered from his recent studies that it was from this point on that he could get a closer look at GreenCorp's giant tower, and hoped greatly to do so, and the surroundings of that modern marvel which was known as Westopolis.

"I am certain that there is huge importance for this event," Horatio continued, Dennis knew that he was a passive partaker in the conversation as Horatio would just educate him from that point on. "When I first found out about it there were several sources stating the time and place that the shower would take place. There were even some early articles stating where the best place to observe the meteor shower would be. But since that time there has been nothing new, nothing promoted anywhere, in fact those sources which I just mentioned have also been taken away."

"Maybe they were just deleted," Dennis contributed his suggestion as he still scanned the horizon, hoping to see something extraordinary pop into view in the very next instance. He noticed that large pipes and overflowing creeks that could be almost classed as rivers started to become more frequent.

"They were deleted, clearly," Horatio agreed, "But even when deleted the articles should still able to be found somewhere. I always download the code and the IP address as well as some other stuff you might not be aware of. I couldn't find them anywhere. They were even scrubbed from my own computer, which would take some serious hacking."

"I know you are a decent journalist," Dennis shared his view, "but I never knew you were so thorough."

"They don't call me 'The Finder' for nothing," Horatio claimed.

"Who calls you that?" Dennis laughed with his response. "The only names I have ever heard you be called, apart from some bad ones which you sometimes deserve, is Horatio or Finny. No-one calls you 'The Finder'."

"Yeah well they should," Horatio replied defiantly. "Because I am the best at what I do. Pure talent over here, anyway mark my words that at some time tonight something spectacular is going to happen and I am going to capture it and discover exactly what it is. What are you looking for?" Horatio seemed to have finally noticed that Dennis was searching for something beyond the glass of the large bus windows. Dennis was not concerned by the question as it was really no big deal.

"Oh, nothing," Dennis half admitted, "I was just noticing how green everything is now. The last time I drove down this road I was being yelled at, when I was a learner driver going to Central West representative training. There had been a plague of locusts at the time and my old man was giving it to me because I kept using my windscreen wipers on all the bugs that kept hitting my windscreen. It smeared the guts all over the glass making it nearly impossible to see. I had to hang my head out of the window to see, which was pretty dangerous."

"Yeah I remember that, it was pretty crazy," Horatio agreed as he reflected upon his own memories. "That all changed when GreenCorp developed and enhanced that aquifer. That Westopolis place is unreal."

"You've been there?" Dennis queried, without trying to sound overly excited. He was simply interested and nothing more. "I was told that you could see it from a fair way off so I was just trying to see if that is true."

"It is true," Horatio answered and then turned to point out his window. "It's right there." Dennis followed his finger to where there was a mountain range, a small gap in the horizon, and then another couple of green spires.

"That's just a lonely mountain out there," Dennis said as he watched.

"Sort of," Horatio replied. "That is the edge of the Goobang National Park. Westopolis sits right in there and takes up all that space. Yeoval sits on an edge of it now. The whole place is built up from the ground. See that point though, the one that looks a slightly different shade of green than the rest? That is GreenCorp Tower." Again Dennis looked and found what Horatio had pointed out. His brow furrowed with misunderstanding.

"I thought that was a mountain," Dennis admitted.

"Most do, in fact the mountain itself is manmade, to cover many of their operations from natural elements above ground, and the tower is then built into that mountainside," Horatio granted. "But it is an inland oasis, a modern masterpiece. I have been there a few times to report on what they are doing there. It's all cutting edge and mind-blowing. Even the new roads that lead you there are amazing. They are all built on massive pipes which funnel water out from the city, trees line the side but they also draw wind energy from the breeze and transfer heat from the sun into solar panels that follow it along, and transfer the energy into more panels beneath the ground. Seriously, check it out sometime. I am pretty sure that they are very close to having a population large enough to be called a city, pretty impressive for a place which is only a few years old." Despite Horatio saying there was too much to talk about in regard to Westopolis he continued to do so anyway. Great parts of it Dennis already knew, but he listened intently to fill the holes of his knowledge. If they could build a mountain and stabilise an entire ecosystem that was suffering, then the person responsible deserved his attention.

What Horatio said was astounding and great portions of it unbelievable. The journalist would jump in between topics regarding Westopolis and then back to the meteor shower. The buildings at Westopolis created more energy than they could use, the meteor shower would be brighter than usual as the fragments were closer to the atmosphere for a longer duration, Westopolis was sustainable for the environment and its workers as no one had ever been fired, the meteors would be a vibrant purple or violet colour which was unheard of.

Dennis wanted to hear more but that was not to be. The conversation in other parts of the bus sparked up once more and the topic changed just as quickly, the last thing anyone wanted to do was talk about a city. Except for Dennis, all he could do

was watch the spire that he had been shown as it stood
unyielding against a naturally amazing background. He watched
it for as long as he could, ignoring all conversation around him.

Westopolis really didn't interest him. He laughed at the
thought. He also wondered why his uncle had so many
reservations about such an amazing place.

"Stand up, hands behind your head, suck in the air you need,"
the order came. Dennis, like many of the other players, had
instinctively bent over to lean on his knees as he tried to
overcome his exhaustion. He obeyed the demand against the
wishes of his body as he attempted to draw in more oxygen to
aid his recovery. Only seconds past but it felt like he was
breathing deeper for minutes. The entire afternoon had been an
exhausting exercise, and although he would be laughing and
joking in triumph usually when he finished he could not on this
occasion. As he sucked in breath he just reflected.

The bus trip had been enjoyable for a short time and then just as
quickly the small luxuries it presented were sorely missed. The
group were not dropped off at the recreation park like they had
imagined, but at a small distance short of their destination
instead. Ten kilometres away at a small village called Mumbil
the bus abruptly came to a halt and all were told to disembark.
All, except the coaches and the physio who were able to stay on
board with their bags and the luggage of Horatio. The bus could
still travel to the desired location no problem, and did so with
those still on board. The players were forced to carry their gear
the remainder of the journey; Horatio accompanied them but he
carried nothing except his camera. To most it was not a
massively big deal, especially those who saw it as a short walk
with their mates, the longer it took the less time they had to do
more rigorous training. Others spent a great deal of time
groaning about the predicament of continuously switching hands

to carry their luggage as it was either too awkward to manage or else there was too much packed and it was heavy. Once it had dropped off its occupants the bus travelled back up the road beeping its horn in response to them. Some players waved cheerily while others raised certain fingers into the air and shouted profanities.

That 'short' walk had only been the beginning.

When they arrived at the camp, after marvelling at the giant expanse of water which gleamed before them, they had been told to dump their gear and proceed to a small hall. The afternoon, they were instructed, was to be filled with numerous simple activities; but first they were to have lunch. Dennis, who was usually one to enjoy his food to excess, particularly if it was delicious or something foreign to him, ate only a small amount. He was suspicious that if the short ten kilometre walk was just the beginning then what was to come would be far worse. Others, it seemed, shared his opinion only eating the bare minimum and drinking a decent amount of water. A few gouged on the delicious food and even sweets that were offered up as well. Dennis thought to himself that those that indulged would almost certainly be tasting the meal at least twice during the coming hours.

Dennis was right.

The first task involved rock climbing. Whilst it sounded enjoyable the task itself was not. The players, four at a time, were to climb a vertical man-made wall with all the usual hard plastic or stone hand holds. But then they were to proceed onto a part of the wall which came back on itself, forcing the climbers to hang by their hands and fingers. When Dennis did it he could feel the few muscles contained within his fingers start to tense and struggle, lactic acid building up in them and in the stronger muscles in his upper arms. His core felt constricted and he imagined that his neck was doing a fair bit of the holding by how tight it was. The consolation of pushing hard through the activity was that those who lasted were rewarded in the next activity, by getting to train for a shorter duration. Dennis managed to hold his own for a decent amount of time. The bigger heavier players suffered and fell quickly, meaning they would be doing more in the next activity. Others, like the tiny, lithe or deceptively strong, persevered and managed to hold on longer. Jet, who had said almost nothing to anybody, was one of those who lasted. He was the last to fall; his body revealed what his face did not. When you looked up at him he hung straight down, unmoving, staring at all those who watched. His expression didn't change and he revealed no stress from what he was doing. His body shook under the pressure but he didn't fall until he was sure he had outlasted everyone. Everyone, including Dennis, applauded the display.

The next activity was thirty minutes of shuttle running. It was a handicapped start, if you went well with the rock climbing you started later than the others, if you didn't you ran for the entire duration. The bigger guys struggled. Dennis just did it. Jiemba was struggling too but attempted to run alongside Dennis. Dennis slowed down marginally to help his friend, if the coaches noticed they said nothing. While many of the incumbent players knew what the coach expected some of those who were new, did not. Despite that, it was easy to know what to do. If you struggled you kept going, you did not want to be seen as someone who would give up or be seen to stop when the going got harder. If you could talk you were expected to, encouraging others to keep them moving or telling a story to keep the pain of the task at the back of your minds. And if you could team up with somebody at a similar level you did it, so you were not alone in your attempt to succeed. Dennis did all of these with Jiemba, and encouraged others who ran past them to do the same, regardless if they were going at a fast pace or almost no pace at all. Dennis had to laugh at Jiemba. When they had started running together Dennis had been encouraging the shorter man to keep his legs moving. It wasn't long before Jiemba grew tired of the encouragement and started his own conversation.

"Whoever invented running must not have liked food, or drink, or fun," he said, and continued the tirade about what he would do to the person who invented running should he ever meet them. Moments later his shirt came off and was wrapped around his head like a turban. Jiemba's stomach muscles hung amongst the concentrated amount of offseason indulgence at his waist. He had gotten leaner over the pre-season training but he hadn't lost it all yet. Dennis would make the observation of his friend's size as a solid, strong, short mass.

"Jeez, my beard is as warm as a woolly jumper," Jiemba muttered openly. He kept lifting his chin to allow the sweat at his neck to soak up some of the cool breeze that sailed past. "Someone find me a shearing shed I am dying over here." The comments continued, but it encouraged others to laugh and share their own stories or funny discomforts. Jet ignored everyone. Only talking to someone to tell them to get out of his way or inform them that he would not help them to succeed when they were failures, and failures weren't welcome in his team.

The event that followed after the seemingly endless running was more enjoyable. They each got a kayak and simply had to follow an instructor as he trailed around the edge of the lake. The wind made it tricky but the players found their groove quickly. Bobbing around with the tiny waves and striking the water with the blade of their oars. The instructor was considerate to them all, initially. He allowed the players to find a rhythm which suited them, he floated with the breeze to let them rest and kept a simple pace for most of the journey. When they had travelled around almost three quarters of the lake, after going around a giant deserted island which appeared from beneath the water off to one side, and they had started heading back into the breeze the situation changed quickly. One of the coaches appeared on the shore with a megaphone and gave them the next instruction.

"There is a road run after the kayak part of the training," the megaphone boomed. "When you finish that run there will be no more training. The first person out sets the pace and everyone else has to keep up. You arrive together." That was all. No sooner had he finished did they realise that the trainer had taken off into the slowly strengthening gale. The chase begun.

Dennis found that the separation of all the players in the water was pretty even. The bigger guys sunk into the water more, but they also had more drive in their arms. The lighter guys skipped awkwardly above the waves but needed to be more focused on how they steered. Dennis found his rhythm and just created a constant and consistent motion that would help him reach the destination. He could hear the splashing of water around him. Some were light and controlled, and some were heavier and more frantic. Dennis didn't turn away from his task to glance at any of them.

He was startled from his trance like focus when nudged by another kayak. The nose of the imposing craft bumping into his arm gave him a small cut which he pulled back from in reflex, causing him to almost drop his double-bladed oar into the water.

"Get out of my way," Jet roared as he pressed past him. He leant forward in his kayak striking the waves as aggressively as the scowl that covered his face. There was no apology just mindless determination towards showing to everyone that he was the best. The players were scattered in their approach to the shore and a few moments later they sporadically started reaching its sandy bank. The instructor stood there, encouraging them on and helping them pull their kayaks free from the water.

"You have to catch up," he told Dennis as he rendered assistance with his kayak. Dennis found his feet, which had not been overly wet by the cool water from the lake, and took off at a jog. Jet was far out in front and he was sprinting away. There was a trail of players that followed, none being able to catch the one in front.

"We have to catch up to that?" Jiemba questioned as he puffed his way to Dennis' side. "What about the blokes behind us?"

"The coach said get there together," Dennis replied, "he didn't say how fast."

"He said the first person sets the pace," Jiemba said in turn. "But that first person should have set a slower pace." As Dennis turned to watch those still struggling to come from the water Jiemba put his fingers to his mouth and let out a loud screeching whistle.

"Oi," he shouted as they turned, holding up both arms above his head. "Stop." All of those that Dennis could see obeyed, some even started walking back down towards them. Dennis waited where he stood and encouraged those behind him to keep going. Once the final player had exited the water he turned to all of them.

"Last activity, we keep up a steady jog, we don't walk though, we encourage each other, and we get there together, agreed?" he spoke to them. They either nodded or voiced their acceptance of his plan. Then they set off.

The instructor had run the journey alongside them, adding his voice to theirs as they made their way back. He also added his voice to those of the coaches when they finally arrived and proceeded to catch their breath. The players had all done it. They were all stoked with their efforts regardless of if they were happy to do it in the first place or not. The coaches walked in around them, patting shoulders and backs, reiterating how the players had all achieved something huge. Everyone was proud of their efforts.

Everyone, that was, except Jet, who stood at the side of the group with arms crossed. His ever staring dangerous eyes never once leaving Dennis.

Upon returning to the camp most of the players had stripped out of their clothes and jumped headlong into the cold lake water. It helped them cool down and sure enough they started playing a rough yet comical version of footy. It ended up just becoming a contest of who would be the last person dunked beneath the water. Dennis chuckled at how even adults found joy in the simplest of things. Once the water started becoming too cold for many, despite it being cool to start with, the players slowly clambered out of the water and towards the warmth of the showers. Gradually they all came to sit around a camp fire which had not yet been lit. Dennis wore an awful Hawaiian style shirt that was covered in bees and pineapples. Promptly Horatio came to sit down beside him with a big smile on his face.

"Is Jiemba organising his surprise?" Dennis asked Horatio who simply nodded with a wink.

"Attention please everyone," one of the coaches stood up from where he sat. A brown cardboard box sat at his feet. "So as not to ruin your bonding tonight we coaches have a few small things to say and do before we leave you to it. We are incredibly impressed by the strength, determination and resolve that you have all shown today, as well as through the rest of the pre-season. It has helped us immensely, to not only assist in picking a team that will start the season in our first grade, but to also allow each of you to come together and realise that together you can do a whole bunch of things that you didn't know you could." He moved to pick up the box at his feet. "We have got these training shirts for all of you in recognition of the effort you have all put in and we hope that you will use them. There are no more so don't lose them, if you break them they are gone, no more. Sorry, not sorry." He passed them around asking sizes and the like and returned to sit down once every player was sorted and wearing their training shirt.

"Everyone get comfortable please and sit around the campfire," Horatio announced from Dennis' side. The players were already sitting in a circle as that was where the chairs had been arranged with the already present logs. All were occupied except for two. "We have something really special this afternoon which I have never been a part of, and I am sure you will be appreciative of what is about to happen. I ask that you are respectful and show as much enthusiasm as I will." Horatio sat down, the expectation sat down with him. No one said anything for a small time and then all had their attention drawn to the movement which came from behind a shack nearby.

Two men came forward. Both wore very little clothing but were covered in some sort of body paint. One of them was far older than the other, his white hair glowing in the twilight that was falling around them, the other had a great deal of his big thick black beard covering his neck and the upper portion of his chest. Dennis caught his eye and smiled, hoping that he was allowed. Jiemba smiled back, before returning to focus on what he was carrying.

"Hi everyone," Jiemba said to the group, who all murmured excitedly in reply. "I have organised something really special this afternoon for all of us. I hope you are as excited as I am, and I am really, really excited." Jiemba laughed nervously, which grew louder instantly and then he stopped. "First I would like to introduce a really special man who is going to explain what we are doing and guide us all through it. Everyone this is Uncle Lue, he is actually my uncle but he is also one of the local elders and we are really lucky to have him here with us this afternoon." The players didn't know whether or not to say hello or wait, none wanting to be the person who did the wrong thing.

"I hope they can play better than they look," Uncle Lue said first, causing nervous laughter to come forth. It helped everyone and the players relaxed a little bit more.

"Good afternoon everyone, my name is Lue, I am a proud Wiradjuri man and I am also a local Wiradjuri Elder. I am first going to welcome you all to Wiradjuri land, I am sure you have all been accepted warmly by my nephew Jiemba where you live, but if you haven't I welcome you to this place. This is the land of the three rivers, the Wambool, which you all know as the Macquarie, which also flows directly into this great lake behind us, the Kalare which is the Lachlan River and the Murrumbidjeri or Murrumbidgee. I would also like to pay my respects to Wiradjuri Elders both past and present, and extend that respect to other nations who are present here today and the Elders of those nations. My name, Lue, means 'chain of waterholes'. On my body you can see the paintings of circles which represent the waterhole but they can also be seen as places of a meeting and a gathering like we have here today. I am here today to perform a ceremonial smoking with you. I will be assisted by Jiemba, if he hasn't told you before his name also means "laughing star", and I know that he lives up to that name as well. We are both covered in Ochre, more white than red but we have both. The white represents the ceremonies that we go through and it is the colour that men wear, the red represents the woman and we wear a little bit because we have a woman side and are from the woman as well. We show respect to the woman as well as the man. Jiemba has his own design which I have helped him with, and on his back and upper arms he has the image of a goanna which is his totem." Everyone once again nodded their understanding but no one else spoke.

"Today, this evening, as I said before, we will be partaking in a smoking ceremony. The ceremony is used so that we can heal together, not just from the long training that you have all had today as Jiemba has told me, but also of the mind, the body, and as a group. We will be getting rid of any bad spirits who may be around you, and also to help your eyes to see what is there. Looking at all of you in front of me, Indigenous and non-indigenous, I am so proud of the brotherhood that you all have together and hope that as a group you continue to help each other and your community beyond your time as a team or a player. Jiemba," Lue motioned to Jiemba who set about his task. He had been holding onto a small bark tray which consisted of leaves from what Dennis guessed was either a wattle or eucalypt. He walked into the campfire area and alongside Lue set about lighting a small fire and then placing the branches on top of them. It wasn't long until they were smouldering and exuding a refreshing scent along with the smoke. Lue walked into the smoke and used his hands and arms to fold the smoke onto himself, Jiemba followed suit and then they both welcomed the rest of the team to join them. One by one they followed the sway of the smoke in the calm breeze and covered themselves in it. The aroma covered them and surrounded them, lingering amongst the cloth once they had retaken their seats. Finally Lue spoke again.

"I want to thank you for inviting me out here with all of you fine individuals. A smoking ceremony is usually only performed at important or significant events. I feel like allowing a young leader like Jiemba to witness and partake in a ceremony is beneficial for him and I appreciate you all for giving him the opportunity. I also feel like this signifies the beginning of an ongoing engagement with everyone here in respect to your communities and showing others who look up to you how to be respectful and positive to all. In my opinion this is significant. The next time you are here I invite you to come and see me and engage with my community as well as your own." The group thanked Lue, but sat silently for a short time allowing the smoke to pour over them and its message sink in. No one moved until the sun had well and truly set.

The coaches were long gone before night had completely fallen. Lue had hung around for a simple meal where he probably engaged in more conversation about football than anybody else. Many of the players spoke to him, thanking him for allowing them all to be part of his special ceremony and being generally appreciative. He then left with a smile shortly after, making the demand that all should look after one another that night, knowing full well that some sort of small party would take place once he had gone.

The players, despite initially wanting to kick on with a small party, sat happily docile. The exhaustion from the days training and the expectation of more the next morning had drained them completely, leaving them more than happy to simply enjoy a quiet drink and the company of one another. The ceremony had also left many of them humbled and unwilling to be disrespectful after the fact, especially as they felt like they had been treated to something quite special. Another fire was not lit, the night was only a touch cooler than the day had been and the chill was nothing a jumper couldn't take away.

Jiemba had stayed in his ceremonial outfit, the pride he had shown in partaking was evident and no one said anything negative about it.

Dennis had pulled up a seat next to Horatio in a reclining chair a little bit closer to the water's edge. Many of the other players had moved down there as well and chatted in small groups.

"I am going to stay out here only a little longer," Horatio said as he finished the remains of the drink he had been sipping at. "It is almost time. While you guys were walking back from the bus I claimed the loft area above the bedrooms. There isn't a bed up there but my sleeping bag will do. I have set up a small telescope which I can use to take photos with at a much closer range. It cost a bit of money but it will be worth it. Did you want to come up as well?"

Dennis' ears pricked up as he heard something else nearby. "No thanks mate," Dennis said as he searched for who was responsible for what he was hearing. "Just show me the pictures when you finish. I will tell you what I can see from down here." He waved Horatio away and climbed to his feet. His body was completely sore. Simply by standing he felt pain in most spots of his body. Luckily, due to the excess of agony within his body, he couldn't pin point all of the locations, but because of his tall stature he knew he still felt more than others though. He arched his stomach forward as his lower back braced, he stepped timidly as the soles of his feet scrunched, his hip felt like it was moving centimetres at a time as it constantly fought off cramp. He believed that he looked like some frail old man, only worse because he was much taller than they were and he stooped far lower and more obviously. Eventually he forgot all that as he found the conversation that he was looking for. He was not surprised by who it was coming from.

"What did you just say?" Dennis demanded angrily.

"You eavesdropping?" Jet said, shrugging off the idea of standing up to Dennis. He was old enough to drink so he had been allowed to do so, but it was still odd to have a school student drinking in front of him, and with him he supposed. No one had had much though and Dennis doubted that Jet had had more than a couple.

"I am going to ask again, nicely," responded Dennis.

"I only said what everyone else here is thinking," Jet said, and this time he did get to his feet, "but you are all too gutless to say it." Dennis could feel he was grinding his own teeth but said nothing.

"This whole thing is a joke," Jet spat forward, he walked a few steps forward revealing his body was well in control. Then he stepped back out of reach of all. "Everything we have done here has celebrated mediocrity. We took a bus to do exercises we could have done back at home, except now we have to stay here, caged together like animals, just to get a number on our backs. I have beaten everyone here at everything we have done and I haven't received the accolades I should have. You should all be trying to aspire to be more like me, stronger, faster, better, but instead you are helping the slobs who couldn't be bothered to get fit. I was the only one who followed the coach's direction in that last activity. Keep the pace. You all slackened off, but the coaches thought it was great. It's stupid." Jiemba had walked over to help calm down the youth.

"Get away from me, you are the worst," Jet snarled. Jiemba smiled in reply; he still took a step back realising the warning. What followed was a non-stop tirade that was not only meant to hurt Jiemba but disrespect everything that he was about and the ceremony that he had help lead. It was abusive, hurtful, and relentless, targeting not only who Jiemba was as a person but questioning everything about his culture and beliefs. When he was finished everyone waited for Jiemba to strike back. He could respond better than anybody in these situations and with a slight on his culture and character no-one would have blamed him if he exploded, as he was justified to do so and had done so in the past.

But he didn't.

Instead he just appeared to sadly accept it. Jiemba turned around, despite heeding calls from the majority of players for him to stay, and walked slowly away, down and along the edge of the water. Dennis knew that apart from what was just said to him something was wrong. Jiemba never did that. He placed it in the back of his head, along with a collection of other instances, for later, but turned to the problem at hand. He wouldn't stand for what he had just been present for.

"Why are you even here?" Dennis spat at the young man. "You are supposedly over-achieving, you have the worst attitude, you like no-one here despite everyone giving you their best, you're an upstart, arrogant, entitled jerk. You are not good enough to be in our company, far beneath the worthiness of

Jiemba's presence, and you do not deserve to wear our emblem on your shirt."

Jet smiled in reply, shrugging off everything that Dennis had said.

"Take it off," Dennis snapped, finally reaching his tipping point. "And then get out. You are not welcome here." His call was repeated by the entirety of the team. A few of them ready to jump in and beat Jet down on the spot for his disrespectful and disgusting behaviour.

"Righto," Jet laughed.

"I mean it," Dennis echoed.

"Why? Because it is the only one without that silly smoke smell on it? Make me," Jet smirked.

Dennis leaped. He grabbed the scruff of the collar and didn't bother hoisting it over the youth's head. He just ripped it clean off. Jet wasn't one to just let it happen and he struggled. Jet's shirt was shredded off but the youth drove Dennis backwards from him as he tore it.

Several uneven steps and they were both staggering into the water. Dennis threw Jet off of him but they both tripped further into the shallow water; shallow water which quickly became deep and deeper. They were finally separated, standing only a few metres apart and staring at the other.

The onlookers on the shore were forgotten as the pair stood waist deep. Dennis' rage was barely hidden below the surface but he was managing to calm himself down, not because he was angry but because he wanted to have more control. Jet's bare chest heaved under the force of his accelerated breathing.

He didn't want to, Dennis thought, he didn't want to strike a student but he might have to. They both stood waiting, and watching, for the other's next move.

Something glistened in the corner of his eye, amongst the bright dazzling stars that were part of the Milky Way high above him.

To Dennis' eye a shooting star travelled slowly up there, moving slower than others he had seen. It was also much larger than the other stars that shone beside it, but none of those radiated a vibrant violet luminosity which stretched into the tail behind it.

"Pause a minute mate," Dennis said in a soft commanding tone. "Check out that up there, regather yourself so you can understand what you have just said and apologise for what you have just done."

"I'm not falling for that garbage," the youth snapped back. "You think I'm an idiot but I am the only smart one out here."

"Not after what you said," Dennis replied. His arms and hands were outstretched showing that he wanted to negotiate, to talk, not to fight. "We can fix this if you apologise, then we . . ."

"I am not apologising," the young man spat. "What I said was true. If you can't see it then there is more wrong with you than anybody else here. You aren't a teacher, you are a liar and a thief."

It didn't take long for Jet to rush him. Dennis had hardly enough time to sink his feet into the mud, clasping at what he could with his toes, before Jet was upon him. It would have been relatively easy to dodge, but then something happened he wasn't expecting.

The small violet light, which he had seen in the sky above, exploded into vibrant brilliance. Dennis was punched through his distraction, but it was only a glancing blow. He staggered, still partially blinded by the ferocity of that light.

The sound came next, as if the moon itself had hit the ground. Dennis only just lifted his hands to his ears before he was punched in the side of the head. This time he stumbled and fell.

From below the muck he could still see the dazzling show which took place in the sky above him. His ears rung, his head pounded and there was a dark silhouette coming towards him. It had limbs, and its hands scooped below the water to where

Dennis was laying on the bottom; reaching out desperately for him. Instead of pulling him up, however, they were pushing him down.

On top of everything else in Jet's rage he was trying to kill his teacher. It was already enough before, but now there were no more arguments to hold back.

Dennis kicked out with both feet, tangling them around Jet's strong legs and tugging hard. He slipped and fell releasing Dennis instantly. Dennis sprung up to his feet, water pouring down from him, and stood over where the boy had fallen. He would rise soon.

Dennis still hadn't decided on what he would do next, indecision blinding him more than the mud which slid away from his face.

A sharp whistling sound could be heard. Dennis hazarded a look up as a building roar echoed around him. That blast of light hadn't just lit up the night sky and released a huge sound, it had sent a huge rock hurtling down towards the ground. Or more accurately towards the water. The meteor shower that Horatio had gone on about for so long had been real and it was about to result in a collision. Prehistoric history stories told him instinctively that the result would not be good. Dennis turned and reached down into the water, yelling at every one on the lake shoreline as he went about the task.

"Everyone run," he screamed. He pulled hard and managed to haul Jet up out of the water. The boy came up swinging almost hitting Dennis again.

"Run you idiot," Dennis shouted at Jet and pushed him back towards the camp.

"What, why?" he barked, still ready for a fight that was now long gone. He had hardly had a chance to comprehend an answer to his own question when the meteor slammed into the centre of the water beyond where the island sat near its centre. It was huge; had it struck the ground it would have wiped out most of the camp. The result was that the water was left shimmering and steaming as it struck. Dennis still urged Jet forward, half-thinking that the result hadn't been that bad. He regretted the thought immediately. He felt a shudder in the water that surrounded his legs, something else had happened beneath the water. A wall of dark liquid suddenly rose high up into the air from the impact zone, blocking out most of the stars in the sky.

"A tsunami from a lake," Dennis called out uncontrollably, "what the heck?" His movement out of the water was slow. His pants and clothing were saturated and the grit and silt at the water's bottom made the ground slick and hard to traverse. Dennis didn't look back. He knew by the sound that Jet was following him, but he also heard that the water was surging forth and falling from that wall of water as well.

"Run, Dennis, run," the team was screaming from the doorway of one of the cabins as they clambered to safety. They had responded to his calls almost immediately, but no sooner had they called out to him with the final players arriving at the building's supposed safety then the door was promptly slammed shut. Dennis knew the reason and could only agree with it as the water continued its large wild surge forward. He was more worried with every step, the light that had been cast by the stars quickly being extinguished as he pressed on, but still he didn't look back. He could feel water droplets start slamming into him. They were small at first but then they came with such ferocity that they stung like he was being hit by darts.

Then the whole wave hit him. He lost his legs almost instantly as the water collapsed down upon him, grabbing at him and dragging him along in its wake. His eyes were squeezed shut, the pressure of the water when opening them too much to bear. His lungs started to squeal in panic, throwing open his mouth and forcing him to drink down large amounts of water. Dennis told himself he didn't want to drown, he didn't want to die, what could he do to stop this? He could do nothing. He felt the water that surrounded him turn from icy cold to warm and welcoming. His ears felt like they were going to explode as oxygen stopped moving through his body. Despite the darkness of the water it still dazzled a purple hue which penetrated through his closed eyelids. He wondered how long the water would surge for and how far he would be pushed. Up felt like it was down, and down felt like it was up; but even then he couldn't be sure if those bearings were true.

His question was answered before long.

Dennis was slammed into something hard, like a brick wall; probably actually a brick wall. Instead of falling down it though he was held in place, pressed hard with no ability to move. Surprisingly the brick wall which he was pressed up against managed to remain standing. That fact was not a relief to Dennis. His mind exploded in a scream of pain which flooded him more than the wave was flooding the camp. He was pressed harder and harder into the building, and he could feel as every muscle was torn, as every bone in his body was broken. He screamed, a howling roar muffled as bubbles as oxygen continued to flee away from his mouth. His breath failing he continued to roar, there was no way to fight it as he tried to force his mind to overcome the overwhelming pain that was ripping him apart. He was giving everything he could to resist it all, to stay awake and overcome his torture, but he could almost literally feel every isolated instance as the fabric of his skin, and the fibres of his body, were slowly torn away from those next to them. He asked himself, how long could he withstand it? He hoped for an end to come one way or another, otherwise there would not be much left of him in either outcome.

Then everything went black.

CHAPTER 5 – THE WHIP

Dennis grunted. Then Dennis groaned. Before too long he was slipping back into consciousness. He set about stretching as he tossed and turned in his bed. His discomfort since awakening was becoming known, but it quickly faded. Dennis had that feeling like he had slept in. His lips were stuck together and he promptly removed the slimy film that rested there. He became aware how bad his breath was, and he was irritated at how the sunlight was coming through his window and piercing his eyelids.

His eyes opened slowly and in the same motion Dennis slumped awake to sit at the side of his bed. His feet collapsed heavily to the floor which seemed to be a lot closer than he imagined, perhaps he had been resting on a low sitting bed. His brain finally started working, looking for clues as to where he was whilst slowly flicking through painful images as he started trying to remember what had happened.

Pain. The thought of pain was the first thing he recognised. It was also the only thing he could remember. Intense, throbbing, relentless pain. His memories of what had happened flashing in and out of focus. The giant wave came back and he cowered as if it was once more casting a twilight shadow over him. The drowning feeling was there too; as was the helplessness that came with it. Slamming into something hard came next. Having every bone in his body broken. He winced as his muscles remembered the conflict, and then he found himself cuddling his torso to comfort his tormented body. What was the thing that came next? Passing out and darkness came next, or perhaps even worse.

Dennis forced his eyes fully open and scanned the room he had been resting in. It seemed familiar. He had not had a chance to actually view his room at the camp properly, perhaps that was where he sat now. Due to the intense all day training, a quick shower and change, and then night time activities he had never had a chance to rest and explore it. He focused his ears but heard nothing. The assumption that the other players were already training hit him. He felt some guilt but imagined that if they really wanted him out there they would have roused him.

Dennis was famished and decided that he had been lying in bed long enough. It was at least mid-morning and well passed time for breakfast. Remembering the pain he been subject to Dennis tentatively pressed up onto his feet and away from his bed, expecting it to all come racing back and lance at his body.

Nothing. He felt nothing. Dennis still fell to the timber floor with a loud thump though. It wasn't the feeling of hurt that had caused him to fall. It was more like an awkwardness of not using his muscles for some time, or rather, more like when your whole body gets pins and needles and you can't control yourself properly. He tried again, this time using the wall to brace himself as he climbed up it. Dennis paused there for a moment waiting for his legs to take the full weight of his body. It came eventually.

Dennis for the first time realised he only wore long pants, no shirt or jersey. The pants weren't his, perhaps he had been leant those by a player. He looked around for his Hawaiian shirt or even the new training one he had received the night before, but the room was empty. He found himself glancing down and staring at his own chest; a chest which normally consisted of weirdly growing hairs and a simple leanness now covered in dense muscle. He poked himself in the stomach. There were no ripples or flab there at all, just what looked like a six pack that was on top of about four other six packs.

He clung to the wall for balance as he started to make his way to the door. When he arrived there he had to stoop a far way to get through. The camp rooms clearly weren't intended for those of the taller persuasion. When he appeared on the other side he stuck to the door frame for a moment. He was wobbly at best but this was not what he thought the cabins at camp would be like at all. He had walked into a kitchen and dining area, but it was decked out with the comforts of home. Pictures hung on the wall, nice looking sofas and entertainment units were pressed snuggly into a wall. He ignored all that in pursuit of nourishment which was close at hand.

Dennis felt his stomach beckon him. He released the door frame and walked tentatively forward. Dennis frowned in annoyance at his progress, he staggered like a toddler as they took their first steps ever. He slowly made his way to the fridge, catching himself from falling again by leaning in opposite directions and flinging his arms out for balance. The fridge was so small he could see over it when standing upright. He leaned for a second and then opened it up, hoping that his team mates had left him something. He was in luck, the best part of a large pizza was in there. Dennis pulled it out and moved it to the bench beside the fridge. He didn't stop to heat it; realising just how famished he was he started demolishing the food immediately. A slice was gone in an instant, followed quickly by another. His hand shot back to the fridge where he collected a pitcher of chilled cordial before proceeding to slurp it down noisily. He sucked down the last drops that hung at the side of the container, draining the jug in no time at all, and moved his attention back to the pizza. He was on his fourth slice before he took his time and stopped.

Dennis had a mouthful but stopped chewing entirely. His eyes wandered back to the fridge and what was covering the front. There were a whole bunch of magnets from various organisations holding down pieces of paper and photos. Dennis stared; his eyes landing on one of the images and staying there. It was a picture of his sister who looked like an almost identical, but clearly younger, version of his mum. Initially he thought it was a sick joke that the other players were playing on him, but as his eyes moved slowly from one picture to another he found they were all of his family. His mum, sister, Dennis, his uncle, even his dad were in these photos.

Dennis shuffled backwards in astonishment. His hands scrambled to grab something before he fell. He collapsed against an island bench which stood behind him; which shifted noisily on the floor under his weight, the remains of the pizza were dragged clumsily onto the floor. His eyes searched the room for what he realised was the first time. He finally took notice of everything. It couldn't be, but it couldn't not be. He was at home, at his mum's house.

The sound of something shattering behind him suddenly sounded. He turned quickly, not hearing the outside door open as he reacted to the arrival of his own understanding. No-one stood there, but an empty and now devastated porcelain cup of tea lay in pieces on the floor. Dennis moved to the window and saw the image of his mother rushing out to the large shed outside. His mum screamed out the name of his uncle. Dennis ignored it for the moment.

None of it made sense. How did he get to his mum's house? How did he travel that distance and sleep, all in one night? How come he felt no pain from what was one of the most terrible experiences? Why was his mum's house smaller than he remembered? His thoughts were interrupted by a loud metallic click.

"Alright friend," came the voice of Scott from behind the barrel of a long shotgun. "Move slowly, it is time for you to leave?" Dennis raised his hands instinctively, in shock and to protect himself, but when he threw them back over his head they struck the roof and he felt the plasterboard give way under the force, showering him with dust and debris. He started stammering in confusion at why his uncle was pointing a gun at him.

"Whoah, whoah, Uncle Scott," he pleaded towards his uncle as his feet shifted and slipped through broken plaster and dirt from the roof. The once pristine kitchen now covered in chaos. "Put the gun away, it's me Dennis." The gun lowered a little but remained pointing at the chest of Dennis. Dennis swept white grit out of his eyes and away from his face. His hands realised more of what he hadn't noticed before. His face was still occupied by a much thicker moustache than he remembered, and he had somehow grown a decent amount of stubble to accompany it. His hair was longer and a swept fringe now hung lazily across his eyes and down the back of his neck towards his shoulder blades. His arms were similar to his chest. Muscle on muscle on muscle showing near boundless strength on his once limber and lean flailing limbs. It took moments to pass before the fragile atmosphere was broken.

"Dennis," his mum exclaimed. She walked towards him, tears flowing down her face as she tried to cover the emotion with her hands. As soon as she came close she embraced him in a hug. She grappled at his midriff as she was now too small to reach his neck. Something had definitely changed, and he could see how tight she clung to him but, oddly, he hardly felt it. His mum remained there for minutes; all he could do was wrap one arm down around her and pat her now dusty hair. She pulled clear eventually, looking up at her son through bloodshot and blurry eyes.

"What's happening?" Dennis asked. "How did I get out here? What's going on?"

"I think you need to come and sit down Dennis," Scott suggested, finally accepting his nephew's claim. The gun was lowered and the bullets removed safely. "There is a lot that we have to talk about."

Dennis sat on an old bike as he tore around the paddocks of his mum's farm. It was a great way to think to himself with no-one else near him. He needed that now. His mum and uncle followed nearby on separate quad bikes, with extra space for equipment at the rear, but were both far enough away to give him solitude.

He felt like he had done nothing but eat since he woke up. During that time he was told what had happened. He had not been asleep for a night like he had thought. He had been asleep for a solid fortnight. He hadn't been sleeping though, he had been in a coma the entire time. Induced by the doctor's once he had been admitted to hospital. The journey from the camp to Orange Base Hospital had been by helicopter, a journey that, Dennis was informed, he had died at least three times.

Dennis had continued eating. The food fuelling his body but also hiding his emotions. His mum cried the whole time as Scott had spoken. There was more to come.

Dennis had broken just under ninety percent of the bones in his body, including his neck, his spine and everything in his chest. As a result he had punctured most of his vital organs including his heart. He had lain in a vegetative state on life support for several days. The doctors had advised that there was nothing they could do apart from the intervention they had provided. When Dennis was stable enough to transport the doctors allowed the request to move him. He would journey to his home with his mum so he could die with those who loved him surrounding his bed. After all, there was no way he could get worse, and he wasn't going to get better in hospital.

That had been over a week beforehand. The patient transport ambulance had brought Dennis into the spare room, ensured that he was comfortable, stayed while his sister had come to say goodbye, and stayed as they removed all the life support apparatus. Then, allowing Dennis to rest in the bed, they left.

Dennis had died multiple times, had no hope of recovery and had been left to die. Now he sat on the back of a motorcycle in the process of rounding up sheep. Everything he was doing he should not have been able to do. His mum had tried to persuade him to rest but Dennis said he had done that and he couldn't do it anymore. He needed time to process and wanted to do it alone. The compromise was that they put him to work, whilst they maintained an almost constant watch on him. His mind was busy and they were putting him to work.

None of his clothes really fit him anymore. His size and physical appearance was another such thing that could not be explained by his family. Dennis had been made to wait a short time as his uncle raced into town and got the biggest clothes and shoes that were available in one of stores. What he found would have to do.

The time spent waiting for his uncle was used to walk around and stretch every muscle in his body. The aches his body used to have from old injuries or fatigue were non-existent. Dennis felt stronger than he ever had before. It was evident almost straight away, apart from how he looked, that things were very different.

Dennis had jumped on his old bike. It was too small for starters but he was determined to ride it. The key turned in the ignition and Dennis had snapped it off as it turned. When he attempted to kick start the bike he ripped off the throttle with his foot. The engine still started, the bike was damaged though, and when he went to take off his wrist twisted and snapped the gear shift off on the handles. The bike died. He had then been forced to use his mother's bigger bike but he hadn't been allowed to start it; his uncle quickly adapted a finger throttle and brought the bike into a warm state so Dennis didn't break this bike as well.

As Dennis rode in pursuit of sheep, while he managed them around the higher hilly areas of the farm, he was lost in thought. He could feel every muscle in his body. Some of them he was being introduced to for the first time, others he had known before but not in their current capacity. He flexed each of them as he discovered them.

The riding had been pretty easy. Scott was driving on one side, his mum on the other, while Dennis followed from behind. The sheep for the most part were pretty obedient with only a few instances of them not doing what the three of them wanted to do. It had been so easy that his uncle and his mum had left Dennis to his own devices the entire time. As they came through a gate he would shut it and the trust was returned to him to do it. Eventually. Initially they had watched him like a hawk but finally, with little concern, apart from Dennis having a small temper at their constant supervision, they let him be.

It was because of this, and also because he had been too engaged in his day dreaming that he lost focus on what he was doing and crashed.

There were rocky parts all through the farm, and even more of them as they entered the more elevated positions on the hills. Dennis hit a hidden rock as he looked to follow the herd and his bike started to throw him. His instinct was to grab the brake and slow down instantly. This action left him with a broken handle bar which instantly made his driving more cumbersome. His bike jerked as it landed hard and took off. The bike was thrown into a wheelie and took off again as the rear wheel tore at the ground. Dennis had tapped the throttle a little too hard. The revs spat dirt everywhere from the wheels before finding grip when they found another rock down below. Dennis imagined that the action resembled a bucking horse that had lost control. He had thoughts of controlling it when the edge of the hill came quickly into view. Without a brake he was not going to be able to stop in time. Dennis flung himself from the bike and away from the danger. He slammed against a neighbouring boulder which stopped him moving.

The impact was one that should have potentially been lethal if not fatal. A broken shoulder or dislocation at the very least. Dennis, instead, just stood up, the only thing harmed was his shirt which was ripped down one side. There was no graze, cut or abrasion on Dennis' skin beneath. In fact the only noticeable difference was that the boulder, which was buried partially in the ground had teetered slightly. Rocks around its base were disturbed and slid down the hill.

The bike had not stopped. It had bounced towards the ledge and flung itself down the other side. There was a small ten metre drop before the hill continued steeply down below. The bike landed hard on the rocky ground and toppled over. It slid a few more metres before it stacked and stayed broken against the base of a tree.

Dennis walked to the edge and looked down. A deep sigh escaped from deep within his body. He had destroyed two bikes today. His mum wouldn't be happy, but all things considered he wasn't sure if she would be mad either. He looked around for a way to get down, and then a way to somehow get the bike back up to where he was standing. He scratched his head a little as he pondered. Then he heard a cry call out from somewhere nearby. He identified it as the bleat of a sheep. There was no animal up on the landing that he could see, the last of the flock well out of view beyond the next gate. Dennis scrambled amongst the rocks as he tracked the sound. It was only a few steps before he saw the creature. The sheep was stuck on a ledge just below him. There was no ramp or steps leading up to it so there was no doubt that it had fallen. Dennis toyed with the idea of leaving it and getting Scott to come back and help him later. It would be a far easier job to roll one of the excavators that he owned over and drop the shovel down to lift the sheep out.

Dennis had other ideas though. He would see if he could get it out himself. He slipped onto his stomach and started sliding backwards across the rocks towards the edge. Each hand and foot was placed deliberately so as to avert a fall, and he spoke kindly to the sheep below him in an effort not to startle it. The attempt was in vein. He grabbed a rock that although appearing stable was actually not. Dennis slid down the face with a startled cry and dropped to the ledge below. The drop was only a few metres and Dennis didn't feel it. He regained his balance and looked at the sheep. It stared back at him, unmoving. He hadn't startled it, but his landing had created a different effect. The ledge, while able to support the weight of the sheep, had not been able to resist the impact of Dennis' drop or their combined weight. It was crumbling slowly, a solution was not desperately needed, but it would be required soon.

Dennis found three options. The first was that he did nothing and the ledge dropped with both him and the sheep falling the half a dozen metres to the hill that continued below. The second was that he jumped across to a tree nearby, hoping that the ledge held and he could come back later. Or the third was that he tried something else.

"It's okay sheep," Dennis said to the sheep, hoping to keep it as calm as it already appeared. It shifted slightly at his approach but mostly just stared back at him. The sheep had been recently shaved and its fleece was quite slim. It wasn't overly large and Dennis thought that there was a possibility he could carry it. He wrapped himself awkwardly around the sheep's torso with his long muscular arms. The sheep allowed him to do so with no protest. He lifted it up easily and placed it across one shoulder where it settled there like a dormant puppy or sleeping baby. It rested there, completely at ease. Not once did Dennis feel any strain under its weight, though the ground below him thought otherwise. Beside the ledge he stood on, there resided another. It was smaller in size but had access to a small ramp that he could use to access his bike down below. There was a divide between the two ledges of a few metres in length. It would have been a stretch for him usually but he felt confident that he could make it, creature over his shoulder and all. More rocks and shale slipped away beneath him and he realised it was now or never. He took the few steps back that he could manage, then took off gaining speed in the small space he still had left. He jumped hard, his right foot pressing against the platform as he leapt, the force enough to make the whole thing collapse. Dennis was happy when he was able to see that he was in fact able to make the jump with a sheep slung over his shoulder. He wasn't happy when he discovered that he had misjudged the jump.

Dennis didn't land on the next ledge over. He didn't fall short though either. His jump had carried him over the ledge completely and towards the grassy slope at the bottom of its access ramp. His mind changed from how to land on the ledge to how to land on the grass. He started pumping his legs, expecting to hear a crack from his ankles as he landed; preparing to tumble upon impact.

Neither happened. His feet found root on the ground and he managed to balance himself rather easily. The sheep bleated something near Dennis' face. Whether it was approval or disgust he couldn't decide. Dennis smiled. He followed the grassy ramp down until he stood beside his crashed bike. He looked down at it, knowing that it was a lot heavier than the sheep. It didn't hurt to try. He reached down towards the frame of it, noticing that there was no pain as his body twisted in ways it shouldn't be able. His large fingers wrapped themselves around the metal of its frame, and he pulled. The strain from the weight was supposed to be enough alone for Dennis to rethink his actions.

The bike came readily, with a little more effort than the sheep. It felt no heavier than leading an infant by the hand as they walked with small resistance beside you. Dennis took the weight easily and looked up for the easiest way out of the small gully. He found it. With sheep over one shoulder and bike curled under his other arm he started to run. A few steps later he jumped vertically.

Dennis landed back where he had fallen from the bike earlier. The giant boulder he had struck still stood there. Dennis rested the sheep and bike to the ground and then placed one foot against the boulder. He hesitated for a moment, thinking through what he was planning to do, and, just because he wanted to try, he pushed. The muscles in his legs flexed. The boulder would have weighed a ton easily, but only seconds passed by before the gigantic rock slipped from its hold and tumbled down the slope with an almighty roar. Dennis closed one eye as it crashed into the tree that would have been his one-time safety choice and splintered the wood violently. The boulder then continued its descent out of sight, ravaging all vegetation in its path as it tumbled down the hillside. He hoped that there wasn't any property bordering close by.

Dennis released another big sigh, but this time it was accompanied by a smile. He turned back towards the gate he should have passed through a short time earlier. He retrieved the sheep and the broken bike before heading back towards the next paddock and home.

Granted it was an odd look, carrying a sheep over one shoulder and a bike slung under the other, but in that moment Dennis felt like big things were happening. He walked his best heroic strut until he met up with others, laughing the whole way at his ridiculous efforts.

"Don't forget you almost died," Scott reminded Dennis as he led him through some of the darker areas of his in town mechanic business. "In fact you did, this morning you were no more than a vegetable and this afternoon you think you are some kind of superhero." Dennis didn't argue, because his uncle was not wrong. He had thought the same thing himself. The incident at the cliff could have seen him killed a few more times under normal circumstances. He was reckless which was not a trait he usually possessed, and one that he wanted to remove.

"You have changed a lot," Scott continued as he strolled past an unfinished rust covered car and between some stripped down motorcycles. "I would love to say that it is a normal thing to get hit by an inland tidal wave, not die, wake up weeks later completely ripped and with abilities you didn't possess before. But that is not the case, and if it was normal then I would have signed up a long time ago. Sit." Scott had decided to take his nephew for a walk into town and was busy showing him through his own mechanic's shed. After shifting long discarded and dust covered products and materials they had finally reached a small nook at the back of the maze-like building. It was clear that this area had not been used for some time. Dennis had been instructed to perch on an old wood and leather swivel chair that had an extra cushion of dust and cobwebs for comfort. Scott rummaged through a lightless cupboard, searching in the dark for something he assumed was still there. A moment later he found what he had searched for, along with a cord for a lamp that sat nearby. Dennis wouldn't have trusted its safety or ability to work, but a flickering light later told him he was wrong.

"Hey, here they are, check them out," Scott pulled the items free, tugging hard as they got caught on heavier items resting from above. Dennis forced a small smile as memories came flooding back, he had enjoyed his time with the items in a previous life, but they also reminded him of his father.

"You used to be pretty good with these I remember," Scott continued. He held them up and gave them to Dennis. In each hand he held a skinny stockwhip. The leather in the handles were worn and they were shorter than his hands were now, so he couldn't wield them properly. That didn't stop him trying. He moved over to a small section of the shed where he could swing safely. The muscles in his hands, that although were new to Dennis, recognised the memories held within them instantly. Dennis swung and cracked the tiny whips time after time. He revolved them faster and faster, twisting and twirling them within his fingers. He lost himself as he pushed his muscles to do more. He wasn't surprised when they slipped from his grip, but the impact was a shock. They were twirling at such a speed that he had thrown a small zephyr full of dirt into the air. When the whip struck the roof after shooting from his hand it dislodged several old wooden planks and a sheet of rusted corrugated metal. Only a small amount of light streamed in as the sun was due to set soon.

"That's why I brought you in here," Scott said with a shake of his head. "Well not to break my shed, but you know." He stood in awe at the talent his nephew displayed but now reprimanded him afterwards. He invited Dennis to sit once more and for the first time Dennis noticed how heavily he was breathing.

"But first," Scott started again, moving to a work table covered in a long faded bed sheet. He pulled it off quickly, sending clumps of debris, animal droppings and more dust into the air. The smaller particles were caught in the light, appearing like a river of atoms dancing under the lingering shine of the sun. Scott coughed. Surprisingly Dennis didn't. He was a long suffering asthmatic who was constantly seen with a puffer in his pocket before or during a physical activity. He had forgotten all about his inhaler, or its whereabouts, and breathed deeper to see if he could force a response from his lungs. None came. He stopped the action as Scott brought something else to place in his hand. He looked it up and down and could not hide his amazement. It was another stockwhip, but this one was much larger, could be far longer, and was not complete.

"This was your dads," Scott said finally. He sat nearby only after he had placed all the materials down at Dennis' feet. "He started making this for you a long time ago. He could swing a whip as good as anyone. He taught you after all, and what he did was very impressive. He was making a much longer and stronger one for you, for no other reason than he just wanted to do it for you. But he couldn't finish it. The handle is done, and he has prepared all the cord that he was going to use. He found it very hard though. He handmade a long fused leather made from kangaroo hide, some equally long bungy paracord and some tightly strung slim rope. Your dad also wanted to add a spine of chain, but it was already hard enough to make. He used the machines in this shed to help him out with this, amongst other things. I was wondering, if you wanted to finish it?" His uncle Scott watched Dennis as his fingers played with the handle and the cord that had already been spun. His mind jumped from place to place and he wasn't sure what he was exactly thinking.

"Do you remember how to do it from here?" Scott interrupted his thoughts. "Do you even want to?" The questions snapped Dennis back to the present. Once more his fingers remembered the trade they had been taught as a young man and they set about finding their way through the materials. He nodded, offering another tiny smile at his uncle, as his hands set to work braiding what was left. There was an abundance of material, too much for the task at hand, but that didn't stop Dennis from setting about with determination.

"That's good to see," Scott smiled warmly. "I was hoping you would."

"You didn't want to do it yourself?" Dennis asked finally, his eyes never left his hands as the pulled the ropes tight together and forced them to hold their shape.

"Couldn't bring myself to," Scott answered back. "Most of the stuff in this part of the shed, and in another more isolated part, belong to your father. I haven't been in here since, well you know." There was silence for a long time, the only sound the rub of his hands on the cord he worked with. "He was working on a lot of cool stuff, some of them we did together. It might be time to get back to that. You might need some of it sooner or later." Dennis was aware that his uncle was asking him to answer a subtle question, but he ignored it.

"No, the reason why I am glad to see you doing that is because that is what your dad used to do. When he was angry or wanted to clear his mind," Scott explained.

"I am not angry," Dennis said truthfully.

"No, I know you aren't. You were always different in that regard. Your father had moments where his passion and drive made him act rashly. Sometimes with bad results," Scott paused again. Dennis saw him out of the corner of his eye. It was odd to see someone who had such a hard exterior struggle to talk about anything.

"But you have always been harder to break. That doesn't mean you don't need time to reflect. A lot of things have happened lately. Just today even. You are a walking miracle, and I am not even talking about the transformation your body has made and what you can do. You should be dead. Several times over, we almost thought. . ." Scott stopped. His voice had remained solid but although he tried to hide it Dennis saw him wipe a tear away from his face.

"Do you know what happened to the others?" Dennis finally asked. His arm muscles were tense, flexed hard as he continued to do work that a machine had struggled to do. He had not asked many questions as his head had swum with too many all day long, coming so frequently that one thought was bumped away quickly by a new one emerging, and so on and so forth. He was calm and collected enough to ask them now.

"The others, your footy team?" Scott turned back to Dennis. "I will admit I haven't spoken to many of them, only a couple, our concern was with you. You were the worst, to my knowledge the others are safe."

"What happened to me?" Dennis asked. "What did that meteor do to me?" Scott looked confused by the question.

"Meteor? I don't know anything about a meteor," he replied.

"A meteor slammed into the lake and caused a massive wave to rise up. I was running away and . . ." another thought struck him. "What happened to Jet?"

"Wow, that's interesting," Scott pondered on the brief bit of information he had received. "I trust what you are saying, but it is so odd that there has been nothing else said about that. A meteor hitting anywhere would be a big deal, let alone only a stone's throw away. I knew of the wave but not what had caused it," He thought some more and saw that Dennis was waiting for an answer.

"I don't know about anyone called Jet," he admitted. "There was another boy who was found in a field just beyond where they found you. He was hurt but not too bad. He was taken by ambulance to a closer hospital. We were told that there was an earthquake. The epicentre was right below the lake, which then caused a surge of water which you were caught up in. Some of the smaller buildings were destroyed. The accommodation all held strong, in fact no water got in them apart from a crack under the door. Some got into the roofs of the closer buildings through open shutters and windows, but there weren't many." Scott paused and thought about what to say next.

"You already know the damage that your body suffered, and the severity," he begun again. "We were told second hand from those who were first on the scene that you were flung within that wave from the shore. You were washed for over a hundred metres before you hit the brick wall of the mess hall. You were pressed against it until the water subsided. It may have been seconds, but most likely a few short minutes."

"You should be dead," Scott said and then nothing was said for some time. Dennis was making great progress with the braiding he was completing. He had gone through a fair amount of material and still had some left.

"I know it is odd to say," Scott finally started talking again. "But I don't want you to get hurt again." Dennis thought that with whatever had happened to his body that wasn't possible anymore, but he still felt his uncle's hurt and said nothing. Dennis respected the knowledge that whatever he had gone through had been hard, but watching him go through it and having to say goodbye, along with the knowledge that he had died already, would have been just as bad.

"What are you going to do with these new abilities of yours? Your body which has somehow changed and miraculously healed?" Scott asked a series of questions all at once. "Will this change be permanent or will it fade? Will you be hurt again? Is this temporary, and should we expect that this miracle will disappear? Will we all have to say goodbye again?" Dennis shook his head, he didn't know the answers, but he knew it was time to reply.

"I don't know," he admitted, "but you shouldn't worry too much. I am not about to go out and get a cape and do something silly. Nor am I going to become a daredevil and do things that are dangerous. Those things didn't interest me before and they still don't. I was merely running tests this afternoon, my tests are finished though," Dennis found that he had come to the end of his cord and, after ensuring that the whip he had made was tight, he tied it off as firmly as he could manage.

"I remember, a long time ago, both you and dad told me something which I haven't forgotten. There are three things that people desire to have. The first is power, the second is wisdom, and the third is courage. Each of them individually is enough to build something special with, mixed together a person could be unstoppable, but by themselves another thing is needed."

"Control," Scott whispered and pondered. "I forgot about saying that."

"Inside somewhere I have all of these properties, and rest assured that I use control more than the others. And I will as long as I can think for myself."

Scott nodded for some time at what his nephew had told him. "I trust you," he said finally. The silence that followed was broken by the sound of Scott's phone ringing.

"Hello, yep, okay," he answered, "sure thing I will be there in a moment."

"What's going on?" Dennis asked with a small amount of concern.

"Nothing much," his uncle shrugged. "Some ring-in and his mates are causing trouble at the pub. I guess I need to go deal with them." He looked at the whip that Dennis had made. Dennis could tell that his uncle was happy with what he had accomplished. "I will finish that off later for you," he said to Dennis. "Did you want to come with me to sort this out?"

"What, like your bodyguard?" Dennis scoffed.

"I don't need one of those," Scott laughed while pressing a hand to his chest showing that he was hurt by the comment. "But it is always nice to have support when facing odds not in your favour."

"Fine I will come," Dennis said. As he stood up his head slammed against a low hanging wooden beam. It shattered instantly, showering him with more muck and gunk.

"Good," Scott replied, starting to lead the way out of the darkness. Night had already fallen outside as Dennis had completed his work. "But remember you have to show control."

"I thought you said that you trusted me," Dennis said slightly taken aback.

"Oh I do," Scott responded, reacting as if he didn't question the fact. "I just don't trust them."

CHAPTER 6 – PICKED ON ABILITY

Dennis felt weird.

He was generally comfortable in his own skin while being well aware of his interesting tendencies. On this morning he was completely befuddled.

Dennis had come to work early in the morning and hidden himself in the back corner of his usual classroom. This was partly because he didn't want to draw attention to himself; choosing to avoid the eyes and interest of both staff and students. The solitude was mostly because he had been in that coma for a long duration of time, and a marginally shorter length of time back at his mum's farm, and he had done no preparation at all for the term ahead. Assessments were needing to be written and reports organised to represent the students' achievements for the first trimester of their schooling year.

It wasn't usual for Dennis to head into work remarkably early, or to hang around late at school. He was efficient enough to get most of his tasks done whilst at work before he left at the end of the day, and as an introverted bachelor he could spend some of his own time finishing off the small bits that remained should the need arise. His time at school in the mornings and during breaks was better spent, and preferably so, interacting with the other staff with jokes and supporting them, as well as getting out and playing or refereeing some sort of sport. His

working at school was out of character for him, and left an odd
sensation, but that wasn't why he felt weird.

Unfortunately it had more to do with him walking out onto
the morning assembly for the first day back. Everyone would sit
in, under or around a large undercover shelter in an exterior
quadrangle area. The principal would lead messages including
one welcoming back all the students from a break. It was
frowned upon to turn up late to the muster, be it students or
staff, and something that Dennis didn't usually do. For staff it
was excusable to simply slide in to their rollcall group unspoken
from the sides or behind. If you were still inside the main
building you had to subtly, with a small hint or embarrassment,
slide past the principal in front of the whole group and make it
to your spot with as little disturbance as you could. This is what
Dennis tried to do, but it didn't work.

As soon as he walked through the large double glass doors he
made an attempt to look invisible but failed. A large gasp
escaped from the crowd and all eyes fell onto the arrival of the
tall teacher. It felt to Dennis like he was wearing a costume to
work and was being greeted by looks of humour, looks of
confusion and astonishment, perhaps even looks of fear. He
could think of multiple reasons why they stared.

Perhaps it was the fact that he had grown at least a foot taller
in the school holidays. Maybe it was because of his clothes. They
were the baggiest he had in his wardrobe but the only ones that
would fit him, as he had completely ignored the requirement to
shop upon his return. The clothes he now wore were slightly less
professional than his usual attire and were almost bursting at
every stitch as well as every seam. Conceivably it was because
that through the gaps in his clothing he was showcasing dense
muscle where he had only displayed skin before. His hair was
also slightly longer than he would have kept it, a comb over that
swept out from his forehead and across his face the current look,
but his moustache although thicker was more pronounced as he

had managed to find a razor and shave off the stubble that had grown wildly there.

It could have been any of those things.

However, Dennis knew that it was most likely the fact that he had walked out into the assembly area as the principal was delivering the best parts of a eulogy in the memory of Dennis. The stabbing eyes and looks of astonishment continued despite Dennis deciding to move away from the small stage. Seeing someone more than two metres tall try to hide from a thousand people by crouch walking in an open space is interesting without the focus that Dennis had acquired. No one laughed or said a word, except for Dennis as he apologised when he stepped over seated students or brushed past standing staff. Dennis had taken his spot at the back of his roll class before the principal tried to save face and divert from what he was saying. With a shake of his head and noticeable puzzlement he continued.

"Anyway like I was saying," he said as he tried to gather his thoughts, "It is great to see that no major mishaps have occurred like the scenario I just mentioned and that everyone is ready to get back on with work for the second term." There was a small giggle from the crowd but the principal changed topic promptly and tried to take the focus as well. Dennis could feel his cheeks warm slightly as he avoided the eyes that he knew were all still placed on him. It would pass, he told himself, but it was something that would draw a thousand questions.

Dennis knew he couldn't answer many of them, but he also knew it was something that he had to get used to.

The best solution to avoid the unwanted attention may have been to pick up a phone and call a whole bunch of people. It would have helped in all manner of ways, but as that was something Dennis wasn't a massive fan of doing he had disregarded the idea. He had had a difficult enough time getting through his own head and arriving at a place where he was even able to function in his usual job normally. There are not too many ways that you can approach the topic of 'so, you thought I was dead'.

"So hi," Dennis started the conversation out loud as he drove to rugby training, "I heard that you heard that I was dead. Well I'm not. Not dead. What's that? Yep, broke every bone in my body, ruptured all my vital organs. Uh huh, died at least three times, didn't feel a thing. How? Got hit by a tidal wave caused by a meteor. I feel fine though, thanks. I am probably stronger than before actually." He chuckled at his own conversation. It wouldn't have sounded right. He did make one phone call though, and he had made it several times. But just like before Jet's parents did not answer.

His principal had been astounded, particularly as he had been one of the first called by Dennis' family as his primary employer. The information that his principal had received was that Dennis had died, was in a coma and would be in a vegetative state with no chance of full revival or recovery. As a result he had been preparing what he would say to both staff and students upon their return. When Dennis had been called in to see him his boss was in a state of relief, shock and annoyance, but it is hard to state your frustration at someone not dying.

That had just been at work.

Dennis was driving his car to training. Upon returning to Orange in his uncle's four wheeled drive ute they had set about altering his little yellow vintage tank of a vehicle. It had already been a tight squeeze but since the changes in his physical size it would have been impossible to manage. Dennis disregarded the idea of a new car almost instantly, so maintenance was the only option. The thoughts, of having both legs touching the roof as he huddled somehow between them to drive, were uncomfortable. Scott pulled out the driver's seat so Dennis could drive with far more comfort from the back seat. It looked odd before, so he couldn't really have appeared any worse.

While he relaxed in his altered car, still heading to training, his mind dreaded what would come. The last time he had seen any of these people they had been having a great time. However the very last time they had seen him was no doubt far different. He had no idea what it would have been like to find his mangled remains pressed against a brick wall, knowing that they couldn't help him, knowing probably that he was going to die if not already dead.

He hadn't called them to say he was okay, and he knew that was a mistake.

Dennis pulled in to the short gravel road that led to the carpark and the club's training fields. He had arrived late so that he didn't have to have the same conversation a hundred times before they got started. He was slinking in, like a coward in his own mind, so as to alleviate some of the stresses he felt. His mum had warned him about training, still not convinced of his condition and preparing for him to drop to the ground at any moment, never to rise again. His uncle had been his saviour in the discussions by siding with Dennis, much to his own detriment no doubt, when he said that he felt better than he had ever done before and that a dead man could do as he pleased. Dennis was not that arrogant to just ignore the wisdom in his mother's words. In her eyes she felt he was being reckless. Dennis wasn't ever that way. He would still be cautious, and behave in the usual fashion. He also thought that the point of not being dead was that you could still live.

He was going to watch training, and maybe get involved a little, but he had a few other objectives for attending. The first was to see if Jiemba was okay. Despite his injuries Dennis had not forgotten the way Jiemba had reacted when he had received the insults that he did not deserve. Something was definitely going on, even before the barrage he had been given, and Dennis knew that sometimes the best thing to do is to just chat about it. One of the other things he wanted to do was to tell everyone he was okay. It wasn't fair that he hadn't done it already, he certainly wasn't going to keep them in the dark any longer.

The other reason was to check on Jet. He had stopped himself short of hurting the youth on that night which seemed like so long ago now, but that didn't mean there weren't things that didn't need resolving. Jet hadn't been at school, his friends hadn't spoken to him or heard from him, and his condition after that event was in serious question. Perhaps he could find him at training.

Dennis walked reluctantly from his car and towards the simple metal fence which would usually separate the crowd from the playing surface. There was only one person standing there watching, and oddly, he saw Dennis and had little to no reaction.

"Hello there Hitman," Horatio said from behind his camera; he seemed unmoved as he took shots of the training session which had already commenced. "How are you?"

"Don't call me that," Dennis replied, leaning on the railing beside him. "Have I missed much?"

"Nah," responded Horatio. "The coaches turned up a little late, plus, you know, most of them were talking about the other thing."

"What other thing?"

"The little rumour that was going around," Horatio answered, "You know, the one where people are saying that you are alive, when we all saw you die." The camera was slowly removed from Horatio's eyes. His hand shot up, it looked like he was busy scrubbing away at the lens cap. Dennis could see that he was actually wiping a tear that had fallen there and threatened to occupy its interior. Each said nothing for a while, until finally Horatio returned to taking photos.

"We will be having a conversation later about this, just you and I, but you better have a pretty good story for them. As soon as they see you they are going to be all over you. You don't just break every bone in your body, then die, and then casually rock up to training as if nothing happened," Horatio smiled. "Even you would have trouble doing that."

"Does everyone know what happened to me before?" Dennis asked.

"Everyone thinks you are dead, or dying, it is pretty hard to not talk about your teammate getting smashed into a brick wall by a twenty metre wave coming from a lake. We also had no way to leave the camp, so, we all lived that, but then again, it seems so did you," Horatio responded. He still didn't seem overly shocked by the appearance of Dennis. Dennis knew however that the threat of a conversation later was a promise and the conversation would be far more interesting. "You better think fast about that explanation, because it looks like you have been spotted." Dennis looked up from where he leaned, already knowing that Horatio was telling the truth. It wasn't just one that came, but all. Every single one of them wearing a face of surprise, a look of glee or a frown of confusion. Dennis really did not know what to say.

It had taken a small amount of time to dismiss the crowd and organise them back into some structure of training. The questions had come quick and fast, so frequently that all Dennis had to do to avoid answering them was to pretend that he was listening to the one that came straight after it. The coaches eventually split the players all back up to join their respective teams and drills. While being bombarded Dennis had searched for the faces of Jet and Jiemba, but neither were present, either amongst his well-wishers or the very small group who had chosen to stay away from Dennis upon his return.

"It is great to see you," one of the coaches commented when the remaining players left. "I wasn't there but I heard the worst. We came to see you at hospital but we were turned away. To be honest we didn't expect to see you again. I assume that you are just here to watch, you know, after your injuries." It was a subtle question, Dennis could tell that the coaches were as confused as everybody else at what was going on, and that number included Dennis.

"No, I can train," replied Dennis, "I came here to see if I could keep up and get some exercise. If I can't I will sit out, I won't get in the way of your team." Dennis didn't give the coach an opportunity to say no to his response. "Are Jiemba or Jet here? I can't see them."

"No," the coach replied, eyeing off the change in Dennis' physical appearance. The coach was purposely standing several metres away so as not to crane his neck up to look at him. "Neither of them have been back. They have been gone for the same amount of time that you were. We assumed Jiemba went walk about, one of his friends said he does that from time to time, especially when he is upset. From what we heard he was pretty upset too. It's a real shame. And Jet, we heard that he went home in an ambulance too but we weren't able to locate him or the hospital he was sent to. Both are missing from the team at the moment."

The coach turned to watch the training as it unfolded and then spoke more slowly. "Listen, we heard what was happening between you and Jet during that first night at camp. To be honest, what you did was probably not too different to what everyone else was thinking. That boy, while talented, is arrogant, obnoxious, self-entitled and a problem for himself and those around him. When you decide to play again, to return to training completely, know that we won't hold your actions against you."

"That's cool, thanks," Dennis replied, he chose not to look the coach in the eye, "but I hold myself accountable for my actions, or rather my inaction. Jiemba deserves better than what he received. Regardless of Jet's actions, which seem uncontrollable, I am in charge of my own. How can I try and get through to someone like that when I am threatening to harm them?" It was a question which he asked aloud mainly to add voice to his own concerns. He considered that the coach was rethinking whether he should have voiced his opinion so quickly.

"Someone has to try to get through to that kid," Dennis continued, "Like you said, he is a real talent, it would be a real shame to lose that, I don't like thinking of any kid as a lost cause. And in regard to turning up for full training. I am already here, let's get into it." Dennis stepped easily over the rail and darted quickly away from his coach. He hoped that he would still be able to hold his own, and through all his guilt and anger he knew without a shadow of a doubt that he would be better than he ever was before. In as many aspects as he could manage.

Dennis' confidence in himself was proven and rewarded quickly. The only fear and worry he had was that he was more afraid for other players at training. He had found it easy and effortless to do any physical activity. His Uncle Scott had informed him that due to the increase in the size of his body that somethings may have changed. Whether that was for the better or for worse he couldn't judge, but the change was massive.

The first drill was full field shuttle runs. It was last man standing, where you kept running until everyone else was out, or you yourself couldn't go on any longer. The threat may have been that lazier players bowed out early, but as positions in the top club team were still up for grabs that wasn't the case. Quickly the bigger players did drop out, followed by those who hadn't maintained their fitness, after that there were only a handful left. Earlier Dennis had been adding his voice to the group to encourage the others who he knew would not be there at the end. As others dropped out he started to really stretch his legs. At first he ambled along trying to remember how to push himself to run. He quickly discovered that his legs remembered, and were stronger, and the strain that were put on them was almost as much as simply sitting still. During a few laps he forced himself to increase his speed. He flew past the quickest of the runners at a considerable pace, but even then he knew he was only running at a short percentage of what he was capable of. He pulled right back, galloping slowly along with the others. One by one they dropped until eventually they were all gone except Dennis. Dennis congratulated the last remaining runner who looked up at Dennis panting hard, trying to regather his breath.

"Gee that was impressive," the other player said. "You aren't out of air, you haven't even broken a sweat." Dennis smiled nervously back at him without explanation. The usual joke he would have spouted off about him just working out a bit lately felt in poor taste as all present knew of his previous circumstances, living on bottles of oxygen rather than hardly needing it. The challenge had been odd for a number of reasons: including that Jet was not pushing along beside him trying to show him up, and Jiemba wasn't present to add some light to the more focused atmosphere. But mostly it was because it wasn't a challenge at all.

The following activities involved some skills with passing and kicking. Dennis was aware that if one thing changed then many other things might have as well. He chipped a kick instead of thumping it hard like the others had done, but even then it still went further. He was able to pass the ball fifty metres with a short flick of his wrist. Just for a laugh he threw a ball with one hand from the goal line of one side of the field towards an inattentive player at the other end, well over a hundred metres away. The throw was precise, deadly accurate even, the pass struck the player at speed on the full in the arm. Despite not striking him in the head the player was instantly knocked out cold. Everyone was too engaged in their own activities to have seen it. That didn't make Dennis feel any less guilty.

The pain that Dennis inflicted didn't end there. The last thing they did was a team run with contact. Dennis could feel that if he hit someone they would be badly hurt. He actively chose not to tackle anybody or even push hard in a ruck or a scrum. That worked for a while, despite the fact that the coaches would have seen him refusing to get as involved as usual. It was for the wellbeing of everyone. That was until someone ran into him. A player on the opposite side had also seen that Dennis was reluctant to engage. He ran straight at Dennis who had been returning to his feet after ducking away from a thrown pass, the player assuming that Dennis was an easy way through the line if he wasn't tackling. Perhaps the player thought Dennis was still injured. Something in Dennis' head told him that he was about to be struck and instinct made him move fast. He vaulted fully to his feet and moved a step to his left, the space where the opposing player had run into. Dennis hardly hit him, but that didn't stop that player from jolting from his feet. He was propelled sideways for several metres before falling into another player who was also knocked over by the force. Dennis didn't know what to think about first. He helped the players up with no exertion and cycled through an ever growing list of things that he was capable of. A vast increase in strength, stamina, speed, accuracy and size. Now on top of that some sort of sensory thing which caused him to act on instinct. It was almost too much. At the very least he wasn't injured. Many others were though, a few more hurt worse, be it their pride or physical harm, stood nearby looking dumbfounded by what he was doing.

Dennis spent no energy doing it, he also knew he could apply himself far more, and had pulled himself back so as to not harm others. None of it should have happened.

As he thought about it, upon completion of training, he realised that by testing himself this way he had actually revealed more questions to which he didn't know the answers to. Most of them scared him. Some were about his new found abilities which were remarkable. Others were about the location of

Jiemba and Jet, hoping that nothing bad had happened to them but knowing that something very well may have.

One of the coaches walked forward, interrupting Dennis' thoughts. They had been busy congratulating the efforts of everybody and reminding them that upon the completion of the next training session a team would be decided upon, as well as all other teams as well. "Dennis, wow," the coach said to him. "That was not what I thought was going to happen, I had half a mind to have an ambulance ready on speed dial, but that, Wow!"

"Thanks, I think," replied Dennis. He did the usual somewhat comical bob of his head trying to relax the coach, while at the same time feeling like he was actually seeming to intimidate him. Dennis pretended to wipe sweat from the sheen of his moustache even though it was as dry as it had ever been after a training session.

"Yeah, listen, Horatio told me to tell you that he would catch you later to discuss something. He said you knew what it was about, but added that it was far more interesting now," the coach shrugged and then tapped Dennis on the arm. "It's great to have you back," he said before turning to leave.

"It's great to be back," Dennis said smiling widely.

He lied.

Jet had returned.

Dennis had spied him at school while walking through the corridors. He was not harmed, sported no limp or sling suggesting injury, but, perhaps unsurprisingly, he walked alone.

Several times throughout the day Dennis attempted to find the youth. He wasn't sure what he would say, nor even if he would be given the chance to say anything. The last time they had stood facing one another Jet had just tried to drown him on the bottom of Lake Burrendong. Dennis knew he wasn't in the wrong at the time, but still he was trying to extend the olive branch in an attempt to repair their broken relationship.

It didn't take long to realise that Jet was somehow very aware of what Dennis intended to do. Whenever Dennis would make an attempt throughout the day to locate him or chase behind him the young man would vanish from sight. It wasn't until almost the end of the day before Dennis was successful, and it had been purely by accident. Jet had all but run into him as Dennis turned a corner at the end of school. The opportunity had presented itself but Dennis said nothing. He just stood there gawping. The image that Dennis had been chasing all day was the same, but the execution was different. For the first time that day they stood near each other and Dennis was seeing a huge transformation.

Jet, much like Dennis, had a varied look. He was taller, much thicker while still lean, his fierce eyes seemed to penetrate through him as they stared, and his blonde hair which was as long as Dennis' seemed almost bleached. Jet glared at the teacher and then left with a sneer that pulled up the side of his nostrils and his upper lip, revealing his dazzling white teeth hidden beneath. The sound of a bouncing bag on someone's back after Jet had disappeared around the corner was enough to betray that the youth had taken flight once again. Dennis made to follow, expecting to see Jet just beyond the corner. Upon rounding it Dennis discovered he stood alone. He jogged quickly to the end of the building and looked beyond. Jet was running away and was still in sight. Somehow he had managed to cover a hundred metres in only a couple seconds.

Dennis until only a few days ago would have thought that such a feat was impossible, but he was the evidence that he was wrong. Considering that Jet was in a very similar situation to him in regard to what had occurred, regardless of result, Dennis felt very little surprise. That didn't mean that he wasn't actually surprised.

He was ready to chase the boy down, to what end he didn't know, but noticed a car that was waiting there. The vehicle was one that seemed to have been comprised of various models. It resembled a vintage car that had been restored, poorly, to look like some form of ugly hot rod. Several young people hung from the windows, drinking and smoking as they yipped and yahooed upon seeing the arrival of Jet. Jet spent no time at all jumping into the silvery polished tray at its rear, revealing his allegiance to a local group of hooligans. Dennis locked eyes with Jet. There were no signs or comments, just a look that was shared. The vehicle didn't wait for the lights to turn green before it burned the rubber on its wheels and took off with a squeal.

That same car made an appearance again. It made a scene as it sped into the small carpark areas at football training; tearing up granite, dust and blue rock as it spun around quickly on its wheels. A cloud was thrown up as it twirled, which was accompanied by a nasty grating of tyres as they crunched to a halt. The same hoodlums and ruffians that Dennis had spied the last time were still present in the car, still hollering and calling out to those nearby. Dennis found it amusing as the sooty dust cloud found its way into the open windows of the vehicle, causing those inside to cough or splutter (and attempt to disguise what was occurring). As loud as the youths were it was a stark comparison to how Jet arrived.

Once again he stood upon the tray, looking out at those who watched him, threatening with his scowl for anyone to say something about his arrival. Either no one cared or no one wanted to comment as he was greeted by silence. Without a word he jumped down from the tray and walked away from the small group he had arrived with, neither acknowledging them nor bidding them farewell. The rest of the players watched as they tore off in a very similar fashion to how they arrived, but Dennis never let his eyes leave the approaching form of Jet. He was surprised that the young man stopped only a short distance away from him. Dennis had been leaning on his car, alone, attempting to organise himself ahead of training. Partly because once again Jiemba, JT and Horatio had not arrived as yet. Jet said nothing for a while, but neither did Dennis.

"I don't want anything to do with you," Jet said finally, the sound of destruction that his colleagues' tyres were causing escaping into the distance. His voice was soft but his gaze was hard. "I never did, but you seemed to be intent on keeping an eye on me regardless whether I wanted you to or not."

"Are you okay?" Dennis asked when a pause was given. It was a loaded question, encompassing a whole bunch of scenarios that Dennis was calculating. Home life, choice in friends, schooling, and pain as a result from what happened. Jet's wellbeing was the foremost thought however.

"I want you to stop," Jet replied dismissing the question quickly. "You mean nothing to me, and you never will. Maybe you didn't understand before, but even if you did I am going to make you a deal. I won't go out of my way to show you up, I won't talk to you, humiliate you or even be present near you, and you won't need to worry about my 'behaviours', as you call them, and all you have to do is just stay away from me and my business." Jet was intimidating before the incident, but the presence he had possessed felt like it was amplified. His physical presence had changed just like Dennis, except Dennis still stood taller and bigger than him. He was not intimidated, but that didn't mean he did not hear what the youth was asking. Sometimes it was better to leave someone to themselves for a while.

"Okay Jet," Dennis replied, "as long as you are alright."

"Like you care," Jet shot back. His voice steady but his words ice cold. "I know who cares, all those who came to see me when I was hurt, that's who. That title doesn't belong to anyone here." The bitterness, spite and resentment held just below the surface starting to bubble its way forth. Jet's eyes, although unfeelingly staring through Dennis, were filled with emotion which threatened to surge forward as tears and animosity. A moment later Jet did something that Dennis was not convinced he was able to do. He swallowed it all back, swept away his emotions, and walked past in relatively calm silence. Dennis said nothing else, simply allowing the boy to walk past unopposed. Dennis watched him go, a part of him relieved that whatever had been going on between them had ceased, but at the same time an even bigger feeling of failure lurked beneath.

The training was simple. All players in the squad would run to a designated location several kilometres away. The older players knew the route well: a long slight hill leading to the top of a plateau in town, progressing onwards into a newly developed area where there was another slope. The gradient there was enough to make you crawl up it, even cars struggled.

The players would run there, and upon arrival of the last person they would be told who would take the positions in the main team by the coaches who had journeyed on ahead, awaiting their arrival. Whether you were successful or not you still had to run back to the club, when players were either in a state of triumph or a slump of shattered despair. Very few felt nothing about the experience.

They started all together, those faster with more stamina taking a quick lead, the slower or less fit players lumbering along in the rear. It wasn't at all slow, as many of the bigger players had improved drastically in that pre-season and were as good if not better than players from other teams in the same positions. This is where Dennis stayed. He knew he could have been up the very front, he knew he could have been leading the pack and beaten everyone in this team to the destination, with probably enough time to do it twice. It was untested but he just knew he could. But at the front of the pack was Jet who was already busy showing his dominance on the other players. Dennis could see that Jet was not the talent he was before, he was far better. There were great differences between them though. Where Dennis held back from using his new strength and speed, choosing to assist those who needed encouragement nearby, Jet was holding back at the front simply to goad others into trying to beat him. Dennis could see that Jet was holding back, and that terrified him. He imagined that the scenario was very possible that Jet had become just like him, that not only made him dangerous, but it made him a weapon. Dennis had no proof, but he imagined it wouldn't take long.

Dennis also thought that using his abilities was a form of cheating and he felt a pang of guilt when using them. He obtained them in a catastrophe which should have caused his death, he wasn't about to flaunt his gifts before he understood them nor promote something so terrible, creating something that could be beneficial. No, he thought, if he didn't have them before he shouldn't be using them now.

The journey was long and arduous for some. Dennis had found it to be nothing of the sort, but had accompanied those at the back nonetheless. Upon arrival he was made aware that Jet had finished first; he had waited until the last turn and a long stretch of road before striding out and making it to the destination point in no time at all. Dennis found it interesting as all the other players described the strength, speed and stamina that Jet now possessed. None of them knew that they were comparable to those that Dennis now wielded, but because of that there wasn't a true comparison.

Dennis was intrigued at how willingly Jet had been to show them off. Jet had displayed them at the first opportunity and stood tall above all others with little to no effort. Even those who previously would have smashed Jet in the endeavour were breathing heavily at his feet. Finally Dennis managed to scale to the top, doing all he could to get those slower than he to the destination. They all thanked him as they gasped for air. Dennis faked his own breathing so it sounded more laboured too, waving away the thanks while offering up his congratulations that they had all made it.

"Now that everyone is here," started the coach as he gathered the team on a vacant block nearby, "we can go about selecting the team." Many players tried to reduce the volume of the panting as they strained their ears to hear who had been successful. It started with the usual clichés about how proud the coaches were, that the building blocks had been established and the team was ready to unite and take on the challenges of the season. Dennis listened to all of it, though he suspected others didn't. It was nice to be encouraged but the players were only there to find out who was in that team. Dennis watched as many continued their attempts to regain their breath, and scanned the crowd watching others.

Jet sat on a small boulder which sat to the side of the block. He watched the coaches with more intent than the others. For a fraction of a second their eyes locked but Jet blinked his awareness away. Finally it came to the announcement of the team.

"In no particular order," they said, which was never ever true. They started running through the list and it took only a few names to identify that they were in order of playing position. All eyes listened along with the ears of the players, searching for their name as well as the names of their friends. Dennis was called out as one of the first names. Jiemba was not. It made sense that his larger built friend had been excluded for not being present; if Dennis hadn't returned when he did he imagined he also wouldn't have made the team. Actually he was certain of that, why would you name a dead person in your team? JT was announced as the halfback despite his absence, but there were some exclusions to policy when it came to working. He was earning a living, not just partying like some of the other youths. Dennis watched as people pumped a silent fist when they heard their name, and as the heads of others dropped due to their omission. Finally the list was complete.

"I think you have missed someone," Jet called out from his perch on the rock.

"No we haven't Jet," the coach responded quickly. "All players were picked on ability, but that doesn't mean that you can't work your way into the team."

"But, that doesn't make sense," Jet stammered trying to restrain the rage he had displayed on countless occasions. "I am the strongest, fastest and youngest person here."

"We agree with you," the coach responded quickly, "but it takes more than individual brilliance to make it to the end of the season we are planning. Ability means more than just talent, which you have got by the bucket load. It takes real commitment, enthusiasm to the team, and a positive attitude towards all those within it."

"I wouldn't even need a team, just give me the ball and I could do it all myself," Jet pleaded.

"That is exactly what we are talking about," the coach dismissed his call. Dennis could see what both parties were saying. Apart from Dennis himself, there was probably no one who could match it with Jet. Jet hated everybody and had a huge chip on his shoulder, making him a liability. That would have been the case in a normal team, but if Jet was enhanced like Dennis was then he may just be the exception to that rule.

"I'm sorry mate," the coaches continued. "You aren't named today." The coaches moved on to encouraging the team before instructing them to return back to the club to continue their training. One by one the players gathered around, offering congratulations and commiserations. They weren't all positive about it but there was nothing they could do at that moment.

Dennis watched Jet as the others left. The boy had not moved from his rock, although he was leaning forward heavily into his knees and staring at something amongst the dirt and grass. The sunlight had vanished and they were left alone under the lamplights. Dennis took a step toward the youth; he wanted to comfort him to let him know that it wasn't the end of the world. Dennis wanted to tell him that he could still help with the things the coaches wanted to see. He had hardly taken a step when he was stopped.

"Don't," Jet commanded softly. He looked into Dennis' eyes for a fleeting moment before looking away. That moment was all Dennis needed to see the pain in his eyes and the shudder of anger in his body. The look of a youth who was completely lost and struggling to contain himself. "Just get out of here. We have a deal." The youth was taking it surprisingly well; there had been no tantrum or tirade of abuse to any player or other individual. The explosion that Dennis had expected never came. Dennis decided it was best to obey and turned to leave.

Dennis jogged a short way down the hill, immediately noticing that even the slowest of the players were a long way off now. He had looked back once to see if Jet remained in his solitude but thanks to the crest at the summit he was lost to view quickly. Dennis had maybe ventured a hundred metres down the hill, discussing to himself at how much Jet had changed including his mental state, when his whole body shuddered with anticipation, a familiar feeling to when he reacted unknowingly. A loud bellowing emotional roar occupied the air, bursting with a cracking sound which was filled with pain. It called out like a wounded lion, no doubt carrying the same distance with its volume.

Dennis had been wrong. Jet was calling out for help. At the same time he was strong enough to physically stop those who tried to assist him. For some unknown reason Dennis jumped instinctively from the road edge and into its centre, but he saw why immediately. A medium sized boulder, no doubt the one that Jet had been sitting on, crashed down beside Dennis. It was too far away from him to be intentionally thrown at him, and it would not have struck him or anyone else due to where it landed, either by accident or design. The rock was covered in dirt revealing how deep it had been buried, but now it crashed down the slope into trees and small bushes as it rolled destructively away. The boulder was yet another reminder of how dangerous Jet was becoming, and he was already dangerous before.

Dennis ran on, the sound of another anguished growl followed him. He didn't look back again.

CHAPTER 7 – FRIENDLY FIRE

Everything was fine, and that was a problem.

Despite everything else that had happened, Dennis felt that his entire world was swirling around one solitary figure in the universe. That figure was Jet. There were definitely other things going on, but no matter how much he tried to pull away he was always drawn back in.

Dennis had given the youth a wide berth ever since the night that he was not named to play. It was partly out of respect to the boy's wishes, but mostly because the boy was volatile and could go off with an unknown ferocity at any given moment. Mostly it was because Dennis didn't know what to say.

That didn't mean that the teacher within Dennis had given up on Jet. Dennis had never done that to anyone in the past and he wasn't going to start now. Especially because he felt like he was the only one who was still trying, but also because if something turned nasty Dennis knew that he was the only one that could help stop it.

There were no lost causes in his book, only more difficult challenges.

But everything appeared to be fine, in regard to what people expected to be normal, and mostly that was because of Jet. Dennis still observed him from a distance. It was hard for Dennis to be secretive when he stood out so easily now, but none the less he was able to make subtle investigations all the same. Jet, like Dennis, also stood out amongst the other students, his own enhanced physical appearance making him look like a plane amongst kites. Dennis had feared that the other students would flock to him and he would encourage an even greater following, but that hadn't been the case. All of them, even those who had called him friend now distanced themselves. Not even the students that Dennis had reprimanded on the first day went anywhere near him. Dennis suspected that this was Jet's wish and that if he desired a following he would have it. Instead he sat alone, pondering something as he gazed out over the sporting fields. In class he was silent and the teachers were happier for him to do nothing then to ask him why. Everywhere else it was like he was a shark in a school of fish as everyone scattered in his wake, but he ignored them without even a sideways look, let alone a threat. So far he had been true to his word.

Something still burned there though. On one occasion Dennis passed by Jet in the corridor, it was entirely by coincidence without Dennis shadowing him. Dennis had been startled by his appearance and Jet had been as well. The younger man only noticing his teacher after the fact. Jet's face, which had been focused on the ground firmly in front of him, immediately glanced up to view Dennis. His stride was unaltered, but his mouth transformed from a look of indifference to a sneer of deep loathing. Jet was gone as quick as he appeared and Dennis had the feeling that he was the only person who had received such a response.

In the last session of the day Dennis sat out on the front lawn of the school. It was partially because he wanted to work outside, his desk and general working space had become too small to accommodate his large frame. He liked being outside as well, but he also had plans to observe the group that Jet was now associating himself with. There was a cool breeze which brought with it a lower temperature. Dennis would usually have felt the drop and rug himself in an ugly knitted sweater or cardigan; but unfortunately they no longer fitted him either, and even if they did he was no longer susceptible to the cold like he once was.

A buzzing sensation was felt in his pocket. Dennis withdrew his phone to see that he was getting a call from Horatio. Dennis was too focused on finding Jet's new friends that he simply pretended that he was in class and couldn't answer the call. It wasn't long before it rang out; better to let Horatio think that Dennis was busy, which he was, than to think that he was dodging the call. A moment later a much smaller buzz came, revealing that a message had been received on his phone. 'JT will be at training this afternoon. He is not happy, your mate might have a problem,' the message read. Dennis sighed heavily. The reference to 'your mate' was clearly Jet due to the proximity the student and teacher shared, also their very well-known aversion to one another was grounds to claim the opposite was true. Dennis wasn't shocked that JT was angry. The last time Jiemba had been seen or heard from was the night at Lake Burrendong, and Jiemba had left the group as a result of what Jet had said.

Jet wasn't the main problem, Dennis thought to himself trying hard not to just dismiss his guilt due to his crusade to help him. Jet certainly hadn't helped, but Jiemba was stronger than that and wouldn't just lay down to that sort of spray, therefore something else was definitely up. Regardless, Jet's tirade had definitely been the catalyst, or at least the last straw.

Dennis didn't blame JT as he too was seeking answers for their friend's disappearance. Jiemba's absence had long since passed the point of concern. Another buzzing and a second message followed the first without response, piling it on top of the other on the screen of Dennis' phone. This one simply said, 'we still need to talk.' Dennis had no idea what about and wasn't sure what to write back.

The hooligan's car jumped back into his mind, not because Dennis could see it but because he could hear it, a booming throb coming from an exhaust under pressure could be heard from blocks away. In fact he had to wait a couple of minutes to see it. Eventually it pulled around the corner and became stationary in the bus bay, which it was not allowed to do. Dennis had already moved to greet it by the time it arrived; as it obnoxiously stopped to spurt black fumes at him from beneath its hull. Dennis wouldn't have been surprised if the thing was actually on fire. Dennis stroked his moustache with quiet amusement at the group but fell short of giving them the satisfaction of swatting the noxious gas away from his face.

"Gentlemen," Dennis said in his most solid teacher voice, "You can't park here." It was not his responsibility to enforce rules on the road, Dennis was instead using their disrespect to begin the conversation.

"What are you going to do about it mate?" one of the youths demanded as he jumped from the open canopy of the backseat. It was clear he acted hastily, not actually realizing the size difference between them; no sooner had he arrived next to Dennis then he was hurriedly stepping away again.

"Lately I have found out I can do lots of things," Dennis was not threatened, and would not have been regardless of his newly found abilities. "I want to have a word with you first though, and then you can leave." The group laughed. There were still three remaining in the car but none of them were venturing out to assist their companion.

"We ain't talking to you," the closest one said again. He was showing his own apprehension as with every word he tried to slink further away. Dennis was certainly not aggressive but nor did he give ground.

"Fine, I will talk to you," he said taking small strides towards the youth that still moved away. A second later he was pressed back up against the ugly looking hot rod without Dennis laying a finger on him. His friends were caught between trying not to laugh at him and continuing their aggressive stares. "I don't want to see you anywhere near this school again," Dennis said firmly, leaning forward to make the command only a whisper from the boy's face. "You don't belong here anymore and you have no business in escorting students to and from the premises in this sorry excuse of a vehicle." The youth slunk out from underneath the teacher's glare. When he was a few metres away he again found his courage.

"Are you telling us what to do? Did you just bag out our car?" he asked without expectation of an answer. He bounced on his feet, seemingly willing himself to take his own action. He glanced around, making sure that there was no one else nearby. He was being encouraged by his friends. "Ain't nobody does that to us," he yelped and lunged with a closed fist towards the teacher. Dennis felt it coming before he saw it, but he made the choice to stand strong without flinching or idea to evade. He watched as the youth ploughed his hand hard into Dennis' upper chest. Then Dennis smirked as he heard a distinct cracking sound. The youth recoiled, clutching at his wrist which dangled limply from his arm. He muffled a scream but as he clenched his teeth spit and foam still managed to come forth. His mates were once more stuck between laughing at him and showing shock at what had happened. Dennis hadn't felt a thing, there was a sensation telling him he had been touched but no nerves telling him he was in pain. The young hooligan on the other hand clearly had a broken wrist, if not a far more serious injury.

"I'm going to ask only once more," Dennis repeated calmly. "Leave this area, and the students around here, and don't come back." His tone invited them to argue but he knew they wouldn't. The boy with the broken wrist sat uncomfortably back in his seat still nursing his hand. He gave a nod to the driver after giving his most fearsome look, the tears that accompanied it took away a bit of the sting. The car lurched forward.

"You'll pay for that," he yelled as the vehicle growled away. It didn't move far, but it was far enough so that it no longer resided in front of the school. Dennis turned to walk back into class and found that he had been observed, for how long he did not know.

"Why are you harassing my friends?" Jet asked coolly.

"Regardless of your connection to them I would have said the same things," Dennis replied evenly. "I make no apology."

"No matter what happens you think you have to get involved with what I do. You have done that ever since you got here," Jet replied and walked down the few stairs slowly. "I have said and done nothing to you, or anybody else at this stupid school. I thought it would make it easier. Why do you keep following me?"

"Because you are better than them," Dennis replied.

"How do you know?" Jet shot back. He stood almost toe to toe with his teacher now, the height difference between them only minute. "You have no idea what I am like, or what I am capable of."

"But I do," Dennis responded. He held Jet's intense gaze and met it with just as much force. "I see all of your potential, you are capable of great things. You could be a leader amongst men, you have a natural charisma and talent. Abilities that could only be enhanced when you apply yourself. I don't want to see you waste it."

"There it is," Jet replied. He shook with anger but his voice remained steady. "A waste. I knew it was what you thought of me."

"You know I don't," Dennis whispered.

"I actually don't know that," Jet took a step back, "just like you don't know me. Everything has changed. I don't need you. I never did. I am going to tell you again, stay out of my way. Sir." He walked past Dennis and headed over towards the car which revved loudly in anticipation of his arrival. Dennis just watched and didn't say a word. He had heard everything that Jet had said and sadly shook his head. Jet slid onto the tray and in a moment he was loudly surging away.

"You will need me more than ever before," Dennis said softly to himself, hoping that he wasn't the one he was trying to convince. He knew, and hoped, that no one else had been around to hear him. Dennis had been the sole intended recipient of the statement. The problem was that he also wasn't convinced that he would actually be able to help.

Just like everything was fine at school everything was equally fine at training. Dennis hadn't responded to any of Horatio's messages and despite JT being at training alongside Dennis and Jet nothing had happened. Jet was training alongside the top grade while assisting those in the reserves. His presence alone was a huge surprise to Dennis as he suspected that he would be gone after missing out on selection; Jet being somewhere that Dennis could see him was a huge plus for the teacher. It wasn't so much about control, but he was happy that he knew what the youth was doing while he was at training.

JT had not said a single thing to him, or Dennis for that matter, and the communication between them that arose out of necessity was civil for the most part. Horatio, who was still apparently injured hovered off to one side taking photos with his camera and videos on his phone. At one stage Dennis saw him interviewing people but he couldn't be sure if it was for his job as a journalist or for the club social media. It may have even been for personal use knowing Horatio.

Despite how ordinary it all looked, it was different to how Dennis felt. Something felt wrong when he knew it shouldn't have. The club carpark was full of cars, and more kept rolling in steadily, suggesting that every player, official, and then some, were in attendance preparing for the first game. The atmosphere was positive and the chat was promoting a similar attitude. Everyone was doing what they were supposed to be doing and the extra patrons were busy talking away about the new season as they observed the players go about their tasks from the sidelines. Eventually Dennis put it to the side and focused on what he was doing. Dennis also noticed that, just like him, Jet was not involving himself in contact or drills like he had done before. He held back, not doing much at all except fill a hole. Perhaps what Dennis had seen in the boy had been false, or perhaps the negative strength that Dennis assumed the youth had possessed, just like Dennis had obtained, had worn out or never existed. Dennis grabbed a clump of strapping tape that someone had discarded on the grass. He placed it in the palm of his hand and when no one was looking he flicked it with his finger. The tape sailed to the other side of the field. If it had worn out for Jet it had not done the same for Dennis.

Finally training ended and Dennis immediately headed towards his small car. Before he got there he heard the commotion behind him.

"I heard what you said," JT called out. Dennis turned and saw that he was only metres behind Jet who did not reply, although he was the intended recipient. "You have the entire pre-season trying to prove to everyone else that you are some big shot, some super player who should be placed on a pedestal and admired for how good you are. That's not what you are. Everyone keeps treading on egg shells around you because you are intimidating, or because they think you can be an asset to a team. But I know what you are." JT stood under the gaze of Jet, looking up at him. His face was a twisted scowl and he was not intimidated despite the size difference. Jet said nothing. "Yeah, that's right. I know. You are the least worthy person here, you are an arrogant self-absorbed jerk. You are the reason why Jiemba isn't here and why everything feels so weird, so wrong."

"Are you finished?" Jet asked sneering. He stepped closer to JT. JT stepped into him, again ignoring the obvious size difference.

"No, there is one more thing," JT snarled. "You're a coward."
The words hung on the brisk night air. Supporters who had been
watching the training inside had slowly begun to make their way
outside. Among them were young children who were now being
hurried away with the expectation of a fight. The risk of seeing
the younger eyes see role models in a compromising situation
too great for the parents to allow.

"Is that all?" Jet replied with indifference, casting a devilish
smile, "I thought we were friends."

"Like you know what that word means, you walk around
thinking you own the place, stepping on everyone nearby. I don't
know why you are still here?" JT was breathing hard but did not
falter in his defiance of the younger man. No one stepped in to
intervene, and no one defended the younger player who had put
himself in this position with how he held himself, and how he
looked down upon others. Jet looked around at those who
surrounded them seeing no security or fondness there.

For the first time in a while Jet laughed.

"Why indeed?" Jet replied and turned away. He took only a
few steps away into the dark night sky, with no one seeking to
stop him or persuade him to stay. In those few steps words
didn't break the tension.

But an explosion from nearby did.

Flames bellowed up into the sky as everyone reactively
cowered in shock, unsure in which direction they should throw
themselves or seek shelter. One moment the silence was
deafening, the next an inferno erupted from where a car used to
sit. The vehicle had been parked away from the group with no
one immediately in harm's way. Inaction was the main motion
as nobody knew what to do. Even Dennis hesitated as he looked
into the darkness while sheltering his eyes from the bright red,
orange and yellow flickers that aggressively danced their way
into the once starlit sky. Dennis was the first to react however,
but it wasn't until he heard a sound.

The loud blasting of an ill equipped car engine roar in the distance, it was so faint that Dennis was surprised he heard it all. Looking around he saw what the others had not, but they wouldn't have known what it meant if they had. Dennis glanced around the carpark with discovery dawning on him. The numerous cars that Dennis had observed were not there because players and supporters alike had flocked to training. No, they were there to cause destruction. Many of them looked like they had been lucky to make it to the training area in the first place, others would not have been out of place in a junkyard.

"Everyone onto the fields, quickly," Dennis called out. He was surprised at how loud his voice boomed in the darkness. Most took the command immediately, while those who didn't swiftly followed like sheep. A handful lingered but when the second car exploded everyone started moving. Dennis scanned the carpark taking care to see that everyone was out or was making it out. In one glance he saw that it wasn't as simple as that.

"JT, help me," Dennis called out to his friend who was one of the few that remained to help out. Dennis led him over to a bunch of cars which sat dangerously close to a large gas container which supplied power to the club.

"No doubt your mate had something to do with this," JT said as he followed.

"I don't know why people keep thinking he is my mate," Dennis replied. "Remember I was the one who called him out at the camp."

"Sorry," JT replied, "I wasn't there. And I am more annoyed now that I wasn't. He is a jerk to everyone, especially you. Yet you put up with him more than others."

"Well I guess I am just a nice guy," Dennis answered as they arrived at the cars drawing his attention. JT ducked to one side as another car exploded. It wasn't close but who wouldn't hide from an exploding vehicle. Dennis knew it wasn't a common occurrence in this neighbourhood.

"How are we going to move these?" JT asked.

"I reckon they are all stolen and they would have left the breaks off so they could cause more destruction, let's just hope that's true or we could be in trouble," Dennis replied. He had a feeling that he could have moved the car by himself, but he was purposely not using the abilities he had possessed so he couldn't be sure. JT had come along so it looked like they had done it together regardless of effort, but it never hurt to have a problem solver if something went wrong. They put their hands on the front bumper and started to push. Dennis discovered the breaks were on as he felt a little bit of resistance, but he pushed past it and urged JT to do the same.

"You got this mate, the breaks are off just like I thought," Dennis lied, "just get those wheels rolling." He saw JT nod as he put a bit more force into it. Dennis could feel the wheels grip the asphalt but without much strain he managed to get them to slide backwards.

"That's it, they are rolling now," Dennis lied again as the car started moving quickly. He was pushing a full weight car basically by himself. It forced his muscles to flex but he felt like he could easily do more. In only a few seconds the car was a reasonable distance away. JT was tired from his effort but with some encouragement they managed to clear the others that had the most potential to cause more destruction. There was no time to stop. Another car blew up, this time launching into the air. As it fell it twisted upon landing on its rear bumper and collapsed against another car.

"Help," cried the anguished, and previously unseen, occupants of that car.

"I will help them," Dennis informed JT while pointing to another car that was attempting to flee, "you take care of those ones." Dennis flashed over to the car, summing up the issues in an instant. Two children were stuck in their child restraints while their parents were pinned in the front seat. It appeared that instead of listening they had decided to try and escape by car.

"Can you get out?" Dennis asked, stroking his moustache down his face as he analysed what to do.

"Get the kids out if you can," the father called back. "We are stuck in here, that car has crushed down on the dashboard and our buckles have jammed."

"JT," Dennis called out to the night hoping that his friend would return. He couldn't really help Dennis but at least he could lead the children to safety once they were removed. Dennis reached into the backseat and immediately started to try and soothe the occupants. The parents were in trouble in the front as Dennis fumbled in the dark with the restraints. Dennis gazed through the far window and shook his head secretly. Some of the cars that had already exploded were blocking the exit, these people weren't going to get out that way even if they were successful in avoiding the destruction.

"Hey it's ok guys," Dennis said to the kids as he managed to click one button, feeling the relief as it came free easily. Even Dennis ducked as he felt the heat from another incinerated junk car spew threateningly past him. A small sob sounded in his ear as the children clenched in terror. It probably didn't help that Dennis was taking up most of the space in the back seat. "I will have you out in a jiffy," Dennis lulled them softly, trying to be as comforting as he could. In the next instant he had them free and standing next to the car.

"You're a coward," JT roared as he returned to Dennis' side. Dennis followed his gaze and noticed he was staring off in Jet's direction who was slinking away mostly unnoticed. Dennis had hoped that Jet really had nothing to do with this but even he had to admit that he had been naïve. Leaving helpless innocent people to a fate they didn't deserve was lower than Dennis was willing to believe was possible.

"JT," Dennis roused the attention of his friend. "I need you to take these kids to safety. I will get the parents out."

"How?" JT asked. He was nodding his compliance but Dennis knew it was valid. There was a car resting on another car with people trapped inside. Dennis felt like he knew what to do but he was reluctant to do it with others nearby, though he would if he had to.

"I dunno," Dennis answered, "I will figure it out but get those kids out of here." It was easier said than done. The children were both infants, Dennis assumed they were not even at school yet, and both fought against JT with all their might. They howled in anguish and terror as they left their trapped parents through a carpark filled with fire and destruction. Dennis ran to the other side of the car.

"Alright," he called to the parents, getting their attention. "I have got something that should help me lever the car on the outside, but I am going to need you to push up on the inside to help me out."

"Will it be enough?" the mother asked through tears and pain.

"I don't know," Dennis replied. After his earlier attempts using his strength he was almost entirely sure that he could do this without their help. They would be distracted though, which allowed him to do it covertly. "On three let's give it a go." He commanded. "One. . . Two . . . Three." He could hear the couple inside push with all their might, Dennis promptly slammed into it with his shoulder. The car moved immediately, rising from the ground and crashing through the barrier protecting another training surface. It was enough for the interior to pop up freeing the occupants.

"Thank you," they each cried out to him as he returned to assist with the removal of their seatbelts.

"Let's get you out of here first," Dennis muttered as he set about his task. A loud crash alerted him to something happening behind him. Dennis turned and watched as the cars that had blocked the carpark were now thrown onto their sides allowing access and escape from the venue. A moment later Dennis saw the only other person who would have been strong enough to move those cars disappear into the trees where he was lost to the darkness of the night. His shape that had been a flickering mirage thrown around by the petrol lit flames vanishing in an instant. Through those same trees that Jet had ventured towards Dennis spied something else; the twinkle of colourful flashing lights revealing the approach of emergency services.

As Dennis returned to his task of freeing the parents he found himself distracted. Jet had cleared a path. There was something in that, he thought to himself. But after what had happened, and what Dennis was sure Jet had been involved with, it was hardly something that brought the greatest satisfaction.

Dennis found himself wondering to himself even more. 'Was it even really worth trying?' he thought to himself. 'I have to,' he decided just as quickly.

CHAPTER 8 – RIVALRY

"That is madness," Kane said, once more draining the pint which sat in front of him. "Do they know who did all that?"

"Police are investigating," Dennis said with a shrug, copying his friend as he too finished off what remained within his own glass. He had been sitting with Kane for the best part of three hours talking about everything that had occurred in the last six months, which was the length of time they had been apart. Kane was Dennis' best friend and rival from when they went to school together. They were equal and opposite in many ways. Dennis was bigger now but they had been of similar height before. Where Dennis had been lean and flexible muscle, Kane had muscle in layers with very little fat. They played for opposing football teams in town, which was a bizarre sort of rivalry in itself, but were always as close as brothers. Kane had a more pronounced jaw which was covered by a handsome layer of multi-coloured stubble, but it didn't make him look any less roguish or attractive.

"Far out," Kane replied rubbing his head with a hand that was a mixture of sweat and paint. "Gee it is all happening for you then. So ah, how do you feel now then, after your accident I mean?" There was very little that was hidden between them, each having shared in the worst or most embarrassing moments of the other's life. So the timid way that Kane had asked that question was slightly off-putting. Again Dennis shrugged it off.

"Yeah I feel fine, don't know why people keep asking me about it. Do I look sick?" Dennis said without looking at his friend.

"It's because you don't look sick," Kane replied swiftly. "The last time I saw you mate you were a complete mess. We were all told to say our goodbyes to you. There were heaps who saw you like that. To be honest I was more shocked that so many people cared about you."

"I don't know why I am surprised that you saw me like that," Dennis said scratching a sudden itch on his brow. "It appears that almost everyone but me were at the hospital at some point."

"Maybe it's because they care," Kane replied, sipping at the foam of his already empty drink. He waved his hand toward the bar, caught the eye of the young lady there and gestured for two more drinks. "Which makes no sense because you are one of the biggest losers I know."

"Do I look like a loser?" Dennis asked, decidedly flexing his arms as they rested on the table. "It is also nice to know that you were there amongst those who care."

"I didn't care about you, I was there for your mum and your sister," Kane's smile returned, raising his eyebrows trying to seem sinister and attractive at the same time. Kane even mouthed a kiss and licked his lips.

"That is very concerning," Dennis shook his head. He could trust his friend to make light of any situation.

"Why?" Kane replied, smirking handsomely while appearing hurt, "they are both fine ladies, I would be happy to look after them, whatever that may look like." Dennis refused to raise to more bait as his friend's smile followed him.

"But apart from people's surprise that you are fit and well, you sure as hell don't look like you're a teacher anymore," Kane scoffed back. "You look like the guy who should be standing at the door to this pub keeping others out, or going for a championship belt in a wrestling tournament, or climbing a beanstalk, basically anything except a teacher. It is easily enough to make people stop and stare." The young bartender promptly placed fresh beverages on the table where the pair sat. Kane gave her more cash than the drinks were worth, as well as one of his most dashing smiles. Dennis shook his head again, his mate was hopeless, but unsurprisingly to Dennis the waitress replied by looking away with a smile, her cheeks turning deep peach coloured with the attention.

"So do you have any other super powers?" Kane asked abruptly as he turned to look back at his friend. Dennis was taken aback not knowing what to say. To the best of his knowledge he had managed to keep his enhanced strength and other attributes to himself.

"What do you mean?" Dennis said as he hid behind a cool sip of his replaced drink.

"I mean you have been drinking as much as I have and you look like you could still run a few laps around the block, I am staying seated because I am not sure if I can walk straight. That never used to be the case, you were always a lightweight compared to me." Dennis had noticed that as well. He felt like he was drinking flavoured water with no adverse effects at all. It seemed that resistance to alcohol and influences of the like were another addition to his lists of positive traits that he had acquired. Dennis still avoided his friend's eyes. They fell onto the screen of an oversized digital television propped high up on the wall. What was initially a ploy to avoid the conversation actually sparked his interest.

"Can you turn this up please?" Dennis called out to the girl behind the bar. She nodded and set about locating the remote. There was a picture of the club inset next to the head of the news reporter. There was nothing new in her delivery that Dennis was not already aware of, except that the police were still chasing several possible leads as a result.

"We have multiple descriptions of those involved," said a police officer who was being interviewed. "The local area task force is linking this destruction to multiple occurrences of stolen vehicles in the last few months. We believe we are dealing with a group of organised youths and their associates, and we are receiving more calls and enquiries every day. It shouldn't be long until we track the perpetrators down. It has also been established that the explosions that occurred were in result to faulty petrol and electrical outlets being ignited. Residents should not be concerned for their safety, but should ensure that they take proper precautions in keeping their vehicles safe."

"Wow," Kane said as he continued to gulp down his ale. "So a big deal, but not deliberate like you said."

"I was there," Dennis replied gruffly, "I know what I saw. Who is that?" His eyes hadn't left the screen as the story had changed. It now showed the ground level of a massive building with a young athletic man in a suit with a slicked pulled back ponytail and neat beard.

"You don't know him?" Kane seemed surprised. "That is Hector Green, the president, owner and CEO of GreenCorp." Dennis continued to watch, reading the blurb which appeared in the news scrawl at the bottom. It said 'GreenCorp and its owners to receive an Australian Service Award for excellence in innovation and technology, and another for focus on renewable energy production with emphasis on regenerating natural resources. To be presented by the Prime Minister.' "Did you read that? Yeah he is kind of a big deal, I heard he is a pretty good bloke too. Not much older than us," Kane continued, "makes you wonder if you could have done more with your life, huh." Dennis continued to watch the smiling CEO and couldn't help but immediately like him. The news changed and Dennis lost interest. Kane drained yet another drink and Dennis could see the effect it was starting to take on his friend.

"I think this one will do me," Dennis offered a way out just in case his friend didn't. "Got school tomorrow, then training, and then we are playing you on the weekend."

"Soft," replied Kane but then quickly withdrew from the claim. "You're probably right though." They got up and Dennis held a hand behind Kane as he made his way to the door.

"You can stay at my place," Dennis suggested. He only lived a few blocks away from the pub they had chosen and it was a better alternative than his friend driving.

"Thanks mate," Kane said shaking his head, "I think I'll taxi this one." Dennis watched as Kane turned to head towards the taxi rank located nearby. Kane turned with a wave and then promptly twisted on his heel to face Dennis again.

"Oh, I almost forgot," Kane stammered a little. His face had a naturally vacant look so passers-by wouldn't have seen a difference in his state. "Coach gave me a call earlier today, he said that one of your players is jumping over to play with us, starting from this weekend. I hadn't heard of him before so I thought I would ask you and get an insight." Dennis hadn't heard of anybody wanting to leave, but he had a feeling he knew who it was.

"Sure, what is his name?" Dennis replied, both dreading and knowing the answer.

"I think his name was Jet," Kane replied loudly, "interesting name huh?"

"Very," replied Dennis with a sigh.

Dennis was trapped inside his own head. The coach was delivering a pre-match speech with the entire team listening around him. Everyone, except Dennis. He had glanced up once or twice, met the eye of their team leader to show that he was paying attention, but then turned away again. His large knees were bobbing up and down, showcasing the nerves that he was feeling. He was listening to the taps and scrapping from metal sprigs striking the concrete ground underneath, from those more excited than he was.

The jersey Dennis wore was the biggest they made and it was skin tight; usually reserved for those with a larger build and disposition around the mid rift the uniform stuck like a glove around Dennis' tall frame. His shorts were the same, several sizes larger than what he was used to as his old ones could no longer hold him, but his socks were entirely different. His massive calves were impossible to cover with the usual socks so instead he wore some on his feet and wrapped the rest of his leg in unnecessary bandages.

His mind bounced between two ideas only, and he couldn't resolve either. The first was portrayed by his own teacher voice inside his head. Over and over again his brain seemed to remind him that with his new power, size, speed, and strength, it was unfair to even take the field and he would gain nothing by doing so. His mind added that if he was successful, which was a given if he tried even a little, it wouldn't matter and possibly in doing so someone would get hurt. He countered his thoughts by arguing that he wasn't doing it for enjoyment, but simply to act as a deterrent should Jet take the field. His brain played both sides in this contest, after the previous argument was made it would repeat to Dennis that he had so far been able to refrain from showcasing his abilities to others. How was he supposed to stop Jet, who Dennis firmly believed had as much potential now as he himself had, without putting himself on display? And if he did do that there was no way that Jet wouldn't find out, and what he did with that information sent Dennis around in circles again. The group around him roared in unison at something that was said.

"What do you think Dennis?" the coach called out to him as he refocused. He hadn't listened to any of it, but he had been in enough huddles to know that sometimes saying less meant more. He stood up finally, observing the range of looks from relaxing and apprehension through to excitement and a show of primal fury. His size helped him, plus he knew that when he stood up they grew in confidence.

"Let's get them," he said with a smile as he rubbed his wrist in a pretend stretch. Whatever the coach said it must have been good. The players were already at a fever pitch before Dennis uttered a word, he felt like he could have said anything to them and they would have responded the same. A whole stream of childish sayings popped into his head, but Dennis, unlike what he used to do, held back from voicing them lest he bring the players down again.

"Stay warm," one of the coaches said as Dennis hunched through the change room door. "I didn't see you stretch, we would hate for you to come off with cramp." To anyone else it was a caring and legitimate comment, but Dennis had no need anymore. He felt no pain, no requirement to warm his body up as it was already primed for movement. Dennis knew he still had yet to discover his own full potential but he also knew that he was always in a state of readiness. He started trotting along at the back of the team line as they made their way along the sideline and onto the field through a readymade tunnel by the players who had participated in the game before.

The team had progressed from their opponents end of the grandstand but instead of the usual hisses and boos which came with a local derby instead there was stunned silence. Dennis could feel the prickle of all the stares that lanced out at him, but no words were uttered alongside their looks. The only person who stepped out to greet him was Horatio. The journalist had no sign of injury any longer and was still filming and taking photos as he usually did, no doubt covering multiple roles like always. Horatio gave a secret wink and continued to cheer the whole team, following along behind Dennis for a short time.

Dennis slowly made his way to the centre of the field, already assuming the look of a big player who was more size than skill and mostly just lumbered along. There were whoops and praise for Dennis for simply taking the field. He encouraged those around him as they waited. He saw beads of liquid finding their way to the brows of several players and almost instinctively he brushed his hand along his bushy moustache and through his long hair to sweep away sweat that didn't exist there.

The ref blew his whistle, to announce that the game was about to begin but also as a warning for their opponents who had yet to arrive. A slow distant roar started to build revealing the approach of the other team. They exploded onto the field, stepping this way and that, soaking in all the cheers from the crowd as they went. Kane lead the way, largely ignoring the cries as he made it out onto the field. The same could not be said for the player who ran out last. Jet absorbed it all and even stimulated the crowd to give him more. Some of Dennis' own team pointed at Jet shaking their heads. Dennis didn't join them though he mostly felt the same way. Jet had probably got more admiration in simply running out to play than he had gotten with months of training with his previous team.

"I'm going to smash you big boy," Kane said as he reached out to Dennis with a hand. Dennis took it and shook it once, trying to pull back his own strength so as not to harm him. He was managing that task better every day. Kane smiled back at him and gave him a wink. "Easy Tiger, I was just kidding, don't hurt me." Dennis couldn't help but smile and was accompanied by his teammates. Kane was well known between the groups and was a friend to many of them. His talent, although being brought to bear on Dennis' team, was all class, inspiration and hard work and he was respected as an opponent.

Jet followed along eventually down the line in a completely different light. He had no respect amongst the team he had left and Dennis noticed that despite his massive frame and ability many of the opposition didn't acknowledge him either. It seemed the crowd just didn't know better but Jet had fooled no one else.

He, one by one, shook hands with his opposing players, and one by one they recoiled from him, clutching at hands that had been all but broken under his vice grip. It continued until Jet made his way to JT, where Jet sought to shake a hand that was never offered.

"I don't shake hands with cowards," JT said simply. Jet looked stunned, but his entire body flexed, bristling at the insult. Dennis could see what was about to happen and luckily was close enough to intervene.

"Is there a problem here?" Dennis said as he arrived behind JT's shoulder. JT was standing as defiant as ever as he looked up into the younger man's killer leer. It looked as if he didn't care about what Jet may do to him, and he was not intimidated. Jet slowly glanced over towards Dennis, perhaps he was contemplating his next move or the odds of its success, but suddenly he smiled.

"No problem here, sir," Jet replied emphasising the title. "Just catching up with old friends."

"Leave it on the field," Kane's deep voice interrupted as he sauntered down the middle of both lines. Jet obeyed with a nod, taking a step back and smirking at JT. "Control your man," Kane whispered to Dennis.

"That's easier than controlling yours," Dennis replied and received a knowing look. A moment later and they were all separated and ready to begin the match. Once more, in the silence that echoed before the starting whistle, all the thoughts popped back into his head. He was the most nervous that he had ever been when about to start a match, and it had nothing to do with the match. The foreboding feeling that something bad was going to happen kept gnawing at him and he simply wondered how long it would be until something bad happened; until he had to intervene to stop Jet as only he could and in the process reveal what Dennis himself could do. Would it be late in the game or early on? How long would it take?

Not long was the answer.

The whistle blew, the ball was kicked off, JT placed himself expertly to catch the ball, jumping as he heard his opposition approach. JT didn't land on the ground immediately, he had to go through some punishment before that happened. His feet never returned to the ground after catching the ball mid-air, instead his chest was met with a shoulder charge from Jet. The hit sent him rushing back towards his goalposts flying parallel to the ground. JT continued in that direction for almost ten metres before he was grabbed and squeezed by Jet once more. JT could feel his ribs breaking under the impact but could do nothing. Wishing the pain ceased, he eventually got his wish, but in the worst way. The ground became the sky and the clouds shifted to grass as he was twisted around in the air and dumped savagely into the ground. JT squeezed his eyes shut, seeing nothing but red and somehow what pain looked like. He was aware that Jet had started to walk away but JT, despite his body ready to collapse, slowly returned to his feet.

"Hey coward," JT called hoarsely with a suffering smile spreading across his face. Jet, who was smirking smugly towards any player who gazed his way, turned with a growl at receiving the same title. "Nice try, but even after all that you still couldn't get the ball from me. Shows just how conceded your ego is huh, even with all your size and strength you couldn't do the simplest task. You couldn't even intimidate someone half your size." The referee blew his whistle to stop play, reaching towards his pocket and pointing towards Jet. "Oh dear, looks like you are in real trouble now, and you have hurt your teammates and yourself more than you hurt me."

JT wasn't fooling anyone. He clearly had a compound fracture or the like as blood was staining his jersey where a bone was protruding underneath. His whole body would be in agony, it was amazing that he was still standing or even conscious for that matter. He wouldn't be for much longer if Dennis didn't step in.

Dennis saw Jet's face twist in rage, and also as he clenched his fist into a powerful ball. Before another movement was made Dennis was between them, no longer at JT's shoulder but rather at his front.

"That's enough," Dennis said calmly with his hand facing Jet. Jet glared at him but made no move. There was no way he could disguise himself now if Jet surged forward. The referee walked forward with a large red card in his hand, a sign that clearly stated that Jet had no further part to play in this game despite it being no longer than fifteen seconds old.

"Are you serious? Is he serious?" the second question was directed at Kane who had made his way over towards the group.

"Looks that way," Kane shrugged.

"Are you just going to let him get rid of me?" Jet squeaked, now shifting his oppressive gaze at Kane.

"Those are the rules of the game we are playing," Kane replied staring straight back at the young man. He was still shorter than Jet but despite that and the clear difference in their physiques Kane stood firm. "And I am not going to argue because I don't disagree with him. We play a sport with rules and etiquette, not something else where we want to seriously maim or injure someone. If you think that you can do that here because you weren't allowed to at their club you need to think again. That is not what we are about," Kane held the stare of Jet for a long moment. Everyone was on edge, awaiting to see how the big teenager would react. He leaned back, flexed his arms and bellowed his lungs out into the sky with a mighty roar. When he had finished he seemed to find the eye of everyone around him, he breathed heavily in a stationary frenzy. Eventually he turned and left. Dennis watched him leave, concerned for the safety of the audience lest they say something that set him off again. None did, all were too scared to even look in his direction. He stormed off the field and in the next moment he clean jumped over a small barbed wire fence which surrounded the whole area and separated it from the carpark beyond. Those who saw that feat shrieked in shock. When finally he was out of sight Dennis turned to face JT, who was now standing with a smile as Kane supported him.

"He's not as tough as he thinks he is," JT said to Dennis. The ball now sat idle at his feet while his hands were covered in blood from touching his soaked jersey. Everyone looked at JT who started to laugh. Everyone joined in, part because it was infectious but mostly because it looked like JT had been hit by a truck despite his defiance. Just like they copied his laugh they also copied his wince when he recoiled in pain. "Ha ha, ha ha," JT laughed again. Then he collapsed into Kane's arms, only semi-conscious.

"I can take him now," the club doctor said as he arrived. "Do I need a stretcher?"

"No I can walk," JT said with muffled breath. Dennis took him from Kane as JT had started to become heavier. It was no struggle to Dennis and despite JT claiming to be able to walk he left most of that to his friend. They made it to the side of the field and the doctor laid him down just out of harm's way.

"I am going to call an ambulance for this," the club doctor said. JT stuck a thumb up as he took a green whistle from the doctor to ease his pain.

"Keep playing," JT said as he reclined against a pillow he had been given. "I'm fine, that guy can't hurt me. He couldn't hurt Jiemba either. Jiemba is my friend, he is tough, best bloke I know. He is. . ." The medication took quick effect. In his delirious state he had been rambling. Dennis felt that despite that, what he said was fundamentally true. Once more he felt a pang of guilt that he hadn't actively been seeking out his friend, but he also did not know how to try.

"He will be all right," the doctor said. "Go back to your game and I will look after him until the ambulance gets here." Dennis returned to the field. He dismissed many of the questions about

JT simply saying that he would be fine. They refocused, and Dennis pretended to do the same. Despite what Jet had done to his friend and at how appalled everyone was at it, Dennis was now very concerned that he may do something similar to someone else. He didn't even know if what Jet had done was all he could do, or perhaps he had just slightly overdone it and could have done far worse. He ignored the new pep talk and resigned himself to his task.

For the next ten minutes Dennis played well within himself and didn't emotionally engage in the game at all. At scrums he took his position and held it, not pushing nor conceding. In the lineouts he stood at the back trying to stay out of the air. When he ran the ball he looked to pass off quickly or find space; he didn't choose to make that space himself because of his concerns. The opposition tried to run away from him, which Dennis was mostly fine with as his teammates would make the tackle instead, but when they did he felt like he was tackling the player much like he was placing a baby into bed. He would slowly wrap them up in his arms and just as slowly place them on the ground with little to no effort. They mostly allowed it to happen too.

At the end of that time, Dennis decided to pretend he was injured. He held in a laugh as he wasn't convinced that could happen to him anymore, before eventually being called over to the sideline. Dennis half smirked, contemplating to suggest that he had cramp just to see the reaction that his coaches would have. He was happy to be substituted as he was not having fun and had no desire to be there. The main reason why he had played in the first place was the same thing that had only recently bounded over the fence. To his surprise he wasn't being pulled from the game because of his injury, instead he was being called over for assistance. The club doctor stood there and behind him was an empty stretcher.

"Dennis I need your help," the doctor said calmly. "JT has jumped up and hopped in his car." Dennis waited for the alarm to show but the doctor seemed to be used to somewhat peculiar emergency situations. "It was unlocked before he jumped in but now he has locked it. The ambulance will be here soon but we need to get him back out of the car before he hurts himself anymore. Can you do it, even with your injuries?"

"No problems," Dennis said, having no issues in overcoming his fake pain. He informed the coaches that he was out of the game with a quick yell. Without arguing the coach nodded, but Dennis could tell that he wasn't happy about it. "Where is he?" Dennis asked, allowing the doctor to point out a lone car in the overflow carpark in one of the old paddocks.

"Cool, I will check to see if his bag is with him first before I go back to the sheds. I will see if he is still alright as well," Dennis didn't wait for a response but received a nod from the doctor anyway. The doctor's phone started ringing and Dennis used it as a means to remove himself from one of the usual awkward conversations he got stuck with ending. Dennis walked to the same fence that Jet had vaulted and grabbed onto the wire. He pretended to swing over the top but his own small leap was enough to clear it, with his hand selling the fact that he was using it as leverage. Dennis jogged over to his friend who he could see sitting in the front seat. He had half expected him to be pretending to drive it, sound effects and all, but instead he saw him leaning back in the seat. Dennis watched for a moment making sure he was still breathing. After an instant of being satisfied and not identifying JT's bag in his car Dennis headed back to the change rooms. He half jogged half skipped not really wanting to sprint but wanting to appear like he was treating the matter with more urgency. He heard the spinning of the wheels from a street not too far away, turned to look out of instinct and saw nothing as was expected, and continued on his search.

Upon entering the change sheds he was greeted with the faces of all the reserve grade players who were in the middle of sharing a beverage and cleaning themselves up. Even amongst his own club Dennis was still receiving the looks of admiration, shock and fright that so many others had showed him since his accident.

"What's up Dennis?" one of them called out as he started to bob his head up and down around bodies; trying to locate his friend's bag while not lingering on body parts he could have done without seeing.

"JT's bag," Dennis replied with a furrowed brow. His ears pricked as he thought he heard the spinning of wheels once again. He didn't search for it within the change room, in fact the room was so noisy he wouldn't have known which way to look if he did. A moment later he had success. He was handed a beverage alongside the bag but he politely declined claiming he was about to go back onto the field. Even as Dennis made the excuse he wasn't sure he would ever play again. Taking a few steps out of the door he started to rummage through his friend's bag searching for the keys. He shook it a couple of times just to hear the jingling sound in an attempt to make the task easier. He felt stupid that it was taking so long to find a set of keys, and just went to show him that regardless of your strength some tasks may have been beyond you regardless how small or big.

That voice in the back of his head spoke out again. 'You could have just ripped the door off,' it said, 'he was asleep and no one would have known. Then you wouldn't have to search for keys. It would be done by now.' The voice was technically right, but Dennis knew it was principally wrong. But he didn't know why he knew that. His abilities were secret and mostly untested. Jet lashing out in JT's presence in such a way could surely just be the tip of the iceberg. It was still a possibility with time that his abilities may still fade.

Success! The keys were found, hidden in the pocket of JT's rolled up dress jeans. The bag was flung over his shoulder and Dennis headed quickly back towards where he assumed JT still slept. As he was alone he noticed sounds, he suspected that he was hearing more than what a normal person would. He heard the whistle blow as something else occurred in the game Dennis had abandoned. He heard the crowd groan and cheer in reply. The crunch of loose stones underneath his own metal studs as he trudged back through the carpark. There were no laces on his boots, they wouldn't have been able to fit; instead they were fastened to his feet with excess tape. There was a helicopter somewhere but he couldn't see it, and a buzzing from some bug that hung around the overheating bonnets of several nearby cars. Then there was the revving sound again.

Dennis started to run. His current jog speed was as fast as his old sprint, if not faster. There was no reason for it but he knew that revving sound, it fit perfectly with what he had heard before. He rounded the corner where JT's car still sat lonely with few others. Dennis spotted the car which sat in his mind immediately. It was further away and, although threatening at that distance, wasn't the main concern.

It was the other car which was lined up to charge JT's which was alarming. While already revving as soon as Dennis came into sight it floored the accelerator. The old wreck of a car lurched forward in waves as its tyres clumsily ate into the loose dirt and bounced over small bumps. A few metres later the driver had found his groove and the speed drastically increased. Dennis sprinted to close the gap hoping that he would make it in time. For the first time he didn't hold back, in what appeared like half a dozen steps Dennis covered at least fifty metres in no time at all. The keys were still in his hand but he didn't fumble with these as he knew that he had no time to do so. Well aware that his secret might be revealed he had decided it didn't matter, not next to the life of his friend. He punched into the glass on the driver side window, showering JT as he slept on, oblivious to what was occurring around him. With his next motion Dennis had gripped the frame where the window had been. He doubted that the other delinquents could see him as they were on the other side of the vehicle hidden from view. Dennis could still hear them though; they appeared to have no problem with the damage one of their members was intent to cause. Dennis clamped down and managed to rip the door clean off both its hinges and lock. The voice that said it would have been better to reach in and unlock had gone for the moment. Dennis didn't hold back his strength either, as the door was pulled clear he hurled it away behind him and was startled to hear it slam into a large red corrugated iron shed. JT looked completely broken making Dennis think twice about moving him at all. There was no choice. Dennis half rejoiced that he didn't have to fiddle about with the seat belt as it hung abandoned, but looking through the opposite window he could see the car only metres away from impact. Satisfied that he held JT tight but without time to turn and run Dennis executed his only other cause of action.

He jumped.

The action carried him clear of the car and the instantaneous collision which occurred thereafter. Petrol immediately ignited in JT's car as the fuel canister had been struck hard; flames leaping up in Dennis' wake as well as covering both cars. Dennis fought hard to stay focused. The leap had no doubt saved his friend but Dennis was not prepared for what his new body could do. He had catapulted high up into the air and had gone as high as the grand stand that still observed the rugby on the far side, and also the red corrugated iron shed with the massive hole in its frame. As Dennis reached his peak he started to panic; his stomach reeling as he started to hurtle back towards the ground. His legs flailed out underneath and he was sure if he wasn't carrying JT his arms would be doing the same thing. Somehow he righted himself mid-air. He prepared for pain as the ground jumped up to meet him, expecting jarred legs at the least but most likely all his bones breaking again. He closed his eyes and opened them after he felt a tiny thump. He teetered for a second but regained his balance on his unbroken legs.

Dennis had landed next to JT's burning car and watched as the driver of the car responsible clambered out from his. He looked dizzy and Dennis suspected would be struggling with a concussion at the very least. Almost as soon as he hit the dirt the culprit was aware that Dennis was watching him. With a great effort and complete lack of coordination he tried to flee. Dennis took a step back, placed JT carefully on the ground where he suspected he would be safe, then took a running leap. Dennis jumped clear over JT's car and landed a metre in front of the youth who had attempted to kill JT. Dennis thought that may have been harsh, but then almost at once disregarded the notion. It could be considered as nothing but. The creep stumbled forward throwing a terrible punch in Dennis' direction. It almost appeared like slow motion, but that may have been due to how poor the punch was, and all Dennis did was watch as it easily missed. The youth looked dumbfounded at Dennis, apparently he suspected it would be a knockout blow as if he was some kind of prize-fighter. Dennis, almost instinctively although completely out of character, returned the favour. He close-hand slapped the young man with some force. It wasn't his full strength but he held back less than he had been doing so lately.

Either way the youth's jaw was broken. It was evident by the sharp snapping noise which Dennis somehow felt in his fingers. The youth crumpled into a heap on the ground after completing several somersaults in the air. Dennis shook his head at himself. He knew that would happen.

For the first time since he decided to take action he searched for people who would have seen him do it. The only people that were near him were the small handful that were still sitting in the grotesque hot-rod which was making its way around the perimeter of the carpark. Their hooting and yelling had ceased, apparently stunned by what they had seen. But there was one other person who had seen it. The hot-rod drove closer and closer to the figure who appeared reluctant to move toward it. But perhaps that was because they were fixated on Dennis. Jet smiled as Dennis took notice of him. Jet had seen Dennis do things that he shouldn't have been able to do. He expected his former student and teammate to say something to him but there was not a word spoken. Jet simply smiled, finally moving towards the vehicle and abandoning his comrade who had driven the car. As soon as Jet was aboard the hot-rod barked loudly as it churned dust up in its wake. Dennis did nothing else but watch as they left. It took a few minutes for the dirt fog to dissipate. When the sky was clear though, he saw, and could also hear, a very welcoming sight. Ambulance sirens and lights lit up the area as best they could despite the beautiful autumn day. As Dennis watched it approach he noticed it was accompanied by a police car. The sight of that car was surprising as he had no idea why it would have been called out to assist with JT's football injury, but he was grateful as it could help him with the broken youth that lay at his feet.

"Damn," Dennis whispered to himself. He wasn't sure why as the only two nearby were both deeply unconscious. He continued talking to himself nonetheless as he placed a hand on his thick moustache and pondered aloud. "How are the police going to question him with a broken jaw?" Then another thought popped into his head. "Well, at least he isn't going to tell anyone what happened."

"My secret is safe," Dennis said a bit louder as the sirens and lights drew nearer. "For a short while at least."

CHAPTER 9 – THE FINDER

Dennis thought that he was a smart person, knowing lots about a lot of different things, but in regard to medicine he had no clue. Hours had gone past as he waited at the Orange Base Hospital alongside JT, whom had been unconscious the entire time. Several different doctors had been called forth to assess him, each marvelling at how an individual had done so much damage to someone while questioning the story entirely. But apart from all the questions they sent towards Dennis, along with a sceptical look when each answer was given, they also stated all sorts of medical jargon in regard to JT's condition. Dennis was as helpful as he could manage but was hoping someone would simply come over and say that JT had broken ribs, a shattered sternum, internal injuries involving his lungs, but otherwise he would be ok.

Dennis wasn't long at the hospital when JT's parents and partner arrived to see what was happening; where again because of the dribble Dennis was being dished he couldn't convey a diagnosis one way or another to JT's concerned family. Dennis discovered that many of the nurses and doctors that walked by knew who he was, maybe not at first but by the time they walked by again they had placed him. That meant that they were either present when Dennis had been brought in the last time or had worked with him, or on him rather. That also explained why many of them looked confused by his presence as no doubt they had all been told that Dennis would be dead before long.

There was a sign saying that the area they all gathered in was restricted to family only, or close friends in their absence. Dennis had spied a security guard make the rounds a couple of times but that man had never come close enough to eject him. In all likelihood, if they had, Dennis would have moved on without a fuss, particularly as he believed JT wasn't in any real danger of getting worse and was in very capable hands. The security guard seemed to lack the courage to make the order despite his large mass which hung well out over the front of his trousers. Dennis understood that a giant moustache wearing man who wore no shoes over his socks and a figure hugging jersey clinging to Dennis' muscular form would have been enough to make the bravest think twice. Knowing that his friend was okay and his family were with him Dennis saved the security guard the trouble and left of his own accord.

Upon reaching the outer doors to the hospital he realised a couple of things. The first was that time was now settling well into the dark hours of the night, with the most vibrant red sunset lingering beneath the far horizon. It would be gone and night would overcome the countryside soon. The room that Dennis had sat in with JT had no windows and therefore no exposure to the outside world. The second thing was that because he had ridden in the back of the ambulance, which was a very tight fit for Dennis who ended up sitting on the floor, he had left his car at the rugby ground and had no means of transport. He suspected that he could simply run home and that it would take neither any time nor effort to do so; with the shortcuts he could take it may even have been a faster option than if he were to drive. Fortunately he wouldn't have to do that.

Horatio Findman sat on an outside bench, apparently waiting for him as the other man rose to his feet as Dennis approached.

Dennis was relieved to see him there, particularly so he could continue to hide his abilities for a longer duration.

"Need a lift?" Horatio asked as he rose to his feet.

"Sure," Dennis replied almost too quickly, "I left my car up at the ground."

"I suspected as much," Horatio said nodding, "I went in to find you but they wouldn't let me in."

"They have signs everywhere saying family only, I am surprised I wasn't thrown out sooner," Dennis said scratching the back of his head.

"You would be the only one who was surprised," Horatio stated gruffly, "in fact I would have loved to have seen them try and move you out. I could say that my omittance might have something to do with that sign, but they know I'm a journalist and unless I have an invite usually I'm not welcome. Anyway my car is over there." He ushered Dennis away who followed easy enough. Dennis was thankful his friend had come to get him, but also because he had a decent sized car. Dennis clambered in loving the legroom in the vehicle, something that he himself had never had in any vehicle he had ever driven; even before he had his size drastically altered. He slumped into the car. It had been a long day but Dennis felt no fatigue. He didn't resign himself to sighing as he sprawled out his legs, he even acknowledged had this been a year ago he would have been stiffly trying to get comfortable to no avail. A lot had changed, but Horatio appeared oblivious. The car started to pull out of the carpark and onto the main highway that flung past the hospital. Once cruising nicely Horatio decided to liven up the conversation.

"I know all about your powers," Horatio said simply, not even turning to see how Dennis reacted.

"What . . ?" Dennis replied making a half attempt at showing a puzzled expression. The other half decided it was indeed time to act tired which would have been usual.

"You don't have to hide it, I am not going to tell anyone. If I was going to I would have done it already, trust me I'm a journo," Horatio continued. Dennis had been practising what to say if he was found out by accidently showing too much, but despite that and all the scenarios that had played out in his mind he was completely bewildered with nothing to say.

"But also I have them too," Horatio added, this time he did look at Dennis, but Dennis had finally found an answer.

"Mate should you be driving?" he asked, implying that Horatio had been involved in some post game refreshments.

"I'm fine," Horatio replied quickly.

"Are you sure? Not being allowed into the hospital, waiting in the dark and now talking about super powers, buddy you are starting to scare me. They aren't real, you know that don't you?" Dennis deflected and hoped that his friend changed the subject. The idea that Horatio had powers too intrigued Dennis but he couldn't just go along with that idea. "Plus, trust me I'm a journo, seriously?"

"Pretty sure, and even if you don't believe me I can prove it," Horatio said with a smile.

"How are you going to show me you have superpowers while you are driving a car?" Dennis demanded, still wishing that the subject would move on, but unable to resist the quest for proof. He still didn't actually know who won the football and would have gladly jumped back into knowing what had happened in the match that he had abandoned.

"I could do lots of things," Horatio replied enthusiastically. "My power is knowledge. I know what you had for breakfast, I know that a helicopter is going to fly over our head by the time we make it back to the ground, I can tell you when the ground was last surfaced, or this car serviced, or whether or not it is going to rain."

"So you are a weatherman, not a journalist?" Dennis laughed but was not greeted with any humour from Horatio. "Knowing that stuff isn't a power, your job is all about finding information so I know you could do it. If this is about trying to get me to tell you that you are good at your job, then you can just stop. You are, one of the best, but observation and knowing stuff isn't a superpower. It is simply a very useful trait. If it was, you would be unstoppable, but superpowers aren't a thing." Dennis released a deep breath which he hoped Horatio wouldn't analyse. He immediately asked about the match to try and distract Horatio for the remainder of the short trip to the field, which Horatio obliged to answer, leaving the superpower thing to the side for the moment.

Despite asking the question Dennis didn't listen past the result. He just wanted to relax in the car and not be interviewed. He hadn't lied when he said that Horatio was good at his job and suspected that given half a chance at discovering the truth he would pin Dennis down and get his scoop regardless of the difference in strength between them. Dennis observed all the things that you couldn't usually see while you were driving. He examined gardens hidden away behind overgrown retaining walls, traced the shadows down nearby alley ways, sometimes he just people watched or pretended not to notice students which laid eyes upon him. It wasn't long until they were turning back into the ground and Dennis' memory was jogged. He laid eyes on the spot where he had unleashed more of his abilities in a stronger fashion; where he had leapt high into the air and sprinted through the car park. He could see a gaping hole where the car door had been thrust through the iron shed wall. Both cars were gone, but the police officer that arrived shortly after the incident had informed Dennis that that would be the case. All that was left was a black patch of dirt where the ground had been scorched by the flames.

"Gee yours was hard to find," Horatio mentioned pointing his headlights at the lonely form of Dennis' car. "How do you fit into that thing anyway?"

"Always with great difficulty, but it keeps me safe," Dennis replied with a grin.

"Like you need help to keep safe," Horatio sniggered as Dennis started to hop out of the car, "I bet you could get hit by a car and you would still be safer than the driver." Horatio watched Dennis who didn't reply immediately. Dennis knew that any answer would be analysed so he took a moment to think.

"And that is because I have superpowers, right?" Dennis closed the door and looked in through the window. Horatio just smiled back at him. "Well, anyway, thanks for the lift, see you around," Dennis tapped the frame and moved away.

"Probably sooner than you think, superhero," Horatio called back. Dennis had almost made it to the car when a thought struck him. A jingle in the air answered his thoughts.

"I guess you're right," Horatio yelled out, "a superhero definitely wouldn't forget his keys."

"A superhero probably wouldn't need them," Dennis called back. Horatio promptly dumped the rest of Dennis' belongings on the ground releasing a small puff of dust. He then waved as the car turned away and drove off into the darkness. When the shine from his rear lights had disappeared down the long access road Dennis finally jumped into his seat. He reflected for a moment.

Reflecting was something Dennis did occasionally, usually when he had a big decision to make or something spectacular, be it good or bad, had occurred and he needed to think. His mind was a hive but there were more bees at work there than usual. The voices which he shared consisted of only two normally, but it felt like there was a party and everyone were yelling. He caught nothing the voices said but understood the tones as being both positive and negative. He started the car and drove slowly to the spot where he had pulled JT unconscious from his own vehicle.

Dennis kept the motor running, which was actually beneficial to his old beast, and stood to one side as he gazed over the scene. It was dark now but he could still see his memories in that space as if they provided their own light. There was that same darker patch on the ground next to some stained soil, small parts of debris left over from the burnt out shells, and leaking fuel which slicked and discoloured the grass. Despite the lack of light Dennis discovered he could still see quite well, maybe not as good as in the day but the difference wasn't massive. He took a step forward and found a big ditch, revealing the spot where Dennis had landed after vaulting high up into the air. That had been remarkable, he thought, but it was just as remarkable that he hadn't been seen. That was with the exception of Jet. Dennis shivered as he thought about the youth even now revealing his abilities to anyone who would listen.

Dennis turned to the spot where he had spoken to the police officer, revealing a story that was mostly true but finished with a lie. He had told them that a group of hooligans had been causing trouble and had planned to ram a vehicle assuming it was empty. The youths hadn't listened, Dennis told them, and Dennis only just pulled JT free, but the driver of the other vehicle suffered serious injuries. There had been nothing else mentioned and the police officer, knowing no better, simply accepted the recount.

"This one and a few of his mates have been getting around lately," the officer had said as he ordered some of his associates to remove the young man. "I'm just glad you're not hurt and I'm sorry that you got caught up in it." Not as sorry as the young man was, Dennis had thought. The officer said that the police would keep in touch if there were any developments and took the youth into custody. Meanwhile, JT had been treated and Dennis went with him.

Jumping back into the car Dennis stayed lost in his thoughts. He was slightly alarmed how he managed to make it halfway across town without even realising he had made half the turns required; even more so that he had not consciously checked any of them and hoped he hadn't had any close shaves along the way. His brain had no doubt gone into auto-pilot allowing him time to digest but ignoring his whereabouts. He needed to relax, to take time to think. He knew that the rest of his team were out celebrating and enjoying a meal together; Dennis would usually have joined them but on this occasion he would have been no company at all.

Before he knew it he was pulling into the street where his house was located. He parked across the road and not in the driveway like usual. The city council were working on paths throughout the suburban estates and there were cones all around Dennis' driveway where they had cordoned off the area to continue that work. Dennis pulled his wallet and phone out of the bag in the seat next to his and walked across the road to his house. He inspected the new cement which was dark grey showing how recently it had been poured, then after marvelling at it he skipped to the side and headed inside. Apart from the few cars that drove down the street shortly after, the night was quiet and undisturbed, which was just what Dennis needed.

The floorboards creaked under his weight. That was an occurrence before he had become bigger in the first place, but still Dennis shuddered as if they would give way at any moment. Around him there was not much that suggested the house was lived in. There were no pictures or paintings hanging along the walls and little for entertainment apart from a television and a chair to watch it in. It was easier to have all his other possessions safely away in one of the bedrooms to avoid being a discussion piece or accidently damaged. He crossed to the kitchen and flung open the door. He stood searching for food for what seemed like an age; despite the fridge being full with all sorts of his favourites, Dennis found nothing. He had resigned himself to the fact that he would go hungry for the moment, but knew that he would probably eat something later and that he hadn't had the inconvenience of being hungry since he had been injured.

Dennis felt his pocket buzzing before he heard it ring. He pulled his phone clear and looked at the number. It was not one that he recognised and he had no desire to talk. He hung up and threw it on the bench. Dennis groaned not sure about what he should do next.

The phone rang again. This time there was no number at all. He suspected telemarketers, and even thought as he reached for his phone that they were overly ambitious to call on a Saturday night. Dennis lurched a finger forward lazily reaching for the button that would hang up the phone. Before he could, the button vanished and the phone answered the call all on its own. Perhaps Dennis had been too close and had answered it accidently, brushing across the toggle that would activate the call. He prepared to hang up when the loudspeaker also sprang to life. This time Dennis knew he didn't press it but had little time to think.

"Dennis," a muffled electronic sounding voice that he didn't recognise called forth. "You are in danger, you need to leave the house immediately and drive to Rushmore Park."

"Excuse me?" Dennis managed to say with confusion.

"There is no time to explain, you must trust me, I am a friend," the voice, although completely unrecognisable with an obscene amount of static, sounded more urgent. "I know what you are and I will let everyone know it unless you follow my instructions."

"So you are blackmailing me?" Dennis asked with annoyance. This was exactly why he had chosen not to showcase his abilities. He had done it once in view of public eyes and there were consequences already. It hadn't taken long for Jet to spread the word it seemed.

"Only to keep you safe, and because I know your powers you should already know that I am no threat to you," the voice crackled back. "But you must hurry."

"Fine," Dennis replied rolling his eyes as he placed a palm over his face. "Rushmore Park? Who are you?" Dennis queried but did not receive a response as the phone disconnected. He clutched at his keys and locked the door behind him. He left the light on and turned on his television so he could watch the football immediately upon his return. Dennis skipped down his front stairs and trotted anxiously to his car. The ignition sparked and the engine roared back to life and in a moment he was driving again.

Rushmore Park was not far away. Only a couple of blocks away in fact, situated on the top of a nearby hill. Apart from some odd rock formations there was nothing interesting about that place, and it was so open that anyone driving past could see everything within its boundaries. Dennis was not anxious about a physical threat but more so about someone revealing him to the world and what that would do to his career, friendships and life in general. He rounded the corner which lead up to the top of the hill and when he got there released another groan.

"You're kidding me," he moaned as he pulled up next to the park.

"I told you I would be seeing you soon, I actually didn't mean now," Horatio said. He smiled but only for the briefest moment. One of his hands swept his long hair over his head to form a sort of comb over before sweeping down to his own substantial moustache. None of his features looked as if he was joking. When Horatio was serious he was deadly serious but even Dennis wasn't convinced.

"You made that phone call to me," Dennis was annoyed but tried very hard not to slam his car door lest it break, "How did you do that? Why did you do that?"

"It was necessary," Horatio replied and pulled his long barrelled camera out of his car. "I will explain most of it later but for the moment I need to show you something." He walked to the far side of his car bonnet and leaned over the front as if about to take a photo before motioning Dennis to his side. "Look through there and tell me what you see." Dennis took the camera with a deep sigh, hoping that there would be something important to see. He took a moment to focus his eyes, a second later he replied.

"That's my house," he said with little surprise, he had seen it a thousand times and although looking at it from another angle and from a distance in the dark was odd it wasn't amazing. "Why are you showing me my house?"

"I'm the journalist so I will ask the questions thank you," Horatio replied. Out of his periphery Dennis could see him looking in the same direction as the camera as he rocked on the soles of his boots with hands clasped behind his back. "For instance did you know that you were followed on your way home?" Dennis did not, but as he had been lost in thought he wouldn't have noticed anyway.

"No I didn't," he seemed slightly shocked and pulled away from the camera. "How did you know I was?"

"Again, I ask the questions and you need to keep watching," Horatio ordered calmly. "I know because I was following the people who were following you."

"Why were you . . ." Dennis started but was met by a stare which reminded him to be quiet.

"I know lots of things, like I said. I also have an idea about why they were following you. Let's see if I'm right." He pointed back towards the camera and flung the same finger in the direction of Dennis' house. Dennis obliged by watching through the scope again. He didn't look away, mainly to avoid being reprimanded again, but for that duration nothing happened. His eyes saw no difference but as he waited his body started feeling all the small itches which come with prolonged annoyance with nothing else to do.

"There do you see?" Horatio said finally drawing the eye of his friend. Dennis removed his eye from the camera, but only to see what Horatio could see. He returned his eye and marvelled at how Horatio had managed to see the movement before him, without an object that could scope for him, and from a greater distance away. Even Dennis had struggled with those things.

A car rolled into view followed by another. Both were old and worn down and hovered in the middle of the street. The first pulled into the driveway which led to the back of the house, ignoring the barriers for the recently laid cement. When it was out of view the second one parked across the driveway at the curb, restricting access.

"What are they doing?" Dennis said half to himself. He had a suspicion that they were up to no good. That feeling arose from earlier events, but also because the cars that had arrived were no different to those that had caused mass chaos in the rugby club carpark at training only nights earlier. Nothing happened for a few moments. Then the revving of an engine could be heard even from the current distance. Dennis was certain it was one of those cars, and his assumption was proved correct a moment later.

The first car which had been out of view suddenly lurched halfway through the living room wall and front door combined. It had been driven straight through the plasterboard from the back of the house, destroying everything in its path, before leaving a gaping hole. The crashing could be heard just as loud as the revving of the engine before. The rubble and dust had been flung up into the air and a small plume existed in the skyline where Dennis' house stood, dirtying the air like the smoke that came from nearby chimneys as the night got colder. Dennis could not look away, aware that his mouth had dropped open by what had happened.

But they weren't finished.

The driver pulled himself free of the debris, looking exactly like Dennis had pictured in his head, and lucky that the ceiling didn't collapse down upon him. His clothes were ragged, torn and dirty, but Dennis suspected that they existed that way before the crash. The driver pulled free the passenger door, stressing the already fragmented wall causing more or the building to shudder and fall. He did something that was obscured from sight and then ran from the site, tripping and stumbling as he watched behind him. In a second he was inside the second car and disappeared as quickly as he came. The squealing tyres could be heard for several blocks before they disappeared.

Dennis looked up from the camera and released a long audible sigh. His head dropped as he contemplated the loss of his house. He looked at Horatio who still watched on.

"I think it is igniting," Horatio suggested, forcing Dennis to glimpse once more and focus his gaze. Dennis saw nothing, he even moved the camera around a bit to see if he was looking at the cars after they had vanished. When he rested it back on his collapsing home he could see what Horatio had meant. A small cloud of smoke was drifting lazily out from the hole, climbing up along the outside and stretching along the expanse of the small roof. It was being coughed out by the car with little showing of fire.

"There it goes," Horatio said, leaving Dennis even more confused. Once more as he looked on, Horatio appeared to have foretold the future. A fire of growing intensity licked forth from the car. Dennis had no time to question how Horatio knew that because in the next instance the car blew up in a magnificent fashion, forcing the already vulnerable dwelling into a volatile state of chaos.

Boom! The explosion thundered, spewing forth an inferno of smoke, flames and debris. Car alarms screamed into existence and dogs suddenly wailed throughout the nearby streets. Dennis had not been prepared for it; almost dropping Horatio's camera as a result. He shook his head, perplexed at what had just occurred. He continued to shake it as he looked at Horatio.

"That's what I thought would happen," Horatio said evenly, finally glancing away.

"Well I am happy you were right," Dennis said sarcastically, "I hope the prize is a new house."

"You seem annoyed," Horatio stated, stepping forward to retrieve his camera. He seemed more put off that Dennis had mishandled it than the destruction of his friend's home.

"I wonder why that is?" Dennis snapped back. "I also wonder why, if you knew this would happen, that you did nothing."

"I told you to leave and now you are safe," Horatio replied calmly. "Had I not you would have been dead. That sounds like I did something."

"Well yes," Dennis responded, now just quietly angry.

"Besides, there was nothing either of us could do to stop them," Horatio stated, before looking straight back at Dennis. "Because if there was I would have maybe acted differently. But no one could have done anything to stop those miscreants unless they had some sort of special abilities, or they could see the future. But no one does have powers, and no one can tell the future. Can they?" Dennis looked away. Horatio was right. A normal person could have done nothing. If Horatio hadn't called him then normal Dennis was a casualty alongside, or trapped inside, his own home. He knew that he might have been able to change that outcome because of what he had become, but even then he wasn't certain.

"Thanks," Dennis said, taking all the malice out of his voice, "I'm sorry for how I just spoke to you. If you hadn't told me then I would be dead."

"Don't thank me yet," Horatio replied smiling. He removed his grin almost immediately. "You don't have a place to stay now, you can come home with me."

"Thanks but I think . . ." Dennis started to say before he was cut off. He was preparing to say he could stay with a teacher or find a hotel but never had the chance to.

"It wasn't a question," Horatio interrupted, "you are coming home with me, and when we get there we can talk more. Like I said, don't thank me yet." Dennis spat air as he failed to dismiss the suggestions. A second later, without any argument at all, Dennis was back in his car and following Horatio away. Fire and smoke bulging at the sky was all that he could see of the remains of his house.

Dennis had an idea about how to get to Horatio's house. He had dropped some stuff off a few times for him but had never been inside. The route he would have taken was not the one that Horatio was leading him along. Dennis was convinced it wasn't a route at all.

Horatio went down every other street, some leading to cul-de-sacs while others led to an avenue which came back on itself. He drove towards every point on the compass and invented a few of his own. It should have only taken a few minutes but it was closer to half an hour before they arrived. That time was made even longer as Dennis continually thought back to his house being destroyed. Surprisingly he was less alarmed by the idea that he might have been hurt, but was more concerned of his possessions that had been reduced to ash under the rubble that had fallen. He was angry about it, but was convinced that he should have been far more emotional than he was. If he didn't have his newly found abilities or the confidence they brought with them he wondered would he feel the same.

Horatio's eyes darted this way and that as he jumped from his car and beckoned Dennis to follow him quickly inside. Horatio shut the door hard after his admittance, dragging the heavy wooden frame along the timber slatted floor. He then bolted shut at least half a dozen locks that ran down the wall next to the door. None of them were the standard push button variety, each had its own key.

"Paranoid much?" Dennis asked. He chuckled as he stooped down, his head touched the roof in the lobby area as the house was tiny.

"You'll see why," Horatio didn't laugh back, but he didn't reprimand his friend for the comment. It was almost pitch black with the only light coming from an outside street lamp, seen from the edges of the dark curtains which hung at the windows. Dennis reached for a switch but had his hand slapped away instantly. He recoiled from instinct not from the pain, as he felt nothing more than if wind had lightly brushed the hairs on the back of his wrist. Horatio led the way shaking his head. Dennis had no idea how he could see, after the first few steps he could feel his eyes adjust but then the house just seemed to get darker. A door opened with a whine and Dennis felt Horatio take him by the hand.

"It might seem weird for me to hold your hand," Horatio spoke quietly, but the silence made it sound like an invasive echo all around them. "But trust me for a minute." Dennis was prepared to say something whimsical or humorous but resisted the urge and simply did as he was told. He could hear footsteps starting to slap down concrete steps. Dennis peered through the darkness trying to identify what was in front of him but found it impossible. Why hadn't Horatio turned on the lights?

Wham!

Dennis let go of Horatio and recoiled a few steps backward ending up tripping and falling. He found himself on the edge of a large hole in the structure, where he suspected a drop down to the hard floor below.

"Oops, sorry," Horatio said from the void, "I forgot how tall you were."

"Yeah right," Dennis scolded him, "you tell me trust you and then slam my head into the doorframe."

"That was the roof, not the door," Horatio replied the correction as if it made all the difference.

"Whatever," Dennis snapped back lightly, "some leader you turned out to be."

"I would probably show sympathy if I thought you were hurt by it," Horatio spoke again whilst once more taking his friend's hand. Dennis didn't argue and Horatio was right. Once again he had not felt any pain, but that didn't mean that his stumble into an unseen solid object didn't leave him embarrassed.

"Would it hurt you to turn on the lights?" Dennis asked but he received no reply. The expectant flicker of an old garage or cellar light bulb flickering into existence never came. Again, just like in the car, the expected route down the stairs was not the one he would have taken. It also didn't make any sense. The stairs should have gone straight down, or spiralled or even turned, but these ones apparently went left, right diagonally backwards and forwards and around invisible objects. Dennis thought apparently because he saw none of it, the room was void of light completely. He knew that from the front door to where he currently stood he had travelled no more than fifteen metres but it felt far longer.

"Wait here," Horatio said finally, making Dennis stand still. "Cover your eyes as well." Dennis couldn't see in the first place but again he did as he was bidden. A powerful glow erupted after an audible clicking of a switch being flicked over. Dennis lifted his fingers ever so slightly to allow his eyes time to adjust beneath his closed eyelids. After several seconds he removed his hands and slowly opened his eyes. His eyes were drawn from the thin carpeted floor and up along the wall. Dennis, without warning or intention let out a massive noise of admiration.

"Whoah," he whispered as he spun on the spot. He glanced back at the stairs he had just walked down and saw how they trailed all the way down in their own unique way. If you walked straight down in the dark you would have been greeted with a fall of a few metres, as several flights had been broken away or removed either by accident or design, and an assortment of solid metal items were piled below to help break your fall. As interesting as the stairs were, Dennis couldn't help staring at what was before him. He was a grown man, one whom had cheated life and obtained extra ordinary powers which few others had, and now he felt like a giddy child. The wall in front of him was covered with television screens and panels, including one massive one at its centre. The wall itself looked bigger than the entirety of Horatio's house upstairs and it probably stretched out its entire length too. At the base of the screens there were multiple computers, laptops and tables all set up to suit a purpose. Every screen was filled with life and they all seemed to be fulfilling some desired function.

"What do you think?" Horatio asked spreading his arms wide as he watched Dennis marvel at what was before him.

"I said it before," Dennis spoke fully aware his mouth hung open. "Journalism isn't a superpower, but you are very, very good at it."

"This isn't for my job, this is just a hobby at the moment," Horatio said with a small laugh, he was also watching the screens now.

"I read books," Dennis said mockingly, "I don't mind the odd video game, watching movies or playing sport. I don't have a book the size of my house though."

"Until recently I didn't either," Horatio replied. He kicked a chair towards Dennis and motioned for him to sit down. The smile had gone from his face as he walked over to the displays, the light from the images reflecting on his features. "I brought you down here to tell you something. Something that I can tell only you." Horatio seemed to watch something that had captured his attention on one of the screens, but then turned as if instantly dismissing it.

"Do you remember the night we were at Burrendong? I don't imagine that you do, and if you did it would be painful. It is all I see though. The night was kicking on, you blokes were all spent after what you had been put through, and festivities were relaxing all of us. I left to go back to where I had set up my telescope in the loft of the large cabin we were staying in. That young friend of yours, Jet, seemed to be agitated, looking for trouble. You stood up for Jiemba and called the young man out. That must have been hard seeing as you had a connection to him. None liked what he said, some stayed but most were so angry by what he had said and were not willing to let it slide. I was already up in the upper rafters in the loft, watching out from where the windows looked out over the lake. Then you were knee deep in the water and so was he, I have never seen you so angry and I wished that I had done what you did. Calling out someone for their gutless actions was what was needed, and I admired you for that. I pulled out my camera and started to take photos, it was only to help you out should anything arise from what happened. You weren't to blame, enough was enough, I just wanted to make sure you didn't lose everything as a result. I can understand the pressures of upholding a certain appearance that being an educator presents." Horatio stopped and looked up as if looking through the very roof itself, stroking his moustache along its length as if for some sort of comfort for what he would share next.

"Then it happened, the meteor shower that I had spoken to you about. I could see it above you and it was all I could do to watch both the stars and you at the same time. Then there was that explosion. I looked up, one hand holding my ear as if that would stop the ringing. I reckon I saw it before you. The meteor hit something, I am not sure what but I believe it was man made, a satellite perhaps, but anything up there should have been moved out of the flight path so I can't be quite sure, yet, but chunks were fragmented all over the place, a bright light erupting in all directions. Everything about that was wrong. The shower itself would have only contained small rocks no bigger than a clump of sand or a small pebble. The smaller stuff looks like a shooting star, the slightly bigger ones look more radiant, but only slightly so. The one that we saw shouldn't have been there, something that size, had it not exploded, could have had the potential to level a city block, or worse. Why didn't we, or even I, know about that?" He stopped for a second, letting the question hang in the air unanswered. Dennis was sure Horatio was making a point of it but he continued without offering a reason.

"I have my suspicions to be sure, anyway, despite the science, it fell down and impacted into the water. Burrendong is a big body of water, although I suspected that there might be some consequences from the impact even I couldn't have suggested. You all started to run and I couldn't say anything. I watched on in horror as I saw the ripples from where it hit. I was immobilised, I consider myself a big brave sort of man but I was scared like nothing else. But then something else happened. I don't know what it was, I have my suspicions, but there was an explosion beneath the water. Regardless the water rose high into the air and surged forth. It was like a tsunami had erupted from an inland lake. It made no sense. Everyone was running. The doors below were opened wide as the players surged in, they barricaded themselves in and managed to get the doors secure, but the cries of astonishment and fear still reached up into the roof. I looked out and, sorry to say Dennis, I knew you were done for. The water came onwards so quick, with such force, I watched as both you and Jet were taken by it. So wrapped up in what was happening I never once stopped to think about what I was doing. Then it came for me. I slammed the windows shut, fumbled with the lock. It was no good, the latch was broken. I held the panes closed but the strength was too much. The glass broke and the shards raced up my arms, slicing through my wrists. I was struck full in the face and I was out cold. Luckily I got only a splash compared to what you got." Once more he stopped, as if remembering what happened.

"I think I woke up a couple of times, I remember hearing people shouting, I saw the glare of a sirens flashing blue and red. Each time I collapsed though. Finally I woke up, it must have been over a day later. I staggered around. All my equipment was broken or missing. My clothes still clung to me, the cuts in my wrists had healed but great gashes remained. I felt little pain, but I was still hurt, I was mostly just confused. I walked outside and everyone was gone. I was loaned a car, surprisingly undamaged, and managed to get the engine started with no effort at all. That's when it happened." Dennis thought his friend was stopping for effect, as was his way sometimes when he had previously discussed some big story or scoop he had been working. This time it was different, Dennis could tell that Horatio was reliving what happened as he retold the tale.

"I thought I was going crazy. I managed to make it back onto the highway. I had intentions to head to Wellington to seek medical help but decided I could make it back to Orange. I drove for maybe half an hour before I started getting headaches. My eyes, it was remarkable. One moment I was looking normally through the front windscreen, the next I could see into the front room of a house that was over five kilometres away, every item seen with vivid detail. I could smell a farm that was going about a late harvest, and I could identify each variety of food they had pulled, and whether it was ripe or not. I could hear a creek bubbling beside the road but I couldn't see it. I checked later, the closest water was again several kilometres away. It felt like my senses were in overdrive. Most of them I could manage, but driving while looking through a randomly zooming lens was a nightmare. I seriously thought I was going to die. I took the longest route in town to arrive at the hospital just so I didn't hurt anyone. When I arrived I was ushered into a bed immediately. My cuts were so bad that they searched for a surgeon, leaving me by myself to wait. I don't remember it hurting even then, but I found myself people watching as I usually do. I watched people as they walked past me without a sideways glance, I didn't know any of them, and then I did. I saw players I knew and others who I had seen you with. They kept coming and going from the same spot. Eventually the steady stream stopped, and I got up and went for a walk. I turned a corner and there you were. Though I wasn't sure at first, the sign on the wall above your head said it was you. You looked mangled, like you were in a car crash, but the car you were in had already been involved with several other far worse crashes. Tubes and bandages covered you. I watched for an age. I could hear when people were coming and wasn't afraid to get caught. I forgot all about my own injuries because next to yours they were nothing but a tiny scratch. I found the doctor's notes and read what had happened. Dead, numerous times, preparing for the worst, family called. Again I just watched. A nurse came to my side, I let her but I had heard her come. She told me that you were dying, and I told her that she was wrong."

"You told the nurse that I wasn't dying, despite the fact that I had already done so several times?" Dennis questioned.

"Yes," came Horatio's simple reply. "I'm sure you have felt the same way since. When for some reason you know something without a shadow of a doubt, without any reason to believe that something should work. I saw you jump clear of that car. Did you know you could do that?" A shake of the head revealed to Horatio that Dennis had not. "I was the same. Where you have gained strength, speed and stamina, I have gained just as much in a different sort of way. I can see, and when I looked down at you I saw things I shouldn't have. I could see your body mending, feel your pulse strengthening, hear your breath consuming more oxygen, your bones shifted under my touch. I knew that despite what you looked like you would get better, any

other time before then I would have been amongst those giving
you up.”

“So, you have been watching me since then?” Dennis asked
after a short pause.

“I have been watching many things, things that have made
me very interested in the happenings of the world, but yes I have
been watching you,” Horatio replied and moved back over to
look at his screens. Dennis shifted nervously on his feet his mind
unsure how to react to such news. “Don’t worry though, I have
made sure that no-one else has been observing your talents. I
have learned many things about what I can do since that day, as
I am sure you have discovered similar things about yourself.”

Most of what Horatio had said had made sense, and Dennis
could not argue with any of it. But to admit it as proof was to
reveal what he was capable of. “Why have you waited this long
to tell me about what happened to you?” Dennis asked. He cast a
quick glance at Horatio’s hands while he was still turned away;
scars still spread along both arms from his ordeal.

“There is a few reasons,” Horatio said with a smile. “For
starters I have been busy; busy finding out what I am and what I
can do, and once I did that I had to search for answers.”

“Answers?”

“Of course answers,” Horatio almost snapped. As jovial or
mysterious as he was on most occasions he had a very serious
side. That side of him could end an argument with or without
evidence that proved his position, and he could make you feel
silly when he did it. Dennis felt a prickle down his back as he fell
into that category. He was older than Horatio and could probably
throw him through the wall if he wanted. Dennis also stood over
his friend like he had always done, but now he wished he hadn’t
asked the obvious.

“Don’t tell me you don’t ask yourself about what you are
now? What can you actually do, how long will it last, what
happens if it goes? But what about the other questions? Why do

you have them in the first place? Why us? Are there others? Was it a chemical reaction, did the energy from that rock change us? And what about that rock, hey? I should have known about that thing entering the atmosphere. The fact that I didn't, and there is no report about it after, smells like a cover up or worse to me," he paused and took a deep breath. Dennis could see that he was gripping the side of his desk quite hard.

"Of course I have asked those questions, many of them anyway," Dennis offered truthfully. "But this is Orange, nothing like that happens here. We are four hours from anywhere important and even then most couldn't find us on a map. What you are saying is the stuff of stories or movies, not a tale within the Central West."

"Yet here we stand, one of us with extrasensory powers, the other a gigantic strong man capable of amazing feats," Horatio breathed deep again and turned to look up at his friend. "And because of that the Finder needs help from the Hitman." He stood tall and powerful. His jaw was clenched back and his moustache held resolutely to his face. There was fire in his eyes. Dennis couldn't return the ferocity, instead after an intense moment, he just laughed.

"What? So we are super heroes now? Is that it?" Dennis did a small lap of the floor as he thought of what to say next. "So you really have named yourself *The Finder,* I get it, Finder, Findman, makes sense well done. I am not *The Hitman* though, in fact I am just Dennis. I have been trying hard to keep everything under wraps for weeks. And I intend to keep it that way. I am also wondering something as well," Dennis was not letting up, but finally Horatio was letting him have his say. "I am not immediately believing anything that you have said. But if you were watching me, and you knew those guys were coming to get me, why didn't you tell me so I could have done something about it? I could have handled them, with or without powers you think I have. Now I don't have a house or any of my possessions."

"Firstly, you have powers. I have seen them, I have the tapes, just let it go. Second, that was only half true, your house did burn down but your stuff is in an upstairs room, well most of it anyway," Horatio smiled. Dennis shook.

"You have my stuff," Dennis said with disbelief. "So if nothing had ended up happening tonight I would have only thought that I had been burgled. A great night either way for me right?"

"Yes," Horatio nodded and moved over towards Dennis with open arms. "And you're welcome by the way. You may not have taken a name yet but it will be better if you do. You can't help others with your own name, your secret won't stay very secret then, will it? I was watching those delinquents, and while you rest upstairs I will continue to search, and I will find them. All of them. I need you to help me. If you want to get them back, for what they did to your house, for what they did to JT you have to trust me, just like I trust you." Horatio held onto Dennis' arms harder, then with a small chuckle pulled himself closer to bury his face in Dennis' chest, embracing him in a warm comical cuddle.

"Get off," Dennis said as he carefully removed his friend. He was still angry but found it hard to be mad at his friend.

"Go get some rest, that was a lot to digest, and I will need you tomorrow," Horatio gestured to the door upon the stairs.

"I never said I would help you," Dennis replied as he turned.

"I know, it feels nice to know that you aren't alone though doesn't it?"

"It does," Dennis answered with a smile. He took a few steps towards the stairs where he glanced over at his friend. Horatio had already returned to the vast screens and seemed to be bouncing between them with intent. Best leave him to whatever he was doing, thought Dennis as he continued on his way.

Horatio was right, there had been a lot to take in, and no doubt there would be more the next day. But there was one thing that Horatio was very wrong about: Dennis was not a superhero, and he would never, ever, be known as the Hitman.

CHAPTER 10 - THE STAND

The scratching in the roof had been persistent. It would be no more than a mouse, but that didn't mean that its constant scurrying along the plasterboard or scratching at the timber was silent. With all his new abilities he found it amusing that he could still be irritated by the soft scrabbling above him. He also laughed to himself that he had no intention of pursuing that mouse either. How was he still afraid of something so small?

Ever since he had awoken from his near death sleep at his mother's house he had found that he required no rest. He went to bed at night and closed his eyes and would drift off into a shallow slumber; but it was out of habit and never required for his recovery. Dennis had been one of those people in his youth who sought rest frequently to reenergise or recover from a hard day whilst preparing for the next.

No more.

As his body healed at an amazing rate he was never tired nor fatigued, and even if he pushed to some state of exhaustion within minutes he would be ready to commence again as if he had wasted no energy at all.

Dennis had tested his theories some nights before. It seemed unnatural and something that he would be recommending against in his classroom, but Dennis cut himself. He did it twice and was uneasy about it both times, he detested self-harm. In this instance though he was testing his body. In the first instance he gave himself a shallow cut with a knife; which still required a decent amount of even his current strength to pierce his skin. It had looked as if his arm had been pricked and torn by some barbed wire. Dennis had watched as his skin went to work and started repairing itself before his eyes. It looked like he had hit the rewind button as it stitched itself back together along the cut he had made. The second time Dennis had to look away. He found a fleshy part of his forearm where he was convinced that if he had done the wrong thing it wouldn't result in him having a serious injury or bleed out. As his eyes had looked at the wall he had driven a blade with his quivering hand through his arm. It was the first time he had felt pain in weeks, and while he didn't enjoy it there was relief that he could still feel that way. It had taken a small amount of extra time but the wound was closed in moments.

Dennis lay shirtless in the dark, thinking of many things; not one scar was exposed on his arm or his torso when there used to be so many. Dennis was not one to lay exposed or present with missing clothing on any occasion. He had looked once or twice at his newly profound physique but it made him feel awkward. In fact the only reason why he had no clothing on his top half was because of the clothing that Horatio had gathered for him. Dennis had been slowly rebuilding his wardrobe as none of the clothes he had previously fit his changed figure. A new set of clothes was expensive and although he had gotten bigger his wages and his wallet had not. Dennis was also no seamstress, at school some of the girls in his textile classes had done the work for him in his assessments; it hadn't been because they liked him, it was entirely to do with how bad he was. The jeans he currently wore were from his kit bag that he had retrieved from his car, but the other shirts gathered were too small.

There was no blame to be laid on Horatio's half for the clothes, he had after all done his best to retrieve them. Dennis was still angry that he had taken no other action to warn others of the destruction of his house. Even if he hadn't gone straight to Dennis there were other parties, like the police, that he could have been informed. The more Dennis thought everything through the more he came to the conclusion that it was his own fault and nothing that Horatio could have done would have worked.

"Hello Mr Policeman," Dennis re-enacted Horatio's made-up conversation in his own head. "My name is Horatio, I have super powers and a possibly not legal video set up in my basement. I am here to tell you that a group of miscreants are going to burn down my friend's house. Why? Because he has super powers too, and I think there is some sort of conspiracy going down around here." Dennis chuckled at the thoughts and relaxed more into the undersized bed with his feet hanging out over the edge. Even he had only understood half of what he had been told. It was somewhat relieving to know that someone else had been affected by the falling space rock at Lake Burrendong. More so that they knew Dennis' secret and were willing to keep it. But the fact that Horatio had been impacted in a different way and had abilities which Dennis did not have was interesting. Whatever had happened seemed to affect people differently, in somewhat unique ways. Perhaps Jet's abilities were not similar to Dennis' like he previously thought.

Apart from the three people Dennis knew of, including himself, he wondered how many others there might have been. He didn't know where to start with completing that thought, but Dennis was brought back to the present as light entered his dark.

"Wake up!" Horatio bellowed as he tore the door open, "I need you now."

"I'm awake," Dennis replied with even calmness. He had learned a long time ago as part of his teacher training that being or showing panic in a stressful situation frequently made a situation worse. "It doesn't hurt anyone to knock or to say please you know."

"Come with me," Horatio demanded without waiting to see if he was being followed. Dennis followed him and expected to be going back down the stairs but Horatio was already at the door.

"Where are you going?" Dennis asked as Horatio continued to assemble what he required.

"Not just me, you too," Horatio replied, throwing an extra layer of clothing over. It was well into the early hours of the morning and it would be chilly outside.

"I'm not going anywhere," Dennis snorted. "I thought you were just going to show me something from your media set up downstairs. I have no shirt and if we do anything out there I will be seen." Horatio didn't question Dennis nor reprimand him; he just found solutions. An oversized oil skin jacket was thrown at Dennis, accompanied by a large dark brown Akubra which matched the colour of the jacket.

"Put those on," Horatio demanded again, "you don't need a shirt, you don't feel the cold, right? The hat and jacket will cover you enough. Oh and don't worry about anyone seeing you and taking a video. It's that dark outside that they would have to be right beside you to identify you."

"Cameras are pretty good these days," Horatio replied, still not actually moving to wear the clothing he had been given.

"True," Horatio admitted, "but they don't work very well if the local communication tower is offline, so unless they have a huge old school camera they won't get a good shot, and if they do and place it up online later I will find it and destroy the image."

"So, you just casually got rid of all communications in Orange? Should I be concerned?"

"It's necessary," Horatio seemed more urgent, "It won't last long though, jump in my car and I will tell you more on the way." A second later he was gone, and a second after that Dennis was locking the door at best as he could manage behind him.

Dennis groaned audibly once Horatio had stopped talking. He had taken Horatio's word that the jacket would be big enough for him, and surprisingly he was correct.

"You never get an oil-skin jacket that is tight, or fits too well," Horatio informed him. "You always have to leave extra room for multiple layers underneath, or, you know. . ."

"What?" Dennis asked with a look of innocence.

"Extra bodies," Horatio said with a broad grin. "You never know when someone else might need to share your jacket."

"Of course," Dennis replied, remarking at his own ignorance. Dennis sat in the front seat thinking that he looked like some sort of exotic cowboy dancer. He imagined what he looked like: a giant shirtless cowboy, abs and all other muscles in his chest exposed for all to see, with a thick powerful moustache hidden amongst his strong features beneath a broad brimmed drover's hat and an oversized jacket which hung down below his knees. At least the hat and jacket fit though.

Dennis had listened intently to the words which streamed from his friend's mouth, and although he had tried to remain calm he knew he showed his displeasure at events. Dennis had not been the only person to lose belongings to fire and destruction. Several cars had been stolen or ransacked and set alight. Sadly, this was not out of the ordinary as similar things had been happening lately in the city, but the amount it was happening at the moment was staggering. Horatio had informed Dennis of the streets and the times and it was almost like those responsible were walking in a straight line, going from one street to another creating an alarming path of destruction.

"So wiping out all communication towers is going to be fantastic for the emergency services who are probably trying to stop this as we speak," Dennis suggested.

"Admittedly I didn't really think of that," Horatio acknowledged. "But it was still necessary to allow our actions to remain secret. It won't be long until they can use them again anyway, the towers will come back online within the next half an hour. Besides you will be more helpful than the emergency services will be." Dennis silently questioned the word secret. Cars had not been the only things destroyed. A few houses had been set alight as well. The occupants had either not been home or had managed to escape to safety quick enough, but each of them had had a connection with the rugby club. Dennis didn't need to be a genius, knowing full well that Jet was probably one of those involved, to see the connection.

"The police are already occupied trying to contain streets where houses are already alight, as are the firies," Horatio explained. "I think that's what these villains want to happen so they can hide what they are actually doing."

"Villains?" Dennis questioned with a frown. Horatio was clearly trying to convince himself of the superhero charade. "And how do you know what they are going to do?"

"Sadly Dennis, your student, whatever his good qualities were, has now thrown his lot in with those responsible for all this chaos. It is no coincidence that this is happening with people involved with our club after the carpark incident. For anybody to think that destruction and injury, which is basically terrorism, is a suitable course of action in any situation there must be something wrong. That is made ten times worse when they have powers like you or me and can amplify their impact," Horatio glanced over from the driver's seat at Dennis who had turned to look out the window. His voice dropped out of its urgent state and sounded full of remorse. "I am sorry to say that Dennis, and I know that you would never abandon a student but something has to be done. I think I know where he is going. The club coaches have both lost their houses, the last one that went up was Jiemba's, but luckily he isn't there."

"Or anywhere else apparently," Dennis said sharply, the report of Jet's state of mind had hit him harder than he thought it would.

"We'll find him another time," Horatio moved on, still driving erratically towards the North end of the city. "I think they are going to move on to JT's place next. His house is nearby."

"He is still at the hospital though," Dennis replied.

"Yeah, but what about his partner and their bub?" Horatio queried. Dennis said nothing. He had actually forgotten that he had either of them; as despite his natural ability on a football field, jovial nature and powerful presence JT rarely spoke of his family, that didn't mean he cared any less about them though. JT was a known fiercely proud and protective individual, which was perhaps why he was lying in hospital at that very moment. "It's up here a bit," Horatio stated as they rounded another corner. Immediately Dennis knew that Horatio's guess had been correct. More cars had been set alight. Some had clearly exploded as they sat in a smouldering heap with a dark black mark shadowing the usually light grey curb side. Saplings and small trees that bordered the street that had been planted by the council were levelled, destroyed or knocked over. The contents of people's front yards, including mailboxes or potted plants, were shattered and strewn across lawns, driveways and the street itself. At a few of the residences garbage bins sat melted whilst still spewing forth toxic fumes. Small slivers of light could be seen from within houses as their occupants chanced a glance out to see if those responsible were still in the vicinity. Just up ahead a small lantern shaped street light toppled to the ground, causing a loud pop as the electricity fizzled into the bitumen. Shadows could be seen now, revealing a car load of vagrants with several others leading or following behind. With a heavy sigh Dennis accepted that he had to step in, which was still one of the last things he wanted to do.

"You should probably stop here," Dennis said to Horatio who slowly pulled his car over. "Stay here," Dennis demanded as he grabbed hold of his hat and fixed it down hard so he could only just see from beneath it. Despite whether Horatio was telling the truth about his abilities or not he was fairly certain he wouldn't be as useful in dealing with this situation face to face as he would be from behind his computer desk.

"Good luck," Horatio said with some silent conviction, "JT's house is up on the next corner at the end of the street." Dennis nodded and started walking.

He chose not to turn around as he slowly pursued those in front of him. Everything about what he was doing was new to him and he was nervous. What was he going to do, just walk up and say 'hey guys can you please stop burning down people's homes and vehicles'? He felt as if it was his first day in a new town and he was wearing a clown suit. People were going to see him, they were going to think that he was odd, and if they questioned what he was doing there he would not be able to give them a definitive answer. He knew he was stronger than almost everyone around, yet he still didn't feel the confidence that should have come with it.

He watched his shadow as it danced around his surroundings, cast by the still remaining street lights or the shimmering fires that appeared around him. He could feel the presence of stares from the houses as people watched him walk silently. He did not acknowledge them, but he did slink further into the jacket which wrapped him like a cape.

Dennis was making some ground on the group and could hear them cheering each other on and whooping with delight as the next item was destroyed. He cared about what they did but his eyes darted around them as he searched for Jet. It wasn't long until he laid eyes on him. Jet walked separate to the rest, nearer the middle of the road. His hands were in his pockets and he didn't appear to be immediately responsible for any of the destruction taking place. None of them had seen Dennis yet, if he could get close to them he could try and stop the car before the group took off. Another street light was torn to the ground, shattering as the glass slammed into the black road.

"What are you playing at?" a large voice called from an open doorway to Dennis' side. He thought initially that the voice was being directed to the group causing all the chaos but it appeared that Dennis had been the desired recipient. Dennis cleared his throat, turning to face the man though he never stopped walking.

"I am here to help," Dennis replied.

"Help?" the man questioned. "They don't need any help destroying the neighbourhood."

"I'm not helping them," Dennis said shaking his head, "I am here to help you." Dennis had stopped now. The group he had been trailing had finally noticed him thanks to the help of this man. He walked out from under the veranda and moved into the light. The man didn't stop until he stood beside what Dennis assumed was his car; his very shiny and very expensive looking sports car. The man was more intimidating to Dennis then the youths he followed. He was a big muscle bound gentleman looking to be of island heritage. He wore dress pants and a white shirt, which had clearly been tailored for him, that had several buttons undone revealing tribal tattoos underneath. His head was shaved bald and the bare spots on his arms and neck revealed the presence of more artwork resembling that on his chest. He was nearly as big as Dennis without all of his accidental enhancements.

"You're here to help?" the man questioned again. "My sister and her children are terrified inside their house. My sons are in there comforting them. Those idiots are walking down the street causing damage as they like, and one of them is pulling street signs out of the ground with his bare hands. What are you going to do?"

"I will do whatever I can," Dennis replied. He really didn't want to talk to him and silently wished him to leave before he told him as much. "Sir could you please go back inside?"

"Sir? Don't you know who I am?" the man snorted with disgust.

"No I don't, and at the moment I don't think it matters anyway. It would just be safer if you were in there," Dennis wasn't sure if he was going to move with the request, and didn't really want to move him though he knew he could. The man stood there looking at him, but then turning to see the destructive group his face changed from contempt at Dennis to a look of alarm, that was filled with fear.

"Watch out," the man called, diverting Dennis' attention. Dennis turned to see what was going on and summed up the situation in and instance. Jet was his focus. The boy sneered in Dennis direction, clearly unhappy at his presence. He had retrieved the fallen power pole, snapped off the cabling at its base and held it casually under one arm. He smiled and then in two steps he had raised the pole out behind one shoulder before throwing it like a javelin. Dennis could see his intention in the first step and had already started moving. The target was not him but the islander man who stood stock still near his car. Despite the size of the light pole it was launched like a bullet. Dennis was moving with intent and then his feet left the ground.

Dennis hit the ground hard but felt no pain. He rolled to his feet, and retrieved his hat from where it had fallen from his head. With a simple look he turned to gaze at the body of the man, who had not been harmed despite Jet's dangerous objectives.

"Now will you go inside?" Dennis asked politely. The man was not hurt although he was completely shaken. The lamp post had never hit him as it had never reached him. Dennis had caught it mid-flight and it was hanging limply, effortlessly, from his hand.

"You got it," the man replied, trying to return to his tall and intimidating posture. "I won't forget this either." Dennis thought no different of him, and didn't really respond to his comment either, he was just relieved that the now shaking form would be removed from the area. When he was gone Dennis turned to watch the group. Jet was clearly annoyed by his teacher's intervention but knew what was coming.

"All of you get up to that house on the corner," Jet ordered the group who quickly crowded the car, aware of the danger. "Destroy it." Dennis was taken back by how quickly the group moved off to accomplish the deed regardless of outcome, but he was also equally irked by how easily Jet gave them the order at which they obeyed. Either way Dennis wasn't going to stand by so that it could happen, he was here to stop it. He swished back the long tail of his jacket and brought the light pole to rest against his shoulder. He watched as the ugly sound of the car revving filled the already noisy dark early morning and tore big clumps of burning rubber from the tyres.

"I really hate that car," Dennis said to himself as he hefted the lamp pole on his shoulder, justifying what he would do next. Then, just like Jet had done before him, Dennis took two steps forward and threw. It was almost like he had been doing it his whole life and the muscles in his body worked to achieve exactly what he wanted. The pole flew straight and true and drove straight into the side of the car's bonnet. The whole car jumped forward a few metres from the impact but the engine died almost instantly, the grinding sound of metal on metal the last cry of the crippled car. Jet looked even more annoyed, bellowing angrily as his comrades immediately abandoned the action they had been ordered to undertake. The target was forgotten; those that were able jumped from the car and sprinted for their lives. Others, who were mostly injured, crawled or limped away hoping that they wouldn't be chased. As none of them progressed up the street, to where JT's house was supposed to be, Dennis chose not to pursue any of them. He may do it later but not now. He was very aware of who the threat was.

Finally it would come to this. Dennis would try talking to his former pupil, but he knew that it would do no good. He would have to fight. He walked casually over to Jet, who, despite his previous desire to destroy JT's home, simply watched him come. Though neither said anything the air was not silent. The crackle of electricity from the broken power cords sparked off to one side, as the blistering of paint on the damaged car and fence wood disintegrating popped every few seconds. The black sky had blood red streaks and dots imposed upon it by the flames, but a rising sun at Dennis' back was slowly bringing natural light to the scene. The sun still wouldn't rise for a while though, giving Dennis time to end this and leave before he could be properly discovered.

"I thought you were trying to help me," Jet called out as he stopped a short distance from Dennis. "But yet again I see that you are the only one willing to fight me."

"Not willing," Dennis replied.

"Just able?" Jet asked, letting the question hang for a moment. "Don't worry, I haven't told anyone. Who would I tell? Who would believe me? I suspected that you were like me the other night, when all the cars were going off at your precious training. Those people were doomed, only some divine intervention was going to save them, and then you did. I didn't want them to be killed, if that is what you think, I just wanted to let everyone know that you were all wrong about me."

"Yep, that was the first thing we thought after you did that," Dennis laughed, "Jet tried to kill us, he must be a good bloke." Jet ignored him and spoke again.

"I had intended to test you out at the game yesterday, it seems so long ago now," Jet continued, he was starting to pace slowly. Dennis followed with his eyes, while subtly moving over towards the cords that were sparking light blue. "But obviously other things stopped that from happening. How is your friend by the way?" Jet smiled as he referred to JT. Dennis again decided to maintain his composure, refusing to rise to the bait.

"He will be fine," Dennis replied. "At least I know where he is, where are your friends?" Dennis thought he had a win with the comment as Jet visibly snarled.

"You don't know where all your friends are though," Jet responded eventually. The statement referred to Jiemba, and it hurt, but Jet was no longer smiling at what he said. "Last time we fought we were interrupted. You even had to make the excuse that you had died, just so you didn't have to fight me. I wonder who the real coward is here. What excuse will you make this time?"

"I don't make a habit of fighting students," Dennis said in reply. "And I would never have been able to stand in front of criminals who are destroying people's lives and ask them to stop."

"See, the real coward stands here before me," Jet chuckled. "The powerless teacher."

"We both know where the coward stands," Dennis replied. "And teachers are not powerless. In fact they wield more power than either of us. They shape and mould the future. They save lives. They lead and inspire countless people. Not just young ones, but older ones too. They never stop trying, even if that means they suffer for their passion. Once more you show that you have no idea about the world that exists around you."

"So moving, are you finished?" Jet groaned, his hands clenching into fists. "I hate to be lectured."

"Then it looks like you still have more to learn, boy," Dennis snapped, and no sooner had he said the word 'boy' then Jet had lunged towards him, with a soul piercing cry. Dennis was glad that he had not underestimated the youth and the powers he may have possessed. He covered the space in a few short seconds. The talking was over, the attempt to avoid a fight had failed, and unlike last time Jet was not holding back and he was not resisted by the water they had been submerged in at the lake. But Dennis was not restricted either. Dennis stepped to the side as Jet's fist flew past, missing by centimetres. He continued to side step backwards and away as the flurries followed after him.

Dennis looked into the eyes of his opponent. Last time they came together he saw fear there, now he saw only desperation and rage. There was no thought of consequence, nor consideration to what his actions were doing. There would be no reasoning, therefore Dennis had no choice but to take action.

Jet threw one more punch, possessing more power than those previous, but once more he missed. Dennis had rocked back on his feet, and in the next moment swept his right hand upwards in a skyward direction, slicing at Jet's face and slamming his jaw shut. Dennis felt the force as it hit, the resistance from his opponent. It was like hitting a bull, the strength that it possessed and the anger that would follow. Dennis should have broken his jaw, and would have done so with that shot without their powers. With them it was a different story. He took a step back as Jet regathered himself. Dennis was astounded to hear the sound of laughter.

"Is that all?" Jet asked. "Was that supposed to hurt?" Dennis was amazed that it did not, and the short moment that he was stunned was all that Jet needed to go back on the offensive. Jet swept a leg out from underneath and connected with the side of Dennis' knee. Dennis crumpled in an instant, feeling a sudden surge of pain. Before he could dwell on it Jet had returned to his feet and was attempting to slam his foot down into Dennis' face.

Dennis rolled back over his shoulders, more out of instinct than intention and landed back on his feet. His knee took his weight easily with no suggestion of injury. Jet noticed it too, and seeing his advantage slide away he moved in to continue his attack. Jet came in close and started beating at Dennis with a barrage of punches. He mostly connected with Dennis' exposed chest as Dennis kept his hands on guard near his face. The assault continued for a moment, which was the time Dennis had given himself to calm himself and remember some training he had participated in with relation to boxing. He allowed himself to be struck by the next three punches, then swiftly moved to one side, shifted back to the other, then led with a jab which was followed by a cross, a hook and then he repeated it all over again. He struck Jet back as many times as he himself had been struck. The boy groaned with the hits, giving Dennis the knowledge that despite what the youth had said Jet was actually hurting with each blow that connected. Finally Dennis let up, jumping back giving the youth space.

"Is that all you've got?" Jet asked. Dennis searched for a way to stop Jet. He would have to knock him down, which would be hard enough, but then he would also somehow have to knock him out. His senses tried to help him. He could still hear all the same sounds, although they jumped in and out of focus. He could hear sirens that seemed to be getting closer, car engines bursting into life as he suspected people fled while Jet was distracted. The buzzing of the blue electricity sounded odd in his ears. Dennis shot a glance in that direction. The wires were still exposed and not too far away. It could work.

Except Dennis had lingered too long.

Jet slammed him with a shoulder and kept driving Dennis backwards. He lost his footing and fell to the ground. Jet was on top of him in an instant. Familiar hands sprang out trying to find his throat, and latched on hard. For the first time in an age Dennis felt the air leave him, and he struggled to find more. His hands flailed as if trying to figure out what to do. Jet was kneeling on Dennis' jacket, helping his cause in keeping Dennis down. Jet was also strong enough to execute his actions. Dennis grappled his hands around Jet's trying to pry them from his throat. It was no use. He looked up into the face of a sinister young man who was prepared to kill him.

Dennis turned his head and saw that the wires still sparkled near him. They were closer now, as he had been driven towards them when Jet had tackled him. He reached out hoping that he could grab hold of them. He stretched. Forcing his feet into the ground trying to grab hold of them. It was no use. His senses flooded. He could hear everything and see everything. His life flashed before him as the sirens blurred his sight and the roar of car engines grew ever louder.

WHAM! Air flooded into his windpipe, the pressure immediately disappearing. Jet was no longer forcing him into the road. But in the space where Jet once occupied above Dennis, there was now the crumpled bonnet of a car.

Horatio's car.

Horatio clambered out with a groan, clearly the worse for wear. He had driven it hard into Jet as he had been trying to suffocate Dennis. The impact had sent Jet flying, but it had also stopped the car dead in its tracks.

"Quick mate," Horatio spluttered as he clung to his car door for support. "Communications are coming back, and he is getting up again." Dennis felt the air surge back into his lungs, rejuvenating him instantly. He leapt to his feet and wasted little time. He grabbed the exposed wires making sure not to accidently touch himself with them. Jet groaned as he started to crawl, lifting himself from the ground slowly. Dennis had no doubt that he would return to his feet shortly. He wasn't going to let it happen.

Dennis ran with the wires in each hand and pulled them along in his wake, ripping them clear from the ground as he sprinted towards his fallen opponent. He could feel the tug as he shredded them through the grass as more wires came free. He could still hear Jet groan as he leapt upon him.

"Sorry," Dennis said as he pinned Jet beneath his legs, "Not sorry." He plunged both wires into Jet's chest. The youth's eyes bulged as the power surged through him. Jet's body pulsed and twitched with the energy, some was transferred into Dennis but still he held on. He had no idea if his attempt would work, unsure if it would make a difference or if it ended up killing the boy. Jet squirmed under the pain, never speaking and staying completely alert. Dennis pushed them in harder, roaring as if that was going to help him out any. The electricity coursed through him too. Dennis had no idea how much longer he could hold on for. Something was calling for him through all the anguish. He was ignoring it like everything else. Then it came harder.

"HITMAN!" Horatio screamed. Dennis became immediately alert. He looked down and saw that although he still convulsed Jet was finally unconscious.

"It's over," Horatio continued, pleading to be noticed. "The sun's coming up, the police are on their way, the power is back fully, which means the cameras are back, and. . . and he isn't going anywhere." Dennis slowly climbed to his feet as he realised everything that Horatio had said was true. He walked the wires back to the side of the road and safely placed them back. He glanced over at Jet; watched his body as it still spasmed.

"Don't worry about him, but if you don't want to be found out then you need to go now," Horatio walked over and returned the Akubra that had been knocked away during the fight. "I will handle this, you head back to my place and be discreet." Dennis shook his head at the scene that was becoming more and more visible by the second as the sun continued to rise.

"How will you explain away this?" Dennis felt that he was going into shock, but he could also feel his own body fight it away. Regardless, his own morals told him that what he had just done, and the cause of it all did not sit right for him.

"I am a journalist remember," Horatio said with a thin smile. "I am an expert on telling a story, whether that story is true or not."

"This all escalated too quickly," Dennis said, still not understanding everything that had happened. He moved over towards Horatio's car. In the next instant he had quickly grappled the damaged grill and bonnet and bent them into a shape that resembled what the car should have looked like. Not properly fixed but able to be used again.

"A great headline to be sure, but I can do the rest. You need to leave right now. Go!" The order was given sternly. Dennis nodded and twisted to leave. Horatio saw the first police car round the corner tentatively. When he turned back all he could see was Jet lying on the road, and Dennis was gone.

CHAPTER 11 - THE WRANGLER AND THE HITMAN

Jet stirred. His eyes were blurred. His neck twitched in realisation of his returning alertness. He knew that he wasn't where he had been, but had no idea about where he was. He was surrounded by light where before he had been surrounded by darkness. There were no sounds here. Everything was calm when it should have been chaos. Chaos that he had created. He had desired it at the time, that was no longer the case.

The slow rhythmic beeping of some device could be heard from nearby but not much else. Jet tried to sit up but found that his arms were restrained. He was not angry about that, they were necessary for what he had just done, he knew, but he was also confident that he would have no problem removing them. He was strapped to a bed with all blankets and sheets removed. He understood where he was. He was in hospital. On the few occasions that he had visited such a place he was in a ward where he could see everyone beyond where he lay. Now he was confined inside a room which resembled a box. There was one other patient who lay in a bed not two metres away. He knew his face but not his name. After a short time the memory of him came back; the other, a youth who was still unconscious, was the one who had driven his car into JT's. Jet knew there would be no conversation coming from him for a while, regardless if he was awake or not.

Jet suddenly became aware of another person in the room. He tried not to look alarmed, but casually cast his gaze to his other side to find he had been correct. A woman leaned against the far wall with a look of disinterest. She was visually stunning, with long flowing red hair resting on the shoulders of a slender, black, expensive looking suit. The woman was older than him, and discovered that she was finally being observed by the young man. She did nothing but flick her eyes over him in simple awareness.

"Who are you?" Jet demanded quietly, he could feel his strength rushing back to him with every passing second. He had no idea how long he had been unconscious for, but he quietly guessed and promised that he would pay back Mr Dodger for every second of it with interest. "Where am I?"

"You are in the security holding for the Base Hospital," the woman replied in a sharp commanding voice. "This is where they put the patients who are in police custody. And you certainly have been a bad boy. You are in a lot of trouble."

"Not really," Jet replied casually. "They won't be able to hold me in here. So I can't really be in trouble can I?"

"No I suppose not," the woman responded. "But what will you do when you leave?"

"That's none of your business," Jet snapped, and in the process he tore both of his arms free from his restraints.

"I think it is," she said unimpressed by his display, with no hint that she had been intimidated. "You leave here and you go into hiding so you don't get caught, or you join up with his lot," she nodded in the direction of his colleague, "a group of directionless vandals who used you for your strength and abandoned you when you needed them. What a waste of talent."

"What would you know about it?" Jet demanded. He had yet to remove himself from his bed.

"A great deal," she replied, "far more than you do. I have seen the videos of what you were doing last night, you have immense strength, great power, but it is unfocused. You have enormous potential."

"I have been told that by a few people lately," Jet said with no emotion, "I didn't listen to them. And it didn't end well for them either. What makes you think that you are any different?"

"I can help you, and you can help me," she stated simply. Not once so far did she change how she had spoken to him. "I can give you purpose, money, power, a means to show everyone that you are more than some thug. You are smart, you show composure, you act young but you show restraint. You are more than anyone gives you credit for."

"That is all well and good for you to say," Jet said, shrugging off her attempt at flattery. "But I don't even know who you are, or how you are allowed to stand by in a supposedly secure room, with someone as dangerous as I am."

"I have my ways of getting most things that I desire," she said with a smirk finally, "which is proved by the fact that I am standing here with you. And in regard to who I am, just call me an Opportunity. I stand here holding the only door that is open to you, offering you a different life by simply walking through it." Jet breathed deeply. He was smart enough to know that his current situation was bad, regardless of how strong he was. There was at least one other person who could stop him, and he had discovered that they were willing to do so. He had to have an edge and at the moment he had nothing.

"You have my attention, Miss Opportunity," Jet answered the lady. "But before I listen to what you want me to do, I have some things that you have to do for me."

"I'm listening." The lady smiled.

"Are you serious? Are you actually serious?" Dennis boomed as he angrily threw down the Monday newspaper.

"What?" Horatio shrugged with confusion, the smile on his face showed that he knew exactly what.

"'The Wrangler to the Rescue', on the front page of your newspaper. You gave me a superhero name. I told you not to do that, because I am not a superhero," Dennis shook his head in disgust.

"I know what you said, but think about it from my point of view," Horatio started to argue his side, "I have to tell a story here. This is a momentous event, someone with extraordinary abilities comes in and takes down someone else, who also has extraordinary abilities by the way, and disappears into the night. You were seen by others, not closely but you were seen all the same. People want to tie a name to that person, I couldn't just call you Frank or Bob, and you wouldn't let me use Hitman, not that that would have been appropriate anyway. It had to be something else, and it had to be something unique."

"But 'Wrangler', why? And I see you stopped short of doing the same to Jet," Dennis slumped further in his chair.

"If you noticed I didn't actually name Jet, partly out of courtesy to you, but also partly because after what he was involved with his name will be spread all over the place before too long by the police and other media. I gave up a scoop for that, you're welcome by the way. And the Wrangler. At the time it fit the headline, I was also trying to fit your look into the name, something country. I had names like the Shepherd, or The Drover, or The Chippendale," Horatio joked.

"That's not funny," Dennis sneered at his friend.

"It totally isn't funny," Horatio agreed, although he said it with a smile. "The Wrangler felt right at the time, I'm not so sure now, oh well, I'm sure it won't stick."

Horatio moved away to prepare his breakfast. It was already late morning and neither of them had attempted to go to work. For Horatio it was normal, for Dennis not so much. He hated calling in sick for work, or taking days off for any reason. The amount he would have to prepare for his casual or relief teacher wasn't worth the trouble most of the time. But on this occasion he had decided to take a day. He would visit JT who was still in hospital and he would just relax. That was in an attempt to get his head around all the other things that time was demanding of him.

The most important thing to him was to acquire items that he would need for the immediate future. Horatio had graciously offered Dennis a place to stay, although Dennis acknowledged quietly that Horatio's superhero building agenda was probably one of the key reasons for that. But Dennis still only had a short supply of clothing and personal items which wouldn't last him very long.

Dennis also had to visit his home. It was completely destroyed but he had been requested by both the police and by the landlord to accompany them so they could do a thorough investigation into the cause and what would happen in regard to insurance.

Dennis was cleared of suspicion quicker than he had thought, a car going through his wall had obviously not been his fault, more or less, but Dennis also assumed the swiftness of the process was because they had to do the same thing with other houses and cars that had been destroyed over the weekend. Before the police officer left he reminded Dennis that he still needed to come down to the station to give his formal report on JT's injury.

"No problem," Dennis replied, left to sift through the debris of his former house. He had been allowed to do so, entirely because the structure had already collapsed in on itself from the fire and he was in no danger for anything else to fall on him. Regardless, there was nothing left to salvage and Dennis didn't stay very long.

"Are you sure you don't want a stint as the Wrangler?" Horatio asked from beside his car. He had offered to drive Dennis around for the day as he had few other stories to cover.

He had done an insane amount of work on what had happened on Saturday night and Sunday morning that his story was spreading like wildfire. Dennis had accepted the offer for a lift, if nothing else than to sell the idea that he had been injured in the weekend game of footy.

"Positive," replied Dennis as he opened the car door.

"It is clear that the city needs something to happen," Horatio continued as he jumped in the driver's seat. "Crime has been slowly on the rise for a while, burnt out cars have become the norm and the people are scared. You could probably change all that in less than a week. If today is any indication the police are already run off their feet." Dennis simply looked at his friend giving him another glare that stated that he was not interested.

"Okay," continued Horatio, "but just so you know this has been my biggest story ever. It has gone viral. Everyone all over the world is talking about it and sharing it. There is a huge demand for superheroes in the current climate. The story has been on repeat in the national news all day. The only downside to it is that there were no photos. What the Wrangler looks like is changing by the hour."

"Fantastic," Dennis said sarcastically, "which means next time I go out as the Wrangler everyone is going to pull out their phones and start recording. No thanks."

"I am working on something to help with that," Horatio replied, suggesting he had given the matter some thought and was well on his way towards a solution. "But for the time being it means that no-one can identify you as they don't actually know what you look like."

"To help with what?" Dennis growled at the initial comment, "I already said no. That stuff and other small crime happens all the time. I am a teacher, not a fighter, or a soldier or anything else."

"That's not what I saw," Horatio said undeterred by the rejection. "To be honest I am actually surprised that you haven't

had to do anything else. Jet can clearly cause damage, I didn't
know that the police would have been able to hold onto him so
well. I thought he would be breaking out at the first
opportunity."

"I did too," confirmed Dennis, "but I can't say that I am sad
that they have been able to contain him. Can we please change
the subject?"

"Sure, I mean the whole world is talking about it, and we are
directly involved, but sure let's change the subject. Where to Mr
Wrangler sir?" Horatio said with a smile, which was not
returned by Dennis.

"Clothes shopping, the police station and then off to the
hospital, thanks," Dennis replied, not showing any enthusiasm
towards either of those tasks.

It was late afternoon before Dennis and Horatio eventually found
their way into the hospital. His statement had taken longer than
anticipated, and he hadn't been clothes shopping for an age. He
knew his size usually and would just grab a shirt and some
trousers and be done. He was usually proud of his ability to be in
and out with essentials quickly but that hadn't been the case this
time. His larger size meant he had to try them all on. The bigger
variations seemed to come suited to accommodate for a larger
chested man, which left extra material hanging around Dennis'
middle which was less than desirable.

Horatio had also reluctantly been cleared to get into the
hospital. His reputation and name had spread exponentially all
day from his report. Hospital staff were both excited to see
someone of his celebrity and nervous about what his skills might
uncover.

Dennis had been feeling some guilt over JT's injuries,
especially after it had been revealed to him that he was not
intended to receive them. Jet had been meaning to test Dennis'

strength and injure him; that was until JT called him out and got in the way.

Hospitals always felt like labyrinths and Dennis wasn't convinced that a map would have been of any assistance. They had also moved JT from the emergency department and into a recovery wing where he was waiting for an upcoming surgery to fix his multiple broken bones.

"Hey Mr Dodger," a voice called down a nearby corridor. Dennis turned to see one of the officers he had spoken to earlier coming towards him. Dennis assumed that he had dealt with them enough and they no longer required anything of him. The officer caught up, glaring at Horatio in the process before turning back to Dennis.

"It is lucky that you are here," the officer continued.

"What can I help you with?" Dennis asked the officer.

"We have been dealing with a young man over the last short period of time," the officer started explaining. "Initially he wasn't talking to us, but then he mentioned that he had become a disappointment to one of his teachers, and he deeply regretted it. He was insistent that before we take him away to be charged that he spoke with that teacher, to tell him how sorry he was. I had no idea that that teacher was you. I was on my way to find you when I saw you in the hall."

"Yeah we had just come to see our friend that was injured the other day," Dennis gave his explanation. "We will go see him and then follow you."

"I'm sorry but I must request that you accompany me presently," the officer refused. "We are all set to take him away so your assistance now would be greatly appreciated." With what seemed like little choice Dennis reluctantly agreed. With Horatio in tow they followed the policeman. Dennis had long since forgotten their route on their way to find JT, now he had no chance without the assistance of signs and staff of finding his way out of there in a hurry.

"Nothing about this seems right," Horatio whispered to Dennis, well out of ear shot as the officer walked several metres in front of them. "You don't seriously think that after everything that has happened, after everything that he has done, that he is suddenly reformed and wants to repent to you."

"I would love to think that," Dennis said in a return whisper. "But looking at things logically, in this most illogical situation, I would not assume that he has changed that quickly."

"Yeah well, you still go in first," Horatio demanded urgently.

"Me, I don't think that is a fantastic idea. Last time that he saw me I was pushing thousands of volts through his body until he passed out. Not the greatest last moment together," Dennis argued.

"Yes, but, he actually wants to see you, and you are strong enough to fight him," Horatio interceded. "Don't forget, I hit him with a car."

"Aren't you a superhero though," Dennis mocked. He turned to laugh but watched Horatio's manner switch from agitation to alarm. Horatio pushed past him, bouncing off Dennis' shoulder as a result, surging forward in the corridor.

"Is everything alright, friend?" the officer asked as Horatio ran past him.

"No, it isn't," Horatio almost wailed. "There is trouble. I think it is Jet."

"You don't know the way though," the officer called after him.

"He'll find it," Dennis informed him as he jogged along behind Horatio, easily keeping up to his friend's frantic pace. They rounded two or three more corners and finally they arrived at the place. Without a sign it was obvious. Two police officers lay beneath a door that hung on a single hinge. The wall was fractured and a red light was flashing on the roof. The officer who had escorted the pair caught up and drew his weapon.

"What happened?" he shouted with concern. One of the guards was out cold, while the other crawled forward, clearly hurt badly.

"We don't know," she said hoarsely. "The door was locked, and then it just broke open. We had no warning."

"That makes no sense," Horatio queried and rushed past the downed officers.

"Wait a minute son," the accompanying officer called as Horatio disappeared into the sealed room. Dennis was also concerned by his friend's eagerness to venture forth.

"Dennis I need you," Horatio called. Dennis was at his side in half a moment. "I could hear a sound, I thought it was Jet, or maybe even someone else, but it wasn't, it was him." He pointed down to the body of the hooligan that had been captured by the police; the one that could make only muffled sounds as Dennis had broken his jaw with a hard slap. The youth was pinned to his bed, while the other bed in the room had been wrapped firmly around it, pressing hard into his chest almost suffocating him. "Jet is the only one who could have done this, remove it or he will die." Dennis shot a quick glance at the door but no one else had ventured inside. Horatio moved to cause a distraction should one of them be brave enough to enter. Dennis started his task. A few seconds was all it took to reshape the metal that had trapped the already injured criminal.

"He is not here," Horatio called out to the police officers. "And that other guy needs more medical help, I think that metal bar has pierced his lungs." All those surrounding them quickly moved to action. Dennis was happy, and expected nothing less, by these people who day in and day out put their lives on the line to save others. The medical staff were ushered forth and quickly assessed the injured boy's status. The police officer jumped onto his microphone and called those waiting in the paddy wagon outside to inform them what had happened.

"If that kid listens to you then you need to help anyway that you can," the officer suggested as he returned his attention to his fallen colleagues. "But for the time being I think the best course of action is to return home. I wouldn't even go to see your friend." Horatio nodded and then lead Dennis away. As soon as they were out of sight Horatio started to run. Despite his exposure to whatever had given him his enhanced senses Horatio hadn't gained any speed as a result.

"We have to get out of here," Horatio demanded. "I am useless in here."

"That's harsh," Dennis replied as he jogged easily beside his friend who was quickly becoming fatigued.

"Not me," Horatio coughed, "my tech. Hospitals have notoriously bad reception, especially down as low as we are. If we can get outside quick enough I can try and find him."

"Why didn't you say so?" Dennis demanded. "Um, this might feel weird but just roll with it. Let me know if you hear someone coming." Before Horatio could ask what Dennis was talking about he had been grabbed and tossed over the taller man's shoulder. Dennis shot off down the corridors at a pace that Horatio couldn't have matched in his wildest dreams.

"Oh, I understand now," Horatio spluttered as his ribs bounced on Dennis' large shoulder. "I will ignore how weird this is. Wait! Person!" Immediately Dennis dumped Horatio back on his feet, but he continued to hold his hand to drag him along quicker.

"Are you okay?" asked one of the staff who appeared before them.

"My friend is sick." Dennis replied quickly, "I need to find a doctor."

"Well I'm a . . ." started the staff member, but before she could finish Dennis had turned another corner and quickly scooped up his friend.

"I need a doctor, really?" Horatio gasped as he carried along helplessly. "In a place full of them you need to think up a better lie."

"I know, shut up," Dennis replied.

"Turn left here, then turn right at the end of that hallway, then go straight," Horatio instructed.

"How did you remember all that?" Dennis asked. He found it humorous that his friend was more out of breath upon his shoulder than he had been when attempting the run himself.

"That is my power," Horatio called back between breaths, "but also I can smell the air outside. This place is so sterile that the outside air smells like chips and gravy to my sensitive snout." Dennis followed the directions and together they ran through the crowded foyer to the outside area.

"Okay we are outside," Dennis said as they stopped in the cool air. "Now work your magic. Hack a camera, sleuth a trail."

"I would normally, but this time there is no need," Horatio replied. He had been fumbling with the screen on his smartphone before promptly turning it to show Dennis. The teacher read it quickly. The focus was on a social media account that belonged to Jet. 'Revenge of the Hitman,' it read, 'get out of my way, if you aren't with me then you are against me.'

"He is doing a live stream as well," Dennis suggested to Horatio. "You can see where he is going. Does anybody we know live over there?"

"I don't think so," replied Horatio. "That area is a notorious bad part of town. I have no idea what he is doing. I think it's clear that he wants someone to follow him, despite the fact he says for people to get out of his way."

"What are we going to do?" Dennis asked, knowing that he would once again have to play a reluctant part in it.

"I have some ideas," replied Horatio, Dennis could almost see the cogs turning in his friends head as he formulated it. "First, we have to acknowledge how interesting it is that Jet has given himself a superhero name, especially as it is your old name. It works on so many levels."

"Don't get excited about that," Dennis reprimanded him harshly.

"Sorry, it's cool though," he avoided the stare he was receiving. "You and I both know that the Wrangler is the only one who can stop him. That being said I will inform the police who are parked out the front and they can follow me. The hat and oil skin are still in my car. Get them now and go. You need to get over to the north-east part of town. If your phone is on I will call you and let you know where you are going. Go fast. Revenge is not a great word when there is someone who is border line psychotic like Jet using it." Dennis nodded. He wasn't going to argue this time. He swooped on Horatio's car and pulled free his disguise. The sun was in the process of setting, so once again he would have some secrecy to his movement. Once he wore them he didn't wait for instructions, he just bolted.

Dennis, for the first time since he acquired his new abilities, put them to the test. He ran as fast as his body could make him, he jumped clear over roads, railway lines and fences, and he pushed through barriers with ease. He also stayed close to the shadows and tried to stay hidden. He had the luxury of Horatio turning off all the cameras last time he tried this, but he no longer had that. In what would have taken fifteen to twenty minutes to make that drive across town, if traffic was kind, Dennis covered in around five minutes. His phone had not gone off to tell him where he was going, but as he grew closer to his destination he found that that information wasn't necessary. I giant plume of black smoke, no doubt laced with chemicals and toxins, erupted into the red streaked dusky sky. It was like a beacon for him and he went towards it like a moth to a flame.

Dennis jogged into a cul-de-sac where commotion was erupting everywhere. Several homes were engulfed in a blaze, as were several vehicles located all over the premises. People were fleeing in all directions as something destructive could be heard rampaging its way through one of the houses. Dennis took a breath, not because he was tired but because he was trying to regain his composure. His eyes took in the scene, and he noticed the look that many of the people there had.

They were all part of Jet's crew, the ones that had terrorised a great deal of Orange only the night before, but they were all running for their lives in panic. One of them was thrown out onto the lawn through a closed window, sending glass raining out towards the road. He was promptly followed by another of his friends, who was not as lucky as he made his exit straight through a fibreglass wall. Dennis had intentions of stopping Jet harming someone, or multiple someones, but as he watched in confusion he could clearly see that all of those present were those who had been responsible for the chaos that had engulfed Orange. Dennis instead of stopping Jet, started to help him. He quickly rounded up and captured all those who had tried to escape as cries filled the air behind him. When he had gathered them all and had them laying in a neat line on the footpath he returned to see the last occupants of one of the dwellings being carried out under the arms of Jet. The young man was breathing heavily, his eyes focused in a rage.

Jet dumped his prey on the grass and walked aggressively over towards Dennis. The teacher clenched his jaw and his fist, waiting for the first inevitable strike that would come from his one time student. He glanced around quickly looking for something that would give him the edge just like last time. He saw nothing, and Jet was closing in fast. How long would this fight last, Dennis wondered, and how effective would the police be when they arrived. In a few more steps Jet would be upon him again.

But then Jet stopped.

And then Jet dropped to his knees.

"I give up," Jet said sadly as he looked up into his teacher's eyes. "I don't want to fight you. I surrender. I will go quietly and without a fuss."

There was no way that Dennis had been able to hide the look of surprise or confusion that he knew he had planted across his face.

"You were right about them, they were no good, I know I have done the wrong thing, I should have listened," Jet sobbed.

"I'm sorry."

CHAPTER 12 - TROUBLE BREWING

"I can't believe you are choosing to watch that," Horatio said as he walked past the chair that Dennis sat upon. "You're punishing yourself man, it isn't worth it, *he* isn't worth it."

"I know," Dennis agreed, though he wasn't sure if he actually did. He had been so confused over the last few days.

Dennis, no, the Wrangler, had been responsible for the recapture of Jet, or the Hitman, as he was now being called. As well as Jet, there were numerous vandals and criminals that he had helped round up who were also in captivity. As soon as the police arrived Dennis had vanished into the night with no desire to hang around. Horatio had been on the scene afterwards, taking everything down; once more claiming some of the most sought after articles in the news world. His only downfall was that he still had no pictures of the Wrangler, although he had plenty of Jet this time. And just because Horatio didn't have those pictures didn't mean others didn't either. The internet had exploded as if there had been confirmation of a UFO sighting, except they had called it Wranglervision. Dennis' attempt to be fast to the scene had left multiple residents with footage of the Wrangler jumping over tall objects, running swiftly through alleyways, or pulverizing heavy barricades. These were all true and each video or picture that was shown came with its own theories. Luckily none of them revealed who the person under the Akubra and beneath the jacket actually was.

Dennis had ignored those and had been focused on what was being shown on the television in front of him. In truth he wasn't watching a program, but Horatio had hacked into the court room cameras that were recording Jet's trial, and it was all he could do to watch it.

"I just find the whole thing confusing," Dennis groaned as he stroked his ever thickening moustache.

"Everything about what is happening to us has been confusing lately," Horatio admitted. He was eating a sandwich while scrolling through website after website on his laptop. A long cord had been dragged up so he could still connect to his extensive setup down stairs.

"I know that," Dennis moaned. "What I mean is this kid."

"The quicker he is behind bars and out of mischief the quicker our lives can return to some form of normality," Horatio replied, filling his mouth and crunching down on a big clump of lettuce.

"You're right, except for kids going to jail," Dennis started.

"He isn't a minor, and he knew full well what he was doing," Horatio interrupted.

"I get it," Dennis agreed, "but what I don't get is that he knows who I am. He knows that I have this power like he does, and he hates me. Why then is he refusing to tell anyone about it? I know that people have asked him and still he denies it. Plus there was that thing where he broke out of a secure room, tore down a whole neighbourhood in a fight for revenge, only to fall down at my feet and surrender. What is up with that?"

"I keep telling you, the kid's a nutcase," Horatio responded with no care. "More importantly what are we going to call our base?" Dennis didn't answer, staying perched on the edge of his seat and observing the screen in front of him. It was early morning and Dennis had all intentions of returning to work after watching the trial. He would still have plenty of time to do so, but he was already well prepared as he sat in some nice winter clothes including an ugly, yet warm, knitted jumper. His laptop bag sat discarded close to the front door. He was hoping to return to some form of regularity after the sentencing.

"You could have at least given him some credit for what happened," Dennis mentioned, "the kid basically annihilated the Orange crime scene in one night. I just had to make sure they didn't leave."

"I'm not about to give the kid anything," Horatio barked, "Besides I am pretty sure I have done him a favour."

"How do you figure that?" Dennis said with a cocked eyebrow.

"Because everyone thinks that the Wrangler is the only person out there with special abilities," Horatio explained. "All the violence and all the damage that Jet has caused has been explained away as juvenile delinquency. You and I know what else he has done, and even though some other people do too, they don't have any proof, so, because no one else saw it conclusively then nobody else is chasing him down chasing a different sort of story because it is unbelievable. If you believe that he has turned over a new leaf, which I don't, then he will get time in jail to have a long hard look about what he has done."

"Hmmph," Dennis snorted.

"What now?" Horatio exclaimed, apparently he had lost his patience on the subject.

"A few months ago, before I turned up, that kid was nothing more than a high school bully," Dennis reflected aloud. "Now he is a full blown criminal. I can't help but feel at least partially responsible for that."

"Well that's your own thing," Horatio replied, and motioned towards the screen. "Looks like he is coming out now."

Dennis watched as the boy was led into the courtroom in handcuffs by multiple security guards. The room was empty apart from the judge, it seemed that they thought the public, and maybe even the jury, were at risk by his presence. Jet looked around the room noticing the same thing, and he looked straight into the cameras before flicking his eyes away quickly. He knew that someone was watching, at least he had no idea that it was Dennis.

"Who is that?" Horatio asked looking over his friend's shoulder. There was a lady who had slunk in behind Jet and moved to sit down in one of the rows at the back. It was hard to make her out as she actively seemed to be trying to avoid detection. She wore a large hat, with long tufts of red hair sneaking out from underneath, and a striking black suit.

"I don't know," Dennis replied. "I don't think it is a relation. I have never seen them. And if it was a relation I don't believe that that is what they would look like. I shouldn't make assumptions I suppose. A lawyer maybe?"

"I don't think so," Horatio replied, "I feel like I have seen her before though." Dennis watched her for a moment longer and then looked back to the youth on the screen. It looked like the proceedings were about to begin. Dennis observed at how relaxed Jet appeared. The judge started.

"Due to the severity of the charges and also to the fact that you have pleaded guilty on all charges, those of vandalism, destruction of property, assault of the public, assault on police officers, running from police, disturbing the peace, and attempted murder, with several other minor charges. This court has decided to pursue a course of action that will lead you, Jet McGrath, to a period of long term incarceration for the duration of five years, with no opportunity for parole at this time. These terms have been accepted and settled upon prior to the commencement of this hearing. Jet McGrath, do you now accept these charges?"

"I do, sir," Jet replied showing no emotion.

"Very good," commended the judge, "I will point out that you and your family were offered legal support in regard to these charges. While you declined the offer we were not able to get in touch with your family members or a next of kin. Could you tell me why that is young man?"

"I am taking responsibility for my crimes, sir," Jet responded without any sign of contempt. "I know I have done the wrong thing. And as to my family I have none."

"What about your parents?" the judge pursued gently.

"They left on a trip at the beginning of the year," Jet replied evenly, "I only recently found out that they were killed in a car accident. As I am eighteen I was allowed to live at home by myself this year. Their absence has taken a toll on me." Dennis gasped at the revelation. It explained why he could make no contact with Jet's parents, it also somewhat explained his anger in their earliest encounters.

"No doubt it has. I am sincerely troubled and sorry to hear of their loss. Is there anything else you would like to say to the court? Knowing that any information that is provided at this point can still be used in regard to your sentence?"

"There is just one thing sir," Jet nodded his understanding. "I haven't had much support in my life. I trusted the wrong people who just wanted to use me, and hung around in crowds who didn't appreciate me being there. I have been told by many people of the potential that I have at my disposal, and, ignoring those same people, I have wasted my talents as well as every opportunity that has come my way. I would like to say that, even though it may seem too late to do so, that I have seen that the actions I have taken, which I am responsible for, have been the wrong ones. In the future I will endeavour to use my ability in a more focused manner, in a way that has purpose and can lead to great things happening."

"Very commendable Mr McGrath," the judge applauded, "anything else?"

"Just one sir," Jet continued, Dennis swore that he saw him glance back up at the camera. "I want to say sorry to those who never gave up on me, and I promise, that sometime, I will return and thank them properly for what they have done for me." The proceedings continued and a whole list of formalities were issued and finalised. Dennis looked long and hard at the lonely figure, more confused than he had ever been before.

"Hey, does this look like her?" Horatio interrupted his thoughts. Dennis glanced over to where the single figure of the woman had been. He frowned.

"Um, I don't know," Dennis replied.

"Well just look at her, then look at the picture on my screen, and tell me yes or no," Horatio responded in a huff.

"I can't," Dennis argued.

"What do you mean you can't," Horatio sounded angrier.

"Because she isn't there," Dennis stated simply in annoyance.

"That isn't possible," Horatio came closer to look. "They lock the doors so no one else can go in or out during the proceedings."

"I believe you," Dennis replied, "but the vision doesn't lie. She isn't there."

"You're right, hang on," Horatio called out. Dennis was the only one there, and he hadn't moved, so the sudden urgency didn't seem necessary. Horatio grabbed his computer and started slamming buttons down quickly. The picture on the screen started to reverse. Nothing changed for a moment, but then finally the figure of the mystery woman reappeared.

"Well that isn't good," Horatio said releasing a huge breath.

"What?" asked Dennis, "what isn't good?"

"Someone is watching this that shouldn't be," Horatio said, worry starting to show on his face. "I know we shouldn't be either, but someone else is doing the same thing."

"Why?" Dennis asked obviously. He climbed to his feet and moved towards the door, collecting his bag in the process.

"I don't know, but rest assured that by the time you get back I will have many theories and leads," Horatio guaranteed.

"Don't you have to go to work?" Dennis asked.

"No, but don't you?" came the reply.

Dennis felt like there had been an enormous breath of relief taken when he arrived back at Orange College. Not just from himself, but by the students and staff as well, even the school buildings seemed to be showing relief. It helped that, even though late autumn was about to shift into winter, the sun shone from a cloudless sky sharing its vibrancy to all below. Once more Dennis had become the focus of mumbled chat. Dennis could hear what they were saying on the most part. Even though his senses were not as attuned to what Horatio bragged his had become Dennis still had an enhanced version of what he once possessed. He smiled at some of the conversations. They ranged from footy, to how he had managed to get clothes that fit, and then onto his huge size again. Some mumbled about the similarities between the teacher and the Wrangler, but many of those in the conversation denied the truth in the opinion. Some of the reasons as to why that couldn't be the case were quite hurtful, others were simply amusing. Most of them spoke about how unlucky he was; having both died and lost his house in short succession. Others spoke about how dangerous it was to be connected to the teacher. One of his best friends missing while another lay in hospital. Some even blamed Dennis for what had happened to Jet.

On the whole the school seemed different though. Teachers had followed Dennis' lead by coming out to interact with several of the students. Students were also making an effort to act positively to one another. It was like everyone had been holding back before, under fear of the consequences if Jet was to hear of them doing the wrong thing, which was in fact the correct thing to do in the first place.

Students piled excitedly back into his classes where he returned naturally to his jovial demeanour; bouncing around as he revealed facts about different time periods in history, delivering anecdotes that were related to sport or real world events, and dropping a mountain of fresh puns or dad jokes if only to hear the unanimous groans stream forth from the children.

In the breaks between periods he interacted with staff members more than he had done so previously. The conversations were fun, but Dennis could feel the apprehension that they had around him. Many of the same concerns that the students whispered about outside were repeated within the staff room. Dennis didn't mind, jumping between intellectual conversations and others that were concerned about where he was living due to the fire engulfing his home, or what his prospects were for football.

Dennis decided to abandon the first of the two football sessions in the week. He knew he could contribute to the team, and by contribute Dennis firmly thought that he could win every game by himself just like Jet had told the coaches that he could have done. Part of his reason to still attend was to be the balm for what Jet had been dishing out and what he had been capable of, which had been proven to be true. But now that was no longer necessary.

By avoiding training he would return home instead, and would walk straight back into Horatio working at full capacity, ready to unveil what he had discovered while Dennis had been at work.

"Have you found anything out about Jiemba?" Dennis asked trying to break up the onslaught of theories.

"Not yet," Horatio replied from deep within his frenzy. "And I won't give up on that, trust me. But there are other things going on that I have to tell you." Dennis rolled his eyes but allowed his friend to continue, hoping that there would be only a few and it would be over with soon.

There were many, not just a few, and they each lasted a long period of time.

"I knew I had seen that girl before," Horatio explained. "Her name is Assumpta Green. She was Hector Green's sister, and a high ranking executive at GreenCorp."

"Was?" questioned Dennis.

"Yeah she mysteriously went missing a few years ago," Horatio continued, "it was thought that she was dead. I have no idea why she would suddenly reappear, next to Jet no less. And then it is even more curious as to why her existence was then erased from the camera footage." Horatio was far from finished.

"And speaking of erasing things. I have been exploring data all day. There are multiple records that have disappeared recently. I was looking specifically for information in regard to the meteor that came and did this to us. The anomaly seems to have never existed. Even some of the research undertaken by Professor Gamut has disappeared. Not only that though. Multiple impact locations and scales that show interference from falling objects are gone. The flight paths of planes, satellites, helicopters etc have also been removed."

"Why are those important?" Dennis asked.

"Come on mate," Horatio groaned. "I know you remember most of what happened that night. The giant violet explosion. The meteor had to have hit something, but we don't know what that was."

The tirade of Horatio's beliefs continued well into the night. The following day repeated almost exactly to the word the speeches that had been shared the night before. Dennis had thought that his friend had come to the end of his fascination with conspiracies, but he was wrong. They continued with even more vigour than they had the night before. The only difference was the topic.

"GreenCorp have been in the news again," Horatio had lost none of his spark. "They are talking about continuing their research into science using water, hydraulics and energy research in attempting to build machines capable of extra-orbital exploration. He has also unveiled the addition of desalination plants at the Northern tip of Australia, to pump more water into the aquifers and building the water table into the central areas of Australia.”

“That sounds like good news,” Dennis was already tired of the conversation. He had received a reprimand from his friend the night before showing disinterest so he attempted to jump in every now and then to appear like he was listening.

“Yes on the surface,” Horatio acknowledged the statement, “but it has led to many other unusual things happening. The visit from the Prime Minister has been moved forward to this weekend, but any information on that has been kept secret.”

“That makes total sense,” Dennis interjected, “seems like that is necessary for security.”

“Again yes,” Horatio agreed, “but the itinerary has already been sent out so people know where the Prime Minister will be at all times. Along with that missing information, things like crime details have been taken away, population data has been altered, as have police records involving crime rates and prisoner transfer.”

“Does that include?”

“Yep,” Horatio confirmed. “It means that Jet’s travel information and confinement details are missing, and he was transferred at some point today.”

“That’s a concern,” Dennis said frankly, becoming immediately interested.

“Sure, but that’s not the worst of it,” Horatio sounded very grave now. He didn’t wait for Dennis to ask him what could be worse, he just revealed it. “There has also been a ton of activity in relation to you, and your family. That information has been deleted.”

“What?” Dennis felt his heart sink. “Who deleted it?”

“I did,” Horatio conceded. “I got rid of all of it. Something is not right here.”

"You think," Dennis barked. "You think something is going on so you decided to delete the digital footprint of my entire family. What gives you the right to do that?"

"It's for their own good," Horatio replied, "so they can be safe."

"Be safe? From what? From some conspiracy that you think is happening. That is really helpful. From now on just keep it to yourself, friend," Dennis boomed. "Don't disturb me, I have marking to do." He stormed from the room and collapsed on his bed. He had had enough of Horatio, his constant superhero chatter and convoluted espionage stories became crazier by the second. Dennis had assumed that he knew that family was off limits, clearly he had been wrong. Foregoing dinner and entertainment was fine for Dennis to remove himself for the time being. It was true that he did have work to do, that was the case for every teacher almost every night, but even that would go by the wayside tonight at least for the time being.

Dennis attended footy training reluctantly. He had avoided Horatio all day. Whilst not a hard task when at work, he did still have to live in his house. Throughout the day Dennis had acknowledged the fact that Horatio had most likely done the right thing. Dennis had been so caught up with what was happening he had struggled to keep his two lives separate, which was what he had desired to do all along. By the end of the day he had accepted that he most likely had an apology to make. He hated making them, it wasn't because he didn't make mistakes; he made them frequently. It was entirely because he always did them poorly and turned a situation into either a far worse one, or he intensified his usual bumbling awkwardness.

Dennis noted that as he ventured into the carpark that most of the burnt out cars had been removed but some still sat off to the side. It was a reminder to Dennis of how quickly everything had escalated. It all seemed so surreal. Dennis found that he had been daydreaming for most of the sessions. He was mostly in autopilot, his body easily doing any task that was demanded of him. He had to snap out of his own head every now and then because sometimes he was doing the task too well. On one occasion he collided with one of the other players. Dennis fell down, surprised by the impact mostly, but attempted to feign an injury so it looked like he was hurt. He rolled over once and noticed that the guy he had run into was actually hurt and having a far worse time than Dennis was pretending to have. His shoulder was dislocated from where he had made contact with Dennis. Dennis swallowed his guilt down hard and followed the injured player slowly from the field.

Dennis sat at the side for a while. He had no interest in participating any longer. There was no adversity he had to overcome here. No goals that he couldn't accomplish. He was only kidding himself. His only desire would have been to continue playing with his friends, but those he cared about were either missing or injured. Dennis glanced around; when he was sure no one else was watching he fled.

He had walked to training, for no other reason than to clear his head. In hindsight it had been a master stroke as he didn't have to worry about his car making a loud stressed noise as it escaped. It was still parked safely in Horatio's driveway where it couldn't cause any damage to anyone.

His head filled with many things on that walk back, none were memorable, and most were cast aside. There were a few that lingered. The first was what he might say to Horatio once he stepped back inside the house. If he prepared something then he would no doubt stuff it up; better to improvise with the best intentions. The second thing was about Jiemba. No one had heard a thing about him, and he felt like he had asked everyone in existence about him. Dennis' heart fell just thinking about it. What was the use of having these abilities if he couldn't help those that he cared about? The last thing he thought about was how care free it was to walk now. Once upon a time he would have been concerned of the chill that was falling, the possibility of being jumped and having his gear stolen, or if he would see something he really didn't want to. He walked through dark parks with no lights and no concern whatsoever.

Dennis was somewhat annoyed when he finally ventured back through the front door of Horatio's house. He expected to find his friend down in his technology filled basement, but he was waiting for him. Dennis started his apology straight away.

"Look Horatio," Dennis began, finding that he was already gesturing wildly with anxiety, "I just wanted to say. . ."

"Save it," Horatio interrupted him promptly. "I have something more important to tell you." Dennis had no mind to listen to more theories or conspiracies. He let out a breath and allowed Horatio to continue anyway.

"I think I have found Jiemba," Horatio announced with excitement, but his face wasn't one of happiness like it should have been.

"But, also, Jet has escaped."

CHAPTER 13 - BEST LAID PLANS

Dennis looked up at the massive central screen. They had both come to the basement where Horatio had set about finding vision from a dozen different sources.

"None of that makes sense," said Dennis in disbelief as he watched the main screen for what was almost the twentieth time.

"That's what I thought as well," Horatio agreed stroking his moustache nervously as he accumulated everything he needed to prove his claim. He looked dishevelled; his hair hanging greasily down to cover his eyes, his clothes bunched in multiple spots, and he was itching random parts of his body whenever his hands weren't attacking the keyboard. "But the more that I look into it, the more I am convinced." Dennis watched as Horatio's fingers frantically slammed at the keyboard in front of him. A booming technological sound suddenly swept into their ears.

"The Finder's query is confirmed," a calm voice that came from the computer announced.

"So it talks now?" Dennis asked. "And you have already got it saying your dumb super hero name as well?"

"Of course," Horatio answered without looking over at him. "I'm shameless remember, nothing is off limits to me." Dennis felt horrible. He still hadn't apologised for lashing out at Horatio earlier, and the statement clearly revealed that the other man was still stung by his words. In the very next breath, before

Dennis could say anything else, Horatio continued, which thankfully dispersed the sudden strain in the air that surrounded them. "I have every angle that I can find and I am going to show you them all at once. It works for my senses but it may be a bit much to take in for you," Horatio stated, and with one last loud click the video all started at once. Some had audio as well but that just made the scene look even more chaotic.

The vision was from the inside of a correctional facility. Obviously it was from within the same facility that Jet had been sent to, as the young man was in the vision, but Dennis had no idea which one that had been or where.

"Wellington?" Dennis asked.

"Correct," Horatio answered, now standing back to observe, arms crossed against his chest. "Wellington Star Five." Wellington was one of the bigger towns in the Central West. It originally was supposed to be the capital of the west but it hadn't worked out that way. The town sat against the Macquarie River and beside a few mountains and hills. It was only a stone's throw away from where they had attempted the training at Lake Burrendong. Several years ago they had established a correctional facility on the outskirts. This was followed by several others. Eventually they had five facilities there. The government became aware that crime was rising as a result and established a police academy and active task force to be continually present in the town. Since then there was almost no discretions, and the town was a thriving beautiful place. Each of the prisons was designated a star and a number so that people knew which one was which. Five Star was the maximum security facility which housed a smaller number of some of the worst offenders in the state.

"You were right about him being able to escape if he wanted too," Dennis admitted. "I guess I knew it was possible as well."

"Yes, but . . ." Horatio agreed, nodding his head and refusing to gloat on the matter. "In this case, I don't know if he actually needs help to get out, but he gets it anyway." Horatio pointed to the screen as if revealing what would happen next. Dennis had already seen patches of it, but running it altogether gave a more complete story. On the screens revealed what Dennis suspected was an ordinary day in confinement. Numerous guards walked along high walls, occupied secure checkpoints and observed from high towers. Only two inmates were out of their cells at the current time, and both were being closely monitored. The place looked immaculately clean, almost as if there was no one present to make it dirty. It would all change within the next second.

Smoke emerged from a small explosion, covering most of the cameras in the blast zone. The unobstructed views showed prison guards spring into action without a second thought. Bodies were in motion, sirens started blaring, and several others jumped onto phones or loudspeakers to direct a response. A moment later the haze cleared and the open two storey cell block could again be seen. A wall had been knocked down and several people dressed in black appeared. One was far larger than the others and that person carried what appeared to be a large battering ram. He glanced around as if unsure of what to do. A call came from one of the cells and he turned towards the sound. The big chunk of metal that he carried was slammed into the door and the whole thing came down.

"I will come back to that in a second," Horatio stated as the vision continued. The sound of the solid bang echoing from several displays. Dennis was not shocked by who emerged, although that had not been the case on the first watch through. Jet emerged casually. One of many confusing things occurred here, again Horatio interrupted, declaring that he had solved another concern. Jet walked up to the large figure who had freed him and started pointing to several other cells. The large man, who had just freed Jet, seemed to be taken aback by the guy who stood before him and seemed to not be listening. The next confusing thing happened then. Jet slapped the man to get his attention. Dennis had expected the tall figure to end up slammed through a wall by the strike; the same ones that Dennis had felt all too well. But instead the man stood his ground and didn't move. The tall man's hood had been knocked clean off his head though. Then the movement started again. The tall figure moved to each cell as directed and slammed in the door, freeing the occupants who hurried out.

"Did you see that?" Horatio remarked as he pointed to several monitors. Each prisoner was grabbed quickly by an intruder, had their heads covered by a sack, and were led back through the wall that they had blasted through. There were at least half a dozen people who were freed. Finally Horatio paused the whole scene. The image was frozen on the closest shot of the tall man as he glanced up at a camera.

"Jiemba?" Dennis questioned with concern.

"Confirmed," Horatio answered. "My computer did a facial recognition scan and it is a complete match."

"The face maybe, but what about the rest of him?" Dennis continued his confusion.

"I think we are in the best position to answer many of the questions raised here," Horatio started explaining. "Are we surprised that Jet has escaped? No, we aren't. It was almost inevitable. As to his new acquaintances, that is more of a concern, but then again not surprising. Jet frequently runs in packs, and he destroyed his last group pretty profoundly, so it makes sense he would join up with another one. I would make the connection with that Green lady returning here, but of course I can't be sure. Then there is the reappearance of Jiemba. It is good to know that he is alive, and yes I am certain that that is him. He took a slap from Jet pretty well, plus did you notice when he knocked the doors to the cells in he did it with his bare hands, and he is enormous, almost as big as you I reckon, suggesting that he has also been subject to the same alterations that we have. He did go missing near the lake, so it seems reasonable that he was still within proximity of that wave when it took out everything. But more concerning is that he is involved with this group, and Jet is now involved with him. Did you see when he paused, before he got slapped, it looked like he suddenly realised who he had just set free. That means he knows who Jet is, which, I will deduce sadly, that Jiemba knows what he is doing and is doing all this willingly."

"What about the others that were freed?" Dennis demanded, trying to change the subject slightly.

"I don't know yet, but I will investigate them next. I hope they are nobody," Horatio admitted.

It was all too much to Dennis. He was a school teacher. Why was he watching footage of a jail break when he should have been training for footy, or marking assessments, or sitting around doing absolutely nothing in the comfort of his own home. He wiped a hand down his face, starting at his moustache. For the first time in what seemed like an age Dennis felt tired. He knew it was a feeling and not reality. It was just the situation. He turned and walked carefully back up the unique basement stairs.

"Where are you going?" Horatio called after him.

"To bed," Dennis moaned.

"I thought you didn't need sleep," Horatio replied.

"I do tonight," Dennis replied, slumping into each step as he made the seemingly long trek to his room.

Dennis could smell something delicious. He opened one eye, and then the other. "Was I actually asleep?" he asked himself in nothing more than a whisper. His senses had roused him, and he was happy about that. He took it all in with a smile as he moved to the side of his bed, which creaked under his weight. He could hear the sizzle and pop of meat being cooked on a pan, feel the grease that hung in the air within a slim layer of smoke, smell the fat and charred flesh as it simmered noisily. He licked his lips.

"Yes you were asleep," the door swung open and Horatio answered. "And just so you know, whatever you are feeling right now, I am feeling a hundred times more. I knew that bacon was fantastic, but I could die amidst this feeling and I would be completely satisfied with how I ventured to the other side." Dennis smiled at his friend and clambered to his feet. Long ago he would have grunted and groaned at the process of getting out of bed, not anymore however. He walked from his room and sat on a chair at the old worn out dining table. Bread, margarine, tomato sauce and some other things like salt and pepper sat there. There was already a plate filled with cooked bacon, piles and piles of it.

"So it seems that even if your body doesn't need much to recover, your mind still needs to refresh to be healthy," Horatio stated. "I am the same by the way, when you take in as much as I do in a day the brain needs a reboot. Dig in, I wasn't sure how much you needed to eat so I cooked a fair bit." Dennis nodded his thanks and set about making what he used to think was one of the greatest creations of all time. He heaped some bread with margarine, covered them in sauce, and then he stacked on bacon. He didn't eat it straight away, instead waiting about a minute for the heat from the bacon to melt the margarine and mix with the sauce. Then he destroyed it. This process was repeated several times. Horatio did something similar.

"This is nice," Horatio said through a mouthful of meat. "I had almost forgotten that we could do this. How good does this taste? Don't answer that, I know." Horatio was gouging almost as much as Dennis. "Look, I wanted to say that I was sorry," Horatio continued. Dennis looked stunned. "I realise that we have both been caught up in something that is bigger than both of us. This sort of thing is what I dream about. A developing story right at my fingertips, that I can explore and investigate, decipher for myself, and impose my own twist on it. This is like all the best stories that you hear about, and not only is it happening around us, it is happening to us. What I am feeling, is almost literally everything, I am running on a thousand percent at all times. But despite the fact that my senses are on overdrive, I didn't stop to think about how you felt about all of it. I was just wanting to get you involved with this and assumed that you would be. This is an epic that we are living, and until this morning I never once considered that it could all end, or that either of us could be hurt."

"That is all I think about," Dennis replied after swallowing half of a sandwich. "I have spent a great deal of time pretending that nothing had happened. I disregarded what people were saying to me, and about me, but at the back of my head I know that I have died several times already. My closest friends and family know that too, so now when they look at me they remember what that was like. I see it in their eyes, hear it in the questions that they don't ask. I am a school teacher, who plays footy, and hangs out with his mates. I was good at doing all of those things. If I never came back to this town then I would still be that guy. I am still trying to be that guy, even now. I am clutching onto the guy who can fix problems in the lives of my students, the guy that can go out and get drunk with friends and not care, or play a sport for the fun of it knowing that I may lose. Those things are all gone."

"You can still fix the lives of students." Horatio intervened, "that hasn't changed."

"Jet is my constant reminder that that isn't true," Dennis replied. He focused once more on the sandwiches he was making, and the supply of bacon that was getting lower.

"Jet is two steps away from being a full blown supervillain, yet you are still the only one who is standing up for him, while trying to show everybody that he isn't what he appears," Horatio showed a hint of irritation but quickly hid behind a big cup of juice.

"I have been told many things in my life," Dennis smiled as he spoke, "some thought provoking, some wrong, some even made me change my mind. There is one thing that was told to me a long time ago that has stuck with me though. I was told that you only fail if you stop trying, that as long as you worked towards something there would be progress, and it didn't matter how small it was it was still progress. The other thing I was taught is that there is no such thing as a lost cause."

"Sometimes there is though," Horatio replied, recreating the infectious smile on his friend's face. "But I guess if you think that way the glass is always half full. Who told you that?"

"It was my dad," Dennis answered with a small pause. "He also used to say that if you think the glass was half full or if you thought it was half empty then you missed the point. The glass could always be filled up again." Dennis smiled even more widely, his mouth appearing out beyond the sides of his wide moustache, remembering a story involving his father. "When he told me about the no lost cause thing we were in his shed. He had about a million parts belonging to a million different bikes. None of them went together, none would fit. We spent weeks sorting them all out into what sort of part they were and what brand of bike they belonged to. There was heaps of all different sorts, except there was only one frame, and none of the parts matched that frame. If we had any other frame then we could have built a complete bike with all the right parts, but with what he had we couldn't. I said it was a lost cause, and he ruffled my hair and told me that there was no such thing. He was a genius and before long he was making all sorts of connections with what he had there, nothing should have worked but it did."

"You must miss him," Horatio stated. Dennis nodded, sweeping a hand quickly to the side of his face to catch a tear that had appeared there. He assumed that Horatio noticed as he quickly stood up to leave. "I can feel the fat all over me, happy to have it, but I am going to go and jump in the shower." He was almost gone from the room when Dennis stopped him.

"Hey, Finder," he said, finally using the name that Horatio had given him. Horatio stopped and turned with a smile. "I never thanked you for all the things that you have done for me. For keeping my secret, looking out for me, giving me a place to crash, even looking out for me and my family. It is a big ask and you have done it like it was nothing. So thanks, and, sorry for being a jerk." Horatio nodded.

"No problem," he replied, "it was easy because it actually was nothing, plus you have always been a jerk so I am used to it." Horatio smiled again and left the room.

Dennis sat in silence, the only sound coming from inside his mouth as he chewed his food in the resemblance of a cow. The bacon sandwiches were delicious and he savoured them in the quiet. It was early Friday morning, the sun had not come up yet and wouldn't for a couple of hours, and he really didn't want to go to work. He glanced at his phone on the charger and reached out to grab it. I have earned a day, he thought to himself. There was no need for any more justification, a casual could easily cover his load for the day. He flicked to his messages and set about sending a text to inform the person responsible for the day that he would not be there. Almost as soon as he started he was interrupted.

The phone buzzed in his hand, there was no ringtone as Dennis hated to be interrupted at the wrong moment so the sound was always off. The caller id said unknown caller. He looked at it for a moment, then decided not to answer. A few seconds later the phone settled and he set about pressing buttons to form his message again. The buzzing renewed. Whoever this was clearly either wanted to talk to him, or was persistently calling the wrong number. He thumbed the icon that allowed him to accept the call and placed it to his ear.

"Hello," Dennis answered cautiously.

"Good morning, sir," the voice said at the other end. Dennis knew who it was immediately. "I hope I didn't wake you."

"No, Jet, you didn't," Dennis replied. He held his voice completely neutral. "In fact I was just finishing my breakfast. It was delicious."

"Always the organised one, sir," Jet continued, "even at this hour. I half expected you to still be sleeping." Dennis let the comment slide.

"How can I help you Jet?" Dennis asked. "Don't tell me you are wasting your one phone call on me at this hour."

"I don't believe that you actually think I am still incarcerated. I have learned to give you more credit than that," Jet responded. "What I called you for is that I would like to meet up and chat, we have a lot to discuss."

"Sure Jet, we can talk," Dennis agreed, "just tell me where you are and I will be there."

"Well the thing is that I can't tell you exactly where I am, it is complicated, you don't know who is listening you see," Jet explained calmly. "But you are smart, so I will let you know in a way that you will understand. I will wait in a spot where we had a shocking encounter." Dennis nodded to himself. He knew exactly where Jet meant. "Oh and one more thing, come now and come alone, if you don't I will go for a short walk and finish what I started." The line disconnected.

Dennis glanced over towards the hall that lead to the bathroom. He could hear the water running suggesting that Horatio was still in the shower. He would not alert his friend this time. Dennis stood up and walked towards the door. He stopped and glanced over to the lounge where he frequently sat, where his hat and oil skin jacket lay abandoned. He grabbed them quickly and walked out the door, shutting it silently to hide his exit for a few moments longer.

The car was parked and Dennis walked up the road in his disguise. It all seemed so familiar, although last time most of his surroundings were on fire and it was dark. He could still see the stains on the road from where cars had leaked oil, fuel had been ignited and the remainder of their contents incinerated. It seemed like police tape surrounded anything on the roadside, protecting the fragments of broken trees, melted bins and small traces of miscellaneous destruction. A few houses were completely enclosed in scaffolding to hide the damage and repair that was about to be undertaken. The pole that Dennis had thrown to destroy the vigilante's car was gone, but the place where it once stood was fenced off with rope which warned pedestrians of the danger which still existed there.

Dennis was the only person on the street. He could feel the black ice trying to make him slip underneath his feet. He knew that if there was another confrontation that the cold frosty conditions gave no one an advantage. Dennis really didn't want to fight.

"Hello sir," a voice called from the lifting fog. Dennis turned towards it and watched as a lone figure ventured forth from the shadows. Jet walked carelessly towards him. His blonde hair sitting handsomely on his head before falling down by his neck. Jet stood handsomely in a newly acquired suit jacket and trousers, his white shirt was unbuttoned at the neck revealing a strong neck and upper chest. He was attractive and his presence was captivating. He smiled at Dennis in a way which he would describe as charming; getting closer as if they were long separated friends. "Thanks for coming to see me."

"I'm here Jet, now what do you want?" Dennis asked.

"For a teacher you don't have any manners," Jet stated; he showed little annoyance though. "I just wanted to talk to you." Both watched the actions of the other, neither wanting to be the first to talk; allowing time for the other to say something. "I have been doing a lot of thinking in the past few days. At the start of this year I was a kid who was lost. My family was gone, and even though I was surrounded by people I found no comfort in those that hid behind me and called me 'friend'. I had intentions of playing sport and then somehow making a go of that. I put no effort into it and had no desire to do extra work. I got everything that I wanted, because if I didn't then everyone was afraid I would do something. They were right because I had done it before. I had the students where I wanted them, I had the teachers running scared, and everyone knew their place. Then you turned up. You helped the teachers, supported the students and returned some form of normality back to the school. Everything changed so quickly. I didn't like it, and I didn't like the person who had changed it. I hated you, sir. All of a sudden it felt like everything was falling down around me, the control that I had was gone, and the worst part was that the person who was responsible was being so damn nice about it."

None of this was a surprise to Dennis. He had spoken frequently about how much potential Jet possessed. But even though he was aware he also knew that this was not the time to gloat. He continued to allow Jet have his say.

"You're so clever," Jet smiled, "you knew all of that would happen, and despite how hard I pushed back you still managed to manipulate others so that the only issue that remained was me, and everyone knew it. Unfortunately I wasn't smart enough to regain control. Then it came to a head between you and I. I thought that if I showed you up, if I broke you down, then I would be seen as the more dominant person at our school and our club. But even those desires you managed to twist to your own means. Everything I had known, everything I was, had become a lie. I was angry. Then that night came. You would know what it was like, but perhaps slightly different. That wave hit us after that rock fell from the sky. I was pushed by that wave and flew across a couple of fields. Help came and I was ignored. I couldn't speak, couldn't scream for help, so I was left there. Some thought I went to a hospital, but I went to no hospital, I got no assistance or aid. I just lay there, thinking of how it wasn't fair. Wanting to kill you."

"I'm sorry," Dennis offered sincerely, finally speaking up.

"Don't pity me," Jet snapped back, but almost instantly his anger diminished and he was smiling again. "But don't apologise either. I should be thanking you. I was reborn that night. The curtains lifted and I finally saw what was important, and it wasn't school or sport or friends. Those things were fleeting. I looked inward while I lay there. I became stronger, faster, better than what I was. I had been given a second chance, I could do things that no one else could do. I thought I was special and unique, but then again I was wrong. I knew that you were like me, it just took me awhile to prove it. When I first came back I jumped back into what life was for me before. I tested myself in that environment, to see if I still fit in. But I didn't, I had outgrown, but that didn't mean that being rejected didn't hurt. And that was the worst thing, that even though I had become stronger than half the world you still looked down upon me like I was broken. I hated that, I got into that group so that I could finally belong somewhere, but all they wanted to do was to use me, which was worse than what you did," Jet smiled at the next thought. "I made them pay, just like how I wanted to make you pay. Now I understand that school wasn't for me, sport wasn't all I thought it was. I have evolved and have people around me who can really push me to reach the possibilities that no one else knew I had."

"I did," Dennis interrupted again gently. "From the first moment until even now, I can see the great things that you could accomplish."

"Not could, can, and will," Jet corrected. "Starting tomorrow I will be taking steps to change the world. I want you to see it."

"Tomorrow," Dennis queried, "why not today?"

"Because today I want to tie up some loose ends," Jet confirmed. "I want to make you pay, want to make you hurt just like I did."

"You want to fight me again?" Dennis replied. "Surely the place that we are standing in is proof to you that that won't work."

"Oh, I know," Jet responded. "I have become smarter remember. You standing here, in your stupid disguise, with your stupid name, the Wrangler is it? Pathetic. I know I can't really hurt you how I would like. So I have thought of another way. If I can't hurt you I need to do something else that will hurt you. Not physically of course, but hurt you none the less." Dennis started to shudder at what he knew Jet was getting at. "At first I thought about getting to you through your friends. But when I thought about that again I realised that it was your friends who were suffering, not you, some even went missing. It wasn't enough. So I thought harder. I discovered that the Wrangler has family. It was hard to find the information I needed, it seems someone or something, apart from you, is working against me. But I found them, and this morning that will be taken care of too."

"What have you done?" Dennis growled. He took a step forward with a closed fist, making aggressively towards Jet. Jet put his hands up in front of him.

"I have done nothing, sir," he admitted. "But my new friends wanted to help me out and, soon, my new friends will be making a visit to your family, and they will introduce themselves on my behalf. They haven't arrived, yet. You have a chance to stop them if you go now. That is the present that goes with my thanks. If you stay here though, who knows what will happen?"

Dennis and Jet looked at each other for a few seconds. Then without a backwards glance Dennis ran hard and fast. He disappeared back around the bend to where his car had been parked and took off as quickly as he could. Jet simply watched him go without saying another word.

Moments went by and Jet remained. The loud, ancient muffler boomed into the night as Dennis sped off and soon even that sound was gone. The dawn seemed to linger, the sun hiding just beyond the horizon as if it knew that something sinister was about to happen. That near darkness would remain for an hour or two. Jet could hear the shuffling of footsteps behind him but he did not turn to investigate. He knew who was there, but even if he didn't he was not scared anymore. Once more he felt like he had regained his control.

"Well done," a female voice congratulated him. "I had no idea that you had that in you. It seems like I had the right idea when I saw you."

"I can't believe you made me do that. It should have back fired because he knows how I feel towards him, the only reason why he didn't see through that charade is because of how stupid and trusting he is. I could have taken care of him right here, and it would have been done with," Jet growled, for the first time returning back to his usual state of mind. He had been acting, for some of what he had said. Most was true but the resentment he still felt for the man was very much there.

"That didn't work out so well for you last time," the red haired lady said. "Besides we need to look forward to what is happening tomorrow. If he had taken you down, or if there was some big incident, it would jeopardise our plans. We could do this a lot easier if you simply told us who he is."

"That is my secret," Jet replied abruptly.

"Why? We could help," she retorted.

"I know," Jet agreed, "but this is my thing, and I will take care of it." Another sound could be heard. It was the lackeys that accompanied Miss Opportunity everywhere.

"Is it done?" Jet asked them.

"I will report only to the lady," one of them replied. He was a big ugly brute, who Jet was surprised had been given a job as simple as this one, as he imagined any task would be beyond him. "Know your place, boy." Jet wasn't angry, instead he smiled. He turned on his heel and before the brute could move Jet had lifted him by the collar so his feet were no longer on the ground.

"I have been told a lot lately that using manners never hurt. You know my name I suggest that in the future you use it," Jet whispered into the man's face. Usually the brute would have overpowered Jet, and all others nearby, no doubt, hence why he was someone who was trusted with the protection of Miss Opportunity. But Jet reminded himself that the brute was nobody and he had to discover his place, just like all the others, or, he had to be made an example of so others never forgot.

"I am the Hitman," Jet growled. The next motion sent the brute hurtling back into the darkness. A loud thud revealed his fate as he slammed into a brick wall. Perhaps he would never be able to say anything again because of the impact. The second lackey stepped forward. She had either learned quickly or was smart enough to see what was going on.

"We have placed a tracking device on the car, but we have also notified our action team of the make and colour. It is a very distinctive model," she said.

"Good and what about the other thing?" Jet followed up.

"We are getting the data analysed as we speak, based on camera footage of the car and the trace on his phone we should be able to find out where he has been hiding," the woman said. Jet nodded and waved her away. A second later she had disappeared back into the shadows, in the direction of her fallen comrade.

"Now it is time for us to go," Mrs Opportunity said, ignoring how easily Jet had taken care of her entourage. "We have much work to do before we set the plan into action." Jet sighed, still wishing that he had taken care of things his way. At the very least his former teacher was out of the way, and soon would be taken care of permanently.

The trap had been set.

CHAPTER 14 - THE TRAP

The little mustard yellow car had never travelled so fast, or shuddered so violently. Dennis had thrown caution out the window. He was not concerned about attracting attention from the authorities, especially as the sun had hardly come up and he took a gamble that police would not be near him. He slowed, originally on corners where he knew that the car might not handle the curve, or the slim layer of ice hiding upon the road surface. But during the rest of that journey his foot was pressed forward on the accelerator pedal to a point where he was satisfied he wouldn't break through the heatshield.

Dennis was conscious of pressing too firmly on the pedals or changing gears too aggressively, hating the thought that he would somehow break them in his efforts and ending his rush home prematurely. Dennis had found that the incidents which had caused him to break things before were entirely due to him not understanding the change within him. He was comfortable within his own, new, skin now and could feel when he was going too hard.

He had attempted to call his home already with no success. Every long stretch he came to he tried again. Dennis even tried to contact Horatio, to get his friend to keep trying on his behalf. Frustratingly despite Horatio being attached to his technology most of the time, he also could not be reached.

Dennis also still wore his disguise. The oil skin jacket had clung on to Dennis as he returned to his car, and without wanting to lose even a second he had allowed it to remain on. His hat sat atop his head, quite suited to being there now. It was a simple look that many other farmers or people who lived out in the area had adopted for countless years. Dennis didn't think that anyone who observed him in the clothing would confuse him with the Wrangler, after all why would a supposed super hero be driving out in the wilderness, in possibly one of the world's oldest and worst performing cars.

Dennis slowed down once he reached Forbes, the last thing he wanted to do was to cause an accident that would result in someone else's death. As soon as he was clear of the town though he returned to pushing his car to, and over, its limits. The dashboard was so old that next to the single stream radio there were three dials, all analogue. The big one in the middle showed the speed. It only reached up to 140 kilometres, about a hundred kilometres less than any new vehicle that was released, regardless if road rules stated that they couldn't actually go that fast. Dennis kept the needle pressed up against the 140 as often as he could. The others showed the time, which didn't work properly, and the fuel level. He had to listen to the car to understand when he had to change gears. The sound it was making at the moment suggested that it was in pain. Odd smells were starting to emerge from underneath the hood, and the odour was accompanied by small traces of smoke that wisped sporadically through the cabin.

Dennis was marginally relieved when he arrived at the outskirts of Clapptown. He had made the journey in less than an hour from start to finish, which, if he didn't feel so guilty in doing so, he would have seen as an achievement. He quickly burned through the centre of town and made for the long driveway that would lead him finally to his mother's dwelling.

The Sun had jest crept up behind him, sending arrows of blinding light from its arrival onto the land. Dennis looked around; he wasn't sure what he had expected to see but was sure that it wasn't what was present before him. He half assumed that there would be mass destruction, buildings or the entire township pulverised, his mother's house burning and in ruins. The light struck his rear-view mirror and reflected as glare straight into his eyes. Dennis swept the mirror gently to the side so as to avoid the distraction. He looked at it, checking where it pointed. He quickly clutched at it and looked closer than he had the entire trip.

"Oh no," he said out loud, turning to look out the back of his car rather than through the mirror. The spears of light still crept towards him, but they were distorted by a cloud of dirt which was being thrown up in all directions. Dust devils, willy willys or mini tornadoes were not uncommon in the dustier areas of the Australian bush. The natural phenomena part of the everyday existence for people who live in the arid environment, even during the colder months. But this one was not natural, it was clearly man made. The roar of propeller blades thudded through the air towards Dennis. He kept his foot firmly on the accelerator pedal in an attempt to outrun the flying nuisance which pursued him. It was clear why it was there, it had no other reason to be there.

Dennis cursed as it overtook him, shaking the car as it flew overhead at a low altitude. The fact that it had ignored the car suggested that it was not there for him. The thought arrived to Dennis that he had been followed. Meaning that the helicopter had refused to take an opportunity against Dennis for that whole duration, entirely designed to follow him to where he was going. Which also meant that Jet did not know where his family had lived, very much thanks to Horatio's best efforts, but now Dennis had lead the new group that Jet had spoken of directly towards them. Dennis swore again.

Up ahead he could see the helicopter descend towards the ground, right beside where his mother's homestead had appeared on the slowly appearing horizon. His keen eyes saw a group of people run clear of the vehicle as it hovered mere centimetres from the ground. Livestock took off in all directions in fright. He had lead them straight to his family and he would be too late to help them.

Dennis bellowed his anger as he forced his car even harder. He tore off his seatbelt and propped open his door so that he could be out of his car the moment he had arrived, regardless whether his car had stopped or not. He cleared the last gate which had been left curiously open, and felt one of his tyres blow as it struck a cattle guard too heavily. It didn't matter. The car lurched savagely off to one side but Dennis was already away from it and charging. The helicopter took flight at his approach and started circling the homestead. Dennis launched onto the deck and lunged through the door.

"Mum?" he yelled out, hoping desperately for a response. "Scott? Are you here?" Neither returned an answer, but that didn't mean there was no noise. The footsteps of several heavy people banged on the wooden floorboard. Dennis could hear the direction that they came from and how fast they approached. His resolve was savage. The teacher in him was gone, and the Wrangler erupted. The lack of response told him that his family was either dead or in serious trouble. The reasoning that Dennis prided himself in possessing abandoned as his grief overcame him.

Dennis roared in agony as he went on the offensive. He didn't care if they heard him coming. Half a dozen steps and he was upon them. The first opponent appeared before him. They were all dressed similar. Heavy duty helmet with communication equipment built in, combat quality uniform with padding, face mask underneath a sensor eye piece, each with a weapon.

None of that mattered to Dennis. He was bigger, stronger, faster, and he was angry.

He reached out, seizing the weapon in his opponent's hands, tugged it towards him savagely which in turn dragged the person holding it. Then Dennis grabbed the man by the scruff of his collar and slammed him through the wall. The next intruder came at him down the corridor, brought his gun up, and fired. Dennis dodged easily. It was reflex and instinct that helped him, he could even feel the bullet as it sailed past. Dennis slid in under his attacker and gave him an uppercut punch which landed firmly on the man's jaw and lifted him into the ceiling, crumpling into the wooden frame and banging against the iron roof. There was one more in the hallway, too close. Dennis lunged out with a leg, kicking the man in his midriff, sending him sailing into the far wall. The way was clear, but the yelling and movement from elsewhere reminded him there were more.

The wall on his right exploded as it was torn apart with gunfire. Dennis lowered into a squat and ran to the corridor's end. He stepped into the next room, a large lounge area, and was greeted by a man holding a small hand gun. The man fired and Dennis was shot. Dennis looked down to his chest where the bullet had come into contact with him. His fingers traced a small hole and noticed some blood dripping free. The man who had fired it clearly expected that to be the end of Dennis. He called in his success to the rest of the group, informing them that the assailant was immobilised.

He was wrong.

Dennis leaped upon him, wrapped his arms around those of the man who had shot him, and looked deep into his eyes.

"It would take more than that," Dennis whispered, watching the fear appear in the other man's face, as his confidence drain out of it. Dennis didn't throw him like he did the others, aware of the destruction that was being caused to his mother's home. Instead he just squeezed him until he saw the lights go out in his eyes and he slumped into a state of unconsciousness. Dennis dropped him to the ground. He walked calmly back out the door and off towards the kitchen. He glanced into the room that he had rested in when he had been pronounced dead, and it remained empty. So much had changed. He fingered the wound which was weeping from his chest and shook his head. He needed to focus. He took a step out into the kitchen area and was greeted by a single word.

"Fire!"

The world erupted around him. The remaining invaders opening fire, turning furniture, ornaments, plasterboard and the frame of the house into shrapnel, debris and small splinters. Dennis hid back behind the wall, ducking as parts of it exploded around him. He wondered if he could take the space between them quickly, hoping he could do so without being shot again. He glanced over towards the kitchen. An idea dropped into his head. He bounded towards it with as much energy that he could muster, diving behind the bench and the cover that supposedly provided.

"And again," one of them called out. A different cacophony of sounds rang out. The bench Dennis hid behind deteriorated under the constant barrage of bullets. The projectiles randomly ricocheting from cooking utensils, pots and pans, and appliances. The hail of fire suddenly stopped.

"Can you lob one in there?" a question was silently asked, but Dennis heard it like the question was aimed at him. Dennis felt his eyes widen as he imagined what that meant. He slid over to the fridge and dragged it free from its position. He lifted it up awkwardly, hefting it behind him, and threw. The fridge sailed through the air as if Dennis had thrown a football. It was greeted by the screams of those who had sought to kill him. They collapsed under its weight, crushing all but one who was bumped clear by the impact. There were still a few who managed to avoid the makeshift projectile.

"He's still alive," one of the intruders yelled as he tried to persuade the heavy fridge to move, lifting it behind himself. The rest attempted to help but it was no use. "Where is the grenade? It's still live."

Bang! Dennis hid back behind the cupboards of the kitchen. He felt shrapnel impact on the other side, and heard the fridge lift from its place, slam into the ceiling and then crunch back into the ground. When Dennis glanced over, when he deemed it to be safe, a portion of the house was missing, blown apart by some sort of explosive device. The wall was crumbling and the ceiling slumped down without the support it had previously been provided. Huge portions of the floor were missing and the dirt that existed beneath the house could be easily seen. Body parts and remnants of the attackers were strewn everywhere. Dennis tried his best not to vomit. He heard the crashing of glass and moved over toward where he heard the sound. One of his attackers, the one that had been bumped clear, had shattered a window and was running clear of the house.

Dennis grunted. He still had no idea what had happened to his family. He needed to question someone. Dennis stepped clear of the rubble and looked out towards where the intruder was making his escape.

"Leave him," a voice spoke to Dennis before he could manage to leave the deck.

"Uncle Scott?" Dennis responded with shocked relief.

"I told you to drop that Uncle stuff," Scott replied. He smiled broadly and then moved over to embrace his nephew.

"I am so happy you're alive," Dennis said truthfully. "Where is mum? How did you stay away?"

"She is safe, I will tell you the rest later, but we are not finished here," Scott reprimanded Dennis. They both watched as the last attacker was picked up by the helicopter.

"He got away," Dennis groaned, watching as the helicopter returned to harassing them from the sky. "And the helicopter is coming back."

"We need to let it," Scott said simply as he watched the attackers return in the sky.

"Come again?" Dennis said with a look of amazement.

"The whole aim of that thing was to come out and destroy you and your family," Scott answered watching as the helicopter assumed a position right above them. "So if they don't do that they can't stop. If they do then we are safe."

"If they kill us we are safe?" Dennis said cocking an eyebrow.

"No, that's dumb," Scott admonished. "If they think they have killed us we are safe." Dennis felt stupid. Of course that is what he meant. "Looks like they are bringing out some bigger guns now." Scott pointed at the large objects which were being held out of the windows. Dennis had no idea what they were, but he wouldn't have to wait long to find out.

Two long streams of fire shot forth from the weapons. Some sort of flamethrower stabbed down at the homestead which sat below the helicopter. Dennis could hear the roof almost immediately succumb to the heat that was being imposed upon it. Crackling and warping of beams and metal giving way before the onslaught.

"Geez it got warm quick," Scott proclaimed.

"I wouldn't know," Dennis replied.

"I need a favour from you," Scott admitted, starting to lead his nephew over to where the massive hole in the outside wall had been created by the previous explosion. Dennis reached down and grabbed the headset from one of the fallen intruders and held it in one hand as he passed. The roof was starting to creak and whine as the pressure from the helicopter continued. "I need you to make it over to the shed, run as fast as you can. I will meet you there."

"What about you?" Dennis asked with concern. "I could carry you."

"If you try to do that I will kill you myself," Scott growled back. "I am not hurt, I will make my own way and meet you there. Are you ready?" Scott asked and watched as Dennis nodded in reply. "Good," Scott acknowledged. "Now go, I will see you there."

As soon as Dennis stepped away from the cover at the side of the house he was almost immediately spotted. Dennis watched as the helicopter changed position and moved over to where Dennis stood. The headset that he carried hissed to life, revealing that the pilot and the helicopter's occupants were preparing to pursue him. The flamethrower spewed forth at the house again, more wood collapsed from within as a result. Dennis looked back to check on his uncle's safety but he was no longer standing where he had been. Gunfire resumed and Dennis found himself running and ducking as he made his way over to the oversized shed; dust and rock being propelled into the air as bullets cracked into the ground behind him. Dennis grunted as once more he felt the sensation of a bullet, or possibly a flying rock, finding its way into his body. This one struck just above his shoulder blade. He didn't stagger, he ran on as if nothing had happened, but still he felt pain there.

Dennis could see his car halfway between his position and the destination. He first thought that he could use it for cover, so that he could avoid being shot at for even the briefest of moments. Another bullet had fizzed by so close to his head and he had no idea what might happen if he received a shot there. Dennis instead gave the car a wide berth, hoping that the action would allow the vehicle to avoid the onslaught that the house was receiving.

He was wrong. A jet of fire lanced forth, no longer focused on the house as it had been, and assaulted the already damaged ride that belonged to Dennis. He felt his heart sink as his pride and joy, which had served him so well for so long, was ruthlessly attacked. The car had been through so much and had proved itself in many situations where a lesser or newer vehicle would have been damaged or destroyed. He hoped it would survive, but he knew in his breaking heart that that was not to be. The flames ruptured the fuel tank and the in next instance the vehicle boosted itself into the air, assisted by a monstrous plume of black smoke and blue flame.

"No," Dennis yelled. He should have felt silly for pleading for the life of his car, but it meant so much to him. He even felt a small tear spring to his eye. He cleared the destruction and made his way into the darkened shed.

Dennis looked around and stared at his surroundings. There were a couple of tractors, bikes and four wheelers around him, as was to be expected. But there was also all sorts of farm chemicals, fuels and machinery. They had been looked after meticulously, but under the barrage of the flames that followed him, Dennis was certain of only one thing. The shed wasn't a sanctuary, it was death trap.

The rattling of bullets on the tin wall accompanying the rushing of the searching flames became all too loud in his ears. He hoped that his uncle had escaped the house as Dennis provided him with a distraction. Otherwise the trouble was compiling, and it was clear that they were both running out of time. One of the beams holding up the roof crunched down on its base before teetering dangerously over to one side. The roof groaned for a heartbeat before the beam buckled, bringing down the whole structure with it. The roof dove over to one side dragging the remaining supports down with it. Somehow they still provided some resistance as the roof stayed high enough for Dennis to remain standing.

As expected several of the fuel pumps and oil drums ruptured, exploding and sending toxic flames up into the air, blistering the metal that protected it and warping the vehicles which were parked nearby. Every few seconds another explosion filled the collapsing shed, echoing the screams of popping rivets and wrenching metal chaos that gushed forth from underneath.

The headset which was forgotten in his hand sparked back to life. The pilot was convinced that the targets were destroyed and occupants deceased. The pilot received acknowledgement from a female voice before ending the communication. The propellers, which were still ear throbbingly deafening as they beat down air, helped spread the furnace that was present under the shed. The helicopter that was responsible suddenly started to lift. The ear-splitting noise produced getting dimmer and dimmer as it gained altitude and then left the area all together.

Dennis was not safe where he stood, but assumed that it was becoming safer outside. He ventured over to a portion of the shed through which he could leave unharmed.

"Psst," a sound came from nearby. "Over here kid." Dennis followed Scott's voice and walked to another part of the shed which somehow had not been so utterly destroyed. When he arrived he found his uncle next to a concrete water tank, watching as the helicopter travelled further and further way. Dennis could see that everything that made the property warm and inviting was completely devastated. The house smouldered nearby, embers jumping between melting wooden parts of the structure and off on the sweeping wind. His car was a smouldering wreak and the shed was prone to dissolve at any moment. Scott gestured for Dennis to follow him quietly. Dennis obeyed. A few short steps later they were at the back of the water tank. Scott looked down at the pump which sat behind it. He appeared to be looking very interested at the motor, before reaching down and flicking a latch. He grabbed hold of a handle, seemingly hidden amongst the rest of the rust, and pulled the whole thing upwards. The pump lifted into the air, folding a hinge on one end, while still operating in its new sideways position. Dennis looked underneath. A large hole had appeared there, and at one side there was a ladder.

"Don't worry, you'll fit," Scott told him as he pointed down into the darkness. "You go first, then I will lock this up behind us." Dennis nodded and reached down into the hole. A moment later Scott had slotted the pump back into place and stood in the darkness beside his nephew. Dennis couldn't see very far, but he could see that they weren't just standing in a hole, they were standing in a tunnel.

"Now follow me," Scott continued as he flicked on a torch, "we have a lot to talk about."

CHAPTER 15 - TOOLS OF THE TRADE

Dennis had walked for some distance. From what he could gather he followed an old mine shaft that had been cleared of any leftover materials and had been reinforced so that the structure was safe. His Uncle Scott had simply led him along the entire route until finally the supporting structures became more rigid and the curves or corners less frequent. There was a stale smell throughout the journey, like stagnant water that had turned due to inactivity whilst still attracting diseased or disgusting vermin. Scott had used his torch to show Dennis the way, but that didn't really help with Dennis identifying the directions he was travelling in.

"This way," Scott directed, finally pointing his light to a spot on the roof, rather than along the floor like it had been consistently. "Up there." Dennis was directed to climb the accompanying ladder first and did so. At the top of the short climb there was an old rusty seal which he easily twisted open. A moment later Scott had joined him. Dennis was very aware of the place where they had arrived.

"What now?" Dennis asked.

"Breakfast," Scott declared, guiding his nephew out of the small room in which they had climbed up into and out into the open.

"I have already had breakfast," Dennis replied.

"That's a shame," Scott shrugged, "because we can't have a discussion over breakfast without having breakfast." Dennis sighed.

"Well I guess a second breakfast never hurt anyone."

Never had Dennis felt so relaxed and so stressed at the same time. He sat in an old plastic chair which threatened at any moment to shift and break under his weight. There were times in his youth where he would swing on his chair purposely to see at what point the chair would overbalance, there were even times in his adult life where he would do that, if he had done so he was sure the chair would break. He sat at a lonely table in the back area of Scott's pub. His uncle was occupied by making a big breakfast for both of them. He had bacon, eggs, sausages, French toast, mushrooms and some other things that Dennis didn't usually eat. There was enough cooking for a family, which again was always his uncle's way. Scott stood in a singlet and jeans, with shades propped on his head, and, despite it only being around eight o'clock in the morning, he was well into his third beer.

Finally, his job done and a mountain of food rising from the table, Scott sat down and set about eating the meal he had delivered.

"That smell's delicious," Scott declared. He grabbed a pair of tongs and started grabbing whatever he desired, before allowing Dennis to do the same. Dennis had to agree with his uncle. Despite already having breakfast he found he certainly had an appetite for more. His hat and oil skin jacket now lay discarded over a nearby chair and Dennis released himself for the moment, refusing to think about anything else apart from the food he was indulging in. His uncle allowed him to do so for the duration of the meal and the time that he was eating. The silence felt odd, but it was definitely appreciated. Dennis wondered how the discussion was going to playout. As always he wasn't shocked at how his uncle started the conversation.

"So, you got shot," his uncle started, after wiping the last remnants of food and grease from his unkempt features. "First time?"

"Yes!" Dennis exclaimed back, spitting a bit of egg out onto the table. Dennis rubbed his own collection of sauce from the hair of his moustache. "I don't go around deliberately or accidently wanting to get shot. Neither does anybody else for that matter."

"Did it hurt?" Scott asked, taking a long slurp from his can.

"What do you think?" Dennis replied sarcastically.

"I think it would have hurt, hell, it probably would have killed me," Scott responded honestly. "But I am not you, so I wouldn't know how you feel." Dennis felt at the wound on his chest. In the time that it had taken for the pair of them to walk through the tunnels and wait for breakfast, Dennis had managed to dig his fingers into both of the holes and, with excruciating pain, had managed to pull free the projectiles that been embedded within. It felt like he had just picked a scab, as it was irritatingly itchy around the wound site. There was no longer a hole there, nor anymore bleeding. Dennis suspected that before he had finished digesting his food he wouldn't even have a scar or something that revealed where he had been harmed.

"It did hurt," Dennis admitted, acknowledging how rude his reply had been. It was not the usual abrupt conversation in which his uncle spoke, joking about everything. This time he was being far more serious. "But not like it would have if I was normal. It felt like someone threw a sharp stick and got me with the point. It stung where it hit, but I knew it would wear off."

"Regardless, I still wouldn't try and make a habit of it," Scott said. It was hard for Dennis to presume the wisdom of the comment if it wasn't so obvious.

"I don't intend to," Dennis replied, then changed the topic back to what he wanted to know. "Where's mum?"

"Safe," Scott answered with a nod. "And so is your sister. They are together and they are safe far from here."

"Thank goodness," Dennis said with relief, releasing a huge breath that he hadn't been aware he was holding. "That's lucky."

"Luck had nothing to do with it, kid," Scott said in spite of Dennis' relief. "We had help." Dennis wanted to know who it was, but before he could ask he had already guessed.

"Horatio?" he questioned.

"Bingo," Scott said. He rose to his feet and started clearing up all the plates and food that rested around them. "But before you think that he just told me yesterday that something was going on, I need to tell you some other things." Dennis was prepared to listen, and helped his uncle clear away the tables so that the conversation could continue uninterrupted. Scott returned with some hard spirits, ignoring the drinks he had already consumed. "You might need something heavier for this."

"There is nothing in the world heavy enough," Dennis replied. He politely took a glass from his uncle and started to drink. Just like he thought, he felt nothing.

"In the hospital, that kid Horatio came up to me," Scott started to explain, settling deeper into his chair as if preparing to enjoy the telling of his own tale. "He told me that even though you had died on the table, numerous times, that you were going to be okay. In fact he told me that you would make a full recovery. Needless to say . . ."

"You laughed at him?" Dennis guessed.

"No," replied Scott a little hurt, "I punched him in the face, did he tell you? Got myself thrown out of the hospital too. Nevertheless he gave me a number to call and told me to call him. I wanted to hit him again but your mum stopped me from doing so. I didn't believe him, not after what we had been through. Then we brought you home, expecting that would be where it all ended for you. Low and behold that a few days later you are up and about as if nothing happened. Do you remember that?”

“I remember you waving a gun at me,” Dennis replied, taking a sip.

“Hey, I just told you I expected the worse,” Scott denied any wrong doing, “therefore a stranger walking through your mum’s home is grounds for a look at my gun.”

“Let’s agree to disagree,” Dennis informed him, “but go on.”

“Right,” Scott was happy to. “Well I was shocked, as were you, as was your mother. The day that you left I rang young Horatio and he spoke to me. Everything that he said was true. He asked lots of questions about you, and told me all his theories which also seemed to make sense. We started talking a lot. I thought it was really funny when he told me later that you were flat out denying what you could do, especially when I gave him that information.” Scott chuckled, but kept on with the story. “I went down there a couple of times, told him to look out for you and gave him a hand with some things he might need.”

“The setup in his basement? That was you?” Dennis asked with astonishment.

“I helped him get it, I don’t know how to use it,” Scott informed his nephew. “My skills lie elsewhere. But, it was obvious, after he showed me, what Horatio could do. So I decided to help him out. I have been helping with a bunch of things for a while, but that isn’t important at the moment.” Scott nodded, seeming to be deep in thought somewhere else, before finally continuing again. “Anyway the other day, when you took down that young protégé of yours, Horatio got spooked. He told me that he expected something big was going to happen soon.”

“And you believed him?” Dennis asked.

“I had no reason not to,” Scott replied. He poured himself another tall glass and continued. “As much as I was helping him he was helping me too, and to date he hasn’t been wrong.”

"In what way?" Dennis asked.

"Like I said," Scott leaned forward, "I am good at other things. Horatio gave me the information to do some other things. We were both working together to help you."

"Why?" Dennis asked the obvious question again. "Why would you both want to help me?"

"I have said this for a long time," Scott replied, standing up and leaning on the table. "So has your mum, and your dad did all the time. You were always someone who could change the world. As a teacher, and how you went about it, you changed lives all the time. Now you have a chance to not only change them, but to save them, and not just students either. Horatio was trying to guide you into it. I was simply wanting to give you the means when the time came."

"What do you mean by that?" Dennis asked, looking both confused at the prospects, and annoyed that his life was being built around in so much secrecy.

"Rather than tell you, how about I show you?" Scott walked past the table and off towards his mechanic shed, beckoning Dennis to follow. "Come on kid, let's go and take a look."

Dennis had lost track of how many times he had been surprised by things lately, or how many times something happened that despite it not being the normal was also not really unexpected. His uncle guided him through the mechanic's shed which was always a lesson in transitioning between places. When you initially walked in the place was immaculate. His customers would always see the shiniest most technologically advanced workshop in their lives, regardless if they were locals or if tourists required the service. As soon as you walked past the space which served as an office, the state of the place declined massively. Dennis wasn't shocked by this. It had become a memory, in fact if it was cleaned he would have been more confused.

The back area always felt like a shrine to his dad. All the jobs that he had been working on still laying unfinished where they had stood at that time. No doubt junkers had come to claim or purchase rare parts from inside and every time Scott would have turned them away. The memory that each possessed too valuable for any sale, and too hard to part with.

Dennis walked past the area where he had tied up his father's old whip. It had been easy, and looking back Dennis imagined that he could do an even better job on it now than he had before. Even that space had been left untouched since his last appearance.

Scott led them even further into the shed. Despite the sun being well and truly up, and part of a brilliantly clear day, there was no light penetrating into the building. It may as well have been night time by how dark and musty it was. They travelled to what Dennis suspected was the deepest part of the premises. To his eyes there was nothing there but a rusted old corner that was filled with tools that no longer worked. Regardless of this, and perhaps it was because of all the time he had spent with Horatio and his theories, or his attention to detail, Dennis could see that the floor and shelving had been disturbed recently and frequently. Again, when his uncle reached out and pulled a handle revealing a secret hidden area, he was not shocked.

He was shocked, however, by what the door had behind it.

Dennis walked in automatically, gaping at what he saw. To his eyes it looked like a mechanic's dream set up, and looked like it had been set up within a sterile hospital environment. The walls were a mix of white and sky blue. The light which shone forth was enough to illuminate most of the abandoned area that they had just walked through. When they were both inside Scott pulled another handle and the wall slid shut, set back in its original position.

"What is this place?" Dennis asked in awe.

"I told you," Scott replied as he started walking through the space. "That my skill set is very different and unique." His uncle seemed to ignore how everything in that first space was arranged perfectly. Here Dennis felt like he could eat his food off the floor, or even use the tools that lined the walls in an operating theatre, because the surfaces reflected brilliance. Due to the standard that was set in that first room Dennis was not surprised that he couldn't find the words to express how much better the second room was. Scott was making his way over to a table positioned in the middle, around the edges of the space were several large cubicle sized rooms which connected to the main room. The contents of each were hidden in darkness and Dennis wished he was able to get a better look in on them to discover their secrets.

"This was what I was talking about," Scott said as Dennis slowly arrived. Dennis could easily see what was located there. He was interested all the same and allowed his uncle to continue. "Horatio has told me that you have constantly been fighting the fact that you are . . ."

"A superhero?" Dennis interrupted.

"No," Scott said shaking his head. "You are different, now, extraordinary even. That doesn't class you as a hero. If it did then others with your abilities would be branded the same, and from what I hear there is at least one other like you who does not fit that title." The image of Jet slipped into Dennis' mind. His feelings were always on the fence about the boy, but after he attempted to set him up and kill his family, despite him already destroying a good portion of a suburb of Orange, he had finally allowed his hatred to rise to the surface.

"Great, I don't like the term superhero," Dennis admitted.

"Me neither," Scott agreed. "But that doesn't mean that you can't see what I see. What Horatio has already suggested. There are people out there who are dangerous. Normally those people are out of our control and have no interest in people like us. But now, like it or not, you have become one of those people who can do something to help, who can change the outcome of events, and who can save lives.”

“I am a teacher,” Dennis interrupted, but his conviction was not as strong as it had been when he argued the point with Horatio. “My whole aim in life to this point is to have fun and help people. I don’t want to hurt anyone, and if I keep following this train of thought then it is likely that I may have to do worse than that.”

“Despite all the things that have happened so far, all of those things being life threatening and dangerous, you haven’t killed anybody yet,” Scott replied.

“I hit a group of people with a fridge,” Dennis retorted stiffly.

“But did they die?” Scott questioned.

“Yes,” Dennis snapped back with his eyebrows raised.

“True,” Scott conceded. “But that was because they decided to recline on an explosive. Which they set off. Inside your own house. Even if you were responsible, which you are not, it seems like you had reason to do so.”

“Perhaps,” Dennis agreed, “but it doesn’t change the fact that it was a close thing, and I am not happy about it.”

“I would be concerned if you had been happy about it,” Scott answered. “That is not the person you are, and I hope you never become that person. But imagine a different scenario. You took no action, and now your mum, your sister, and even me, are all gone. The feelings you have right now would be far worse. I don’t wish to have your abilities, because now if you stand by, knowing that you can be the difference, and someone gets hurt or worse as a result, then you will feel as if you had been the person responsible.”

“I understand what you are telling me,” Dennis confessed. “But to accept that role I would stop being everything that I am.”

“No, you’re wrong,” Scott shook his head. “Because if you stopped being who you are then you are not the person who would care enough to help in the first place. It simply means that you may have to give up on other things. You can still be some form of teacher, player, rogue, just not in the same capacity. That is a decision that you need to make for yourself, down the track. But you and I both know that you are the only one at this moment that can make a difference in the case of your young friend."

Slowly, reluctantly, Dennis nodded his acceptance of what his uncle was saying.

"I will do what I can," Dennis said finally.

"I understand," Scott said, slapping Dennis on the shoulder and smiling at him. He spread an arm over the bench in front of him, as well as something that was hidden underneath a tarp nearby. "And I will try to help you out, however I can. Let me show you some things that I have been working on. Don't interrupt, I have been working on my spiel for these. All of these are one of a kind, especially designed and made by me, with some assistance from Horatio, with only one person in mind." Scott smiled expecting some sort of emotional outburst from his nephew. As always Dennis remained composed but was stroking his moustache and his lower jaw with interest.

"Okay here we go," Scott continued. "First I have tried to help out with your look. The big oil-skin jacket and hat for concealment. It is interesting but I have added some things that could be useful. This jacket is a little heavier than the one you already have. Why? Because this one is bulletproof. I made this before I knew that bullets were as effective as a wasp sting to you. However, not being shot could be considered a bonus, and if you are protecting someone else it may come in handy for them. It is also, very warm, again not that you need it, but just in case." Scott smiled but didn't wait for any input from his nephew before proceeding. "Next is your hat. This one is also heavier, bulletproof, again, but all the way to the edge of the rim. The edge also has a sharp metal tip, you could throw it and it could do some damage even from far away, but then of course you wouldn't have a hat for concealment, so, you know, try your best. This little thing is an ear piece," he said holding up a tiny device which was no bigger than his finger nail. "It connects to a closed frequency which only myself and Horatio are tapped into. As soon as you put that on you will be able to connect to us. It also has a microphone in built, no long cord or anything, which will hear whatever you say. And remember, even if you whisper, Horatio can hear what you are saying."

"Next, weapons," Scott said. Dennis cocked an eyebrow at the word, but, as requested, refused to interrupt. "We have established that you don't want to hurt someone, or kill them, but we are also aware that it may come to that."

"Not if I can help it," Dennis finally said.

"True, but . . ." Scott continued. "These should be able to assist with that. The first is the whip that you made the last time you were here. I said at the time that I would fix it, and I have done so. This thing is so tight that there is no chance of it breaking. The tensile strength is amazing, I reckon you could hold a train back with this bad boy. I have attached a chain into the lower half to make it stronger there, I reckon you could break bricks with it, and with the tip I have attached a magnetic claw. If you need to wrap it around something it should definitely grip, and if it is metal it will attach. In the handle there is a button that when you press it will reverse the polarity and allow you to release the whip. I am proud to say that this is definitely the best whip in the world, sorry Dennis I am still going to take all the credit for this one. Next . . ."

"Is that a sword?" Dennis asked. His eyes had jumped to the next device several times.

"No, it isn't a sword," Scott sounded hurt. "It's a cattle prod."

"A cattle prod that is shaped like a sword with a pretty sharp tip?" Dennis questioned again.

"The tip isn't sharp," Scott explained. "It is solid though, perfectly for stabbing into solid things and making a hole, the rest of it is sharp. I promise that it is a cattle prod though. Look." He pointed to two buttons on the side of the handle. "If you press this one it creates an open electric circuit, which makes the entire thing, apart from the handle, electrified. The other button ignites it from several small fissures, giving you either a torch or a device that can burn."

"And it is shaped like a sword," Dennis repeated again.

"Yes of course," Scott finally admitted. "Swords are cool. Now there is one more thing." Scott turned and stood behind the big tarp that covered something nearby.

"This, this one is special," Scott said, gripping and re-gripping the covering sheet. "It is more of a gift for you, but I am sure that you will be able to use it." Scott had clearly waited long enough, flinging the giant tarp over and away, revealing what was hidden underneath. Once more Dennis could not stop his mouth from hanging open.

"Wow," he said with astonishment.

"Great to hear," Scott smiled. His voice wavered as he explained the latest revelation. "This is a gift from me and your dad." Before him stood an enormous motorcycle, sparkling and finished to perfection. Scott removed his singlet and showed Dennis one of his tattoos. "You have seen this bike before, I know you remember because of how you reacted to this. Your dad started making this a long time ago, with all sorts of things, and what he called only the best parts. It is so big and is an absolute monster to drive. I couldn't handle it and I don't think he could either. It is as if he knew this was going to happen to you."

"It's amazing," Dennis admitted with acclamation.

"Your dad was a genius," Scott told him. "He helped me set up this place years ago. He called it his lab. Most of these rooms are still filled with things he started, inventions he thought of, projects he loved. This bike has all the best of him in it. I know that he wanted you to have it." Dennis looked at it over and over again. It was a tank of a bike. Despite it having features from many different styles it didn't look out of place. It had the frame of a World War 2 Harley Davidson, but it also had shocks and wheel guards from a Yamaha dirt bike, and the sleek speed design from a Ducati. Dennis was impressed. He could have marvelled all day at what had been presented to him but he knew that he couldn't.

"Horatio seemed to think that something big would be happening soon," Dennis admitted to his uncle. "I am sure that all this will come in handy, even if I don't know what exactly it will be used for."

"Horatio is working on that as we speak," Scott replied, sliding his singlet back over his head. "He thinks that it is linked to the visit from the Prime Minister, and he will let us know whatever that is as soon as he knows. I trust him to do that. Your bike will be able to get you there in almost no time at all, that thing is a beast." Scott rested a hand on the shoulder of his nephew. "Just like I am trusting Horatio with what he does, we need to make sure that you can use all of this stuff properly when the time comes. So from now, until we get a call that says that you are needed. We are going to work on using this stuff perfectly. And then we are going to relax and share a beer together, because we just don't know when we will be able to do that again."

"Sounds like a plan," Dennis agreed, placing his own firm arm on top of his uncle's shoulder. "When do we begin?"

His uncle smiled.

CHAPTER 16 – NO SENSE

"How do you feel?" the electronic voice said in Dennis' ear.

"Everything about this feel's weird and wrong," Dennis replied. He was tearing up the highway at close to two hundred kilometres an hour. He had no helmet, which was a huge no-no to Dennis as he was almost always promoting safety first. His new Akubra was suctioned to his head, showing off one of its many new functions despite the gale force wind that opposed him. His bulletproof oil-skin jacket was wrapped snuggly around him as the tails of the jacket fluttered boldly in the breeze. On one hip he wore his whip, wrapped up tight and stuck magnetically to his side, unable to unwind unless he commanded it to. His sword/cattle prod occupied the space at his lower back, the grip easily reachable from his other hip. Nothing about what was happening felt normal.

"Perhaps," Horatio said in his ear. "But essential. I hope you are ready."

"Ready?" Dennis blurted out, feeling an odd sensation as his mouth vibrated on the wind. He was sure he would attract a bug into his mouth soon enough. He may not have been able to be hurt as easily as before but he was still pretty sure he could choke to death. What a way to go, he thought to himself. "How can someone ever be ready for something like this?"

"It would have been easier if you hadn't slept in," Horatio sparked back. "And you had your communication equipment ready to go."

"Look I'm sorry," Dennis replied truthfully, though he hadn't been asleep so he couldn't have slept in. He had helped Scott with some last minute chores around the pub, it was only fair as his uncle would be cleaning up the mess that had been made at his mother's farm all by himself. "I'm on my way now though."

"There will be a lot to do once you get here, so I hope you got back all your energy while you rested," Horatio said with contempt on the line.

"Hey," Dennis barked back. "I was shot you know. Twice. Anyone else would be out of action for a while or for good."

"Is that right?" Horatio did not sound sympathetic nor impressed. "But you aren't just anyone, which I assume after your long chat with your uncle you are very aware of now. So you get nothing from me, except more belligerence if you don't arrive soon."

"Fine, I get it," Dennis replied. He remarked at how well his bike was taking corners, as well as maintaining its speed throughout the duration. He had made the hour and a half trek in less than half an hour. He was impressed, but he wouldn't have time to admire the bike for too much longer. "I am on my way in, let me know what is going on."

"Everything and nothing," Horatio responded quickly. Dennis had established early in the conversation that Horatio had set up his screens so he could manage everything that was happening within Orange. He could spare a few screens if something else sprang up, but it seemed that everything that Horatio had identified as a problem had occurred within the towns proximity. Horatio was prepared to be in Dennis' ear the entire time, happily admitting that his skills would be far more useful there. Dennis had found it challenging to repeat half of what Horatio said he was doing, let alone understand it or do it himself, so admitted that he was happy for this to be the case. One less person for Dennis to worry about if his friend was in a safe place and out of harm's way. Dennis thought about his friends for a moment.

"Is Jiemba amongst them?" he asked, concerned that he may have to confront that mysterious form of his friend.

"No," Horatio responded quickly, before swiftly drawing Dennis' attention to what else was happening. "Okay here is the long and short of it. My main concern is at the airport. The Prime Minister intends to set down and travel from there by car. The runway and all other non-essential personnel have been cleared from the area as that is the only flight coming in in the morning period. Cars including support vehicles will be on sight, and the Prime Minister will be met by the federal member of the local area."

"Mr Egg?"

"Yeah, do you know him?" Horatio asked.

"Not really, I taught a few of his children at one point," Dennis said feeling slightly abashed. "Sorry to interrupt."

"Noted, I will go on," Horatio continued, sounding only slightly annoyed. "The mayor will be there along with some other high profile notables. There is nothing happening at the moment that proposes any wrong doing, or suggests that that is likely to change. I just know that something will happen. All over Orange there are multiple crimes being reported. Cars are being stolen, vandals are breaking into homes all over the south of the city, and there are multiple incidents of assault, road rage and vehicular crashes. It is my estimation that each of these things is a distraction. The fact that these things are happening in broad daylight this early in the morning is unusual. None of them requires your attention as they can be dealt with by the police. The problem is that the local area police are not responding. The other emergency services are but the police have not appeared. I think that something is happening at the station. I have alerted the commands from surrounding towns using various mediums, asking for assistance, and they are responding, but they will also take some time to get here. My other concern apart from the police not responding is that there appears to be two major areas of people gathering, at least at the moment, with the likelihood of more emerging after the fact. One is in the middle of town at the local shopping centre, the other is at the showground where they are closing down the Easter show. In both cases I have identified groups of wrongdoers gathering and I surmise that soon they will all act."

"So what is the plan?" Dennis asked. "I am happy to follow your lead on this."

"I think that when the extra police arrive they can deal with the smaller matters, which leaves those big areas. As I said, I think they are a distraction, which means you shouldn't have to deal with them, but that also means you might have to if the local police aren't. That's a problem. Get to the local command and engage them to that task, I would not be surprised if they need your help first. Start at the police station. Head straight there and no matter what else you see on the way don't stop. There is less than an hour until the Prime Minister arrives," Horatio gave his directive.

"Can't they just divert the Prime Minister to somewhere else?" Dennis asked.

"Usually they would," Horatio replied, "regardless of how much planning has gone into this. I suspect that everything I have told you has not been conveyed and therefore nothing has gone wrong and there is no reason to divert. Something must be up with their communications. Besides, because I have emptied a few surrounding areas of their armed forces those places would not be much better."

"Lucky I have you then," Dennis laughed. He had finally entered the city and had hardly slowed down. With no police around and countless other issues he could see few reasons why he would be stopped. He had to help resolve the situation, and fast.

"You have no idea how lucky you are to have me," Horatio said with no measure of modesty. "I imagined that I might be doing something like this with my new abilities, but never quite like this. I will requote what you said earlier, this has indeed escalated quickly. Now get on with it."

A buzz and then a click sounded in Dennis' ear. He wasn't sure if Horatio had disconnected or terminated their discussion, but he knew that both of them would be busy regardless if the other spoke.

Dennis was not someone who got excited about cars, bikes, heavy machinery, or anything which had a particularly loud noise. But he had to admit he had largely enjoyed the ride, and the booming reverberating sound that his motorbike screamed out. He could feel the vibrations all through his body, and it reacted to his every whim at the slightest touch. He had decided that he would endeavour to look after it, and should both of them survive what was expected to happen, then he would name it as well. Dennis became easily aware that there was next to no traffic on the roads despite it being early on a Saturday morning. Usually there would be cars going in each direction as kids went to Saturday sport, or families set about their weekend rituals and tasks. Perhaps the residents had also got wind of what was happening. Either way it made his job easier.

It also gave him a glimpse of the beautiful streets at their most controlled. Every other side street was filled with trees and older style homes. In the late autumn days Orange really claimed its name as the colour city. Every colour that you could think of was on display, from vibrant purples and reds, to the browns, oranges and yellows as the leaves prepared to fall, and the constant greens that remained resolute despite the drop in the weather. On a day with less happening Dennis would probably have slowed down to admire the sight. Of all his unique traits, stopping to enjoy the little things was always something that he made time to do.

Another day perhaps, he thought.

Dennis rode his bike right up to the front door of the police station. In accepting this role, and the information he had received from Horatio, he had finally accepted that the ideals that he held onto usually, had to be rested somewhat. Dennis took great care in making sure the bike was in a spot where he could easily jump on and drive away quickly. He also ensured that it was locked and standing safely on its stand. Then he walked over and knocked on the door.

Dennis could see inside, and watched as the single police officer sat and watched him. The sliding door did not open, nor did the officer make any attempt to open it. Dennis stood in all his Wrangler clothing. He knocked politely again. The officer once more did nothing, neither allowing him to come inside nor telling him to leave. Dennis rapped his knuckles one more time. He didn't expect any difference in reaction, and he didn't receive it. He simply acknowledged that Horatio had most likely been right and something was wrong at the police station. Dennis looked up at the sliding door and analysed it briefly. He resolved that he could remove it without much effort, and then proceeded to do so. It took no longer than thirty seconds and the officer made no attempt to stop him or to seek help. Dennis placed the door to one side and took half a step beyond the door. Dennis looked up and saw a camera there pointing in his direction. He was not concerned that it saw him, but he was suspicious.

"Finder?" he whispered seemingly to himself. He had resolved to use Horatio's code name whenever he was within his disguise and where other people could possibly hear him.

"Yes sir?" the snap and crackle appeared back in his ear.

"I am standing in the doorway of the Orange Local Command," Dennis continued almost silently. "There is a camera on me. Can you see me?" There was no sound for a moment, as Dennis assumed Horatio was checking.

"No Wrangler I cannot," his friend replied. "Nor on any others, despite the fact that they are on and I am receiving a feed. That can't be good. I will see what I can do."

"I will try and do the same," Dennis replied. He expected the worst but decided that he would show nothing but confidence. The male officer looked at him. Dennis had suspected that he may have been unconscious or drugged by his lack of action, but he was very much conscious. Immobilised with fear was probably more accurate.

"Can I help you?" the officer asked as Dennis came closer.

"I sure hope so," Dennis replied and looked nonchalant around the room. He turned back to look directly at the officer. Perhaps he was an intruder. The long beads of sweat that ran freely from his brow suggested that he was real, and so was his terror. "But perhaps I might be able to help you first."

"I don't understand," the officer replied, trying his hardest to remain composed throughout the exchange.

"I will make it obvious," Dennis informed. He could feel some of his old school tendencies return from when he used to deal with upstarts at difficult schools, or jerks in everyday situations. "I suspect that something is happening in this place, and my intention is to go through every room and help out. But first I need you to show me the way." Dennis had spoken hard at the officer. Usually he would no doubt feel safe as he sat behind a strong Perspex glass wall and was a button press away from help. He shouldn't have been as scared of Dennis as he projected. The officer looked straight at Dennis and held his gaze. A moment later, and only for the briefest of easily, missable moments, the officer's eyes shot down to his feet. It was all the prompt that Dennis needed. He leaned down below the counter where a plaster board wall held up all above it. Dennis drew one hand back and punched straight through it. His hand fumbled about for a second as it searched, and then found, something that didn't belong. As soon as he had a grip Dennis pulled hard, destroying the remaining portion of wall as he pulled forth someone who had no reason to be there. Dennis was not surprised in the military-like attire that the person bore. It was all too similar to the garb that those who had destroyed his mother's house had worn.

A garbled yell and the click of a weapon were the sounds that were heard before Dennis slammed the man into the brick wall at his side. The man slid down the lower part of it and crumpled to the ground. Dennis had no doubt that he had broken several bones in the man's body, but nor did he care. He retrieved his weapon and threw it across to the stunned officer.

"How many are there?" Dennis whispered.

"Too many," the officer replied weakly, barely able to comprehend what just happened.

"Where?" Dennis said with an edge.

"Everywhere," the officer replied and found a little bit more courage. "Many of the officers have been placed in the holding areas. Some are being kept in the carpark underneath. The command centre was taken quickly, I don't know who by. If they hear a noise then who knows what will happen."

"I can help," Horatio's voice sprung to life again. "I have hacked back into the cameras, sorry that it took a while. Someone really didn't want anyone else to see what was happening there. I can tell you where they are so you can sneak in and remove as many as possible. I also have an idea when you get to the holding areas. Listen to my instructions and we should be fine. Ready?"

"Stay here," Dennis ordered the lone officer, "make sure no-one touches my bike."

"Left door," Horatio told him. Dennis obeyed.

"Ready," Dennis declared quietly.

"Good, three in the first corridor as soon as you are in. All side rooms are empty. All three are armed. Go," Horatio revealed. Dennis pulled the lock clear of the hinge as he started his siege. Apart from the initial door he slunk through quietly. Knowing the extent of who was inside was a great relief. He was behind the first in a heartbeat and, after slapping the man stiffly in the jaw, discarded his body in a vacant side room. The second and third were easily spotted just a little further on. Neither were aware of the breach and sat around waiting for some direction. Both were easily dispatched by Dennis and likewise dumped in an adjoining room.

"Cleared, next?" Dennis whispered.

"There are three more on your floor and that is it. The rest, and I count there to be at least a dozen, are all occupying areas where they are keeping hostages. They are a floor down. The three remaining are in the room furthest away from you," Horatio informed. Dennis silently made his way across the space. He imagined that this would be easier if he wasn't so tall, but he also realised that he should probably be complaining about back pain as well. Think about what was going on, he told himself.

This door wasn't locked. He opened the door swiftly, stepped through, allowed his figure to take up most of the space, frightened the occupants who did not belong there, and three strong punches later left the intruders piled on the floor.

"Next?"

"The stairs along the west wall lead down to the holding area. There is a guard in front of each cell, three are hidden behind the desked area, and two more are in the office behind. Stealth won't get you to all of them, speed will be your friend here. I suggest getting to the guards first and then taking out the rest. If they call for help you will have to act fast though. I have an idea, but you will have to go through the door next to the elevator to access the parking garage," Horatio finished.

"Is that all?" Dennis chuckled to himself and then took a deep breath. He was confident that he wouldn't be harmed, but he wished he could say the same for the captured officers.

"No, we are running out of time," Horatio added.

"Thanks friend," Dennis groaned. He mentally counted to three and then jumped down the flights of stairs. He felt like a lion as he entered the small area. His speed almost made him fall as he twisted and turned through the space. He heard them shout as he appeared. He took little notice of the sounds that followed. He drove his shoulder into the first intruder, altered course marginally to drive into the second and third. All the guards were taken care of but Dennis wasn't finished. He dumped all three bodies over the desk which threw the occupants into disorder. Dennis cleared the space and jumped through the glass into the next room. It shattered in all directions, as did the intruders who had hidden there. Dennis closed the gaps and after a moment of frenzied strikes he stood alone amidst wails and groans.

"The door straight ahead," Horatio yelped into his ear. "Quickly, and close your eyes as you go through." Dennis ignored the pain in his ears, and the cries of the officers who remained locked behind closed doors, and obeyed. They would be safer there for the moment. He reached the door and it opened easily before him. He closed his eyes as instructed. The shades of light behind his eyelids faded from bright yellow, orange and red, and into darkness. The lights were gone and confused murmurs replaced them. Dennis carried himself towards those sounds preparing to go on the attack again.

"Keep them closed," said the voice in his ear. Dennis obeyed and was grateful. All the lights had been turned back on. But with an additional hit of electricity. The result was a blinding light and the sound of popping as several bulbs burst unable to contain the extra energy. Dennis smiled and then, while gazing firmly at the ground, he opened his eyes and made his presence known. It took less than a minute to dispatch all that were there. Many of the remaining lights exploded, unable to continue absorbing the energy that flowed through them, adding to the confusion. The security lights were turned on, adding to the minute shafts of light which appeared from gaps in the building that lead outside. Cheers started to sound from the officers he had rescued. Dennis understood their glee and happiness, but he would have none of it.

"Quiet," he demanded, and to his surprise all fell silent. "This isn't over, there is far more to do and I need your help." One of them, a senior officer Dennis supposed, stepped forward and addressed Dennis. "Did I lose anyone?" Dennis whispered so no one could hear him.

"All intruders are accounted for. All appear injured, not deceased. The police contingent are safe and all relatively unharmed, from what I can gather, but to be honest I haven't checked the whole building. I was happy to help, but don't expect this next time."

"Thank you young man," the senior officer said, "they overran us so quickly, we are sorry. The local area command does not operate like this."

"Well it is time to make up for it then," Dennis addressed the man as if he was one of his students. "Your city needs you. Get everyone you can, send most of them towards the showground, there is about to be a whole lot of trouble there. Then send the rest to help ease the disturbances which are happening all around the town. You should get some assistance shortly from extra police from other regions."

"Of course, all that I can manage will be called in. The local command will move out and start to deal with the problems," the officer obeyed, showing how he still felt foolish for what had happened. "Where will you be?"

"I will be helping you elsewhere," Dennis explained. "If I need your help, or if you need mine, my friend will be in touch. I will try to be everywhere. I don't think anyone is going to forget what is happening here today. I trust you and your people to help resolve this."

"I'll help, sure thing," Horatio blurted into his ear, "but you don't have time for this." Dennis turned around, preparing to run back to his bike.

"But what do we call you?" the senior officer shouted.

"You can call me the Wrangler," Dennis called back, hiding his distaste in referring to the name, but in the next second he was gone.

With the police force active it took some of the weight from the shoulders of Dennis. He was confident that they could deal with the problems that were arising. He hated micromanaging people and was sure that he could turn his attention to more important matters without having to watch his back from this point forward.

"I am not joking about the time," Horatio spoke into his ear again. It was only a few blocks from the police station to the shopping centre that Horatio had outlined. "We will be cutting it fine to help out here and then make it out to the airport."

"Has anything happened at the airport yet?" Dennis asked.

"Not yet," Horatio replied. "I would bet any moment now though, otherwise they will be cutting it fine too, and all this nonsense in town would be useless. Too many annoying, yet valuable, resources would be wasted. Both the showground and the shopping centre have shown an increase in activity. The mall has communicated a small explosion in its centre portion. Several masked assailants have appeared. They are shouting. Many of the occupants are fleeing but some remain."

"How many bad guys?" Dennis asked.

"Bad guys?" Horatio sniggered slightly. "It's good to see that you are finally taking this seriously."

"Well, what else do I call them when in a hurry?" Dennis called back. "I don't know their individual names. How are Flynn, Corben, Angus and Noah looking as they attack? Perhaps tell me how Zoe, Ruby, and Lacey are planning to harm others."

"Good point, interesting use of names too, bad guys it is. I count no more than ten, and they are all together, although they are still spread out. By the time you get to one the others will either flee, or have time to do who knows what else," Horatio informed him. "The showground has also shown an increase an activity, but I can see that multiple police units are inward bound to the scene now. Get in and get out quickly, Wrangler."

The duration of this conversation, however brief, was all that occupied the time taken from the police station to the shopping centre. Dennis could see the large double doors that opened into the complex ahead of him, and through them he saw a constant stream of people who fled for their lives and out into the streets. The roar of his bike gave him a fair bit of attention, the growl of his voice allowed him to be granted a divide in which he could enter quickly. The screaming of those people almost covered the sound of his bike, but not completely. The bellowing thump of his engine was powerful enough to make everyone think twice as he surged forward.

"It's the Wrangler," a lady in the crowd called out, seemingly identifying Dennis as he sped past. More people accompanied her cries in both amazement and relief. Whooping and cheering replaced the cries that he had heard. Dennis wasn't sure how to feel about the recognition. It seemed at the very least to aid the people in removing some of their anxiety. Dennis had no time to think or dwell on it now. These people weren't the only ones who recognised him.

"Here he comes," a loud brutish voice belted out. "Take him down in whatever way you can." Dennis smiled. His intent was never to hurt anyone, or even to throw the first punch, as he was never certain that it was the right course of action. He felt that after the big guy's acclamation that he was pretty safe with whatever actions he took. Dennis didn't slow down his bike, driving it straight toward the man who had made the call. He hoped that this was a case of cowardice, where if he took the main person down then the rest would surrender. The big guy glared at him, but didn't move as he approached. Dennis saw a gun get pulled clear from under the man's overcoat and pointed in his direction. Then it was fired. The loud rattling from an ammunition clip being emptied echoed through the area, accompanied by more screaming from frightened civilians as they searched for cover. Dennis kept his head down and charged.

Thump.

The bike slammed into the big guy and sent him sailing into the wall behind him. Dennis watched to see if he would get up, but he was well and truly out of the fight. Unfortunately others were not. There were still a few who surrounded Dennis, too far away to cover them all before they overcame him. It was time to put his tools to the test. His whip came free and he swept it over his head in one massive arc. The whirring of the cord and the snap as it struck was terrifying without Dennis adding his own presence, strength and skill. He let it revolve for a second time, attracting all the attention of those around him. Then he struck. Snap, crack, bang. Prompt and direct strokes downed three more in an instant.

The fourth who had stood against him started retreating, fleeing straight toward a nearby crowd. Dennis feared what he would do once he reached the people there, and he was too far away for his whip to reach easily. He switched his whip into his left hand and removed the hat from his head. Dennis held the edge firmly between his thumb and two additional fingers, took one step forward, and flung his hat towards the villain. It covered the space quickly, making a noise as deadly sounding as his whip had. It covered the ground almost instantly and struck the target square in the shoulder. Dennis heard the sound as it struck the man, sinking deep into his flesh and impacting on bone, shattering the joint in the man's arm as he fell to the floor whimpering. Dennis looked around quickly and noticed the rest of the would-be bandits were no more than school students. They had no stomach to stand up to the Wrangler, and Dennis had no idea about how they had been brought into this scheme. They all cried under his gaze and turned to run for any exit they could reach. He let them go, allowing the suddenly active security presence to give chase instead.

"Well done," Horatio spoke into his ear again. "I think you have got a good eye for this."

"Shut up," Dennis barked. He regathered his hat, strung the whip back into its holster and returned to his bike. "Tell me what is happening." Dennis started the engine, revving it loudly within the halls of the shopping complex, regretfully leaving a giant black mark as his rear wheel revolved violently on the polished white tiles, and shot off towards the nearest exit.

"It's a mix of good and bad news I'm afraid," Horatio confirmed ruefully. "Police from other areas have started to arrive and are slowly starting to deal with the smaller incidents plaguing the city. The local area command has made its presence known at the showground and are taking control of the situation. But. . ."

"But?" Dennis questioned as his bike shot free from the corridors of the shopping centre. He turned toward the road that would lead him towards the airport, however, he slowed his bike just in case he needed to divert somewhere else.

"But that red haired woman, I'm sure it is Assumpta Green, has appeared there as well. Her goons are accompanying her and a riot has broken out," Horatio explained.

"Jiemba?" Dennis queried after his friend.

"Not present from what I can see," Horatio confirmed, "but regardless you are out of time. As much as you want to help them, and I would like to have a conversation with Miss Green, there is activity at the airport. You are needed there immediately. No matter what happens you need to get out there and make sure that those very important people arrive safely. I haven't seen young Jet anywhere yet, but I would put money on it that he is out there. Don't stop for anything, everything else can be dealt with later."

Dennis gritted his teeth. "I will back you on this," he said. "I sort of have too. You haven't led me astray yet, and I probably should have trusted you earlier. I guess what I am also trying to say is. . ." Dennis began to make his apology that he had attempted once already, and provide the confirmation that he now acknowledged what Horatio was saying, when he was cut off abruptly. The roads were once again almost empty and Dennis found no difficulty in speeding along to his next destination.

"Hang on," Horatio interrupted, "I hear something. It's coming from outside. Something is wrong here."

"Hang on, Finder, I will be there in a moment," Dennis was suddenly panicked, where only moments before he had become supremely confident in his new abilities.

"No, don't," Horatio yelled back at him. "I said don't change target for any reason. Even me, I . . ." The transmission clicked and the feed ended.

"Finder?" Dennis queried, receiving no response. "FINDER," he roared. His bike came to a bridge which stretched over several railway lines. Dennis brought his bike to a screeching halt and stared over the nearby trees in the direction where Horatio's house stood. He could feel his heart beat faster than it had ever done before. His brain was rolling through a thousand scenarios of what action he should take next. He doubted each scenario until finally one was confirmed.

Boom.

A massive blast shattered the silent sky, followed by a rising plume of smoke and fire. Dennis had no question about where it had come from, as he had been starring in a straight line directly at it. There was no doubt that the blast had come from Horatio's home. The cloud grew larger and larger in the sky, polluting the serene blue that had existed there before hand. There was no secondary blast, nor sounds of other activity. It was over as soon as it had begun.

"FINDER!" he howled.

Dennis felt his stomach drop. His head dropped as if the motion was going to help him release the vice that had gripped at his heart. His breathing became irregular as his body went into shock. His vision blurred as tears rolled freely down his face, after drenching his lids. He sniffed loudly and ignored everything else.

No matter what happened, the memory of his friend's voice called out to him. He lifted his eyes finally, smeared the tears using the back of his right hand. His left had removed his hat, in a sign of respect. When he returned it he wore the desperate and angry look of someone whose soul was in distress. He grappled the throttle aggressively and tore through his thick back tyre.

"Thank you," he growled out loud. "I'm so sorry." Dennis released his brakes and took off down the street. "Nothing can make up for what has just happened," he continued. "But I know something that might help."

Dennis headed straight towards his target.

Nothing was going to stand in his way. It was a promise that he had made to a friend, one of the best he had ever had.

Nothing and nobody.

CHAPTER 17 - THE LOST CAUSE

Dennis had his head down. He could see just underneath the rim of his hat as he took yet another corner over the crest of another hill. There was no one using this road, but that was the norm of the route not the exception. Farmland surrounded the road on all sides. At one point there was a large water catchment area with several visible dams flowing down by way of a creek. On the other there was green pasture that was being enjoyed by several varieties of cow.

Dennis had a friend who had lived out this way once, he had also been someone who had dreams of being a teacher. That friend had long since left the area, but regardless Dennis still knew the road as if he had travelled it only minutes before.

His bike bounced as he dipped down into another small valley. He was not concerned, he was getting close now. His mind swam with all sorts of information, his brain analysed many more scenarios and situations, and his heart pumped with all manner of emotions. The trip out had been slower than he would have initially desired, but he took more time to resume control. An erratic version of himself was far less useful than a knowledgeable and practical version.

One more bend and he saw the flat paddocks in which the Orange airport stood. A windsock appeared before him, showing that he was at the far end of the airstrip. The road followed around the perimeter fence until it arrived at the airport's main entrance. Despite its importance the premise was not massive. A car park big enough to hold a hundred or so cars appeared just beyond an old brick gateway, and the recently renovated building stood just behind it. There were more cars than usual, but if Horatio had been correct then there should have been a great deal more people expected to greet the next plane, and to exit from it.

Horatio. Dennis blinked back a tear, and settled his body that was tense with the memory of his friend. His friend whom was no longer around to help him. Dennis would have greatly desired to have his voice in his ear now; because he was his friend but also because his insight was invaluable. Dennis would have to do this next part on his own.

Dennis casually rolled his bike in through the gates and knew that he was being watched immediately. He slowly guided his bike to a vacant spot, and it purred under his touch. He had enjoyed how much power and speed it had given him, but also appreciated the vehicle when it was under spoken as well. When this was all over he hoped that he could take it for a long ride. The destination of that ride was not important.

He kicked a stand out and gently let his bike slump down upon it. The bike was heavier than most, so Dennis had no concern that someone else would take it, but he still had no desire to scratch it any more than he had already done.

"Can I help you?" a softly spoken voice asked from next to Dennis. He had noticed the appearance of the two guards but had paid them little notice.

"I'm just here to meet a friend," Dennis replied simply. He smiled warmly and spread a hand across his moustache, pinching its edge and curling it slightly. It was uncommon to be met in the carpark. In fact it was uncommon to be spoken to at all at the airport. Your task was usually just to get in, wait patiently, and then get on your plane. The process was not so hard. He understood that things should be different when the

Prime Minister was coming, but Dennis had no idea what that process looked like or if these people who had appeared were part of that entourage or actually imposters. "It seems to be busy today," Dennis continued, "I am happy to wait at the fence if the inside of the terminal is too crowded."

One of the pair, a young female, returned his smile. "Of course," she said, turning and beckoning him to follow her. It appeared like she was going to lead him to the spot he had mentioned.

"I don't need an escort," Dennis informed them, he followed along politely anyway. He also understood that a person as tall as he was, looking like he was, who just left one of the most impressive bikes ever seen, was probably intimidating. She didn't seem intimidated though, which meant, that if she was anyone who had read the news or watched television, that she was aware of who the Wrangler was.

"I insist," the female replied. She smiled at him as she showed him the way. Her partner, who was a young man but had showed Dennis nothing but a scowl when she had offered a smile, followed along behind them. Dennis noticed that despite his professional suit and clothing that he walked as if he had just had a long session at the gym and wanted everyone to see his results. His upper body was rigid as he flexed his arms and chest outwards in a dominating display. Dennis, regardless of his own appearance, laughed at the actions.

"Why do you insist?" Dennis asked subduing his joy.

"No doubt you have heard that there are some important people coming to the region today," the lady spoke easily.

"Really?" Dennis looked shocked. "I had no idea. Who?"

"I can't reveal who," she told him shrugging off the notion with a shake of her head and her accompanying smile. "But I can tell you that the Mayor of Orange, and the local member will be here to greet them."

"Mr Egg?" Dennis questioned. He had finally made it to the fence which stood as a barrier between a small grassed area and the black bitumen of the tarmac.

"Yes, Mr Egg," she replied. "I am one of his secretaries."

"Oh really?" Dennis smiled. He switched his gaze from her, then towards the runway and then the sky. There was no sign of a plane having already arrived or on course for a landing. He still had a little bit of time at least. "I knew his children once. How is his eldest? William. I heard his business is doing well overseas." The lady who claimed to be the secretary smiled at Dennis. He saw her eyes narrow at the question.

"William is doing fine," her male counterpart provided the answer. "And Mr Egg claims that his business is doing quite well. He speaks about him often." For the first time the male in the suit smiled at Dennis.

Dennis smiled back heartily. Then swiftly punched him in the face.

The man's whole body flung back and struck the grass hard. He made no show or sound that the impact had hurt as he was out cold before he hit the ground. Dennis ducked as a leg swept towards his face. He suspected it wouldn't have hurt but his reflexes were so focused it was entirely instinct. His hand shot out at the same moment as the woman clasped at a hidden microphone attached to her wrist. Dennis crushed it.

"You're not a secretary, are you?" he questioned, still smiling at her. She brought her hand up and punched him in the jaw. He felt bone break under the impact, but it wasn't his, it was hers. She dropped down to her knees clutching at her hand and wrist which had shattered as they struck him. But she wasn't finished. She swung a leg low, attempting to trip him or injure him. It failed. Dennis merely stepped over the attempt, but brought his foot down to stomp on her ankle. Again the bone broke. She attempted to scream but Dennis grabbed her cheeks and held on firmly.

"Enough of that," he warned. "Now you will answer me with a nod, or I will break something else. Do you understand?" She nodded. "Good. Now, how many are there?" He received nothing. "Sorry," Dennis slapped his head with his other palm. "You need yes or no questions, my mistake. Are there more than a dozen of you?" A nod. "More than twenty?" Again a nod. "Less than thirty though?" Nod. "Okay, have you taken the minister and his entourage hostage?" Nod. "Are they inside the terminal?" Nod. "Armed?" Nod. Dennis thought for a moment. That was a lot of people to help with a lot of people standing in the way. Another thought occurred to him. "Is there a young man that goes by the name of Jet among you?" He received a look of confusion. He squeezed her mouth as a warning and then let go. "I don't know all the names," she admitted. "But we have multiple leaders inside, and people who are stronger than you."

"I doubt that," Dennis replied, letting a small hint of bravado show.

"And there is one other, I don't know him, he is new. But he calls himself the Hitman," she said. She alternated between rubbing her hand, ankle and face. Of course he calls himself that, Dennis thought to himself.

"I don't hold with violence against women, or anyone else for that matter. I hate people getting hurt for no good reason," Dennis explained to her. "But you and your friends are not nice people. You intend to harm others, and," Dennis paused. "You killed my friend." He paused again. "When this is finished be grateful that I only broke your ankle." He looked down at her feeble form, and that of her unconscious friend and left them there. He walked over towards the main doors. Again he appeared casual but he felt nervous.

The majority of the terminal was mostly glass, with the exception of the side walls near the outside fence that were solid rendered concrete. From inside you could see everything happening in the carpark from one side of the building, and from the other you could see all the activity on the landing strip. Dennis knew that whoever was inside could see him as he entered the building. He also suspected that if Jet was among them then they were aware of what he was capable of. The big sliding doors opened wide for him. And he ventured inside.

"Well, that escalated quickly," Dennis voiced as he discovered what awaited him. The inside of the terminal was a massive open space. Vending machines lined one wall, toilet facilities occupied another along with access to the runway past a series of desks and security devices. Chairs were spread out throughout the remainder of the complex. Apart from large stone pillars there was nothing else to see, normally.

Today, right now, there was a large group of people who occupied one corner. They huddled together there, hands on heads as they kneeled helplessly on the floor. The rest of the space was filled with people who did not appear to be friendly. They looked familiar to him, as they wore the same garbed uniform and carried the same equipment; each of them had some sort of heavy machine gun or handgun pointed straight at him. At least all of the people he had come to rescue were off to one side. Dennis glanced from one foe to the next; analysing size, shape, percentage of risk to him and a whole range of other factors. His head told him that he shouldn't be in this situation, that he was a teacher and everything that he had just walked into was wrong, was dangerous, and despite having to do with him was likely to get him captured or killed. His heart said otherwise. His heart said that this was something that he had to do. His heart told him that he was the only one who could and despite everything else he knew he had to. His heart also told him that there weren't enough to stop him.

What a frightening thought, for so many reasons, Dennis told himself. Then he spoke before anyone else could.

"I just thought I would ask you guys a couple of things," Dennis started, with a small smirk on his face which he covered with his hand and he stroked his thick moustache. "The first is, I don't like violence, so, if any of you are like me and you don't want to get involved with a fight now is the time to leave." No one moved, but nor did Dennis expect any of them to. "No one, okay. Next, formalities. I will introduce myself. I am the Wrangler, and at any point if you need to go to the bathroom they are over there." He pointed in the direction of the facilities and noted how the group reacted to his movements. He took a careful step forward which was followed by every weapon, but none fired. "Does anyone want to tell me their name?" Again silence. "Okay, that's fine, we won't use names," Dennis continued. "I would have forgotten them anyway and just started calling everyone mate. The last thing is, I was wondering if you could give me a bit of help. You see I brought the wrong thing here," both of Dennis' weapons were concealed beneath his jacket and unable to be seen by all those around him. Dennis had been slowly making his way forward into a space where he could easily use them without concern of striking a hostage or a pillar. He was convinced he was in that space. They surrounded him. At no point had they attempted to talk to him; to persuade him to leave or to motion him into the corner with the others. They knew what he was there for, and they had prepared for it to some degree, without really knowing what he was capable of. It was time to show them.

"Stupidly, I missed the meeting, and I brought a whip to a gunfight," Dennis told them. As he finished the statement his body was thrown into motion. As soon as his hand was clear of his jacket the whip he held was being swung hard around his head. Gunfire exploded into the air around him aimed at the spot where he had stood; the spot that Dennis had leapt away from almost as quickly as he had drawn his weapon. Bullets darted past him, striking the door behind him and shattering the glass instantly. It disintegrated spectacularly with an entire sheet buckling under its own weight and collapsing noisily to the ground.

Dennis found that he had been told the truth. He counted close to two dozen adversaries within the terminal. Not all attacked him at once, choosing to invoke some resemblance of strategy as they kept moving forward and back in and out of a suitable position. It made it easier to count. Dennis moved faster than his opponents, but that didn't mean the gunfire was any less dangerous. He felt the impact as bullets found his jacket and ricocheted from the rim on his hat. His speed was key in him taking down all who opposed him, and he did it with ferocity. The whip shot forward in an arc from Dennis' side. It collected weapons and body parts as it whistled through the air. The second wave swept past at head height. Dennis felt the vibrations in his hand as it struck solid bone in its path. In the first two swings he had removed half of the danger either by removing the weapons that searched for him or by staggering his assailants with a multitude of wounds. He dropped his whip and moved forward in a blur, punching, kicking and throwing all in his wake. His jacket flicked out behind him like a rogue breeze from a tornado. Each strike that he threw resulted in another person exiting the fight. There were men and women who opposed him in the group, almost equally numbered, and he dealt with them all the same. A scream erupted in front of him as one foe tried to block one punch with his forearm, the bone almost wrapped around Dennis' hand as it collapsed under his force. He dodged a kick, grabbed the leg and swung that person hard into their companion. Both were down and wailing. The next person came forth received a hard driving kick and was sent straight into a vending machine; the plastic advertising shattered and a shower of energy drinks rained down on their collapsed body. He punched one into the roof, tackled another into one of the concrete pillars. He whirled around jumping from one to another. A moment later he stopped and found that he was breathing heavily. There were three opponents remaining, and each of them stood near the corner, pointing the guns they wielded in the direction of the hostages.

"Make one move, just one," one of the soldiers remaining threatened. "And you will be responsible for the death of the hostages." Dennis contemplated how quick he could make the space between them, but he wouldn't be fast enough to stop a bullet if it fired in that time. He looked around at the scene of carnage that he had unleashed, the pile of bodies piled around or limping for cover appalling for any to see. To his eye no one had been killed by his hand, though he hadn't been around to check on any of them. A moment ago he had been unstoppable, now he seemed to be almost out of options.

Almost.

"I surrender," Dennis declared raising his hands harmlessly out in front of himself. The action itself seemed to shock not only the guards that were left but the captives they stood over.

"Open your jacket," one of them demanded, knowing that although the whip had been discarded it had appeared from underneath the clothing. The small sword clung to the small of his back, the handle hanging loose from Dennis' left hip. "That sword," the guard continued. "Place it on the ground and kick it over to me. No funny business or we will shoot them and you." Dennis moved one hand slowly and retrieved the weapon. As he pulled it free he noticed how many dints and marks there were all over his jacket. Clearly he had been hit numerous times under the onslaught of those villains inside the terminal. He hadn't felt a thing and had naively thought that he had been so fast that he had been untouchable. A stupid thought, and one that he would remember.

Dennis pulled the sword forth and placed it delicately on the ground. The guard motioned for Dennis to kick it carefully over, and said as much to him. "Kick it over, nice and easy, and then put your hands on your head and get to the ground."

"As you wish," Dennis accepted the demand, clicking a single button as he removed his hands from it. He slid the sword slowly over the tiled ground and moved to the floor with hands on his head. The guard who had the demands, and appeared to be in charge of the other two, clearly did not trust Dennis. He motioned for one of the others to move forward and retrieve the blade from where Dennis had kicked it just short of them. The second man walked forth and stepped into the weapon.

Dennis immediately reacted.

The sword had been switched to its electrified setting. As soon as the second guard had touched it he had been jolted with a serious amount of electricity, immediately becoming incapacitated and falling momentarily paralysed to the floor. Dennis had flicked his fingers along the edge of his hat and swung it from the top of his head. It whirred through the air to strike the last guard across the bridge of his nose, scuttling him backwards to slam against the wall. The guard who had been in charge looked shocked by what was happening, unsure of who to help or how to act next. Dennis leapt to his feet and charged straight at him. He hollered loudly as he approached, trying to draw all of the man's attention. Dennis took three steps and then finished with one swift punch. The man flew backwards, breaking the toilet door as he slammed straight through it.

Suddenly there was silence. Dennis ignored those that he had released for a moment as he retrieved his whip, his sword, and his hat. He walked around quickly and ensured that none of those that lay strewn across the floor would be a threat to anyone, and then promptly made his way over to the group.

"Is anyone hurt?" Dennis asked the group. Some were obviously traumatised at what had befallen them, others were too afraid to respond to the giant ruffian who had saved them. "Is anyone injured?" he asked again.

"No, we are all fine," one of the men stood up gingerly, "thanks to you. Who were those people?" Dennis knew the older man to be the Mayor of Orange, and as he rose to his feet and asked the question he helped others as well.

"Your guess is as good as mine," Dennis replied, also assisting some of the people as he checked for any who were seriously hurt. "I can only assume what they were here to do."

"That seems rather obvious," a tall man said stepping forward. Dennis knew him to be the local member. Dennis kept his head down, as they had met before, to avoid him having a guess at his identity. "We have to call the attendants of the Prime Minister and inform them immediately."

"An attempt has already been made, but it is my understanding that something is happening to block communications within the plane," Dennis explained and watched as Mr Egg withdrew his phone and attempted to make the call anyway. A moment later he removed the device confirming what Dennis had said.

"No good," the minister remarked. "What are we supposed to do now?"

"I will have to stop this here, and ensure that the Prime Minister arrives safely," Dennis told them.

"Well, we could help you," Mr Egg said, walking bravely forward. "There are only a few of them left." Those around him seemed less happy about the idea, in particular those that Dennis deemed to be security personnel.

"Thank you, but no," Dennis replied. He looked away out the window expecting the plane to land at any moment. "It is too dangerous. I don't want to place anyone else at risk. I don't know what they have in store for that plane, or anyone who steps foot on that tarmac." Dennis couldn't even see anybody moving out there. "There is at least one of them who I might not be able to stop." The group seemed both relieved at his dismissal, but also taken aback that someone could be more dangerous.

"We can't just sit here and do nothing," the mayor stepped forward. "There must be something we can do."

"There is," Dennis admitted and pointed to those that he had disabled which lay all over the place. "Make sure that all of these fools don't go anywhere. Tie them up or lock them in a room for all I care. Then get onto the police. They have been busy this whole time, but if they have anyone they can spare then get them out here."

"What are you going to do?" one of the other hostages asked.

"Whatever I can," Dennis replied confidently. He left them without a second thought. They should be capable of dealing with a group of imposters, who were all either injured or unconscious. Their weapons had already been removed from them and the threat that remained was tiny. He hoped that should any police arrive then they could render the captives with some more assistance.

Dennis walked through the area that normally would have been the security and quarantine space. Lights flashed and alarms went off as he walked through the metal detector. He didn't slow. The tinted glass doors slid away to reveal the bright day beyond. He could see four figures out on the runway, all of which had been hidden from view by a baggage collector transport. They turned and saw him; all wearing matching suits to the pair that he had incapacitated in the carpark area. They appeared to be waiting for the incoming plane but as soon as they saw Dennis they abandoned the idea. They turned and started to run perpendicular to Dennis, in a direction that would take them to one of the hangers nearby. Dennis had no idea what they intended, but regardless he knew he must stop them. As he turned to pursue he realised that Jet was not with them, when he was informed that he should have been.

The thought came too late.

Thump! A blow came from a blind spot to his right. Dennis felt every bit of it as he was knocked from his feet and fell to the ground. The bumps from the ground were minimal and not worth thinking about, the initial hit had done some damage. He was quickly feeling his face with one hand as his instincts told him to move. He rolled to the side as another blow came for him; only just missing but slamming and crushing the concrete below him where he had lain a moment before. Dennis sprung to his feet and turned to face the person who had struck him. There was only one person it could have been.

"I knew that you would be here," Jet told Dennis as he walked closer. The youth was also dressed in a handsome custom suit, the same one that he had worn at their last meeting. Despite everything that had happened Dennis still had to admit that the young man looked the part. His long blonde hair which had appeared like a mullet at their first meeting was tied neatly into a ponytail at the back of his head. His shoes were polished, his jacket and slacks pressed, and his metal accessories sparkled with care shown. Jet smiled his most dashing grin toward Dennis; displaying his confidence at the power he was displaying in that moment.

Dennis felt his hands slick with blood at the blow he had been delivered. Jet had a couple of new accessories. On each hand he wore steal moulds with the knuckles showing huge bulges that could do some damage.

"I knew that they were incapable of dealing with you," Jet continued. His smile was so deceiving that it fooled Dennis into inaction. Jet surged forth, fainted to his left and then struck hard with his right hand. The blow was thrown into Dennis' guts where he doubled over, trying to keep his eyes on the young man. "I didn't know that someone who claimed to be nothing but a teacher, someone who wanted to help those around him at all times, could be the biggest problem to this organisation."

"Organisation?" Dennis questioned as he fought for breath. "I thought you were a leader not a follower."

"You are right, sir," Jet agreed. "Don't think that I haven't learned from you. Initially when you arrived I saw a threat, someone who was there to upset everything that my life was about. But then I realised that you had actually allowed me to see. To see those who were using me, to see those who were holding me back. The possibilities are endless now," Jet threw another punch into Dennis' face, knocking him to his knees and gasping for oxygen. Jet continued. "I feel like you and I are so similar, you were just the version of me that was holding me back. I have surpassed you. I don't need you anymore. You are a bump in the road, and after today the possibilities, as I said, will be endless."

"Whoever this organisation is, you never told them who I was," Dennis said as he staggered to his feet. "Why? They could have taken me out in my sleep."

"That is true," Jet admitted, allowing Dennis to stagger in front of him. "There were times when I could have done that myself too."

"Why didn't you?" Dennis continued. Jet hesitated. It seemed like he was trying to decide whether he should say anymore.

"I don't know," he said finally. "I think I always had some respect for you. I have been told for a long time that I was no good. That I would never amount to anything. That I was a lost cause. All of that hurt so much. Then you came along. I knew you were just like the others, but no matter what I threw your way you just absorbed it with a smile. I wanted to prove that I was better than you, and oddly it had to be in a fair contest. I was compared to you, which, as much as I didn't like the idea, meant that we were similar. If I was like you then you were like me. I found that I kept learning, kept finding ways to be better. That has led me here. I wouldn't be here, be the person who I am without you. I can't deny it, but after today I won't have to live with it anymore." Jet smiled at Dennis. "There is just one more thing left to do and only one person who is standing in my way. It ends now."

The onslaught began. Dennis had recovered enough after his surprise blow to react. His stalling tactics had been necessary as it gave him the time he needed to endure what was to come. Jet thought that after he had landed some easy strikes that the rest of his assault would be easy. It wouldn't. He lunged forward with a bunch which should have landed, but missed. Dennis ducked, swept a leg, and knocked Jet to the ground. Unlike his previous opponents Jet was back on his feet in an instant. The metal fists sliced through the air as they swung toward Dennis. Jet got in close, missed the target twice allowing Dennis an opportunity after a side step to slide back in and slam down with an elbow. Jet didn't let up. He took the pain, landing two prompt knees to Dennis' sternum and then slamming a fist across the bridge of his nose.

Their dance continued. Each blow one that would have killed any other person. Despite their heightened pain thresholds and resistance they each grunted and cried with every subsequent hit. The awareness that each blow hurt apparent to both parties. Dennis was allowing himself to be driven back towards the hanger in which the other imposters had disappeared. He grappled the whole way, taking blow after blow and retaliating with his own strength as well.

Jet grabbed hold of some discarded iron and used it as a weapon. Dennis dodged it and utilised some small machine parts to return the favour. Jet was not backing down, every attempt that Dennis made to subdue only increased his resolve. Bigger and heavier items were being hurled in Dennis' direction. Grating along concrete or slamming with a screech into nearby buildings after they missed.

Finally Dennis was drawn into the hanger. He immediately saw, and heard with a whining whirring sound, what the others had planned to do. On the back of a quad bike a helicopter was being driven out of the huge shed. His momentary lapse of concentration was a benefit to Jet.

Wham! Another well aimed punch brought itself to bear across his face. Dennis staggered and fell to the ground. They had fought ruthlessly across the tarmac. Dennis could feel, as he sat on the smooth concrete, heavy painful bruises and possible broken bones make themselves aware to him. By the way that Jet stood Dennis believed that he was in a much similar condition. Dennis knew however that Jet was firmly in control and was not showing the same injuries that Dennis carried.

"You, know," Jet said as he walked closer. "There was a small moment when I thought that you understood what I was about, and because of that I almost asked if you would join me on the path that I am on. But, I then realised, that as much as you have come to know me I also know you. You are one of those people who would never stray from what they think is right."

"You are right," Dennis said with a shallow breath. "I wouldn't do that. But you were also right with another thing."

"What?" Jet spat, but smiled down at Dennis.

"I never give up on someone, on anyone," Dennis looked up into the eyes of the young man. "I never stray from what I think is the right course of action, whether others think that it is a lost cause, or it brings me great pain, or even kills me." Dennis matched the stare of his former student. He watched even as a smudge of tears dribbled from within the boy's eyes, as Jet's smile changed into a scowl of pain, as the suited villain walked over to Dennis, preparing to finally end it all.

Blam, blam, blam! Punch after punch rocked forward and slammed into Dennis face as he laid on the ground, and not once did he try to block them or fight back. He felt the first few blows, then the rest became numb. They kept coming, ferociously, a boy screamed, his voice wretched in agony as if he was the one receiving them, not Dennis. Eventually Dennis slumped hard onto the floor.

"You don't know me," Jet said, the words quivering. "No one does. I'm a lost cause. Now because of you our plans have had to change. The outcome hasn't changed, just the execution. If you are smart, you will stay down, and never stick your head into my business ever again." He turned and walked slowly away. Dennis didn't hear any of those words; he had already passed out.

Get up. A voice was calling out. Get up Dennis. He leaned forward, pain throbbing, pulsing, through his body. He was not where he was. He was in a large space, pristine, sterile, clean, safe. He could hear footsteps. Heeled boots tapping and echoing off from the polished floor.

"Come on you must get up," the voice said more clearly. Someone was speaking to him. He gazed around searching for them, his eyes seemed like they were only half open and his vision was hazy. He guessed at the voice and also at his surroundings.

"Uncle Scott?" he asked. His lips were numb and swollen, and the words hurt, but he could hear his voice.

"No, boy," the voice said soothingly. "Not Scott."

"But that means," Dennis felt even more discomfort as his brain processed what he thought was happening. "Dad?" he asked.

"Yes Dennis, it's me," his dad confirmed.

"But that can't be true, you're dead, wait, am I dead?" Dennis starting to feel his body as if it would reveal to him the truth. He no longer wore his disguise, sitting in a pair of jeans and a slim fitting tee-shirt. His dad laughed.

"No, not dead, not this time," his father confirmed. "Though you have been giving that a red hot go lately."

"Then what is happening? Is this a dream?" Dennis asked.

"Yes, well sort of," his dad answered. "You are in your own head, so this has been made entirely by you. But while I am here there are some things that I need to say to you."

"That I am a failure," Dennis suggested. He didn't look hurt in his dream, but he still felt it.

"Ha, ha, no," his father admonished him with a smile. "Although failure isn't so bad, you learn more from that than you ever could if you were only ever successful."

"But it is so hard," Dennis replied. He felt like he was a small child again, complaining to his father after things had not been going his way.

"What is so hard?" his dad asked, seemingly confused. If he was truly in his own head then surely he would know.

"Being the Wrangler," Dennis told him. "Being this person that is super powerful, that has these great abilities, the expectation that people have."

"You have it wrong mate," Dennis' dad said as he kneeled down beside his son. "Being a character called 'The Wrangler' is easy. Jet is a version of the Wrangler and he does it as if it's nothing. What is hard is being Dennis Dodger. Being who you actually are."

"That makes no sense," Dennis shook his head.

"It makes total sense," his dad finally growled at him, meaning that Dennis was getting angry at himself. "If you were just the Wrangler this fight would be over already. You wouldn't have brought a whip with you, you would have brought something else. If you didn't care about Dennis Dodger, the person you were born to be, there would be no need for a disguise. But you are Dennis Dodger, you are a caring, intelligent, confident young man, whose power is not measured by how fast you are or how you can lift heavy things. Your strength comes from a different place, which makes you never give up when things look the hardest, when something is a lost cause." Dennis smiled.

"There are no lost causes, Dad," Dennis replied. He was helped to his feet and somehow his dad still made him feel silly; ruffling his hair as if he was a toddler.

"And your mum thought you never listened," he said looking up at his son. "You know what you have to do now?"

"Yep," Dennis replied, with a massive sigh. "It isn't going to be easy though."

"Good thing that you are Dennis Dodger then," his dad said with a shrug, "never forget that son, but, having the Wrangler around might help as well." The walls started to disappear around them. "The Wrangler really is a terrible name though."

"I know," Dennis agreed. His head pounded and he felt like he was being pulled away. "Hey Dad, what was the thing you said you wanted to tell me?" Smoke swirled now, the scene was fading and his dad was almost out of sight.

"I am proud of you Dennis. I always have been, and I always will be," his dad said. Then he was gone.

Dennis grunted heavily. His head swam and he wanted to vomit. His face had opened up, his left eye was swollen over and blind, and he could feel the breeze as it cooled the blood on his face. A loud whirring sound had been executed from the engine of a nearby helicopter which was sputtering into life.

"Oh yeah," Dennis said, reminding himself what he was in the middle of. The helicopter rotors needed more revolutions and speed to take off. Dennis still had time, but he had also been seen.

"He is coming," one of the four remaining imposters called out, gaining the attention of Jet who was already on board. Dennis heard the roar of frustration which came from the youth as Dennis regained his feet unsteadily. He could stand though, and a few short steps later he knew that he could do everything else too.

"Doesn't he ever give up?" Jet bellowed. "Take him out." The direction was given to one of the two remaining plebs left on the tarmac. "And you, get that quad out of the way. No, hit him with it. I have greatly wanted to see him get hit by a car." Both subordinates advanced toward their tasks. The first pulled forth an automatic weapon which hung at his side and opened fire immediately. There was space between them but Dennis could cover it quickly. Not without being shot though. He pulled his oil-skin jacket up around his shoulders and over his head, so his body from knee to head was completely covered, and then he charged. The sensation was odd. The bullets which rained down upon him felt like raindrops as they pattered on the ceiling of a tent as he hid from a storm while camping. The material bounced back slightly but nothing penetrated. He silently thanked his uncle for making it for him, but cursed loudly as his legs took a couple of hits. Then he exploded out from behind his jacket right on top of the gunman. Clearly the man had thought that his barrage would be successful, the confusion and fear evident on his face before Dennis punched him hard across the face. The man spun multiple times through the air before he hit the ground.

The approaching quad bike revealed itself with the sound of an over revved engine. The rider had managed to get some speed up as Dennis had been busy avoiding his companion, and headed straight at him. Dennis stood his ground. He planted one foot behind the other, bracing for impact. As the quad bike came towards him Dennis reached out, grabbed the bars that sat on top of the bike's front section, and flexed his muscles. The bike's wheels spun uselessly as Dennis lifted the bike into the air. He used the momentum that it already had, allowing it to twist naturally with centrifugal force, and then dumped it upside down on the tarmac. The rider was thrown clear but his vehicle was crushed. Neither were moving.

Dennis turned and ran after the helicopter which was already gaining speed away from the hanger. Dennis swore. In the air just off to the right he caught the glare from the sun, reflecting from the shape of an approaching aircraft. Time had run out. Dennis caught up, crouching as he ran to avoid the blades. He arrived undetected, the occupants must have been watching the plane coming down toward them. He grabbed the landing skids and pulled with all his might. The wheels stopped rolling forward and helicopter halted. The loss of movement lasted momentarily, it was enough for him to grab hold of the petrol cap and break it, jettisoning fumes and flammable liquid all over the craft and himself. Jet rushed out from the cabin and dealt Dennis another brutal blow. He didn't see it coming as the youth had approached from the side of his now blind eye. He crumpled to the ground but he was not pursued.

"Get in the air now," Jet ordered. The demand met with immediate response as the helicopter lurched into the air and climbed quickly. "Go straight at it, it must not get away," Jet boomed from inside. Dennis slowly climbed to his feet, doubting whether he could vault up to reach the escaping helicopter. He had few options. His hand jolted to his waist and pulled his whip clear. In two revolutions he had the speed he needed and shot the tip out towards the helicopter. Skilfully he found his target. The cord wrapped around the landing skids near where Dennis had a hold previously. He felt the helicopter jerk under the new pressure. Dennis was dragged for a moment but held on with every ounce of his remaining energy. When he had managed to slow his grind he started pulling back on the whip cord. The helicopter skipped and bounced in the air under the opposing pressure. Dennis slowly made progress as the vehicle flew lower in the air. A second later Jet and another appeared at the open doorway. Jet worked his way down to where the whip cord was attached, whereas his companion opened fire on Dennis who was a sitting duck on the runway. Dennis clicked his finger over the whip cord making sure that the magnet tip that Scott had installed was still attached, although he knew that Jet could most likely pry that off. It wouldn't take long, there had to be another action.

Dennis slipped forward as he released one hand from the whip handle, fumbling about behind his jacket as he reached for the sword. He pulled it free and held it aloft. Dennis looked at the point, that his uncle Scott has described as being able to penetrate metal if desired. Dennis would back his arm. If he could throw it while it was alight then he could try and ignite the petrol which was dribbling freely from the vehicle. He rose the blade with one arm, struggling to get a good look with his one remaining eye as he was dragged along holding the whip with his other arm.

"Arrrggh," Dennis yelled. Blood sprayed from an open bullet wound on his sword hand. He had been shot and pain laced through him. He couldn't throw it with that hand now, and to switch hands would mean to lose his hold on the whip, leading to the escape of the helicopter and no chance of intervention. He was out of options.

"Ha ha," Jet yelled down to him. "You tried your best, but it was not good enough. I told you it was a lost cause."

Almost, out of options.

Dennis still held the sword shaped cattle prod. His hand shook fiercely as he moved a finger to flick the switch that would ignite the fire. It sparked to life and the flames grabbed onto the metal of the blade.

"There are no lost causes," Dennis yelled aloud. He swiftly pressed the blade to the side of the whip and watched as it caught alight. The cord had been doused in the petrol as it gushed away from its canister. It lit up as if it was being chased along the length of the rope, sending a trail of blue flames and smoke along with it.

"Aaargh," the yell came from Dennis. He was on fire as well, the petrol had soaked into his clothing as he had been standing beneath the struggling helicopter. Dennis could hear Jet's desperate pleas even though his eyes were no longer open.

"He is going to kill us all, take him out now," Jet screamed at the other man. "Let go you fool. You will kill yourself as well." Dennis didn't let go. He dropped the cattle prod, his hand unable to grip the blade any longer. His injured arm moved to assist his other failing arm. Both his hands were blistering and turning red, his arms burned and smelt like he had placed them into a barbecue. Yet still he held on.

An explosion blasted above him. The fuel canister had ruptured. The helicopter was in its last death throws. Dennis glanced up and saw that Jet was preparing to abandon the vehicle.

"No," Dennis wailed. He knew that if Jet made it to the ground he still had a chance of bringing the plane down. Dennis knew that his strength was gone but he had to try and stop that from happening. He gripped the scorched handle of the whip with everything he had left. He pulled with all his might, and he started to swing the helicopter into an arc. It resisted his movement, but Dennis didn't give in. It twirled back towards the hanger and Jet was thrown back into the cabin out of sight. Dennis could feel the rope in his hand snap, a second later the rest of it had evaporated into ash. Dennis slumped to the ground with nothing else left that he could do. He was fatigued and his breathing was heavy. He rolled painfully on the ground, starving the flames of oxygen and removing the roasting sensation. The fire that had burned all over him subsided, but all Dennis could do now was watch.

The helicopter had lurched forward after being released by the whip. The nose of the vehicle had dipped as the rotors swung over the top. Another explosion, bigger than the first, coughed through the air. The tail boom was severed and the rotor gone. The helicopter had lost all direction and vibrated viciously in the air. Then it twisted and shot down towards the ground. The helicopter slammed into the hanger, bringing the grating tin and heavy steel beams down along with it. It hadn't even struck the ground before the whole scene exploded.

The helicopter engine could still be heard choking as it tore itself apart. Dennis looked on, knowing that Jet was no longer a threat. He had been pounded to a bloody pulp by the boy and even after all that he could not stand back and watch as he lost his life. Dennis told himself that Jet could still be saved. Slowly he managed to walk himself, stumbling with every step, towards the hanger where the helicopter screamed for aid.

Dennis was thrown clear off his feet as a surge or energy exploded angrily towards him.

The hanger pulsed outwards with the sonic boom, sending loose debris and fire out in all directions. The building collapsed around the helicopter and the raging inferno that consumed it, igniting everything else that was caught inside. A moment later you wouldn't have known that there was a hanger there in the first place. Oil drums, fuel stations and machinery all engulfed and erupting in a brilliant show of destruction. All that remained was a towering black spire-like furnace that melted everything within its kiln.

The sight didn't make Dennis happy, but he was suddenly filled with relief.

He rolled to his side and watched as the Australian Air Force plane that had carried the Prime Minister landed safely on the runway. He didn't need to be here any longer. He slowly walked back to his bike without another look.

Dennis was gone before the first person exited the plane.

CHAPTER 18 - UNFINISHED BUSINESS

"What will you do now?" Scott asked his nephew. Both stood at the foot of a tree, looking over a procession which numbered in the hundreds. Dennis had chosen a spot at the back so as to avoid as much attention as he could. He had multiple reasons to want to avoid the eyes of others; the main one was that he simply didn't want anyone watching him.

It was a week after the events that had taken place at the airport. So much had occurred, not only in that week but in the six months prior. There weren't many happy memories, but most had been extraordinary in some degree. The injuries that he had received were still only just healing. The burns on his hands and arms, while all of a serious and life threatening nature to any other person, had almost faded away completely, leaving only a tingling sensation in his nerves which Dennis was sure would pass. The wounds from shrapnel and ballistics were long gone, and the black and blood shot eyes that he had sported for the first few days were also completely removed from his features. Dennis had allowed himself a haircut, and had trimmed the sides of his moustache lightly. He had also indulged in buying himself a new suit that was cut precisely for his size. It was the first time he had taken this much care when selecting his apparel.

Dennis had purposely not answered the question that his uncle had asked. He would, just not yet. The answer would be for his ears only and he didn't trust any crowds anymore, especially several of those in this one. It wasn't that the crowd was bad, however the majority of them were qualified reporters who always seemed to be listening. Dennis acknowledged a few people; he didn't know them they had just been looking over in his direction. He smiled and returned to his usual awkward head bob as he wasn't sure what else he should do.

The crowd started to disperse and the people made their way indoors. Dennis hung around a little longer, to pay his respects.

The funeral was for Horatio, and the wake was to be held inside the rugby club. After the events at the airport Dennis had somehow made his way back into town. He rode his bike immediately to his friend's home where he had scrambled through the wreckage. He had painfully, with a broken body and damaged hands, searched through the ruins until he was well into night. No one had helped him and no one had stopped him. The police continued rescuing the town from all its problems and nobody cared about one house that was too far gone to save. Dennis had dug down deep with his bare hands, his blood was now mixed in with the dirt and mortar. He tried feverishly to find any clue that would lead him to his friend. The house had been levelled, there was nothing left. Dennis had burrowed as far as he could to locate the secret basement, but that too was gone. All that was left was a huge crater. Then Dennis had driven all the way back to Clapptown. He had no idea how he got there, but he slept for days upon arrival. The only disturbance to his slumber were his tears as they soaked into the pillow.

Dennis looked at the coffin which lay before him. He would have felt more attached to its occupant if he believed that any part of Horatio was actually inside. He hesitated, wanting to say sorry, wanting to say anything. The words didn't come. He wiped away a single tear before following the rest of the group.

His friend would be sorely missed. Even if Dennis had found his voice there would have been no words that could relate how much he appreciated what Horatio had done, as either the Wrangler or as Dennis Dodger.

"There are things that I still have to do," Dennis responded finally. "Some unfinished business that needs my attention."

"If you need any help, you know all you have to do is ask?" Scott said quickly but said no more, allowing Dennis to be alone with his thoughts. When they entered the clubhouse Dennis once more sought out the refuge at the back of the room. He had no need of refreshments or food, and he couldn't make small talk with other friends or family members in his current mood.

The television that hung on the wall above their heads was powered on. Dennis glanced in the screen's direction and saw the same news story that he had seen for the last few days. The Prime Minister had extended her stay in the Central West, mostly so that each area that had been rife with conflict could see her and be inspired by a resounding speech. The Prime Minister was a lady by the name of Evelyn Darcy; who had a striking presence with her strong blue eyes, beautiful blonde hair and knowledgeable intelligence. Dennis had caught many of her speeches as they were shown while he rested, and had to applaud much of what she had said. The most interesting press conference was when she arrived at Westopolis Central, the area where the GreenCorp Tower stood. Around her she had her entourage which included the local member Mr Egg, and his counterpart from an electorate that was further west. Hector Green stood behind her, ready to engage in discussion involving several of his business strategies and future exploits, as well as how he was helping the local economy. There was another man that Dennis hadn't been able to find a name for. Regardless, he knew him as the heavily tattooed islander that he had rescued when he had first revealed himself to Jet. The man had asked then if Dennis knew who he was speaking to, Dennis had no idea then and he had no idea now. The only clue was that he was some technological expert who had been invited to attend the meetings by the Prime Minister's request. Dennis assumed that he wasn't overly welcome by Hector Green due to the look that the pair shared when they thought no one was watching.

The police had been thanked numerous times for their actions in the week that had passed, and alongside every news story the name of a mysterious figure known as the Wrangler was present. Dennis hadn't read any of the stories, and he had no interest to do so.

He looked through the crowd and identified several people that he knew, but didn't want to speak to. His eyes shot between them and then landed on one person. He was met with the glacial stare of someone he knew quite well, JT. Despite everything that Dennis had been through, all the battles he had fought and won, he could not hold the gaze of one of his friends. He knew what JT was thinking, it was the same thing that Dennis was thinking. Where was Jiemba, and why wasn't anyone looking? Dennis had one final look over the crowd and then walked out the door.

"Where will you go?" his Uncle Scott asked as he followed behind Dennis.

"There are many things that I need to look into," Dennis told his relative openly; he doubted people were listening, but he couldn't be sure so he remained vague. "Horatio had a list of things that he was suspicious of, that he was looking into in the area. I have given my notice to the principal at work and am not intending to work for the foreseeable future. In this time I am going to investigate what Horatio could not. The meteor, Westopolis and a few other things. But first I need to find a friend."

"Where will you start?" his uncle asked.

"I will go to Wellington first, that is the last place that Jiemba was seen. I may even revisit the camp and see if there are any clues remaining from his initial disappearance," Dennis informed him, shuddering at the thought of returning to the place where he had died, "then I will move on from there, I don't intend to return until I have found him. One way or another."

"Well if you need anything let me know," Scott told him. They had entered the carpark and stood next to his bike. It had been given a new coat of paint; mostly to give it a new identity but it also helped to cover all the minor damage that Dennis had caused it. "The bikes all packed. You have your new jacket, hats and weapons all ready to go. Almost exactly like they were. There are a few new surprises too, just in case."

"Thanks Uncle Scott," Dennis replied. He didn't shake his hand as was their usual custom, instead choosing to wrap his arms firmly around him in a warm embrace. He heard Scott sniff loudly as his uncle returned the hug.

"You are welcome back to Clapptown any time," Scott said trying to make his voice sound deeper to remove any suspicion that he had shed a tear. "And while you are gone I will be working on some things that can help you out down the road." The pair shared a look, then they smiled warmly at each other. Dennis kicked his engine into life, then, after a small wave goodbye, Dennis was gone.

"Take care boy," Scott said as he left. "Come back to me safe." The loud muffler roar as Dennis drove off down the road was his only reply.

EPILOGUE

The job that Frank had taken on as the maintenance man out at the airport, in charge of rubbish, simple ground keeping and small jobs, was supposed to be an easy one. He wasn't qualified to fly a plane, nor was he a mechanic and allowed to fix one, so generally he was confined to looking after the main terminal and the surrounding gardens. His days were usually boring with little expectation and that was how he liked them.

The past week had been a nightmare for him. He had been in touch with about a thousand different agencies dealing with all sorts of dilemmas ever since the hanger had blown up and the terminal had been overrun by criminals. Travel, tourism, aviation and insurance agencies were only some of the contacts that he had chasing him for answers to questions he had no idea about. He had been busy dealing with the police and emergency services in an attempt to get the facilities up and running again as soon as possible but everything seemed to be wrapped up in red tape.

It was the worst week ever.

Frank slammed his phone down after spending the best part of two hours on hold as he tried to get a sign off for some other documentation that he needed. He had been so focused on his work that he hadn't seen the approach of a small group of people.

"Who are you?" he asked rudely, sandpaper was not as rough as how Frank spoke to the newcomers.

"We are from the Aviation and Travel Insurance Agency," one of them said in a soft voice. Every part of that statement was music to Frank's ears. He glanced over at the one who had said it. She was a tall, slim woman with striking red hair and an expensive looking suit.

"Are you here to check out the damage?" he asked her in a far nicer tone.

"Yes," she replied with a smile. "I would appreciate it if you could show us the way immediately, so we can help sort out this mess." Frank didn't have to be asked twice.

"Follow me," he instructed them as he led the way out the door. The group that followed him didn't seem to be interested in the runway itself, but why should they, he thought. They were all professionals and apart from the crumpled carcass that used to be the air hanger nothing else looked of concern. Police tape cordoning off the site surrounded the destroyed building, and since the fire had been extinguished no one had been inside. Everything had to go through the proper channels.

"Hey what are you doing?" Frank called out as the group ignored the barriers and walked into the dangerous section.

"We are doing our job," the lady replied, she sounded sweet yet controlling at the same time. "We must be allowed to inspect the damage of the space and vehicles before any decisions can be made. I am sure that you don't want to be dealing with this mess any longer than you have to." Frank wasn't going to argue that point.

"So be it lady," he responded. "Just be careful in there, I don't want to have to fill out any more paperwork." Frank turned and left. "Call me if you need me." They watched as he walked away, every few steps grumbling something under his breath.

"Mistress Green?" one of the other women in the group said, getting the attention of the red haired lady.

"Spread out," she ordered. "You know what you are here for."
They needed no other direction and set about the task. Assumpta
Green followed along behind and looked at what had unfolded.
The amount of destruction was impressive, but ultimately her
plan had failed. She was not pleased by what she could see. She
stepped through the outer shell of what remained. Her people
spread out everywhere. There was a large hole in the ceiling
where a helicopter had crashed through. Parts of it were evident
in various areas of the interior. She walked to the front of the
remaining frame and looked inside. The pilot was still strapped
into the seat, but what remained of him was mostly cremated.
He was the best part of burnt.

"Black box located," the young girl called out as she returned
from the far end of the hanger. Assumpta ignored her, looking
down at the floor. Another person lay there, also crisped from
what had resulted. This one's body had melted and stuck fast to
the floor.

At least someone had paid for this failure, she thought to
herself. She was not one to share her thoughts with those that
were beneath her.

"We have what we need, time to resume our previous
instructions," another woman called out as she neared her
leader, but noticed how she seemed distracted. "Is there
anything else you need, milady?" Assumpta had heard her but
declined to reply. Something else had in fact caught her gaze.
There was movement near the centre of the building where
there had been the most destruction. Machines had been melted
and vehicles sheered into multiple components. There was
definitely movement. It could not have been a mouse, bird or
other small animal. While she suspected those creatures would
be nearby none would have been able to move the fallen steel
beams that were being disturbed in front of her. She walked
faster, which in turn made her subordinates quickly follow suit.

"Lift that metal sheet," she ordered as she stepped through more debris. They obeyed without question. With the sheet removed it became clearer what was happening. The floor was blackened, no doubt as a result from an extremely hot oil fire which had erupted beneath; boiling all plastics and some metal which had been trapped underneath. There was also another body, which had been hidden below the wreckage.

Yet that body was moving and showing signs of life. Assumpta gasped with astonishment. She paused to check if any of her colleagues had seen her, she was not one to show emotion so freely. She was convinced that they had not noticed.

"Get him out of there, now," she ordered. She hoped that no one was waiting outside, but she didn't really care if there was. She could deal with that just as easily. She watched as they all set about their tasks. Assumpta moved closer to the body and looked at the metal beam which still hung across it.

"Move this," she demanded, and at once the steel was gone. Assumpta kneeled down beside the body and took hold of one extremely charred palm. "You are going to be alright," she whispered, not knowing if that was the truth or not. "And when you are better, we will finish what we started, and you will be given the chance to find those that did this to you." The hand gripped for a moment and then fell limp as the body slipped out of consciousness. There was still life there, and if his strength returned than he would be a valuable asset. The boy would live.

Jet, the Hitman, would return.

Books by the author:

Following the Leader
Creek Crew: Kingdom of the Creek
Warriors of Westopolis: The Wrangler
Warriors of Westopolis: The Bigger Man

About the author:
Drew is a qualified primary school teacher who resides in the city of Orange, within the Central West of New South Wales in Australia. He is a lover of sports, media, reading and exploring whatever the world has to offer. Drew shares his time between working as a teacher, spending time with his family, and, on rare occasions, writing. Drew can be found on social media platforms including Facebook.

www.facebook.com/drewbaleauthor